BIG CITY,
BAD BLOOD

BIG CITY, BAD BLOOD

SEAN CHERCOVER

WM
WILLIAM MORROW
An Imprint of HarperCollins*Publishers*

BIG CITY, BAD BLOOD. Copyright © 2007 by Sean Chercover. All rights reserved. Printed in the United States of America. No part of this book may be used or reproduced in any manner whatsoever without written permission except in the case of brief quotations embodied in critical articles and reviews. For information address HarperCollins Publishers, 10 East 53rd Street, New York, NY 10022.

HarperCollins books may be purchased for educational, business, or sales promotional use. For information please write: Special Markets Department, HarperCollins Publishers, 10 East 53rd Street, New York, NY 10022.

FIRST EDITION

Designed by Susan Yang

Library of Congress Cataloging-in-Publication Data

Chercover, Sean.
    Big city, bad blood : a novel / Sean Chercover. — 1st ed.
       p. cm.
    ISBN: 978-0-06-112867-7
    ISBN-10: 0-06-112867-8
    1. Private investigators—Illinois—Chicago—Fiction. 2. Chicago (Ill.)—
Fiction. 3. Organized crime—Fiction. I. Title.

    PS3603.H47B54 2007
    813'.6—dc22   2006046766

07 08 09 10 11 JTC/RRD 10 9 8 7 6 5 4 3 2 1

To Martine, who made it good again

And to the memory of
Alexander "Sasha" Neyfakh (1959–2006)

Acknowledgments

I owe a great debt of gratitude to many people.

To my parents, Barbara and Murray Chercover, for their love and support, and for instilling a love of books in me when I was very young . . .

To Denise Marcil and Michael Congdon for their belief and guidance, and to the team at the Denise Marcil Literary Agency . . .

To my editor, Lyssa Keusch, for making this a better book, and to May Chen, Susan Yang, and the entire team at William Morrow . . .

To Ruth and Jon Jordan for welcoming me into the mystery community and into their home, and making me feel like family . . .

To Lt. Robert Biebel, Dennis Bingham (Retired), Sgt. Robert Cargie, Det. Michael Puttin (Retired) and Kristina Schuler at the Chicago Police Department. To Angela Bell, Special Agent Frank Bochte and Special Agent Ross Rice at the FBI. To Det. Sgt. Neill Murchinson at the LASD. And to John J. Flood and Jim McGough at the Illinois Police and Sheriff's News . . .

To Dr. Erin Boynton (ace surgeon) and David Evans (physio Yoda) for the new shoulder . . .

To my co-bloggers at www.theoutfitcollective.com, and to the many good folks at rec.arts.mystery . . .

To R. Aguilari, Franklin Ashley, Jill Brickman, Sean Bryson, Ann Chernow, J. and M. Chicco, Larry Copeland, P. Corallo, Jane Cornett, Anne-Marie Dean R.N., U.S. senator Dick Durban, Fred Gardaphe, Bear Graves, Paul Carter Harrison, Christopher Jackson, A. Jones, Jennifer Jordan, Crad Kilodney, Alexis MacDonald, Krista MacFarlane, Dave Martin, Kit Martin R.N., Howard M. Marx, Rik Morden, Sandy Morris, Chicago alderman Burt Naturus, Scott Parker, Patricia and Soren Pedersen, John Purcell Jr., Kat Richardson, Gary Robertson, Emmett Sanders, Keith Snyder, Junko Tokumaro, J. Tosoni and Michelle Woods . . .

But most of all, to Martine . . . for everything.

CHAPTER ONE

In the shadows of the John F. Kennedy Expressway, surrounded by warehouses, factories and auto-body shops, stands Villa d'Este, a family-run restaurant that serves generous portions of decidedly untrendy Italian-American food at reasonable prices. The restaurant was there more than thirty years before the expressway slashed the neighborhood in two and I imagine it'll be there long after the Kennedy collapses under the weight of bureaucratic neglect and political corruption. In Chicago, some things never go out of style.

I paced the restaurant's black and white checkerboard marble floor, waiting to ask Johnny Greico if he planned to kill my client. I didn't know how he would take such a question and I decided not to think about it. So I thought about other things.

I was doing my pacing in the Library Room, an ornate lounge they only used at night. Since it was just past noon, the room was closed and I was alone with my thoughts. Thinking, *Maybe I should have called ahead for an appointment.*

Sal Greico and his $3,000 suit strutted into the room.

"How are you, Ray?" He squeezed my hand harder than he needed to.

"Sal, good to see you."

Sal gestured to a pair of faux-nineteenth-century Florentine chairs. He tugged at the top of his trouser legs as he sat, to keep the razor-crease. Throwing caution to the wind, I neglected my crease and just sat down.

"Big John is very busy," he said. "What can I do for you?" Big John was Johnny Greico, Sal's uncle, and nobody outside the family called him that.

"I don't mind waiting. I only need a few minutes of his time."

"What's it about?"

"Well it's not about you, Sal. Either I can see him or I can't. But I think he'll be disappointed if you send me away."

We stared at each other for about a week. Finally Sal said, "Every-body gets screened, Dudgeon. That's the protocol."

Protocol is a pretty fancy word for a guy like Sal Greico, but I left it alone. No use being a wiseass.

"Sorry, no disrespect intended. I'll just wait."

Sal stared at me for another week, then stood up and left the room. On his way out, he closed the door harder than he needed to.

I stood and wandered around, just to save what was left of the crease in my pants. The room had no windows and I wondered if the snow had started. There had been little snow this year, which was fine by me. Gus the barber had bemoaned the possibility of not having a white Christmas, now only a week away. Sitting in his chair, I'd made sympathetic noises, but I wasn't looking forward to Christmas and I certainly didn't care what color it was going to be.

I had sent out Christmas cards, not because I was taken by the spirit of the season but simply to remind previous clients that I still existed. One of those cards had gone to Johnny Greico.

Greico was what most people call a Mob Boss. He was probably the fourth-most-powerful organized crime figure in the Chicago Outfit, which made him pretty powerful. It was said that he controlled most of the bookmaking and loan-sharking operations in the Midwest and I had no reason to disbelieve it. The feds had tried for years to make a RICO case against him and had twice gotten indictments, but never a conviction. During the first trial a key witness turned up dead, and during the second, evidence went missing from police custody. Johnny Greico had clout. Johnny Greico was not a man you wanted to screw around with.

So about a year earlier, when I got a message that Mr. Greico wished to have the pleasure of my company, I wasn't about to say no. Sal had picked me up in a dark blue Lincoln Continental driven by a big boy named Vinnie Cosimo. I recognized Vinnie because he had played some college ball. He was a pretty good defensive lineman but they said he lacked the killer instinct and he never figured to go pro. Sal and Vinnie had brought me here, where I met Johnny Greico in a wood-paneled office behind the kitchen.

Greico was worried about electronic surveillance and hired me to sweep the office and the three cars he used regularly, and to check the telephone lines for wiretaps. He never said why he picked me for the job and I never asked. I suspect that he may have thought someone from inside his organization was involved, but that still didn't explain how he came across my name.

As it turned out, there were no bugs to be found. There was a tap on his phone line but it wasn't on the premises; it was located in the JWI terminal. That meant it was a police wiretap and there was nothing he could do about it, except to have his lawyers ensure that a warrant had been properly issued to place the tap.

Greico accepted the news without question and let me sell him $8,000 worth of electronic countersurveillance equipment. Plus three days of my time at $600 a day. I spent one day sweeping for bugs and checking the phone lines. On the second day I tracked the location of the wiretap and installed tap detectors on the phones. And on the third day I trained Vinnie in the proper use of tap detectors and bug-sweeping equipment. Vinnie surprised me by being a lot smarter than I expected and it only took a few hours, but I was charging by the day.

In the end, I came out with a decent pile of cash for only a few days' work and I put Johnny Greico on my Christmas card list, not that I ever wanted to work for him again.

Some people would say that working for a guy like Greico, even once, is unethical. Maybe. But I had been asked to do a perfectly legal job and turning it down would have made an enemy I can live without. Besides, most of my work comes through law firms and I often don't even know the client's name. It's not like on television, where you can always tell the good guy from the bad guy. In real life, you just do your job and sometimes your client is the bad guy. And sometimes everybody is the bad guy.

Anyway, I knew that Sal would keep me waiting just to make a point. I examined the bookshelves for something to occupy the time. Most of the titles were unfamiliar and many were in Italian. I decided upon an English translation of *The Autobiography of Benvenuto Cellini.*

The dust jacket told me that Cellini was a famous artist in the 1500s. He worked in rare jewels, gold, and marble and he had lived "a life consecrated to passion and pleasure, to vast and delicate creative enterprises and to dangerous escapades."

How could I resist?

Benvenuto spent the opening chapters of his autobiography trying to convince me that he had some important ancestors who had won the approval of Julius Caesar and of God. Quoting his father, Benvenuto wrote, "Whithersoever the wheel of Fortune turns, Virtue stands firm upon her feet." Maybe that was true in sixteenth-century Florence but it seemed to me that, these days, Virtue usually landed flat on her ass.

I worry about the old girl sometimes.

Just as Benvenuto was starting his apprenticeship as a goldsmith, Vinnie Cosimo came into the room. I looked at my watch: 3:45.

"I don't know what you said to Sal but he's been a bitch all afternoon." He let out a barrel-chested baritone chuckle. We shook hands.

"It's good to see you, Vince," I said, meaning it. A year ago, I had learned that Vinnie preferred to be called Vince, so that's what I called him. I think his wife was the only other person to grant him that small favor. Personal transformation can be difficult for those who never leave the old neighborhood.

Vinnie produced an electronic handheld bug detector from his jacket. I raised my arms and he passed the antenna over my body, just as I had taught him.

"You packin'?"

I swept my jacket back to show that the horsehide on my belt was empty.

"Okay." He patted my shoulder with a meaty paw. It was a friendly gesture and I smiled back at him.

It was time to see the man.

The previous afternoon, I sat in my office with my feet on the desk, listening to the El train rumble-rattle down Wabash Avenue, twelve floors below my window. I'd just wrapped up an insurance fraud case, so there was a little money in the bank and I didn't figure to work again until the new year. Which suited me just fine.

The phone rang. I considered ignoring it, but being a detective and all, I am possessed of a natural curiosity. The call display told me it was Terry Green, an old friend and former colleague at the *Chicago Chronicle*. I picked it up.

"What's the scoop, Betty Boop?"

"You still gonna be there in half an hour?"

"I can be."

"Then be." And he hung up.

Twenty-eight minutes later, Terry Green entered my office, along with a man I'd never seen before. The man was just under six feet tall, weighed about 230 and wore a beard, perhaps to make up for the hair that was beating a fast retreat from his forehead. The man was white. Terry is black. For what that's worth.

"Ray Dudgeon, meet Bob Loniski," said Terry. I shook hands with

Bob Loniski. He seemed nervous. I asked them to sit and they did and so did I.

Terry continued, "Bob has a problem and I figure I owe you one, so here we are, bringing his problem to you."

"You owe me several, Terry."

"Be that as it may . . ." Terry gave me a palms-up shrug and a grin. If I were a winking sort of guy, I'd have winked at him, but I'm not, so I just grinned back.

Loniski spoke up. "Look, if you guys aren't going to take this seriously . . . I mean, I haven't hired you yet."

"What seems to be the problem, Mr. Loniski?"

"There is no *seems*," he sputtered. "They're going to kill me."

"That would be a problem. Who are *they*?"

"The Mafia, I guess." I shot a glance at Terry.

"Where are you from, Mr. Loniski?" I asked.

"Los Angeles. I've been here three months."

"Okay. I don't know how it works in Los Angeles but in Chicago we like to call them the Outfit."

Loniski flushed. "I don't know who you think you are," he said. "My life is in danger and you're joking around and playing semantics? I'll find someone else." But he didn't move. I figured I should say something.

"Mr. Loniski, I understand you're on edge. Let's just start at the beginning and tell me what makes you think the Outfit wants you dead."

It was a complicated story and it took him almost an hour to tell it. Here's the not-so-long version: Bob Loniski was a locations manager in the film industry. His employer, Continental Pictures, sent him to Chicago to work on a couple of movies that they were shooting here. He would scout locations, take photos, drive the director around to look at his top choices. Then he would negotiate with the various owners of properties they wanted to use, write up contracts and work with the city's film liaison office to arrange permits. He also arranged for police officers to be on location during shooting and hired additional private security. There was a lot to be done and he usually worked twelve-hour days, six days a week.

Scouting around the South Side for a warehouse, he came across one that he thought would be perfect for the film. There were a few tenants on the ground floor—an artist's studio, a silk-screening shop and a cabinetmaker. The upper floors were vacant. The cabinetmaker gave him a name, Frank DiMarco, and a phone number.

He called Frank DiMarco and offered to rent the upper floors of the building for five days of shooting at $5,000 per day. DiMarco asked for ten thousand and they agreed on seven. Loniski showed the building to the director, who liked it fine. Loniski then met DiMarco at the building and they signed the contract.

The trouble came three weeks later, during filming, when a man named Steven Novak arrived and demanded to know what was going on. It turns out that Novak was, in fact, the owner of the building.

Novak was a transplanted Chicagoan living in Boca Raton. He had purchased the building as a speculative investment—he planned to hold on to the property, keeping it vacant and closed, until gentrification spread south. Then he would sell it.

Steven Novak had never heard of anyone named Frank DiMarco.

Obviously, the police took an interest. From Loniski's contract, they traced DiMarco to a mail-forwarding service on LaSalle Street. With a judge's warrant, they got DiMarco's real address and made an easy arrest. DiMarco was charged with *felony theft by deception* and was not saying a word.

Bob Loniski didn't want to be a witness but the tenants were of marginal value. They would be called to testify but Loniski was the only one who could say, with certainty, that DiMarco claimed to be the owner of the property. And Loniski witnessed DiMarco's signing of the contract, while the tenants were renting month to month with no leases. Loniski was deposed and ordered to be available to testify at trial, which was scheduled for mid-January. In the meantime, DiMarco was out on bail.

Then the cabinetmaker died. A simple mugging, it could have happened to anybody. But two nights before, a voice on the other end of the phone told Bob Loniski that testifying would be bad for his health. The voice also said it was *connected*. Two stale clichés, but both effective.

Loniski was terrified. He called the police and they told him there was nothing they could do until someone actually makes an attempt on him. They suggested he hire a bodyguard.

Having told his story, he sat slumped in the chair, looking like a man who didn't expect to be cashing any Social Security checks.

I glanced at my watch. It was 4:37. My first-cigarette target time for today was 4:30. I quietly congratulated myself by lighting a cigarette—and looked at Terry.

"What's your interest here?"

"I was in the courtroom prospecting for stories when DiMarco was arraigned and I talked with the assistant state's attorney," said Terry. "It's a story, for sure. The way I figure it, this DiMarco's not getting rich on three tenants, so he's probably got other buildings going."

"Running a bold version of the 'long con' Fake Landlord Scam."

"I figure. You know Sam Christensen?"

"Yeah, in the fraud squad."

"Except now they're calling it the Financial Crimes Division. Anyway, he drew the case and he agrees with me, but they found nothing in DiMarco's place. Not a shred. Also if you want to rent out some vacant building, you want to make sure the owner's not gonna just show up. So I figure DiMarco *knew* that Novak lived in Boca. Had to."

"So you figure he's got a friend in county government who can cross-check records and match vacant buildings to absentee landlords."

"I'm looking into it."

"All right guys, fascinating," Loniski cut in, "but what about me?"

"I don't know yet," I said. "I've never heard of Frank DiMarco, but then I've never heard of a lot of people and some of them are connected. Keep in mind, there are loads of people who claim to be connected to the Outfit. It's kind of like Woodstock."

"Woodstock?"

"The music festival? Hippies, free love, Jimi Hendrix?"

"Yes, I know."

"Well if you took all the people who *claim* to have been at Woodstock, you'd have roughly the population of Chicago."

"And St. Louis," added Terry.

"And St. Louis," I said. "Claiming to be connected to the Outfit is kind of like that. So don't panic, at least not until I check it out."

"I've got some feelers out," said Terry, "but so far, the smart money is on DiMarco not being too much of anything. He's an associate but he's not a made guy."

"Why not?"

"For one thing, his attorney. He's represented by Stearns, Jephcoat & Associates. Now, they are an Outfit firm but his lawyer is just some junior associate. If he was a made guy, he'd have rated a partner."

I turned back to Loniski, who didn't look reassured. "It's likely that DiMarco simply learned that the cabinetmaker went off to the great woodshop in the sky and he saw the chance to intimidate the other witnesses."

"Or he actually killed the guy," said Loniski, "and I'm next."

"It's a possibility." I stubbed out my cigarette. "Let me check on DiMarco first. Then we'll see."

"Are you going to protect me?"

I glanced at the Ernie Banks bobblehead doll standing on my desk and tapped on the bill of his baseball cap. Ernie nodded in the affirmative. Ernie was usually right.

"We'll see. Write me a check for six hundred dollars and I'll poke around tomorrow and see what I can find out. Then we'll talk about the bodyguard job." I gave him my business card and told him to call me at the end of the following day, or sooner if he got another threatening call.

And he gave me a check.

The next morning, I called around and learned that Frank DiMarco had posted a $50,000 bond to cover his bail. The arrest had taken place in the late afternoon and bond was posted just before noon the next day. Another good sign. If he were a made guy, the Outfit would never have left him to cool his heels overnight; he would've made bail in time to be home for dinner, even if they had to post it in cash.

I rented a car and visited Sergeant Sam Christensen at the Financial Crimes Division. For the price of a hat, he let me look at DiMarco's rap sheet. It told me that DiMarco was thirty-seven years old and that he had spent eight of those years in jail, on three separate convictions. Keeping a place of prostitution, possession of a trunkload of unlicensed firearms with filed-down serial numbers, and beating the snot out of a guy who owed Bennie Schwartz, a midsize bookie on the West Side. Since Bennie Schwartz was a bookie, he came under Johnny Greico's authority, which was lucky for me because I knew Greico.

Christensen also let me see the case file. It looked like an easy win for the good guys, assuming the remaining witnesses lived to testify. I wrote down the names and addresses of the two other witnesses—the artist and the owner of the silk-screen shop. The dead cabinetmaker was of no use to me, but I wrote his name in my notebook anyway.

His name was Chester Kolarik. The name meant nothing to me and his death meant nothing to me. Maybe he had a wife, kids, parents. Maybe his death meant something to them. Or maybe they didn't like him much. Maybe Chester was a complete bastard who beat his wife and yelled at his kids and ignored his parents. Maybe they struggled to produce the appropriate noises of grief, crying around the coffin while hiding a secret relief. *Better him than me.* And maybe they felt guilty for that thought and then their noises of grief got louder and more convincing.

Or maybe Chester Kolarik had no family.

After leaving the Financial Crimes Division, I stopped for a burger at Blackie's, washed it down with a pint of beer and drove to Villa d'Este with the intention of asking Johnny Greico if he planned to kill my client.

After making sure I was clean, Vinnie led me downstairs to the basement, through a long corridor that ran under the kitchen, back upstairs and along another hallway and into an office. There was a sentry posted at the door but he seemed to be expecting us and he stepped aside as we approached. I entered, with Vinnie right behind.

Johnny Greico sat at his desk, holding a clear plastic cube that contained a baseball signed by Ron Santo. I couldn't see the signature but I remembered it from a year ago, when I swept the office for bugs. Sal sat on a brown leather couch along the left wall. Tony Bennett sang from an unseen stereo. I sat in a chair facing the desk and Vinnie leaned against the door behind me.

"You like their chances next year?" asked Greico, without taking his eye off the ball. Perhaps the only thing he and I had in common was an abiding love for the Cubs.

"Dusty's doing fine, so far," I said. "I have hope. But they've got to upgrade the bullpen, big-time. If not, I worry."

Greico put the ball back on his desktop. "Me too." He looked at me, finally. His eyes were hard, dark and dangerous. A young man's eyes set into the wrinkled folds of an old man's face, topped with a thick mass of curly white hair. He was a small man, no more than five and a half feet tall with his shoes on. And he carried a lot of weight, but rather than looking flabby, he looked round and taut, like an overfilled balloon.

His small hands reached forward and opened a cigar box. The label on the lid said *White Owl*. With thick little sausage-fingers he extracted a cigar. Sal moved silently to the desk and lit the cigar, then returned to his place on the couch. Sal wasn't just showing respect; he was helping. I noticed the old man's swollen knuckles and a slight tremor in his hands. He'd aged a lot in the last year. Greico blew a stream of smoke at the ceiling and I wondered why a rich man would smoke cheap cigars. Again his eyes fixed on mine.

"What's so important, you gotta see me?"

"I have a client who seems convinced that Frank DiMarco is going to kill him."

"So?"

"So, I know that DiMarco has done some work for Bennie Schwartz."

"So?"

I didn't want to insult Greico but he wasn't letting me come at this gently. I wanted a cigarette but I'd set a target time of 5:00 for today. No smoking before five, damnit. The clock on the wood-paneled wall behind Johnny Greico said 4:07.

I chose my next words carefully. "Mr. Greico . . . I know that you're an important man with many interests in the community, and I know that you hear about most of what goes on. My client has hired me to protect him. If DiMarco is acting on his own, I'm sure I can do that. If, on the other hand, there are other interests at work here, I certainly wouldn't want to create any unpleasantness between us."

Greico was getting a kick out of watching me dance around it. But I was playing straight with him. If DiMarco was on his own, I would take the case. If the Outfit wanted Loniski dead, then he was dead, and nothing would be served by my getting dead along with him. I would simply advise Loniski to develop a case of amnesia before trial.

The old man rested his cigar in a large glass ashtray. "You think you can take Frankie?"

"With all due respect Mr. Greico, Frank DiMarco's a punk."

Greico seemed to stop breathing for a second. I know I did. Then the corners of his eyes crinkled and he broke into a wide smile and picked up his cigar. "You're right there, Dudgeon. Yes you are. Frankie's a punk. He's Paul Tortelli's cousin and all, but he's still a punk. Weren't for Paul, I'd a cut him loose a long time ago. He don't do what he's told and he does what he's told not to, like he's a free agent or something. And another thing," Greico waved his cigar in a small circle, "he's braggadocio. I think you probably could take him."

So we agreed that Frank DiMarco was a punk and that I could probably take him. That was a start. I waited to hear the rest of it. The old man sat and smoked. Tony Bennett wailed about leaving his heart in San Francisco, which seemed like a careless thing to do. And I waited some more.

"Okay. Just so you know, Frankie's present troubles are his own. He gets clipped making a play for your client, it don't bother me. He made his bed. And I doubt he'll try it anyway. Even if he goes to college for this recent thing, he'll do a nickel, at most. Not worth killing for."

That was all I needed to hear. Greico had no interest in seeing Loniski dead and Frank DiMarco was on his own. I stood up.

"Thank you very much for your time, Mr. Greico. I appreciate it."

He reached forward to shake my hand, something he had never done before. "I'm glad you came and checked with me, you're a smart kid." We shook and I turned to go. When I got to the door, the old man added, "Dudgeon. You oughta come by the restaurant for dinner one of these days. Just make a reservation and it'll be on the house."

"Thank you, sir. I'll do that."

Gus the barber was getting his wish. As I scraped snow off my rented car, I decided not to let it affect my fine mood. Johnny Greico had made a good point—DiMarco would be stupid to make a play for Bob Loniski. He would try to intimidate, sure, but he could do five years easily and probably wouldn't have to do even that much for his little landlord scam. Once he learned that Loniski had a bodyguard, the stakes would just be too high. So I had a new client and the job should prove to be both lucrative and easy. I wasn't about to let a little snow get me down.

On the way back to my office, I stopped at Powell's bookstore. If anybody was going to have a copy of *The Autobiography of Benvenuto Cellini*, it would be Powell's. I don't know why, but I was eager to read more about the passions and pleasures and dangerous escapades of my new friend Benvenuto. Or maybe I was just hoping he could convince me that Virtue really does stand firm upon her delicate little feet.

They had two copies, a new paperback and a used hardcover. I prefer the size and weight of a hardcover and I like the way an old book smells. The used copy was in good condition and bore no marks from a previous owner, so I bought it.

I took my new used book back to my office, where there were six messages on the answering machine. Terry Green had new information on the DiMarco case and wanted to meet for a drink. Some salesman wanted me to know that he was having a Christmas special on carpet cleaning. And Bob Loniski had called four times, each message sounding slightly more agitated than the last.

I lit a cigarette—first one of the day—and called Loniski and he picked up on the first ring. There had been no more threatening calls but he had apparently spent the day imagining all the ways in which Frank DiMarco could end his life. When I told him I would take the case, he calmed considerably. He wanted me to start that night but I said I had some things to do and I'd meet him at his office in the morning. I told him not to worry.

Terry Green was still in his office and still had work to do. We agreed to meet at midnight in the Boathouse Bar at Trader Vic's. I always like to make plans to meet at midnight . . . it makes me feel like Humphrey Bogart. And I always expect to run into the ghost of Peter Lorre at Trader Vic's. Never happens, but I live in hope.

As I hung up, I remembered that I had a date set for the next night with Jill Browning. I picked up the phone and dialed her number from memory. She answered on the third ring, sounding like she'd been asleep.

"Hey, it's Ray."

"Oh my God, Ray," she said. "Was it tonight? I thought it was tomorrow night. I'm not even close to ready." She had lived in Chicago for ten years but still had an undiluted English accent that, for some reason, I found both arousing and funny.

"No, it was tomorrow night. But something's come up."

"Oh? What's her name?" she said.

"Her name is Bob Loniski."

"You're standing me up for a girl named Bob Loniski? That is disappointing."

"I'm really sorry, Jill. It's work, and I'm going to be tied up for at least a couple weeks."

"Well that's no way to pitch woo."

"Can we meet tonight?"

"Um . . . all right. But you'll have to come here. I've been on nights and I switch to days tomorrow, so my internal clock has gone haywire and I don't much feel like going out."

On the way to Jill's apartment, I stopped and picked up a bottle of good red wine at Binny's and some enchiladas from the El Jardín Café. The El Jardín makes some of the best Mexican food in Chicago and it was close to Jill's place on Belmont, so the food would still be hot when I arrived.

As I drove along Clark, it occurred to me that Jill might be intending for me to stay the night. Everything seemed to be heading in the right direction. We enjoyed each other's company and there was sexual chemistry in abundance and we'd come pretty close to naked on our last date. But Jill wasn't sure that she could be in a relationship with a guy who carries a gun and disappears for days at a time and makes enemies of violent men. I was trying to convince her that she could and I seemed to be succeeding, if slowly.

We first met in the emergency room at Rush Presbyterian. She was a nurse and I was a guy with a black eye, a broken nose and two cracked ribs. I'd been working on a case for a chain of hardware stores. Merchandise had been disappearing from their distribution warehouse, so I went undercover in the shipping department and worked there until I knew the names of all the employees involved. I testified against them and they were convicted. But their fence, Pat Delany, was upset that I'd cut off a major supplier, so he sent a couple of hard guys to make me hurt. Which they did.

When you arrive at the hospital in such a condition, they automatically call the cops. Jill listened as I told my story to the two uniforms who responded to the call. After they were gone, she said, "Seems like an awfully difficult way to make a living." To which I replied, "Would you like to have dinner with me?"

That was three months ago. My ribs still tingled sometimes but it had been worth it, just to meet Jill. She was smart and funny and pretty and had all the right curves in all the right places. She was sexy and she knew it and she wasn't afraid of it. Neither did she try to flaunt it.

And it went deeper than that. While we were moving slowly on the physical relationship, the emotional connection had developed almost immediately. On our second date, something just clicked. Something beyond sexual chemistry and shared interests.

Jill was working the night shift at Rush, so we met for a romantic lunch at a little Italian joint called Sotto Le Stelle. True to its name, the place had hundreds of little white lights set into the ceiling, which was painted to resemble a night sky with scattered clouds. The restaurant's windows were tinted black and there were candles on the tables and it really did feel like dining under the stars. We shared a bottle of Chianti with our lunch, and as the waiter refilled our glasses, it struck me. Normally during the early dating phase of a relationship, you project an image of your best self. It's a sales job, really. But this was only our second date, and it felt completely authentic. I didn't feel like I was projecting an image of my best self. I felt like I *was* my best self. And I had the sense that Jill was feeling the same thing.

Walking down Armitage after lunch, Jill took my hand in hers. I glanced down at the swell of her hip and felt an erection growing. She stopped and kissed me softly on the lips.

"I want you to do something for me," she said. "I want you to show me something in this city that is special to you."

I took her to the Shedd aquarium, where we wandered the tropical reef exhibits. Jill had never been diving and asked a lot of questions about the animals in the massive tanks and artificial habitats. I pointed out the different sharks and rays and eels and schooling fish and corals. Jill held my hand throughout. She never asked *why* this place was special to me. It seemed enough for her to just know that it was, and to enjoy it along with me.

Walking back to the car, I said something funny and she laughed and I watched her face in the afternoon sun—her small ears, her sharp nose, the fine lines around her mouth and next to her eyes that would only deepen with time—and I was struck by a feeling so pure and so certain. I could see her as she would someday look, a woman in her seventies, and I could see myself, still walking with her.

I could see myself growing old with this woman.

And on the dates we'd had since, that feeling had only become stronger, but Jill was still uneasy about my chosen profession. Now, driving to her apartment, I was hoping that she wanted me to spend the night and at the same time hoping that she didn't, because I had to meet Terry later. What the hell . . . if it came down to it, Terry could wait. Professionalism be damned.

And then I noticed the green Ford in my rearview. I'd spotted it outside the liquor store when I picked up the wine. Just a car with two guys in it, idling at the curb. Two guys who just happened to pull away from the curb and into the flow of traffic two cars behind me and who just happened to be following the same route to Lakeview. But that didn't mean they were following me. When I stopped at the El Jardín Café, the green Ford kept going and I put it out of my mind, determined not to be paranoid.

Now it was there again.

In an effort to ease Jill's concerns, I had stopped wearing a gun whenever we went on a date. So my gun was back in the office, locked in my desk. Clever.

The green Ford was now one car behind me. I passed Jill's apartment building without slowing. Three blocks later I slowed and turned right, right again on the next block, and again, slowing even more. Thinking, *What's the first rule of gunfighting? Bring a gun.*

They were still behind me. Circling the block slowly ruled out any possibility of coincidence and probably gave them the impression that I was just looking for a parking space. I opened the glove box and grabbed the small can of Mace that I kept there and put it on the seat beside me. It didn't make me feel invincible.

I parked on Kenmore, near a row of two-flats. The green Ford passed me and parked ten yards ahead. The two guys got out of the

Ford and stood talking, pretending to be looking for an address. They made a big show of it, gesturing at a building across the road and wondering too loud if they had the right address and if Jimmy was home yet. Even with the help of acting lessons, these guys would never play the Dane. Rosencrantz and Guildenstern, maybe. Maybe with a lot of lessons.

I took stock of the situation. The driver was a big guy, about six two, with a lot of muscle. The other guy was about my size—five nine, 170 pounds. And they might be armed. I was armed with a small can of Mace, a bottle of wine and six enchiladas. I would have to take the big guy first.

A few deep breaths got my heart rate down to a manageable level. I took the Mace in my left hand and balanced the paper bag of enchiladas on top to conceal it. In my right hand I held the bottle. I got the door open, stepped out of the car and walked straight toward one of the two-flats. I heard them approaching from behind, footfalls crunching on fresh snow. Closer to the house, I found their reflection in the front room's bay window and when they were about twelve feet behind me I turned to face them. And smiled.

"Hey, fellas. You know who lives here?"

"Don't give a fuck," said the big guy. "Got a message from Frank DiMarco." My smile turned upside down.

"Don't think I know him." They were coming closer now.

"Don't matter," said the little guy. The guy about my size. "Mr. DiMarco says you wanna stay outta his business." They stopped about six feet in front of me.

"Okay. Message received. Thanks a lot." I tried to smile.

"Not good enough," said the big guy. From his pocket he pulled a pair of lead-weighted sap gloves and began putting them on.

I tossed the enchiladas at the little guy's face and fired the Mace at the big guy, who screamed "Fuck!" and went to his knees, gagging and rubbing his eyes with the back of his hands. But the little guy was fast and he kicked my hand and the Mace went flying and I swung with the bottle but missed. His foot slammed into the bottle and it sailed away and landed on the snow. He was on me and I took a fist to the mouth and returned the favor and took another to the solar plexus and the wind went out of me but I managed to kick him in the nuts and he went down. He dropped the roll of nickels he'd been holding in his right hand. I stood there, doubled over, drooling blood and trying to suck wind. The little guy vomited and moaned. The big guy was done wiping his eyes and came at me. His right fist slammed into my left eye and I went down on my back, hard. Through a veil of red dots I saw him coming closer and I rabbit-kicked him in the gut and he stepped back. I rolled over and grabbed the bottle and swung blindly. The heel of the bottle caught him on the chin and I heard his jaw break and he was down and out. I swung again in the direction of the little guy but he was about ten feet away, limping back to the car.

Then everything went black.

CHAPTER TWO

I wasn't out very long. When I came to, something hot was pressing against my right cheek. I opened my eyes and realized that it wasn't hot. It was cold. I was lying on my side in the snow. I tried to sit up and got it right on the third try. I made it to my hands and knees and then my head started throbbing and I got dizzy and threw up. I crawled over to the wine bottle and was surprised that it was intact. I picked up the bottle and, with a Herculean effort, got to my feet. I stood there, swaying, trying not to vomit again.

It's funny how the mind works at a time like that. I staggered over to the bag of enchiladas and picked them up, thinking, *Jill will be disappointed if I show up without dinner. I promised dinner, and a gentleman keeps his word.* Then I staggered to the car and fell in. I couldn't find my keys. I checked my pockets and on the seat beside me and then I found them. They were in my hand.

Although I have no memory of it, I must have driven to Jill's place because the next thing I remember is standing at her apartment door with the cold enchiladas and the bottle of good red wine. I heard the bolt turn and the chain come off and then the door opened.

"Oh my God!"

"Sorry I'm late," I mumbled, "and the food is cold. But I brought wine." This was definitely no way to pitch woo.

"Get in here."

Jill pulled me inside and took the enchiladas and wine and put them on the kitchen counter. She helped me out of my jacket and shirt and began examining the patient. No nonsense; she was in full nurse mode. She felt the area around my left eye and palpated my solar plexus with her fingers and felt my hands for broken bones and asked me to open and close my hands.

When she was done she lit a cigarette and put it between my lips and then another for herself.

"Did you lose consciousness?"

"Just for a minute or two."

"It doesn't matter how long, Ray. You've got a concussion."

"Sorry." I don't know why I said that. I opened the wine and poured two glasses.

"That's probably not a good idea," she said.

"I've been hit in the head before, Jill. This one's not so bad."

I went to her and put my arms around her. Her arms went around my waist and we stood there for a while, saying nothing, just holding each other.

"Go take a shower, you smell awful." She forced a smile. "You can use my robe, it's hanging on the back of the door."

I stood in the shower and the spray felt like little daggers. It removed the coagulated blood from my lip, which started to flow again. I watched the red-stained water run down my body, over my left foot, across the white floor of the tub and into the drain. I wondered if this incident would make Jill call the whole thing off. I couldn't blame her if she did, but the thought of it put a lump in my throat.

I got busy with the soap and shampoo and turned my thoughts to practical matters. How did DiMarco know I was on the case? Had Greico told him? And was Greico playing straight with me when he said he had no interest in DiMarco's fate? I decided that he was. If

Sam Christensen was a bent cop, he might have told DiMarco that I'd paid to see his sheet, but I figured Christensen for a right guy. Maybe Loniski told someone who told someone. Or maybe Terry told the wrong person.

Shit, Terry. I was supposed to meet him later. I rinsed off and cut the water and dried myself. I slipped into Jill's robe, which was too small. And pink. In the living room I phoned Terry's pager and told him I couldn't make it and I'd call him tomorrow.

Jill was in the bedroom. She sat on the bed, propped up by a thousand pillows, drinking wine. My wineglass was on the bedside table. An ice pack sat next to the glass. *The Gentle Side of John Coltrane* played on the stereo. I sat with my arm around her and we drank the bottle of wine that had saved me and listened to the music without talking. I held the ice pack to my swollen left eye, five minutes on, five minutes off. We finished the wine just as the music ended.

"The trouble is," said Jill, her voice thick with wine and the onset of sleep, "I think I'm in love with you."

I stroked her soft hair for a minute and started to say something, but the rhythm of her breathing had changed and I knew she was asleep.

The mid-July sun blazed off the Atlantic Ocean, off the white gunwales of my grandfather's fishing boat, off the gleaming metal line that ran out from the reel. I sat in the fighting chair, my bare feet braced against the footrest, the rod butt secure in the gimbal, and I let the line run just as Grandpa had taught me. The line slowed some and the reel's ratchet clicks became more distinct.

"Good," said my grandfather from behind. "Now get ready to tighten up a bit." His sinewy arm reached around and adjusted the drag lever ever so slightly, like a bluesman fine-tuning the G-string of an old Gibson. Even in this small action, he moved with the smooth precision of a tomcat, and as he finished tweaking the drag lever, I wondered if I would move like that someday, when I was a man.

Grandpa's right forearm bore a faded blue tattoo that he'd gotten in the navy, and a lot of hair. His skin had the leather texture and deep bronze color of a man who spent his life on the water. I was still prone to sunburn, but my own arms were increasingly hairy and I'd recently started sprouting chest hair as well. A significant milestone in the life of a boy.

I was fourteen years old and I'd been living in Georgia with my grandparents for almost a year. A difficult year. Yankee boy, big-city boy, Chicago boy, abruptly transplanted to St. Simons Island. I'd made only one friend, a black kid named Randall Curtis whose dad was a fisherman like my grandfather. The other kids, black and white, wanted nothing to do with me and Randall lost a few friends as a result of hanging out with me, so he'd recently backed away.

A difficult year. But at times like this, out on the water with my grandfather, I could feel the promise of happiness almost within reach. I leaned back in the chair and pulled gently on the rod. And then all the tension went out of the line.

"Damn," I said. "Got away. Sorry." I reeled in the slack line and Grandpa patted my shoulder.

"Not your fault, son," he said. "You did nothing wrong. Sometimes they throw the hook. Sometimes you just lose 'em." He opened the cooler and rustled around in the ice and came up with a new bonito and smiled at me. Like the color of his skin, the deep smile lines in his face gave testimony to a lifetime spent in the sun. "We'll get the next one."

A strange rush of happiness flowed over me, through me.

"I love you, Pop," I said.

My grandfather's smile vanished. He checked his watch, looked at the sky, cleared his throat. "Well we're never gonna catch dinner if you don't bait the damn hook," he said. He thrust the dead bonito into my hands and turned his back to me and I felt my cheeks burn with embarrassment.

I didn't understand the need to tell my grandfather that I loved him, or the need to hear him say it back. Nor did I understand why he reacted the way he did. I just knew that I hated myself for having said it and I longed to turn back time and *un*-say it. But I couldn't. The long afternoon passed in awkward silence, intermittently punctuated by forced small talk.

The memory-dream of my grandfather was still sharp in my mind when I woke to the smell of bacon. I was lying on Jill's bed, on top of the sheets, still wearing a pink robe. I swung my feet over the edge and stood up. Inside my head a little man went to work with a jackhammer. The pain moved in waves over the top of my skull, from front to back. Its epicenter was just above my left eye, which had swollen into a constant squint. At least I could see through it.

I was still tired as hell. Jill had set the alarm so that, every couple of hours throughout the night, we woke up and she checked my pupils and made me say my name and where I was and what day it was. She had explained that she had to be sure my brain wasn't swelling, or something like that. So I now felt like I hadn't slept at all.

I moved slowly into the living room. Jill was in the kitchen, frying eggs. She smiled at me, but the effort showed.

"Breakfast's almost ready," she said. "Your clothes are in the bathroom."

I went to the bathroom and took a good look in the mirror, not liking it much. The puffy area around my eye was a riot of color—mostly purple and brown, mixed with blue, green and a little yellow. Pretty. My lower lip was swollen but not as much as I'd expected. The back of my right hand was bruised and the knuckles swollen. I opened the robe. There was a bruise in my gut but it didn't look too bad. I felt stiff all over. Brushing my teeth was an adventure, but I got it done without reopening my lower lip.

I took a quick shower and the hot water loosened up the stiffness in my muscles. I toweled off and got into yesterday's clothes and went back to the mirror to brush my hair. It seemed like there were a dozen more gray hairs than yesterday but I told myself that I was just more aware of them this morning.

I was still a couple years shy of forty and I always thought gray hair on a young face looked distinguished. But today my face looked anything but young. I wondered how many more beatings it could take before it turned ugly.

In the cabinet behind the mirror I found a stick of Secret antiperspirant and put it on. *Strong enough for a man, but made for a woman.* It sure smelled like a woman. I hoped that the other half of the slogan was as accurate.

Breakfast was an awkward affair. Twice I tried to talk about the night before and twice Jill raised her hand to stop me, without taking her eyes off her food.

"Not now, Ray. I'm just not up to it." She sipped her tea.

"But I . . . you're too important to me to let this go."

"We can't solve it over bacon and eggs," she said. "You're about to disappear for two weeks and I'll be here every day, wondering if you're alive or dead. Or at work, waiting for them to wheel you into emerg."

"I'll call you—"

"No, I'd rather you didn't. Just do what you must, and call me when it's over."

"And you'll keep seeing me?"

Her electric-blue eyes were swimming. "I don't know," she said.

Back at my apartment, there was a message from Terry waiting on the machine. Terry told me that Frank DiMarco's lawyer had filed a bunch of motions, which would likely push the trial date back to the end of January. And he said that he'd be at Trader Vic's again at midnight, unless he heard from me. I called him back and he said hello and I told him midnight at Trader Vic's was fine.

"Good," said Terry, "just got something on DiMarco. Apparently he's now running Division Street."

"Now, as of when?"

"Like now, now. Started this morning, the way I hear it. The general buzz is, since DiMarco's awaiting trial they can't exactly send him around breaking deadbeat thumbs, so maybe he's on loan to Paul Tortelli, collecting street tax from pimps. Anyway, there's a lot more and I'll fill you in later. Gotta run." The phone clicked in my ear.

My soul needed a lift, so I made a pot of strong coffee and put Sonny Rollins's *Saxophone Colossus* on the stereo. Whatever my problems, Sonny could always make it better. At least for a little while. In a different life I'd have been a musician. But in this life I was utterly without talent. I'd proved that to myself and to a succession of tolerant music teachers in my younger years. Eventually I learned to be content with listening. One must accept one's limitations.

Max Roach laid down a playful rhythm and Sonny's horn danced a jazzy calypso and I began to feel human again. While the music played, I shaved and changed my clothes. Black trousers, cream shirt and a jacket that looked black from a distance but had a subtle dose of blue woven in. Checking my reflection in the mirror, I decided that, from the neck down, I looked pretty good. I chose to forgo the tie. Movie people are casual dressers.

My everyday gun was still at the office. I selected a Colt Detective Special and put it in an inside-the-waistband holster on my right hip.

My ensemble was complete.

I took a look around the apartment and wondered what Jill would think of the place. Not much, probably. It wasn't a dump but it wasn't much of a home either. The living room had an entertainment center with a large stereo and a small television, accurately reflecting my entertainment priorities. There were close to a thousand compact discs from which to choose, covering most types of music. A ton of jazz, a ton of good old rock & roll, a half ton of blues, a half ton of reggae, a generous helping of Cajun and just enough classical to fool visitors into thinking that I was cultured. But most women are not impressed by obsessive music consumption. It's usually a guy thing. There were large ersatz bookshelves, made from stacked milk crates, and a good selection of reading. The furniture was mostly Pier 1 stuff, with some used junk thrown in for a bohemian flair. A Papadum couch and matching chair, wicker side tables and a coffee table made from a battered piano bench. There was an old dining table which I'd picked up at a flea market. The legs didn't exactly match the top, but it looked good together and it was solid and could seat six. It served as a desk.

On one wall were large framed black-and-white photos of Dexter Gordon and Thelonious Monk. On the facing wall were photos of Hal Russell and Dizzy Gillespie. Above the couch hung a framed print of Salvador Dalí's *The Phantom Wagon*. The bedroom contained a plain set of dresser drawers and a queen-size futon, which lay on the floor. I'd intended to get a bed frame for it but never got around to it. There was a full-length mirror on the back of the bedroom door, but nothing on the walls. There was a second bedroom, which I'd converted into an exercise room complete with recumbent bicycle, heavy bag, speed bag and a bench with assorted free weights. Nothing on the walls there either.

I finished my coffee by the window. Thinking, *What is wrong with you, Dudgeon? Why so many bare walls? Why not decorate a little, like a normal person? Put up some photos, maybe. Something personal. A narcissistic graduation photo. Pictures of the grandparents. Dear old Mom.*

I put my head against the window and looked to the left and caught a glimpse of Lake Michigan reflecting the morning sun. The apartment building was almost in the South Loop, fifteen blocks south of the gentrified Printer's Row neighborhood, where I'd lived until all the buildings went condo. Gentrification was spreading south but hadn't quite reached my place. Pretty soon it would again chase me from the neighborhood. My apartment windows looked toward the increasingly desperate areas on the South Side. If you craned your neck to the left you could see the lake, but if you didn't, there wasn't much to look at. A landscape of rooftop water towers and broken sidewalks and lost hope.

So it wasn't the kind of apartment that would trigger a girl's nesting instincts. Maybe that's why I hadn't brought Jill there. I'd brought other women home but those women weren't looking for a place to nest—just a place to spend the night. Now I wondered if Jill would ever see the place.

"You'll keep seeing me?"

"I don't know."

Damn.

The film production office was located just off Halsted Street, near the river. There were a lot of warehouses in the area and some had been converted into soundstages where movies were shot. I pulled into the gravel parking lot next to a giant gray box of a building. About a dozen cars were parked in the lot but there was no "Continental Pictures" sign, or anything else that would suggest occupancy. I wondered if Bob Loniski had given me the wrong address.

I got out of the car and walked to a glass door in the side of the building. Taped to the inside was a simple piece of paper that said: *Final Revenge*—Production Office—*2nd Floor*. Loniski had told me that the movie he was working on was called *Final Revenge*. It sounded like a stupid name to me, but most movies were pretty stupid these days, so maybe it would be a big hit.

The production office looked like hell. The industrial carpeting was old and worn, the Salvation Army furniture was beat-up, and once-white walls cried out for a fresh coat of paint. From here, the movie business seemed less than captivating.

A twenty-something girl sat at the reception desk. Her dyed-black hair was tied back and she wore black jeans and a black sweatshirt. Even her short fingernails were painted black. A Rolling Stones song came into my head: *I see a red door and I want it painted black . . . no colors anymore, I want them to turn black . . .*

The girl who liked black made a disgusted face when she got a look at mine.

"Oooh, that's gross. Does it hurt?"

"Yes, it hurts." The handful of aspirin I swallowed at breakfast had helped only a little. Now it was wearing off.

"I bet."

"I'm here for Bob Loniski."

"*You're* the bodyguard?" She giggled without even trying to conceal it.

"Don't be a brat. Get Loniski."

"Oh lighten up. It's funny." She picked up the phone and dialed. "Bob, your slightly damaged bodyguard is here."

She had a point. It was funny, just not to me, not at that moment. I sat on an orange plastic chair and lit a cigarette. My target time for today was supposed to be 5:30. No smoking before 5:30. To hell with that.

"You can't smoke in here."

"Oh lighten up," I said, and smiled, which made my lip hurt. Bob Loniski strode into the room and stopped short.

"Holy Christ."

"Yeah, I know. Let's go where we can talk."

Loniski took me down a hallway and around a corner, explaining along the way that we were about to meet with the film's producer, Alan Diskin. He added that Diskin was a *very powerful* man in Hollywood and that his time was valuable.

"You'd think such a powerhouse could get better digs."

"Oh this," said Loniski. "This is just a temporary production office, they're always like this. The head office is unbelievable. Best of everything. Designer furniture, over a million dollars of art on the walls, fully staffed private restaurant, everything. You should see it. It's right on Wilshire, you know."

"Hot diggity," I said.

Diskin came around his desk to greet me. He wore blue jeans with a sharp iron crease, brown ostrich cowboy boots and a beige cashmere turtleneck sweater. Over the sweater he wore a gold necklace. He had hair plugs and capped teeth and a salon tan.

I didn't like him.

"Ray, good to meet you. I'm Al Diskin." I shook his hand and sat in one of the guest chairs. He took his place behind the desk and Loniski sat in the chair beside me. Diskin gestured toward my face. "What happened, you get caught banging the wrong man's wife?" Loniski forced a short laugh that told me Diskin was the kind of boss who expects you to laugh at his rotten jokes.

"A couple of Frank DiMarco's guys tried to convince me to call in sick today."

Loniski gasped. "So the Mafia, uh, the Outfit, really does want me dead."

"DiMarco's landlord scam was his own invention and he did it without authorization. But even on his own he can afford a little muscle."

"So my life is in danger."

"Probably."

"Jesus fucking Christ." He looked like a man who'd forgotten how to blink. We sat in silence for a minute.

"You know John Stone," said Diskin.

"Sure." John Stone ran Stone Security, one of the top firms in Chicago. They specialized in providing security guards to film productions, rock concerts and anything else that seemed glamorous.

"John provides all our security when we shoot in Chicago. I asked him about you and he vouched for your skills. In fact, he was very enthusiastic."

"Uh-huh."

"But I must say, you don't look like what I expected. I mean, not like a bodyguard."

"I'm not a bodyguard, Mr. Diskin—"

"Al, please." So we were buddies.

"Al. I'm a private detective. Sometimes I do executive protection work, which is a little different from regular bodyguard work."

Diskin leaned back in his chair and put his cowboy boots on the desk and flashed his perfect teeth at me. "What's the difference?"

"Most bodyguards are big and scary-looking, kind of like nightclub bouncers. And about as effective. They can clear a path through a crowd for you, shove paparazzi out of the way and make onlookers say, 'Oooh, he has a bodyguard.' Which, for most people, is enough."

"But not if someone is trying to kill you."

"Right. If someone is trying to kill you, it doesn't matter if your bodyguard is big and scary-looking. He has to be quick and aware and calm and able to shoot. More important, he has to take steps to head off vulnerable situations before they occur."

"And the big guys can't do that?"

"Sure, some of them can."

"Interesting."

I didn't think I'd said anything particularly interesting. Diskin took his feet off the desk and leaned forward. "And you can protect Bob ably?" He said it as if Bob were not in the room.

"I can protect Bob more than ably. But you need to understand, if DiMarco is determined enough and patient enough and has enough resources . . ." I let the rest of the sentence go unspoken.

"Oh great," said Loniski, looking ashen.

"Best anybody can do," I said, "is make it difficult, dangerous and very expensive for him to try."

"I have to go to the bathroom," Loniski said, and left the room.

Diskin picked up the phone and punched two buttons. "Emily, do me a favor and intercept Bob on his way back from the can. Yes, tell him to wait in his office." He put the receiver down and sighed. "He's out of his mind with worry. Couldn't you have been a little more comforting?"

"No, I couldn't."

Diskin laughed as if I'd told a joke. The laugh and its associated smile ended rather abruptly and he put his face into a new expression that was supposed to convey his deep concern.

Diskin said that Stone Security provided armed guards to protect the film equipment in the studio downstairs. One of those guards would be assigned to Loniski whenever he was in the building. Loniski's assistant, Kathie, would handle the location scouting and bring back photos for him. On days when Loniski had to be on location, I was expected to stay with him, but most of the time I would simply be required to pick him up each morning and drive him to work and then get him safely home again each night. The furnished apartment that Continental Pictures had rented for Loniski's extended stay in Chicago was in a secure building with a doorman, so I would not be expected to stay overnight. He added that he didn't want Loniski to feel like a prisoner, so I was to accompany him whenever he wanted to go out for dinner, or shopping, or whatever.

I said that was all fine.

"Now in a few days," Diskin continued, "we break for Christmas and go back to L.A. to be with our families. Can you go with Bob? I know that'll take you away from your family here—"

"I can go with Bob," I said. "But I don't have a concealed-carry permit for California."

Diskin smiled broadly. "Continental Pictures is not without influence in the state of California. We'll have it arranged before you arrive."

"Okay then."

"Which brings us to the little matter of your fee," said Diskin.

"Six hundred a day, plus expenses."

"What sort of expenses?"

"Gasoline and mileage for carting Bob around, bullets if I have to shoot somebody, that sort of thing."

"Let's hope it doesn't come to that."

"Let's."

"But I have some trouble with the six hundred. Most days, you'll only be working about an hour, just driving Bob to and from work."

"And getting in the way if Frank DiMarco tries to kill him."

Diskin continued as if I hadn't said anything. "Why don't we say, six hundred for each day in L.A. or when you're on location, and the days when Bob goes out on the town . . . and two fifty for the days when he just comes to work and goes straight home."

"Why don't we say six hundred dollars a day, plus expenses. You want someone else to stand between Bob and DiMarco's gunmen, that's fine by me. The fee is not negotiable."

"I don't think you're being reasonable."

It wasn't a question and didn't require an answer, so I just sat there and listened to my head throb. After a while Diskin flashed his teeth at me again. "Well you can't blame me for trying," he said and leaned forward to shake hands.

I shook his hand, but I did blame him for trying.

Their pitcher hits one of your batters, you hit one of theirs. That's the way it works. I had to send a message to Frank DiMarco. Doing nothing would send an even louder message. Doing nothing would say, "Feel free to kick me around whenever you get the urge."

I parked my rental car on State Street, a few blocks from the Hadleyburg hotel. The Hadleyburg was the kind of hotel that rents rooms by the hour and changes the sheets weekly. In recent years, the Outfit had gotten out of the street-level prostitution business in Chicago. Of course they still ran the vast majority of the sex trade—the escort agencies, massage parlors, strip clubs and porn shops. They'd divested themselves only of the bottom tier, and Chicago's black and Latino gangs now controlled the streetwalkers. But because of its proximity to Rush Street, the Hadleyburg was a valuable asset, so Paul Tortelli had saved that one for the Outfit.

The hookers who use the Hadleyburg as their base all work for a low-life pimp named Booker T. Washington. His mother must have had higher hopes when she named him. Booker was a successful pimp, but strictly street. He would never manage expensive call girls; never move up in the world. Which was okay by him. He seemed perfectly content to run the Division Street sex trade and turn 50 percent street tax over to Frank DiMarco each month as a gesture of respect to Paul Tortelli and, by extension, the Outfit.

I first met Booker almost two years earlier, when a couple from Warroad, Minnesota, hired me to find their daughter Laura, who had come to Chicago to attend art college. She'd disappeared after the first semester of school. It was the same old story. Laura was probably the most talented artist in Warroad, but she couldn't hold her own against the competition in the big city. She got into drugs, dropped out of school, took up with a scumbag boyfriend who got her a job in a strip club. And it's just a small step from peeling to whoring. She ended up working for Booker Washington, doing the frat boys and tourists at Rush and Division, and buying food and crack cocaine with what little money Booker allowed her to keep. I found her all right and she wanted to go home. So I had a few words with Booker and he reluctantly let her go.

Booker Washington was not on my Christmas card list. And I was not on his.

I was still aching from the previous day, especially the swollen knuckles of my right hand. I brought along a large Maglite, the kind cops use for breaking bones. Lifting the flashlight from the trunk, I felt the heft of six D-cell batteries packed into the Maglite's aluminum tube and I decided that this would be more than adequate for a punk like Booker. Unless he had an army with him, my gun would never clear leather. Flashlight in hand, I walked up to Division Street, then west on Division for a few blocks and across to the hotel.

I entered the dark lobby of the Hadleyburg and waited for my eyes to adjust. It was just after noon but whoring is a round-the-clock racket. On a tattered couch in the corner of the lobby sat Candy, a hooker so old she had probably sold blow jobs to Moses. She wore a stained, threadbare sundress. Candy was her street name, of course. I didn't know her real name.

"Candy," I said with a smile, "how you doin', babe?"

Candy glanced up toward me and said, "Mmmm," and then turned her attention back to a disposable lighter that wouldn't light. A long cigarette dangled from her too-red lips, lipstick smeared all over the filter. "Fucking thing," she said.

Up close, she looked like Keith Richards in drag. "Let me help you with that," I said, and spun the wheel of my Zippo. She sucked the flame into the end of the cigarette.

"Mmmm, thanks," she slurred. "You're a true gentleman." Her breath reeked of cheap gin.

"Anytime," I said.

Her head rolled back slightly and she made unfocused eye contact. "Wanna fuck?"

"Gee, I'd love to," I said, "but I can't. I'm working."

"Working," she said. "See what I mean? A true gentleman. Most guys 'round here just say, 'You shriveled old cunt, you make me puke . . . I wouldn't fuck you with someone else's dick.' " Her eyes welled up. She dragged deep on the cigarette and hacked out a blue cloud. "But not you. You'd love to, but you're working. A true gentleman."

I sat down next to her on the couch, fished two twenties from my pocket and slipped them into her hand. "Listen, Candy," I said, "this is for you. You didn't earn it, so you don't have to give it to Booker. It's a gift, for you only. Understand?"

Candy nodded, staring at the money in her palm. "You know, I graduated third in my high school, you know," she said, talking really to herself.

"That's pretty good," I said.

"Sure is," she said, still looking at the money in her hand. "I coulda been something else, you know. Third, outta five hundred kids."

"That's real good," I said. "Listen, where's Booker, I gotta talk to him."

"He's in the fucking office, as usual." She waved her hand in the general direction of the office.

"Alone?"

"Hell, I don't fucking know," Candy said. "He could have the Queen of England in there, for all I know." She folded the money and stuck it in her bra.

I approached the office door, stood and listened. Through the door I could hear the muted tones of music but no voices. I held the Maglite in my right hand, opened the door with my left and entered, closing the door behind me.

Booker Washington sat behind the desk, reading—or rather, looking at—a copy of *D-Cups* magazine. A boom box on the desk played "The World Is a Ghetto" by War.

Booker dropped the magazine on the desk and his expression told me that he was searching his memory banks for my face. After a second, he found it.

"The fuck you want, peckerwood?" he said.

"Nice to see you, Booker."

Booker reached for the telephone on his desk and I brought the barrel of the flashlight down hard on the back of his hand, crushing some metacarpals.

"Shit!" He pulled his broken paw back and cradled it in his good hand. He stood up. He was about six foot one and weighed maybe 160 pounds with his pockets full of loose change. "You crazy? I'm protected, man."

I tried to look impressed as I came around the desk and rammed the end of the flashlight into his solar plexus. He grunted and doubled over, his good hand braced on the desktop for support. I slammed the flashlight down and heard more bones break. I brought the flashlight down a second time, just above the wrist, and the sharp white end of a broken bone popped out through the skin, squirting blood on the desktop. I felt a little light-headed but I pushed the revulsion from my mind and focused on what Booker did to girls like Laura and Candy. It worked, and my anger returned.

Booker fell back into his chair and held his mangled, bleeding hands in front of his face. "Come on, man," he whined, "stop it."

I considered breaking one of Booker's kneecaps, but decided that two badly broken hands and a compound fracture of the wrist were enough. Booker Washington would be out of commission for a while.

"Tell Frank DiMarco that Bob Loniski is off-limits," I said.

Booker looked at me and nodded. "Bob Loniski is off-limits," he repeated as a tear snaked down his left cheek.

"Very good," I said. I stopped at the door and turned around. "And make him believe it, Booker, because next time I'm gonna take out your fuckin' kneecaps."

On the way back to my office, I stopped in an alley and disassembled the flashlight and wiped it down to remove my fingerprints. Then I wiped the batteries clean. The flashlight went into a Dumpster and the batteries went down a sewer. It was a shame to throw it away but there was always a chance that Booker Washington would swear out a complaint against me. I could afford a new flashlight more than I could afford to lose my detective's license. While disposing of the evidence, I thought about the message I'd sent. Frank DiMarco may be protected, but I could still damage his business interests.

Their pitcher hits one of your batters, you hit one of theirs. That's the way it works.

CHAPTER THREE

I **entered the lobby of the Richmond Building** just before 3:30. The Richmond Building is on the east side of Wabash, just north and across the street from the Palmer House hotel. It's a good building, with Art Deco elevators and lobby. And it hasn't had a face-lift in a very long time, which means I can afford to keep an office there. There's a thirteenth floor, which most buildings don't have, and the landlord gives what he calls a "bravery discount" to tenants willing to occupy it. So my office was on the thirteenth floor, and because my office was number 1313, my rent was the lowest of all.

Even with the bravery discount, there was usually a vacant office on the floor, while there was a waiting list to get into the rest of the building. People are strange. Anyway, I'd been there almost eight years and I liked the place. But I also stepped on cracks in the sidewalk and petted black cats. That's bravery for you.

I got off the elevator at the thirteenth floor and turned right, toward my office. There were no ghosts or lycanthropes in the hallway but Vinnie Cosimo was propped up against my door, reading a book.

When I was about ten feet away, he dog-eared the page he was on and closed the book without looking up.

"Good timing," he said. "My feet were startin' to hurt."

"Hey Vince." We shook hands as if we hadn't just seen each other the previous day. "How'd you know I was gonna show at all?"

"I didn't. That's why I brought along some reading."

"Who sent you?" I unlocked the door and we went inside and I switched on the lights.

"You kidding? Shit, Sal would kill me if he knew. You don't mind, do you?"

"Always welcome," I said. "You want a beer?"

"That'd be great." Vinnie squeezed his large frame into one of my client chairs and I got two bottles of Goose Island Christmas Ale out of the little bar fridge that doubled as a table for my coffeemaker. I opened the bottles and handed one to Vinnie as I went around my desk. I sat and took a pull off the bottle and lit a cigarette.

"Those things'll kill ya," said Vinnie. "You should give 'em up."

"Yeah, I know, I'm trying."

Vinnie drank some beer and took in the room. "Man, this place is cool. Like going back in time to one of them old movies."

"Thanks. It helps sell the image." Which was true. Selling the image is a big part of success for a private detective and I had decorated the office with that in mind.

All of the furniture was pre-1960. There was a burgundy leather couch along one wall, a matching desk chair and a couple of oak captain's chairs with leather seat cushions, for visitors. On the wall above the couch hung a framed replica of the Declaration of Independence and a map of Chicago, circa 1871, the year of the Great Fire that may or may not have been started by Mrs. O'Leary's cow. On the facing wall there were built-in bookshelves and an up-to-date map of the city. Back by the door there were some cupboards and a sink and the little bar fridge with the coffeemaker on top. The door itself was my favorite part. An old oak door with a frosted window, and RAY DUDGEON INVESTIGATIONS painted on the window in gold.

Behind me were large windows, which looked out over Wabash Avenue. On the little bit of wall between the windows hung my bachelor's degree in journalism, my certificate from the American Security Training Institute, and my State of Illinois private detective's license. Below them stood an oak filing cabinet that matched the desk. An old Turkish rug covered much of the hardwood floor.

Truth be told, I couldn't have afforded to decorate the place with new furniture, at least not of any quality. So I'd put the office together, piece by piece, over time. Garage sales, estate sales, flea markets—that sort of thing. You could see it as a bunch of used junk, but I liked to think of it as a collection of pre-antiques. I was perhaps overly proud of it but it did help to sell the image. I had even removed the fluorescent bulbs and scattered old lamps around the place. The only nods to modernity were the laptop computer, the all-in-one printer/scanner/fax gadget, the combination telephone–answering machine and the coffeemaker. And there wasn't much I could do about that, since I needed all those things.

But Vinnie Cosimo had not come to help with the Surgeon General's fight against tobacco or to compliment my abilities as an interior decorator. He took another swig of beer and so did I.

"You know, I think I could be a pretty good private eye," he said.

"You come to fill out a job application?"

"I guess you don't think I'd be any good." His face held a worried look I'd never seen on him and I wished he would just get on with it. He took another long draw on the beer.

"I think you'd be fine," I said. "Could you pass a background check?"

"I've never even been arrested," Vinnie said, with some pride.

"Would the Outfit let you walk away?"

"Mr. Greico would be okay. He knows he can trust me and I think he knows I'm not that happy with what I'm doing." Another swig of beer emptied the bottle. "Besides, I'm just thinkin' out loud . . . I'm not goin' anywhere while he's around."

"But he's not getting any younger and you don't want to work for Sal," I guessed.

Vinnie sat and looked past me out the window. The brakes of a northbound El train screamed at us from below as it pulled into Washington Station. I took Vinnie's empty and went to the fridge and got him a fresh bottle. It seemed to me that he was wrestling with how much to tell. I sat back down and we both drank. I swallowed a bunch of aspirin with my beer.

"I got a theory about Sal," said Vinnie. "My theory is, Sal has a hard time living in Mr. Greico's shadow. So he comes on like a hard guy, more than he should. But that don't make him a bad guy. My theory is, maybe when, God forbid, Mr. Greico's gone, then Sal will ease up a little." Vinnie was no dummy.

"Maybe," I said. "Or maybe he has even more to prove when he tries to fill the old man's shoes. Maybe he gets worse."

"Yeah, maybe." Vinnie drank some more and looked out the window again. He was having trouble with eye contact. He needed a gentle push.

"Vince," I said, "you come here to see me and you sit in my office and drink my beer and talk about your career options . . . which is fine with me, but that's not why you're here. My face looks like it lost an argument with a meat tenderizer and you don't even mention it. So I have to assume that the two are connected. As much as I enjoy your company, can we get to the fucking point?"

"I shouldn't even be here."

"Yeah, but here you are and you know I'm not going to drop a dime on you. So spill."

Vinnie examined the label on his beer bottle as if it could tell him what to do. Apparently, it told him to spill his guts. It all came out in a rush of words. "Yesterday after you leave, Mr. Greico calls Frank DiMarco in. He tells him not to be a numbskull. He says that you're protecting this Loniski guy and Frank should just take his chances in court and that he wouldn't get by you anyway and he shouldn't a been freelancing to begin with. And Frank says, 'You can't tell me what to do, I got Paul Tortelli backing me.' And Mr. Greico says, 'Fine, you can work for Paul, because you don't work here no more.' And he picks up the phone, right there, and calls Tortelli and tells him about it. I don't know what Tortelli says but I can see that Mr. Greico don't like it. Then Frank says 'go to hell' and marches out and Mr. Greico is pissed. He tells me and Sal to take a walk, he wants to think."

"Uh-huh," I said.

"So I thought I should warn you that Frankie's off the leash"—he pointed at my face—"but I guess I'm a little late."

"It's the thought that counts," I said.

"I guess. So, you okay?"

"Fine."

"How many were there?" That he assumed there was more than one pleased me.

"Two. The big guy was almost as big as you and maybe five years older. Has a broken jaw now. The other guy was about my size, fights with his feet. He'll be walking funny for a while. You know who I mean?"

"Think so. Both Tortelli's guys, but not his personal guys. Probably work for Frank now."

"That's a safe assumption."

We didn't seem to have any more to say to each other and Vinnie had already said more than he should, so I thanked him again and reminded him he was always welcome and he left. When he picked up his book, I caught a glimpse of the title. *Covert Surveillance & Electronic Penetration, Volume 2*. It was a standard text in the field and it was not a light read. Vinnie Cosimo was no dummy. And he probably would make a good private eye, if he could ever bring himself to leave the Outfit.

After Vinnie was gone, I sat and smoked and thought about what he had said. *Frank DiMarco was off the leash*. More than that, DiMarco told Johnny Greico to go to hell. No matter how much of a punk he was, he wouldn't have stood up to the old man without Paul Tortelli's okay. Not a chance. But why would Cousin Paul allow DiMarco to quit Greico? As far as I knew, Tortelli's position in the Outfit was a few rungs down the ladder from Greico and this would be seen as a major slap in the face. It didn't make sense. And whatever Tortelli said to Greico on the phone had reinforced the point. Could Tortelli have designs on Greico's operation? It seemed unlikely, but I had no other theory.

The two knuckleheads who had tried to put the arm on me were Tortelli's guys. Even if they were on loan to DiMarco, they would surely report to their real boss. So Tortelli must also be sanctioning DiMarco's plans for Bob Loniski. That didn't make sense either. Why wouldn't Tortelli just tell DiMarco to keep his mouth shut and do his time? Five years, out in two.

I had no answers for these and other questions that occurred to me over the course of three cigarettes and two mugs of coffee. And I found myself wishing that I'd known all this before my visit to Booker Washington. I called Terry and got his voice mail. I told his voice mail that I'd see him at midnight, unless he heard from me between now and then.

I unlocked my desk drawer and got my everyday gun, a Para Ordnance P10 Limited, and put it on the desk. Thinking, *Jill doesn't approve of guns.* Jill was a nurse, she had that luxury. But this gun had saved my life.

The first time I shot another human being was just after I got into the investigation business. I was serving papers on a guy who was being sued for beating someone unconscious in a bowling alley. The lawyer who hired me had warned me to be careful—the guy had a short temper and a long history of assaults to prove it. I found the guy in his driveway working under a rusty Trans Am. I called him by his first name and he wiggled out from underneath. I dropped the subpoena on his chest and said, "You've been served, sir. Have a nice day," and walked away without waiting for a reply. But his reply came from behind in the form of a crowbar blow to the head. A simple "fuck you, buddy" would have sufficed. Luckily, his aim was imperfect and the iron bar glanced off the back of my head and came down on my left shoulder. I fell to the ground and rolled on my back and drew the gun and shot. The bullet entered through his upper lip and the back of his head came off in a shower of blood and brains and skull fragments. He stood frozen for an eternity, the crowbar still poised to strike again, then crumpled on top of me in slow motion. I rolled out from under him and began to hyperventilate. A woman across the street saw the whole thing from her window and called the police. It didn't take them long to ascertain what had happened, and they ruled it justifiable homicide. I didn't like being connected to the word "homicide," so I called it "self-defense," which is the same thing.

I'd shot a few other well-deserving people since then but the first one sticks in your mind forever, like the death of your first dog. It gets easier as you go along.

I got up and went to the fridge for a beer. From the cupboard over the sink I got a roll of paper towels and spread them out on the desk. I opened the bottom drawer and took out a gun-cleaning kit. I popped the magazine out of the pistol, ejected the round from the chamber and emptied the magazine. I put the bullets off to one side, counted them, and then stripped the gun and scrubbed it thoroughly, leaving just a thin coat of oil where necessary. I reassembled the gun, loaded the magazine, jacked a round into the chamber, applied the safety, popped the magazine out again, inserted one more round and reinserted the mag.

I was mindful and methodical about the work and it took almost fifteen minutes, start to finish. But I once knew a guy who shot himself while cleaning his gun. He had been around guns all his life, had even served in Vietnam, and could strip, clean and reassemble a weapon while blindfolded. He just got careless one day and it cost him three fingers from his left hand. I wasn't going to make that mistake. I might get shot one day, but I sure as hell wasn't going to shoot myself.

Okay, so Jill didn't approve of guns. It was hard to blame her. But to me, disapproving of guns was simplistic and naive. Like disapproving of violence, without making any distinction between an aggressor and a victim acting in self-defense. What I disapproved of was the *initiation* of violence.

And this gun had saved my life.

I wasn't going to shoot myself but I didn't really want anyone else to shoot me either, and that was something I could not completely control. *Control the things you can, and don't be distracted by the things that you cannot.* So I did what I could, and arrived at McSorley's Gun Shop just after 4:00.

McSorley's is on West Madison, on the border between declining Puerto Rican and black neighborhoods. Low income but not destitute. At least not yet. Being where it is, the clientele is a mix of cops, drug dealers and solid citizens. Until you assess which group you're dealing with, you keep to yourself. There is a palpable tension when different types of client share the range.

The shooting range itself is a dump. The lighting is terrible, the walls are decorated with bullet holes and graffiti and ventilation is nonexistent. The acrid odor of spent gunpowder, brass and sweat hangs heavy. But all of this lends to a more realistic practice session. In the real world, there will be more than a palpable tension to deal with and the lighting is rarely perfect.

I had the range to myself, so I set up in the middle lane. On the shelf in front of me were a stack of paper silhouette targets, a box of .45 caliber bullets for the Para-Ordnance, and a box of .32s for the little Seecamp that I sometimes carried as a backup piece. The Seecamp isn't powerful enough for a primary weapon; it would only come into use if someone got the .45 out of my hand, and in that case they'd be standing close enough for the .32 to do its job.

I attached a target to the bulldog clip and wheeled it out along the clothesline-type mechanism to about ten yards. The range was twenty-five yards long but most shootings take place at about ten feet, so ten yards seemed plenty to me.

I always shoot respectably well but today I had *flow,* practicing Zen shooting, putting nice, neat holes in the X-ring. I put a new target out there, then walked two lanes over and wheeled out a second target, about six feet past the first. Back in my lane, I alternated between the two, putting a double-tap in each, back and forth, with the precision of Benvenuto Cellini carving a gold pendant.

I was good and I liked to be good, because this was something that was important to be good at. Benvenuto could always melt down the gold and start over, but I might not get a second chance if I missed my target. And I couldn't take back a stray bullet that might kill a bystander.

After I'd put a box of ammo through the .45, I set a new target at about twelve feet and went to work with the little Seecamp. I shot both right-handed and left- because if the first gun was gone I might not have a right hand. The left-handed groups were not as tight but they hit the silhouette and that's all that mattered. With the target up close, I kept seeing the faces of Tortelli's thugs on it. I didn't feel one way or the other about shooting them. If I had to, I would. There was no like or dislike.

I felt like Yoda.

Bob Loniski was staying at the Balderstone Apartments, a modern sixteen-story building on Oak Street, in the fashionable Gold Coast neighborhood. The building was quite secure. The rear emergency exit only opened from inside and the elevator from the underground parking garage only went to the lobby. To get up to the apartments, you had to pass a security desk on the way to the main elevators or stairwells. If your name was not on a list of expected guests, the guard called up to the tenant. The tenant could tune his television to channel one and see closed-circuit video of the lobby, so he could be sure before giving the guard permission to let anyone up. On the guard's desk was a video monitor that displayed four multiplexed views of the underground garage.

It was a good system. The only flaw in it was that the guard did not wear a sidearm. But I doubted that DiMarco would be coming in hard, anyway. Easier just to write off the apartment as a target and take Loniski out when he was in transit.

Loniski introduced me to the guard and told him that I was to be allowed access whenever I wanted, but no one else. The guard was a skinny black man in his middle sixties, but he looked scrappy and he seemed like a retired cop. Despite his age and size, I figured he could look after himself.

The guard's name was Sylvester. I asked if he'd been a cop and he said no, but he was in the military for over thirty years. He'd seen action from Vietnam to Grenada and had retired a major.

"I'm still one tough Marine," he said with a confident smile. I agreed that he was.

"All the guards in this building are retired military," he added. "You don't have to worry about us."

I showed Major Sylvester my identification and explained that Loniski had received a threat, so special attention was in order. He took a Polaroid of me and put it beside his monitor for the guards on the other two shifts.

The apartment was on the eleventh floor, second door to the right of the elevators. There were stairwells at either end of the hallway. The apartment had a metal door with a wide-angle peephole and a useless chain and a better-than-average dead bolt. It was one of those generic-furniture executive suites that rent out to traveling business folks who are in town for an extended stay. Loniski's lease was for nine months, with six left to go.

I searched the apartment and found nobody hiding in the bathtub or under the bed or in a closet. Large windows spanned the living room wall. Through them, Chicago's Magnificent Mile glittered greedily, proffering all the requisite garbage for another consumer Mc-Christmas. The John Hancock Building towered over everything, its roof antennas sticking up like ice picks threatening to blind the sky. I closed the drapes and told Loniski that they were to stay closed.

He was still nervous as hell. On the drive from the studio to his apartment he had chattered incessantly and asked repeatedly if we were being followed. I had assured him that we were not.

I didn't tell him that Tortelli's thugs had been watching from a car across the street when I picked him up. Different thugs from yesterday, but it was the same green Ford and they made sure that I noticed them. Still, they hadn't followed us and there seemed no reason to rattle Loniski's cage. He was already a mess.

"You think this building's good enough, I–I mean safe enough?" Loniski stammered.

"It's fine. Better than most. Just keep the drapes closed and the door bolted." From the fridge, I got us each a beer.

Loniski sat on the couch and drank his beer. I took off my jacket and draped it over the back of a chair. He stared at the gun on my hip.

"Try to relax, Bob," I said. "You look like your head's gonna explode."

"Easy for you to say, you deal with this shit all the time."

I didn't deal with this shit all the time but saying so wasn't going to reassure him, so I said nothing. I opened the gym bag I'd brought and got out my supplies and put them on the coffee table. Loniski stared at them like they were alien artifacts from the planet Krypton.

"This is a portable door brace. You put this end under the doorknob and jam it forward until the rubber foot is secure. No one will be able to force the door." I took the door jammer and showed him how. Then I unlocked the door and yanked like hell on the doorknob. The door didn't open.

"Of course, you still keep the door locked," I added, taking nothing for granted.

"Wow. That's really neat," said Loniski. At least he didn't say *Neat-O.*

We sat back down and I showed him the next item on the list.

"This is a simple door alarm. Put the metal loop around the doorknob and turn on the switch. If anyone touches the knob in the hallway, it'll go off. And it's loud." I decided that a demonstration wasn't necessary. "Every time I leave, you dead-bolt the door, put the jammer in place and turn on the alarm. Got it?"

"Sure."

"If the alarm sounds, you don't go near the door. You call security downstairs, and then page me. Don't leave a voice message. Just punch in 911 and I'll come running."

Then I showed him how to work the stun gun. It was a Security Plus 500,000-volt model—the Cadillac of stun guns, or so said the guy who sold it to me. I told Bob to keep it on his bedside table.

I gave him a four-ounce can of Mace and told him to carry it at all times. The stuff I'd used on Tortelli's thug was only a 5 percent concentration of pepper spray, and it hadn't been potent enough. This stuff had a 10 percent concentration of OC pepper, plus CN tear gas. It would stop a small bear.

While Loniski took the stun gun into the bedroom, I looked around the kitchen for any sign of food and found none.

Loniski wanted to order out for pizza. I explained that his food delivery days were over until this Frank DiMarco business was finished. I told him to make a list of groceries and I would get them. He reluctantly made the list but he didn't like the idea of me leaving. It was nice to feel wanted.

I drove to the nearest grocery store and bought everything on the list. It was all preprepared crap. Evidently, Bob Loniski was not a cook. I pushed my squeaky-wheeled cart full of crap to the front of the store and paid for it. The checkout girl didn't try to kill me.

Then I stopped at a liquor store and picked up two six-packs of Goose Island Ale and a couple of bottles of Faustino V, the same wine that I'd used the day before to crack a guy's jawbone. Loniski's list just said beer and wine, so I figured I was free to choose something I liked. The old man behind the counter didn't pull a gun, or suggest that I stop protecting anyone.

Finally, I stopped at Edwardo's to pick up a flat-guy. I started with their popular spinach pizza, to which I added Italian sausage, anchovies, mushrooms and roasted garlic. Nobody there tried to kill me either but the shapely young woman behind the counter gave me a nasty look when she caught me admiring her assets. I was tempted to explain the difference between leering and admiring, but I didn't want the pizza to get cold, so I just paid for it and left.

Bob and I sat on his rented living room couch and ate pizza and drank beer and watched the post-MJ Bulls lose another game. Just a couple of guys. And Bob told me about his life.

He was a California kid, always wanted to be in "the industry," and even studied film at UCLA. At school he wanted to be a director, just like everyone else. But he admitted (as if it needed to be said) that he was a bit of a nerd, and he wasn't very good at selling himself. In Hollywood, selling yourself was what it was all about. So he settled into locations managing and he made a good living out of it.

He had been married once, to an assistant film editor. They had a son who was now in the seventh grade. Bob left his wife and son during his inevitable midlife crisis a few years ago. He saw his son every second weekend and got along fine with the ex-wife. They were still good friends, he insisted, and he even got along fine with her new husband. I didn't understand that, but I'm not from Hollywood.

I was staying sober but there was no such obligation for Bob, who was now on his sixth beer. His eyes were glassy.

"You got a kid, Ray?"

"No."

"Too bad. Greatest thing you could ever do." Yeah. So great that he left his.

"I know what you're thinking and, yes, I miss Josh when I'm away like this." He didn't have a clue what I was thinking. The motherfucker *had* a family and he threw it away. "But there's lots of ways of being close," he continued. "We talk by e-mail every day." Another swig of beer. "Every damn day. He tells me everything. I bet there aren't many fathers who can say that."

I didn't want him getting maudlin on me, so I agreed with him and changed the subject back to the movie business. He went with it, and proceeded to list the titles of all the movies he'd ever worked on. I didn't recognize most of them. Each time I admitted as much, he told me how much money it took in at the box office, as if that would spark my memory.

I picked up the remote control and switched to the nine o'clock news. The top local story was a suicide. An unidentified white woman had walked out the window of her sixteenth-floor apartment. The building was in the fourteen-hundred block of South Michigan Avenue. She was believed to be in her early forties. Police were not releasing her name until they notified her next of kin.

The fourteen-hundred block of South Michigan, sixteenth floor. Where had I seen that before?

The video that went along with the story showed Michigan Avenue with police cars scattered about, lights flashing. It showed yellow crime-scene tape blocking the sidewalk, an ambulance that was of no use to anyone, and uniformed cops directing traffic away from the curb lane. It showed a green plastic tarp covering the remains of an unidentified white woman in her early forties. When I saw the numbers above the building's entrance, I made the connection. I knew that address.

And I knew that this was no ordinary jumper. The dead woman under the tarp was the artist who had rented space from Frank DiMarco.

"But you didn't tell Bob about the jumper?" Terry sipped his single-malt Scotch in the dim light of Trader Vic's Boathouse Bar. I was drinking dark rum on the rocks.

"No reason to. He doesn't know where the artist lived, so to him it was just a suicide."

"Her name will be released."

"Eventually. Right now Bob needs to focus on his own situation."

"And he's okay where he is?"

"Nobody's going to get to him in the apartment, as long as he does what he's told."

"What about you?"

I'd given Terry a full account of what had happened since he brought Bob Loniski to my office, including my night with Jill, my meeting with Booker Washington and Vinnie's visit. Terry was a guy I could tell everything to, without seeing it printed in the *Chronicle* the next morning. We had that kind of relationship.

"I'm fine."

"Don't look it."

"Thanks. What have you got for me on DiMarco?"

"Got this—our boy DiMarco's been fucking up for a while now. The last time he got pinched?"

"Muscle job for Bennie Schwartz."

"Yeah. DiMarco was supposed to, you know, *emphasize* to some guy the importance of not falling behind on his payments. Break a finger or two. Like that. But he goes wild on the poor bastard, damn near kills him."

"Uh-huh."

"Which was stupid because the nearly-dead guy is so scared he tells the cops all about it and when they pick DiMarco up he's still carrying his brass knucks and they've still got the vic's blood on them."

"So DiMarco goes away for a while. Big deal."

Terry sipped his drink and smiled. There was no use rushing him.

"It gets better. Once inside, DiMarco can't seem to keep his mouth shut, trying to develop a badass rep for himself. Talking about how his cousin is Paul Tortelli and how nobody better fuck with him. And word gets back to Tortelli, who's not happy. So Tortelli pulls some strings and gets DiMarco moved into a cell with Dominic Salviati. Know him?"

"No."

"He's Outfit muscle. But real muscle, not a lightweight like Di-Marco. Anyway, Salviati's job is to look out for DiMarco and make sure he keeps his mouth shut. Which he does. Word is, it wasn't easy. DiMarco came pretty unglued in there."

"Okay," I said, "but everybody knows that DiMarco is Tortelli's cousin, and everybody knows that Tortelli is an Outfit capo."

"What I hear, Tortelli has shared a lot of family business with Cousin Frank," said Terry. "DiMarco may not be a made guy but he knows a lot more than he should."

"That explains why Tortelli's nervous about DiMarco having to do another stretch."

"Could be."

"But it doesn't explain why Tortelli would disrespect Johnny Greico."

"No it doesn't."

"Tortelli get a promotion I don't know about?"

"No. Still runs the sex trade."

"Is he ambitious?"

"Maybe," said Terry. "Why?"

"Maybe he wants to move up but there's nowhere to go. Greico's getting pretty ancient and maybe Tortelli wants to run the bookmaking operation."

"Never gonna happen. The Outfit would never allow it. Everybody knows that Sal's being groomed to take over for the old man."

"So why would Tortelli risk making bad blood with Greico?"

"Haven't got a clue. What's that got to do with keeping Loniski alive?"

"Nothing, really. I'm a curious guy."

Terry tossed back the rest of his Scotch and rattled the ice around the bottom of the glass. "Don't take your eye off the ball, Ray. The thing is, we now know it's important to Tortelli that DiMarco not go back to jail. Which means, it's important that Loniski die. Which means you're facing off against a lot more than just a jerk-off like Frank DiMarco."

"I know."

"And Tortelli won't be thrilled about you fucking up one of his pimps."

"I know. I thought Frank DiMarco was acting on his own." I took another sip of rum, which burned against the inside of my split lip. "Anyway, I don't see how I could've played it any differently, regardless of Tortelli. The day I start laying down for beatings is the day I'm finished."

"Want to know what I think you should do?"

"Always," I said, and signaled across the room to the bartender for another round. Terry stared at the ice in the bottom of the glass, thinking. I lit a cigarette and waited.

"I think you should finish off this case and then go back to being a reporter, which is what you're really good at, and then marry the girl."

"I'm really good at this too."

"No, I know, I didn't mean it that way."

A pretty Polynesian waitress in a pretty tight Polynesian floral-print dress deposited our new drinks on the table and picked up our empty glasses and changed the dirty ashtray for a fresh one.

Terry sipped his new drink. "You think there's a future in this thing you've got going with Jill?"

"I'd like there to be."

"She say she loves you?"

"She thinks so."

"What about you?"

I hadn't said the words "I love you" since that day on my grandfather's fishing boat, a million years ago. I drank some rum and thought about Jill and got that light-headed feeling that always came when I thought of her.

"I haven't said it yet but, yeah."

"Okay. So you're a couple of lovebirds and spring is in the air." Terry grinned. "What is she, thirty-three?"

"Thirty-six."

"She want kids?"

"Jesus, Terry. I don't know."

"Well you might want to find out. And if she does, you might not want to waste her time. Girl's thirty-six, she's probably got the need to breed. Most of them do."

"And?"

"And she deserves to be happy. She deserves to have a father for her kids that doesn't run around pissing off gangsters."

"You piss off gangsters. Angela seems happy."

"That's different. Folks are reluctant to clip a reporter. It just brings more heat down. Last time a journalist got hit in this town was about thirty years ago, and he was playing both sides. You know the rules— cops and journalists are off-limits, as long as they're playing square. Besides, Angela recognizes that there's a paucity of quality husbands in the black community."

"Paucity."

"A definite paucity." Terry grinned again.

"She didn't have to marry a black guy."

"Yeah, well, there's a paucity of quality husbands in the white community too."

"Maybe somebody ought to tell Jill that."

"She's been dating you, man. I think she already knows."

CHAPTER FOUR

The Chicago Police Department Area 4 Headquarters stands at the corner of Harrison and Kedzie. From the street, it looks like any number of featureless brown brick public school buildings that sprang up everywhere in the 1970s. But inside, it's all cop shop.

I waved at the desk sergeant and climbed the stairs to the detective division. The floor was a whirlwind of activity—detectives in shirtsleeves tapping on computer keyboards, talking rapidly into telephones, taking witness statements and doing a variety of other detective things. Nobody broke into applause upon my arrival, but a couple of familiar faces nodded hello and another one sneered at me. Two out of three ain't bad.

Lieutenant Mike Angelo was the commanding officer of the Area 4 Homicide Section, so he rated a private office. I knocked on his door and he answered it. He was not quite six feet in height but he more than made up for it in width and he gave the impression of being a Big Man. He wore a disciplined mustache and a brown JCPenney suit.

"Dudgeon, don't you look like shit." He shook my hand.

"Hey, Mike," I said. "Have you put on more weight?"

"Don't look so smug. You get to my age, you'll have a pot too." Mike waved me into his office, left me sitting there for a minute, and returned with a Styrofoam coffee cup. He opened the window and then sat on a squeaky chair behind his desk, took a sip of coffee and made a face.

"No coffee for me, thanks Mike," I said.

"Hey, I'm doing you a favor. This stuff sucks." He took another long sip and made another face and put the cup on his desk. He pulled a pack of Marlboro Lights from his shirt pocket and lit one and dropped the match into the coffee. "Ashtrays are not allowed anymore," he said, and offered the pack to me. "Neither is smoking, but what the hell."

Before falling off the wagon the previous day, I'd worked my target time up to 5:00. No smoking before five. But yesterday I'd smoked all day, and it wouldn't be fair to force my system to wait until 5:30. I looked at my watch. It was just after ten in the morning. Bob Loniski was safe at work, so I'd already accomplished one stressful task today without smoking. Okay. I'd start at ten and work my way up the hill again. Like Sisyphus.

I took a cigarette and lit it.

"Times change," I said. "The puritans are winning the culture war."

"Don't get me started," said Mike. He dragged on his smoke and dipped some ash into the Styrofoam cup. He looked at me and his eyes said he was out of small talk. They were not cruel eyes, but they were often cold. Today they were bloodshot and a little glassy and I wondered if he'd been up all night working, or if he'd just been drinking. It was hard to tell with Mike. He drank regularly and he drank a lot but I'd never seen it affect his speech or movements or judgment. Only his eyes. And even then, I could never be sure. "You come to confess, don't bother," he said. "I already know."

"What?"

"Don't fuck with me. You've been working for Johnny Greico again."

"Absolutely not," I said.

"Bullshit. A very fuckin' important informant went AWOL a few weeks back and we've been watching Greico's place. You were there Tuesday for almost five hours. Don't say you weren't, 'cause I fuckin' know it."

Mike was upset. It's not just that he was a straight cop, which he was. But he was also Italian, and he took the existence of the Outfit personally. I'd heard him rant on the subject before and I knew how violent his feelings were.

I took my time and explained my visit to Johnny Greico. I told Mike all about Frank DiMarco's landlord scam and the dead cabinet-maker and the threats to Loniski. I told him about Paul Tortelli's thugs and how my face came to look the way it did.

Of course I didn't tell him about Booker Washington, or Vinnie Cosimo's visit to my office, or about Terry Green working the story. No use complicating things.

"What makes you think Greico would tell you if he had plans for your client?"

"I told him that if he wanted Loniski dead, I wouldn't take the case."

Mike let out a derisive snort. "Jesus Christ, Dudgeon. You're some piece of work. As if I need to tell you, getting chummy with Wiseguys is a very bad idea."

"I'm not chummy, Mike. I asked the man a question, he answered me and I left."

"You hang around barbers long enough, you're gonna end up with a haircut. *Capisce?*"

"*Capisco.*"

"Hope so." He dragged on his smoke. "So what do you want?"

"The jumper on South Michigan last night."

"What about her?"

"Her name was Jeanne Gosselin. She was a painter."

"And?"

"And she didn't jump. She was helped out the window."

"Uh-huh." Mike's half-smoked cigarette let out a dying hiss as he tossed it into the cup. "You got any ideas on who helped her?"

"Frank DiMarco."

"Shit." Mike stood and walked to the window and watched the sunlight turn snow into puddles. He peeled off his jacket and hung it on the back of his chair and sat down again. From a desk drawer he produced a yellow pad and slapped it on the desk and plucked a pen from a ceramic cup. He pushed the plunger on the pen about a hundred times as he gave me his hard cop-stare.

I tried not to wilt. "Look, I know you don't want to hear it, but I—"

"No. I do want to hear it. But you're not the guy I want to hear it from."

"None taken," I said. Then I told him that Jeanne Gosselin had been one of DiMarco's tenants. "Also," I added, "I think DiMarco's working for Paul Tortelli now, and I think Tortelli's sanctioning these hits."

"And how do you know all this?"

"I don't know. I think."

"Okay, why do you think?"

"Can't say."

"Can't, or won't?"

"Call it a hunch, Mike. I'm just telling you what I think. I'm not holding out."

"Better not be. That license you got can be taken away." Mike lit another cigarette and I tossed mine into his ersatz ashtray.

"I came here to give you information about a possible homicide," I said. "I know my responsibilities."

"Right."

"DiMarco had a third tenant who, as far as I know, isn't dead yet." I flipped through my notebook. "Name's Andre Hanson, owns a silk-screen shop. Might be in line for police protection."

"If it turns out that DiMarco actually did your jumper."

"Well that's for you to decide. Anyway, you can get the background from Sam Christensen at the fraud squad."

"Fine. If there's nothing else, I've got work to do."

I stood up. "You're welcome," I said, and walked out.

I drove south to Thirty-fifth Street and stopped at Buckeye's for a hot dog and a beer. Sitting by the window, I looked out at the monstrosity now called U.S. Cellular Field and the parking lot where the original Comiskey Park had once stood. I suppose it was an economic inevitability, but it made me sad to think about them tearing the old girl down.

A lot of Cubs fans took great pleasure from the fact that Sox now played in such a terrible ballpark. Not me. I didn't understand Cubs fans who rooted against the Sox. To me, being a fan was about rooting *for* something, not *against* something. I had no hate for the White Sox. In fact, they were my favorite team in the Junior League. My idea of nirvana would be watching the Cubs beat the White Sox in game seven of the World Series. And that could never happen unless *both* teams made it to the Big Dance. Defeating a worthy opponent is true victory—there's little sense of achievement in beating an unworthy opponent. Baseball players get this—I wonder why so many fans miss the point.

I ate my hot dog and drank my beer without tasting either and realized that the meeting with Mike Angelo had left me in a foul mood. Mike had every right to be angry—my courtesy call to Johnny Greico was not something he could easily dismiss.

And I could ill afford to tarnish my relationship with Mike. On television, the private eye always has a high-ranking cop for a best buddy. But that's not the way it really is. Cops, as a rule, hate private detectives. We run fewer risks than they do and often get in their way. Unless you're a retired cop turned private, you don't get a lot of cooperation and even less respect.

Still, Mike had always been fair with me. Mike was a cop the way I'd been a reporter. He did it right and didn't back down. He was born into the job—his father had been a beat cop and both of his brothers were cops. Good cops. Mike had risen higher in the force than his brothers but he'd reached his zenith at lieutenant. He didn't suffer fools gladly—even fools of higher rank—and he refused to play politics. He was clean, yet he'd break the rules when the rules were wrong. He was an idealist and a homicide cop, which seemed to me like a hell of a high-wire act. The politics and corruption all around him must've taken a toll over the years. This, I suspected, is why he drank so much and why he bitched constantly about the job and why he would never leave it.

Which made him a lot tougher than me. Journalism was my childhood fantasy. More than that, it was a remote and wished-for goal, then maybe even a reachable destination. Ultimately, it became my lifeboat and *If I could just get there* . . . became my teenage mantra. I was obsessed by the idea of working as one of "society's watchdogs." I was firmly hooked—and there were reasons for that. But when the real thing fell short of an untainted pursuit of Truth and Justice, I bailed. Working as a private detective was never a dream for me. But I do it honestly and there's no publisher or editor or advertising department to mess with that. When I take a case, I see it through. Period. Moral relativism may be the order of the day but *something* has to be absolute. Someone has to stand up and declare himself dependable.

I recognized that declaration in Mike Angelo and I think he saw it in me. Mike and I were not best buddies, but I'd brought him a few leads over the years and I'd even helped him out with a sensitive personal matter, so we'd developed a certain mutual respect. And the closer I got to guys like Greico, the more that respect would erode.

So I was angry with Mike for being angry with me and I was probably even angry with me for making Mike angry.

The only solution was to order another beer, which I did.

Back in my office, I made a pot of coffee and called Stone Security and asked for John Stone. I thanked him for giving Al Diskin a good report on me and warned him that the threat against Loniski was heating up. I suggested that he tell his guys to upgrade to Condition Orange at all times.

"Ten-four," he said. "Notify us when you're bringing the Primary in, and our operative will be waiting in the parking lot. And when you pick up the Primary, our operative will accompany you to your vehicle." By "the primary," he meant Bob Loniski.

To me, cars were not "vehicles"; they were cars. Security guards were not "operatives," and if I mean to say yes I don't say "ten-four." But that kind of talk was just John selling his image. It was not my image, but it was John's and I shouldn't begrudge him that.

So I just thanked him and rang off. Then I called Binny's and had them put a bottle of W. L. Weller on my tab and send it to John Stone at Stone Security, with my compliments.

There were some leftover Christmas cards on the desk. I addressed an envelope to my grandfather and wrote a note in the card:

> Pop,
> Working on a case that will take me to Los Angeles for a week, so I probably won't get the chance to call and wish you a Merry Christmas. May have a car by spring, would love to see you. Give my best to Randall and the guys at the marina.
>
> Save some fish for me,
Ray

I sealed it up, put a stamp on it and dropped it in the mail chute by the elevators and returned to my desk, where I drank my coffee and smoked and resumed my time-travel visit with Benvenuto Cellini. But I couldn't concentrate. My mind was full of Jill.

I picked up the phone to call her but then remembered she was now on days at the hospital. It was probably just as well since I'd promised not to call until the case was finished.

Five hours later I stood on the front steps of Jill's building and chewed gum. I wanted a cigarette but Jill could show up at any minute and I also wanted my breath to be minty fresh. I told myself that it was just a matter of priorities.

At least the weather had improved. The snow had melted on this most unseasonably warm December day, save for a fringe of brown slush in the gutters, so the sidewalks were wet and clear. With only five days to go, I put the line on Gus the barber getting his white Christmas at 2 to 1. I wondered if Johnny Greico or Bennie Schwartz would make book on that bet.

People came and went along Belmont. They wore heavy coats, scarves and gloves. It seemed they didn't trust the freakish weather we were having. It seemed they expected Mother Nature to unleash a sudden blizzard, cackle like a witch and say "fooled you!" I didn't share their pessimism. I was wearing a standard Marshall Field's overcoat and I hadn't even bothered with the buttons.

Maybe that was because I wanted to be able to get at my sidearm quickly but to passersby I just looked like an old-fashioned Midwestern optimist. I wasn't even wearing gloves.

My naked left hand, curled around the stems of a dozen near-frozen roses, was getting a little numb. My watch said 7:18. Jill's shift ended at six. Of course she could have gone out with coworkers for a drink. Or maybe a nurse on the night shift called in sick and Jill was pulling a double. Or maybe she accepted a dinner invitation from some handsome doctor who had a stable income and whose idea of risk was playing golf on a cloudy day.

There wasn't any percentage in thinking that way, so I settled into people-watching. A woman passed, wearing an aging fox jacket, tight jeans tucked into black leather boots and too much makeup. I decided she was a struggling actress in her mid-thirties, unmarried and lonely, with a cat or two at home for company. She made the rent waiting tables in an upscale restaurant. On weekends she visited her parents in the suburbs and told them everything was swell.

A young man in his mid-twenties swaggered past. His light brown hair was cut short and kept in place with some sort of gel. He wore a charcoal cashmere overcoat and $500 cordovan shoes. I decided he was a corporate lawyer and he would make partner before his twenty-ninth birthday. He worked out at the health club five days a week and always placed first in the house-league squash tournament. He was in great shape but he couldn't take a punch and, luckily, would never have to find that out. He probably lived in a Lake Shore Drive condo. He was on his way to visit his girlfriend, who he would enjoy for a while but would later ditch for the frigid daughter of one of the law firm's senior partners.

Then came a striking beauty with straight hair that stopped just above her shoulders. She walked with her head held high, shoulders back and her hips slightly forward. Confident. Her eyes gleamed with intelligence but there was a sadness that crept out around the edges. The sadness looked incongruous with the rest of her. I decided that the man in her life was the cause of this sadness.

She walked up and kissed me on the mouth.

"I thought you promised to leave me alone," she said.

"I promised not to call. And I didn't." I handed her the roses.

We went inside and took off our coats and Jill put the flowers in a vase. I couldn't decide if she was happy to see me and, looking at her, I got the impression that she couldn't decide either.

Jill made us a couple of gin and tonics, with lime. To me, gin and tonic was strictly a summer drink but Jill drank them year-round. How very English of her. I suddenly had the image of her lovely body in a one-piece bathing suit with the Union Jack printed all over it. We were drinking gin and tonics on a deserted tropical beach.

I was just about to remove her bathing suit when her long fingers touched my face and brought me back to reality. She'd left the drinks on the kitchen counter and was standing so close I could feel the warmth of her breath on my throat.

"Your eye is looking better," she said. "How do you feel?"

I kissed her. She started to pull back, then leaned in and returned the kiss. Her lips parted and her soft tongue found mine. My arms went around her and drew her close, the full length of her body pressed against me. Her hands slipped behind my neck and pulled my head forward and the urgency of our kiss was almost unbearable. She pulled her head back and her hands rested on my chest and her eyes locked onto mine.

"Wow," she said.

"Wow indeed," I said.

"I missed you," she said. Her hands slid down to my waist and around. Her left hand bumped into my pistol and jerked back like she'd stuck her finger in a light socket.

"Damn!" she said, and stepped away from me. The sadness in her eyes took over and the passion was gone. Just like that.

She turned to get our drinks. I didn't know what to say, so I lit two cigarettes and said nothing. She traded me one of the drinks for one of the cigarettes. She sat on the couch and sipped her drink.

I removed my jacket and draped it over the back of a chair. If the gun was going to be an issue, I might as well bring it out in the open. I sat beside her on the couch, withdrew the gun from its holster and placed it on the coffee table, pointing away from us. She stared at it. I stared at her. I still didn't know what to say.

"Jill, it's a gun. It's not plutonium. It's not a rattlesnake. It's just a gun."

"Don't patronize me."

"I'm not," I said. But of course I was. I was angry that such a beautiful moment between us had been ruined for no good reason, and I wanted her to know it. We sat in silence for a few minutes.

"Okay," I said. "Sorry about that. But last time I didn't have a gun and you saw the result."

"And that's my point, isn't it? It's not just the gun, it's everything that comes with."

"Well that's what I do. You want me to be a florist?"

"I just don't think I can handle all this . . . the violence, the uncertainty. I know it's what you do and it's who you are and I don't want to change you. But I can't sit by the phone waiting for bad news."

"Most people go their whole lives hoping to find what we've got," I said, trying to keep my anger down. "Eventually they just settle. You want to play it safe, pass this by and settle on some accountant you feel fondly toward. Then one day he gets hit by a bus or has a heart attack. Good choice. Sit by the phone and wait for that call."

"That's unfair," Jill shot back. She stubbed her cigarette in a glass ashtray and pushed her hair back. "There was a man . . . wanted to marry me, in London when I was in nursing college. A sweet and gentle man, who loved me truly. He was studying property law and had a good job lined up." Her eyes met mine. "He was a safe choice. And I cared for him very much. But it wasn't love, at least not as I imagined love could be. So I broke his heart and ran away to America. And now you make presumptions . . . That's just really unfair . . ."

Anger had gotten the better of me and now Jill was crying. A steady flow of tears without any sound. I put my arms around her. Thinking, *Dudgeon, you are such a jerk*. She put her head on my shoulder. I still didn't know what to say and what I'd said so far hadn't helped any. So we just sat like that for a while and finished our drinks.

Jill lit a fresh cigarette. "Really, Ray, I'm not trying to change you. I'm just trying to understand. You're smart and caring and you could do anything you want for a living. I need to understand."

It was too hot inside the apartment. I removed my tie and dropped it on the coffee table, next to my gun. "I tried the journalism racket," I said, "and it didn't suit me. This does. I don't know why. Why are you a nurse? Everybody has to do something."

"That's too dismissive," said Jill with a shake of her head. "I know why I'm a nurse. I became a nurse because it was a way to save people." On our fourth date, Jill had told me that her parents died in a car accident when she was nine years old. That seemed like awfully personal information to share on a fourth date but I figured that's what normal people do, so I told her that my father had died before I was born and my mother when I was thirteen. I didn't say how they died and I don't suppose it matters. "I didn't know it at the time," Jill continued, "but now I know and I realize that, no matter how many people I save in the ER, I'll never bring my parents back." She put her hand on my knee. "Are you trying to save people, Ray? Trying to save your parents?"

Shit. I don't want to get into this. Why can't people just live in the present? Why do we always have to open up our lives for inspection? Why perform the autopsy when the body is still living?

"I don't know. Maybe that's it, I don't know." *Bullshit. You know exactly why. Three reasons . . . Shut up, I don't want to hear it . . . Three simple reasons. One: you sometimes get to save people . . . Stop it, I don't want this . . . Two: you might get killed and part of you hopes for that . . . Fuck, not now, stop . . . Three: and once in a while, once in a while you get to . . .* "Christ, Jill. I can't do this. Navel-gazing may be the official pastime of our generation, but it's wrong. It's wrong to live inside your head while life passes you by."

"It's just as wrong to run away from what's inside your head," said Jill as a new tear ran down her cheek. "I'm trying . . . I'm trying to know you."

"People don't get to know each other by exchanging psychobabble," I said. "It takes time." *Keep a lid on it, Dudgeon. Just don't say it.* "Goddamnit, Jill, I love you. Okay?" *Shit. You idiot.*

"You say it like it makes you angry."

"Look, I'm not . . . this is not easy," I managed.

"If you love me, then you have to trust me. You have to let me in." My head began to throb and I closed my eyes. "Ray—"

"I'm doing my fucking best!" I snapped. The pager on my belt went off. Bob Loniski was ready to be picked up from work. "Look, I—"

"You have to go," she said.

"I can be back in a couple of hours."

"Please don't. I need some time. I'll call you later."

"I'll be home," I said.

I delivered Bob to his apartment without any trouble and went straight home. There was a message waiting on my answering machine.

It was Jill. The message was as hard for me to listen to as it was for her to leave. She was crying into the telephone and I had to play it twice before I understood it all. The bottom line was, she was in love with me but she would not see me again. There was stuff about how she couldn't bear to lose me but it was better to lose me now than to live the rest of her life waiting for the day I don't come home. And there was other stuff about trust. There were a lot of half-started sentences that ended in sobs and the whole thing ended with her begging me never to call her again.

I opened a bottle of bourbon and got very drunk and smashed some things and passed out in my clothes.

CHAPTER FIVE

Bob Loniski and I arrived in Los Angeles on the twenty-third of December, in the early afternoon. The flight had been uneventful. In fact, the last couple of days had been uneventful, which was a good thing because I'd been having a hard time keeping my mind on work.

I'd been thinking about Jill and about how my world seemed smaller and darker without her in it. I was desperate to make contact with her but I knew how destructive that would be after the message she left on my machine.

Maybe Frank DiMarco would shoot me and the ambulance would take me to Rush and Jill would be on duty at the time. That was one way I might get to see her again. But that's a lot of maybes. I decided that it was best if Frank DiMarco didn't shoot me. Anyway, he wouldn't get the chance until after Christmas unless he wanted to make a working vacation out of it and come to California.

Bob and I flew business class, where there's more legroom and they treat you better and the booze is free. Bob had several screwdrivers but I just drank water, which is free all over the plane.

For the last two days I'd gotten Bob to and from work and then gone immediately home and gotten myself drunk. It was time to put an end to that foolishness.

Bob and I walked down the gangway into the terminal building at LAX, where families and lovers and uniformed chauffeurs waited to greet disembarking passengers. One of the chauffeurs held a hand-lettered sign that read CONTINENTAL PICTURES. Behind him was a guy wearing a photographer's vest and holding a Nikon, and a little runt of a man I figured for a reporter. As we got closer the photographer started snapping pictures and the reporter thrust a Dictaphone toward us.

"Mr. Loniski," the reporter called out, "Julian Davis, *Los Angeles Post*. How does it feel to have a price on your head?"

A glance at Bob told me that he was as shocked as I.

I muttered, "Don't say a word," just loud enough for Bob to hear. I gave a sharp nod to the chauffeur and we followed him. We walked fast but our uninvited companions had no trouble keeping up, even with the photographer snapping pictures and the reporter barking questions at us.

"Mr. Dudgeon, are you confident that you can keep him alive?"

We kept walking.

"Mr. Loniski, are you still planning to testify against the Mafia?"

The little reporter got next to me and I stuck my foot out and came to a quick stop and he pitched forward and fell. His hands went instinctively to break his fall and the Dictaphone hit the floor and clattered out of his hand.

"Be careful," I said. I started walking again and ground the Dictaphone under my heel. The photographer stopped taking pictures and bent down to help his partner up.

As we walked away, the reporter yelled something about suing me for everything I owned. Not knowing how little I owned, he had no idea how funny that was.

We picked up our bags and the chauffeur led us to a black limousine that was not quite as long as the *Queen Mary*. Bob and I climbed into the cavernous mobile living room, where Al Diskin sat with a Cheshire-cat grin on his face.

"Welcome to sunny California, boys," said Diskin as the limo rocked gently into motion. "How was the flight?"

"There was a reporter waiting for us at the gate," said Bob.

"Of course there was. I hope you gave him a good quote."

"Are you nuts?" I said. Diskin ignored me.

"Listen, Bob. This could be the best thing to happen to your career, and to *Final Revenge*. Check it out." He handed some trade papers across to Bob.

There was *Variety*, *The Hollywood Reporter* and a few I didn't recognize. Also, the previous day's business section of the *Los Angeles Post*. They were all running stories about how Bob Loniski, locations manager for Continental Pictures, had run afoul of the Mafia while working in Chicago. According to the stories, Loniski had seen something he shouldn't have and now there was a Mob contract on his life and Alan Diskin, senior producer at Continental, had hired Ray Dudgeon, a Chicago private investigator, to protect Loniski.

Diskin was the only source quoted throughout the articles. My favorite quote was:

> At Continental Pictures, we always strive for authenticity, even if it means shooting in dangerous locations. It is this commitment that makes our movies so true to life, and *Final Revenge* is no exception. Bob Loniski is a valued member of the Continental Pictures family, and we will spare no expense to ensure his safety.

As Bob and I skimmed the articles, Diskin chuckled and rubbed his palms together and said, "There's going to be a hell of a bidding war for *Final Revenge*. I've got international distributors lining up at my fuckin' door since this story broke."

"This story didn't break, Al," I said. "You planted it."

Again Diskin ignored me. "Bob, you've become a celebrity in this town," he said. "I'm afraid I'm going to have to give you a raise to keep you from jumping to Universal."

Bob sat dumbfounded but a brief smile played across his face when Diskin mentioned the raise. Diskin reached into the little bar and poured some Scotch over ice and handed the drink to Bob. He turned to me and I held up a hand and shook my head. He shrugged and refreshed his own drink.

"Relax, Ray," he said. "Everything's great." He gestured toward the papers. "You know, this is good for your career too."

I settled back into the leather seat and hated him. I looked out through the tinted windows. Along the edge of the freeway, an evenly spaced line of palm trees stood like sentries guarding the palace gates. Porsches and Mercedes and Range Rovers shared the multilane freeway with airport limousines, taxis and rusted-out beaters. In the slow lane an ancient pickup truck chugged along, its skin covered in primer, still waiting for the new paint job that wasn't coming. About a dozen Mexicans sat in the payload, breathing the blue clouds of exhaust that belched from a gash in the muffler. Their hands and clothes were black with dirt. Each time the truck hit a bump, the Mexicans grabbed onto something solid and held on and bounced around the metal deck. They all managed to stay on board but none of them looked particularly happy about it.

Welcome to America.

We rode the rest of the way to Bob Loniski's house in silence. Bob read and reread the articles and Diskin let him. Diskin knew what he was doing. Working in a town and an industry based on celebrity, it must be strange to be one of the thousands of anonymous workers who make the big machine go. Directors and even producers could become famous but locations managers were destined to toil in complete obscurity. Bob had probably never seen his name in print. Now he sat and read about himself in the same papers that everyone else in the industry reads. Now he had evidence of his own existence.

And it wasn't going to make my job any easier.

Bob Loniski's house stood high up in the Hollywood Hills, on Sierra Mar Drive—a steep, narrow, and winding street that could just ac-

commodate our stretch limo. The property was built into the side of
the hill and from the street it was well hidden by trees. There was a
two-car garage, a tall iron fence all around and an iron door that had
to be opened with a key, or from an inside buzzer. Beside the door was
an intercom.

Bob opened the iron door with his key and we went through and
up a flight of flagstone steps which led to an expansive patio. Behind
us, the chauffeur struggled along with our bags. Once we were all
through, the door closed itself with a solid reassuring clang.

The house was a marvel of modern architecture, all white and
open and airy, walls of glass flooding the interior with light. The main
floor was open concept—a spacious living room complete with full
bar, connected to the dining area and a large kitchen with breakfast
bar. There was a McIntosh stereo, a huge plasma-screen television and
modern art on the walls. French doors opened onto a pool deck. Beside them stood a telescope on a tripod. Not large enough to view distant planets but more than adequate for looking into the private lives
of your neighbors down the hill. The furniture was modern but looked
comfortable and it all went together perfectly and you just knew the
place had been decorated by a *professional*. I wondered how a locations manager could afford such a place.

The chauffeur took our bags upstairs and then told Diskin he would
wait in the car and left. Diskin went into the kitchen to use the phone.
I went upstairs. At the top of the stairs was a large home office, complete with all the latest gadgets. Then a hallway, with a guest bedroom
to the right, a bathroom to the left and the master suite at the end of
the hall. In the guest bedroom, I unpacked and then reassembled my
gun and loaded it.

When I got downstairs Bob was behind the bar pouring Scotch
over ice. Diskin was sitting on the sectional. A very tall man wearing a
beige suit stood looking out onto the pool deck. He turned to face me
as I entered the living room. He was as hard as granite, with sandy hair
and pale blue eyes. It seemed a safe bet that he had once been the star
quarterback on his high school football team.

"Ray," said Diskin, "this is Deputy Sheriff Mullins."

Deputy Mullins and I shook hands and he didn't even fake a smile.

"I've got some papers for you, Mr. Dudgeon," he said, "and I need you to sign."

He led me to the dining table, where I read some legalese and signed in triplicate for my pistol permit. Concealed carry permits are issued by the sheriff of Los Angeles County and bear his signature. Of course the sheriff of Los Angeles County is a busy man, so a civilian clerk in his office hands out the permits. Because Al Diskin had clout, the permit was delivered to Loniski's house. That I could understand. But why send a deputy to do a clerk's job?

Deputy Mullins inspected my gun, wrote down the serial number, and handed me the permit. To Diskin he said, "All set, Mr. Diskin."

"Thanks Deputy. And tell Ed I appreciate it."

"No problem, sir."

Deputy Mullins gave me a long look. He walked through the French doors and onto the pool deck. I followed and closed the doors behind us. The pool deck was, of course, gorgeous. There was a kidney-shaped pool, plenty of teak furniture and an unobstructed view. To the left was downtown Los Angeles with its skyscrapers and slums. Straight down the hill was Hollywood. To the right were Beverly Hills, Santa Monica and the Pacific Ocean, which glittered like a field of broken glass. Beyond that was Japan.

"Look, Dudgeon, I'm not too crazy about this arrangement," said Deputy Mullins. "And to be frank, neither is Sheriff Boyd." So this was why the sheriff sent a deputy instead of a clerk.

"Then why did he issue the permit?"

"Don't be a fool. You know this is a company town."

"And Continental Pictures is the company?"

"One of many. But an important one. And my boss is a politician, and that's the way it goes." He looked at me the way you look at an inanimate object. "But I don't know you and I don't think I like you much."

"That's okay. I don't like me much either."

"Whatever. The point is, we follow orders—"

"And somehow I became your responsibility and the cop in you doesn't like it." Mullins nodded. "Okay. Where do we go from here?"

"We don't go anywhere," he said. "Just don't act like a swinging dick around my town. Because if you do, I'll be right up your ass."

"Buy me dinner first?"

Mullins hit me in the chest with his index finger, which hurt a lot. "See, this is the kind of shit that's gonna make me mad, asshole. You're a fucking amateur and you don't even have the brains to know when to shut the fuck up and nod your fucking head."

I shut up and nodded my head. Mullins sighed. "Just don't shoot anybody."

"Unless I have to."

"And if you have to, make sure they're dead. I don't need a witness against you. I don't need to explain to the DA why the sheriff's office issued a permit to some amateur with a handful of shootings on his record already." He had done his research and he wasn't wrong to bring it up but I didn't love him for it.

"Clean shootings," I said.

"Maybe. But I don't need the headache."

"Couldn't you just tell the D.A., 'My boss is a politician'?"

"Fuck you, Dudgeon."

"Point taken," I said.

Bob Loniski and I went to the Beverly Center to do his Christmas shopping. We drove there in Bob's BMW 745i Sport. I did the driving while Bob expounded the virtues of his car, ad nauseam. It was a fine car—in fact it was one of the best I'd ever driven. But I wasn't about to say so. What bugged me was that Bob got such an ego boost from his car. What bugged me was that he was *selling* me on it. If he had said nothing, then I'd have told him that it was a fine car. But he wouldn't shut up about the goddamned thing.

What really bugged me was that I didn't even have a car. After dumping untold dollars into my old Pontiac to keep it running, I finally sold the dinosaur to a mechanic for parts. I could afford a new car but not a good one, so I was saving up. In the meantime I'd been relying on the Chicago Transit Authority to get me around. Or taxis, when I was feeling like Daddy Warbucks. I'd rent a car whenever I had a client but otherwise it was public transit.

At the Beverly Center, we squeezed in and out of a thousand over-priced boutiques where hordes of plastic pretty people rushed to get their last-minute Christmas shopping done. All the women had face-lifts and fake breasts and all the men had capped teeth and fake tans. The men over fifty had face-lifts, too.

Bob bought a matching pair of his-and-hers TAG Heuer watches for his ex-wife and her husband, a Pelikan Toledo 900 fountain pen for Al Diskin and a diamond tennis bracelet for his assistant, Kathie. Together they cost a shade over four grand, plus tax. Bob didn't say why he chose these gifts but it wasn't a mystery. The watches were supposed to send a message to Bob's ex and her new man. The message was, "I'm doing just fine, thank you very much." The pen was chosen to tell Diskin that Bob valued him as more than an employer; that they had a meaningful bond. And the bracelet was Bob's attempt to convince Kathie, and perhaps himself, that he was a great and generous boss. As nice as the gifts were, there was no thought about what the intended recipients actually needed or wanted or liked. Bob's discussions with the salespeople were centered on what items were *must-haves* among Hollywood's elite.

The stumbling block came when Bob Loniski tried to find a Christmas present for his son. After a half hour of aimless browsing, I found myself singing along with the Muzak . . .

. . . Then all the reindeer loved him
As they shouted out with glee:
"Rudolph the red-nosed reindeer,
You'll go down in history."

That song always bugged me. Those reindeer punks used to hate Rudolph. They never let him join in any reindeer games. They even laughed and called him names. And why? Just because he had a red nose. Superficial bastards. Now that Rudy's a celebrity, they suddenly love him. I always wanted Rudolph to tell all of the other reindeer to get stuffed. They didn't deserve his friendship.

I told Bob it was time for a break and we retreated to one of the mall's restaurants for a burger and a beer.

"I was going to get Josh that new video game console and some games," said Bob. He took a sip of his second beer. I had limited myself to one, just in case one of the plastic pretty people made an assassination attempt. "But Suzanne and Vick already got it for him." Suzanne and Vick were Bob's ex-wife and her husband.

"What else does he like?"

"He spends a lot of time playing video games. He's already got a computer and everything. I gave him a digital camera for his birthday."

"How old is he?"

"Thirteen."

"Into sports?"

Bob thought about this for a minute. "He's not a real jock or anything, but he plays baseball on his school team."

"There's a sporting-goods store on the upper level, how about a new ball glove?"

So we braved the crowds once again and made our way to the sporting-goods store. They had a fine selection of gloves. Bob moved from one to another, looking at the price tags and putting them back on the rack. Finally he selected one that pleased him.

"This is a beauty. Two hundred and sixty bucks."

"It's a first-baseman's mitt, Bob. Does Josh play first base?"

"Uh, I don't know."

I selected a smallish outfielder's glove from the rack and handed it to him. "Here. This will work whatever position he plays, so long as he isn't a catcher."

Bob frowned at the price tag. "It's only a hundred and thirty."

"It's a fine glove, Bob. You really want to show the kid you love him, buy two and play catch with him."

Bob's face flushed and his eyes darted around the store, avoiding mine. He grabbed another glove from the wall. "Good idea," he said, and marched off toward the cash registers. I followed behind, stopping to pick up some glove oil, a few baseballs and a bat. I figured Bob wouldn't have those things hanging around the house.

Bob didn't stock Mount Gay Extra Old or El Dorado Special Reserve or even Appleton Estate in his home bar. No accounting for taste. But at least he had Captain Morgan Private Stock, so I poured some over ice and checked my messages.

There was one from Mike Angelo and one from Terry. Both left the same message: call back ASAP, it's urgent. There was no message from Jill. I wondered how long it would be before I stopped hoping for one.

I called Mike first. The cop who answered told me that Lieutenant Angelo was on the street and would call me back, and I gave him Bob's number. I had better luck with Terry.

"Has Hollywood turned your brains to mush?" he said.

"Something bothering you, Terry?"

"It bothers me that chasing headlines is suddenly more important than keeping your client alive. Wiseguys read the papers too."

"Whoa. Alan Diskin planted those stories."

"Well he's gonna get his employee killed, and you too."

"I appreciate your confidence in my abilities."

Terry breathed through the phone line. "Ray, listen up. DiMarco's third tenant was murdered this morning. And it wasn't made to look like a mugging or a suicide or an accident."

"What happened?"

"As he leaves his house on the way to work. Car pulls up, stops, and they put about a zillion slugs into the poor bastard. Then they cut out his tongue. Which is unusual because they usually save that nuance for their own guys who turn squealer."

My throat felt dry all of a sudden, and I became aware of the tongue in my own mouth. It was not something I wanted to part with. "I see."

"Do you? Because I'm starting to wonder."

"I get it, Terry," I said, a little peevishly. "Tortelli read the papers and he's sending me a message."

"That's likely. What are you going to do?"

"I'll talk to Loniski and Diskin. I can scare Bob easy enough but Diskin wants to play this for publicity and I don't think anything's gonna change his mind."

"I talked to my editor about this story," said Terry. "He's letting me run with it now that there's a splashy murder."

"Making any headway?"

"Some. Nothing that's fit to print yet. But it does look like something's brewing within the Outfit. Something a lot bigger than Frank DiMarco."

"See? I told you. Tortelli's after Greico's turf, isn't he?"

"Maybe. But I haven't found anything that would suggest he could get away with it. I've only got a few rumors to work with and none of my sources seem to know anything that would back them up."

"But that's the angle you're pursuing."

"Yeah." Terry paused. "Ray . . . I talked to my editor about you, as well."

"What about me?"

"You know, he might be willing to take you back at the *Chronicle*."

"Not interested, thanks."

"Just think about it. That's all I'm saying. I'd hate to have to buy a new suit for your funeral."

"It's not that I'm not grateful," I said, "but I don't have any use for the journalism racket."

"You used to."

"Long time ago."

"Now you're a little older, maybe you can come to terms with the compromise."

"Don't think so, Bernstein. But thanks just the same. I gotta run."

"Stay alive, Woodward," said Terry, and hung up.

The compromise. So that's what it was called.

When Terry Green and I became friends, there was never any talk of compromise. We were just a couple of arrogant journalism students, supremely confident in our ability to change the world. We were going to be Woodward and Bernstein. We were going to expose hypocrisy and corruption wherever we found it. And once we had enough bent politicians on our trophy wall, we were going to ease into the journalistic penthouse inhabited by the most respected columnists. Terry was going to be Clarence Page. I was going to be Mike Royko.

After graduation I took a job reporting for the *Morning Dispatch* in Columbia, South Carolina, and Terry worked at the *Rockford Daily News*. We both worked like hell and within two years we were both able to affix *Investigative* before *Reporter* on our business cards. Terry then uncovered a big money scandal within Rockford's city hall and by the next year he was back in Chicago, working at the *Chronicle*.

My career took a different path. I successfully broke a story of racial discrimination by a couple of local banks. The banks were keeping black families out of white neighborhoods by denying them mortgages. But when the same family applied for the same size loan for a home in a predominantly black part of town, they were accepted. My piece in the *Morning Dispatch* caused a stir in local and state government. I got a raise and a promotion. Then I set my sights on rumors of NCAA violations in the recruitment of college athletes.

That was a big mistake. The newspaper's publisher was a big booster of college sports. As was everybody else who mattered in the region. My editor killed the story. It wasn't his decision and he felt terrible about it, but that didn't make any difference to me and I threatened to go public with the cover-up. We worked out a deal. I applied for a job at the *Chicago Chronicle* and he pulled all kinds of strings on my behalf and I got the job.

So Terry and I were back in business. Woodward and Bernstein.

We often worked as a team and we had some early successes. We were even starting to get a reputation as the Next Big Thing in Chicago newspaper journalism. Working together, we uncovered irregularities in the management of a union pension fund. We didn't yet have enough to go to print but we were close. Then somebody important had a word with somebody else and somebody else made a phone call to another guy and another guy applied pressure in just the right places. And we were pulled off the story.

Just like that.

I was bitter as grapefruit rinds, but Terry was more philosophical. He saw it as a bump in the road and even spouted clichés about losing the battle but winning the war. Maybe he was more mature. Or maybe, having grown up black in Chicago, he had fewer illusions than I. But it was the second time in as many years that I'd seen powerful people protect corruption by killing a perfectly legitimate news story. And if they could do that whenever it suited them, then our society's watchdog was truly dead and I'd been worshiping at the altar of a false God since childhood. Anyway, I couldn't handle it and I walked away from the whole stinking journalism racket.

I didn't know what to do with myself but I figured I could put my skills to use as a private detective, so that's what I did. I never intended to do it forever. Once in it, I found that it suited me. A client would hire me to find out the facts about something, and I would. Simple. Pure.

To hell with changing the world.

The rum in my glass had evaporated, so I poured some more. Through the French doors, I saw Bob out on the pool deck and went to join him. He was talking on a cordless phone. I hung back quietly and listened.

"Yeah? Uh-huh . . . well sure I'm concerned about my safety, but I see it as my civic duty . . . and what kind of example would I be setting for my son if I didn't testify? Right . . . no, I think Continental Pictures is taking good care of security . . . Yes, it's Ray Dudgeon . . . D-U-D-G-E-O-N. That's right . . . well, you know, it's a bit strange, having some guy with a gun around all the time . . . you met him, you know what he's like . . . yeah, a bit of a hard-ass, but he's okay, in a Midwestern sort of way . . . no, no, he's confident that they'll leave me alone when all this is over . . . I mean, it's not like I'm testifying against the Godfather or anything, it's someone not that high up . . . no, I'm really not allowed to talk about specifics . . . well, in Chicago they call it the Outfit . . . okay . . . thanks, Julian. And sorry again for that thing at the airport. Yes, okay, good-bye."

"What the hell was that?"

Bob jerked his head around. "What?"

I sat on a chair across from him and lit a cigarette and pointed at the phone. "You just gave an interview to that prick from the airport."

"Yes, but Al said I should, and—"

"I don't give a shit what Al said. I'm trying to keep you alive and I said you shouldn't. You think getting this in the papers is gonna help your chances?"

Bob looked at the pool. He sipped his drink. "It's like you said, Ray. They probably just want to intimidate me."

"They don't just want to intimidate you, Bob."

Then I told him about the murders of Jeanne Gosselin and Andre Hanson, and all the color drained from his face. He looked like he was going to throw up or pass out, or both, so I left out the detail about the tongue.

"But I thought . . . I mean, Al said it was no big deal and—"

"Let me ask you something that's none of my business," I said. "Al Diskin owns this house, doesn't he?"

Bob looked at me like I had just pulled a quarter out of his ear. "How did you know?"

"Tell me about it," I said.

"Not much to tell, really. Al owns the place and I lease it from him."

"But you don't pay market value."

"Of course not. I pay twenty-five hundred a month. He could get at least seven thousand on the open market and I could never afford that."

"And what does he get in return?"

Bob took a large swallow of his drink. "He gets . . . access. A few times a month, he calls and I have to vacate the place for an evening. He reimburses me for the hotel bill of course."

"So it's his little love nest."

"It's difficult to find privacy in L.A. And you know, he's married."

"Sounds like a swell arrangement. How do you feel about having to leave your home whenever he wants to get it on with some popsie?"

Bob examined his shoes for a while. "It's not so bad. If you were from here, you'd understand."

"I understand fine," I said. "Everyone who rented from Frank Di-Marco is dead. And you're next. Al Diskin uses people—he doesn't give a shit about you or anyone else. This publicity is good for *Final Revenge,* so it's good for him. If you get clipped, what's that, compared to millions of dollars at the box office? He'll just have to find another sucker willing to rent this place and get lost whenever he wants to cheat on his wife."

Bob examined his shoes some more. His eyes welled up with tears but he managed to fight them off. "What are we going to do?" he whimpered, and his eyes welled up again.

"You're going to stay here with the shades drawn and let nobody in. I'm going to go see some people."

I stood and walked to the end of the patio and looked down at the skyline of Los Angeles. The sun was sitting in that perfect spot in the western sky where everything is bathed in a warm orange glow and the world looks more three-dimensional than usual. Photographers and movie people call it *magic hour.* I stood there and smoked and waited for Bob to compose himself.

After a minute, I returned to where he was sitting. I glanced up into the hills. There were at least a dozen places where someone could set up and take him out with a high-powered rifle and a decent scope.

I'd made the assumption that Frank DiMarco wouldn't make a play for Bob until we returned to Chicago. But DiMarco didn't have what it takes to pull off an execution like the one on the guy with no tongue. As Terry had said, something was brewing within the Outfit. There was no way to know how high up the chain of command this hit was sanctioned or how far they might come to make the hit. Or who they might send.

"What do you say, Bob? Are you going to play it my way or is Al Diskin calling the shots?" I stood looking down at him.

"Okay. But there's two things I have to do. Otherwise, I'll do whatever you say."

"Yes?"

"One is spending Christmas with Josh. I'm supposed to go over to Suzanne and Vick's in the late morning, spend some time, and then Josh comes back here with me for the afternoon."

"Agreed."

"The other is the Continental Pictures Christmas party tonight."

"I think you can skip a company Christmas party."

"No I can't!" snapped Bob. He took a breath. "Look, this party is at the Starlight Bar. Do you even know what that means?"

"I guess I don't."

"The Starlight Bar is not just a bar," said Bob. "It's *the* bar. On a regular night, no way I could get in there. Too exclusive. They keep a list of maybe three thousand people in this town. If you're not either on the list or with someone on the list, you don't get in. But tonight only, because of this party, I'm on the list and right now everybody's talking about me. I make a good impression tonight, maybe I can get on the permanent list."

"Is that worth risking your life?"

"For me, yes it is." Bob squinted at the Pacific Ocean. "Sixteen messages on my machine when we got in, some from people who normally don't even know my name. Important people. Everybody wishing me well, hoping I'm all right." He finished his drink in one long swallow. "Al's right—I'm a celebrity right now. I know it won't last. Once the trial is over, I'm just Bob Loniski, locations manager. But if I can make an impression on the right people tonight . . ." He didn't finish the sentence.

It was sad as hell. Bob was desperate to convince himself that he could stretch his fifteen minutes of fame into a lifetime. He was a bit player in this town, the friendly fat guy they kept around for comic relief, and he wanted to be the leading man. He needed to believe that this was his big chance, even though he had no chance at all. Sad as hell.

"Okay, Bob. We'll go to the party."

I took Bob's BMW and drove down the hill to the West Hollywood Sheriff's Station, which sits on the corner of Santa Monica and San Vicente. I used the car phone along the way. Mike Angelo told me what Terry had already told me, without the gory details.

"So I guess you didn't put police protection on the guy," I said.

"We were getting around to it. Had to investigate first . . . you know, like cops?"

"Not much consolation to the dead guy."

"The wheels of justice turn slowly." I could picture his grim smirk.

"Listen, Mike. I need a favor."

"Uh-huh."

"I got a CCP from a Deputy Mullins today and I was in a bad mood at the time."

"And now you need his help."

"Maybe you could give him a call and tell him I'm a right guy."

After an uncomfortable silence Mike said, "Are you?"

"Come on, Mike. I know you're pissed I went to see Greico—"

"First you go visit the asshole, tell him you won't take on a client if he wants the guy dead. Then you take the case because the asshole lies to you. Now what are you gonna do when they come after your client? Ask Greico for permission to defend the guy?"

"It's not like that. Anyway I don't think Greico is behind this. I think it's Tortelli."

"Grow up, Ray. Tortelli doesn't move against Greico's wishes."

"I think now he does."

Another uncomfortable pause. "You got something to tell me?"

"I still don't know anything. But I think Tortelli's got something going against the old man. Right now it's just an idea and I've got nothing to support it. As soon as I learn anything, I'll be in to see you."

"If you're still alive."

"Yeah." Through the phone I could hear Mike light a cigarette.

"Okay," he said. I gave him the number for Deputy Mullins and hung up just as I arrived at the sheriff's station. I leaned against the car and smoked, to give Mike time to make the call.

Across the street, a group of teenage Chicano boys stood around posing and making crude comments to passing women and generally trying to out-tough one another. The leader of the group wore mirrored sunglasses, baggy black pants, a black do-rag and a white muscle shirt. His bulging arms were covered with tattoos. The rest of the boys looked so similar that it might've been a uniform.

The leader noticed that he'd caught my attention.

"Hey, pig," he called. "Hey, pig! You know wha' choo are?"

I had a pretty good idea of what I was but I couldn't be absolutely certain. And I didn't want to engage the young man and force him to prove his toughness, so I just kept smoking and said nothing.

"Hey, pig, I'm talkin' to you! You know what wha' choo are? You are a Fart Smeller!" The other boys thought this the height of wit.

"Hey, Fartsmeller," he called. Through the fabric of his baggy pants, he grabbed his crotch. "Why don' choo come over here an' arrest this, Fartsmeller?" That was even more hysterical and the boys convulsed with laughter and exchanged high fives.

Their leader flexed his tattoos at me. I considered removing my shirt so I could flex my own tattoo back at him. But neither my tattoo nor my muscles were any match for his, and doing so might just embolden him. Then he might come over to show me how tough he really was and I might have to shoot him. And I suspected that Deputy Mullins would not approve.

I could hear the conversation in my head: *"Why did you shoot the kid?" "He called me a Fartsmeller."*

So I kept my shirt on. I tossed my cigarette into the gutter, smiled at the kid and made the shape of a pistol with my hand and shot him with my finger. And went inside to see Mullins. Oh, I was a tough-guy, all right. Almost as tough as a tattooed teenager.

Deputy Mullins sat at his desk. Only his eyes moved to greet me. He didn't offer a chair.

"Just got off the phone with your boyfriend in Chicago," he said.

"Deputy Mullins, about earlier . . . I was having a bad day."

"You know what? I don't give a rat's ass."

"Okay. But this thing with Bob Loniski . . ."

"Not my problem."

"Did Lieutenant Angelo tell you about recent developments?"

"Told me that you're a swell fella. Told me that some people got whacked in Chicago. Told me that your client, according to you, could be in jeopardy."

"That's right."

"Well your say-so may be good enough for the CPD but it doesn't mean shit to me."

"He's the last surviving witness against a known bad guy, you can check it out."

"So he can apply to the Witness Protection Program."

"He doesn't qualify, the guy on trial is a small fish and it's not a federal case."

"Again, not my problem." Mullins squeezed out a thin smile. "Besides, I don't see how he can be in any jeopardy, what, with a hard guy like you watching his back."

I sat in a little metal chair facing the desk, and chose my words.

"Look. I don't want Loniski to get dead just because you're pissed at me for being a smart-ass. I'm asking for your help here. Just one deputy and only until I can get Diskin to spring for more bodyguards. At most it's a couple of days and we're back to Chicago and out of your hair. Please."

Ray Dudgeon—The Groveling Detective. Not a pretty sight. But if the Outfit sent a real pro, he would get by one bodyguard easily. They wouldn't make a play against Bob Loniski with a uniformed cop standing next to him, and I needed time to assemble a proper team. An advance man, two body men including me, two sets of professional eyes—front and rear—with long guns, and a driver. Minimum.

After a full minute of silence, Mullins said, "We're not rent-a-cops, Dudgeon. If Mr. Loniski wants to come in and sign out a complaint and if the CPD copies us on a case file that supports his claim, we might consider the merits of a protection detail. But I can tell you that it is not going to happen in the next few days." He fixed me with a firm stare. "We're a little busy with the holidays."

"And if he gets clipped on your watch, after you turned down my request for help?"

Mullins's face got even harder. "Take a hike," he said.

I did.

Driving back up the Hollywood Hills, I called Al Diskin and his secretary said he couldn't be disturbed. I told her it was an emergency. Diskin came on the line just long enough to learn that Bob was still alive. He said anything else could wait. I told him about the murder that morning and he said we could discuss it at the party later. Then he hung up in my ear.

I passed Bob's house and continued up Sierra Mar Drive, winding this way and that until I reached the summit. Then down various roads, stopping wherever there was an unobstructed view of Bob's property. I was looking for the same thing a professional sniper would be looking for. A spot near the road so he wouldn't have to venture far from his car. A spot secluded by foliage so he wouldn't be noticed while waiting. A nearby wide shoulder so the car could be parked without attracting attention. A spot neither too far east nor too far west of target, to avoid aiming into the sun. I worked quickly and within an hour I'd surveyed the eight most likely positions. I didn't see any signs of reconnaissance—no cigarette butts, no tramped-down grass. I cut a yellow plastic shopping bag into strips and tied a strip to a tree branch at each location. I also used a digital compass to take the exact heading of Bob Loniski's front door and wrote them in my notepad. The light was fading. Tomorrow I would come back and cut back the foliage as much as possible. I would have to gamble on the assumption that a sniper would not be shooting from private property. There were just too many such places to do anything about it.

And besides, I had a party to attend.

CHAPTER SIX

My psychic says I was born to study the Kabbalah."

"That wouldn't work for me, I'm Virgo with Libra ascendant."

"I've been deep into aura work. Very cleansing."

"Look, Steven's here tonight."

"Oh my *God*, he's with Julia."

"That bitch."

"I mean, *really*."

"I'm convinced there are simply *no* good screenplays anymore."

"Brian says they're just not *high concept* enough."

"I just finished one . . . it's very *Die Hard* meets *Dead Poets Society*."

"Send it to my agent, I'd love to read it."

"That's the latest Hugo Boss, you know. That jacket, the one Tom's wearing."

"I only wear *German*-made Hugo Boss."

"You know what I heard? Next time he's playing a *villain*."

"No way!"

"Yes. I heard it from his own mouth."

"We leave tomorrow for the Peru shoot and I am *so* not looking forward to the thin air."

"Oh! Look who's had another *procedure*."

"What is that, four now?"

"Five, if you include the nose."

"I must get the name of her surgeon. He does beautiful work."

"Simply *gorgeous*. He's a true artist."

On and on it went. Listening to the nonstop mindless prattle made me want to put a bullet in someone's head. Or my own. Bob tried to gossip along with the Hollywood phonies but he wasn't very good at it. They didn't really see him as part of the fashionable crowd but he was a temporary celebrity, so he got a lot of attention and he loved it.

There were dozens of little groups of people scattered around the rooftop deck of the Starlight Bar. We moved from clique to clique, spending a little time with each, and each time Bob got to tell his Mob story all over again. He told the story the exact same way every time, almost word for word, and I realized that he had been rehearsing it while I was out visiting Deputy Mullins and marking sniper locations. Thankfully he made it a short story and everyone seemed to enjoy it, but people were more interested in talking to a "real live private eye," so the inevitable questions were directed my way and Bob stopped introducing me after the first three cliques. Which was fine by me. I just stood at his side, looking Midwestern and hating everyone.

The bar was on the eighth-floor roof deck of an overpriced hotel on Sunset Boulevard. The location offered a spectacular view of the Los Angeles skyline sparkling in the night, although nobody seemed to notice it. There was even a swimming pool, but not for swimming. Hundreds of lit candles floated aimlessly in the pool and the effect was otherworldly. Placed around the pool were five king-size beds with massive silk pillows, where people lounged, sometimes four or five to a bed. The large bar had a thatched tiki-style roof. The only thing missing from the scene was a team of muscular, half-naked Moorish slaves with giant ostrich-feather fans, cooling the kings and queens of Tinseltown.

Model-pretty waitresses, dressed like Santa's elves, moved with android precision amid the crowd and nobody's drink was ever allowed to run dry. I drank plain ginger ale. I wanted to be drunk and I didn't expect an assassination attempt but a professional has to make certain sacrifices.

Then I saw Virginia Lane standing at the bar. I recognized her from the movies. It had been a few years since she'd made one, or maybe I'd just missed the ones she'd been in lately. She stood out from the crowd, even more beautiful in person than on the screen. She carried herself with a certain grace that seemed lacking in the others. She had a lot of wavy red hair and I assumed it was her natural color, since it had always been red. She was now creeping into her mid-fifties and although she looked young for her age, she didn't seem absurdly youthful, and there was no evidence that she'd ever visited an artistic surgeon.

She caught me looking at her but didn't seem to mind, so when our eyes met I just smiled and kept looking. And so did she. She picked up her drink from the bar and walked across the patio, straight toward me, without breaking eye contact.

"Hello, Chicago," she said. She offered her hand and I took it in mine.

"Hello, Red."

"You guys know each other?" said Bob.

"Not yet," said Virginia Lane, still looking into me with those deep brown eyes. "But I've been reading about you two in the papers. You're the talk of the town."

"It'll pass," I said. "I think we've got about fourteen minutes left."

Virginia Lane and I just stood there looking into each other. Bob turned and resumed his conversation with whoever was standing next to him. I became aware that I was still holding Virginia Lane's hand, and I let go of it.

She watched it fall back down to her side. "Such a shame," she said, and walked away. I watched her walk and mentally kicked myself for letting go of her hand.

Bob seemed to be finished with this group, or they with him, so we moved on and he told his story to a new audience.

"And you're the private eye?" a shapely young woman asked me when he finished.

"Excuse us," said Bob. We walked to the far side of the pool. "Listen, Ray . . . you're doing a great job, and—"

"How would you know?"

"Uh, what I mean is, I appreciate you looking out for me. But can you, uh, do it from a distance?"

"Cramping your style?"

"No, it's just . . . well you know how it is. I think I've got a really good chance of getting laid tonight and I—I just need some space. A man needs a little room to work." He tried to give me a conspiratorial man-to-man smile but it came out looking apologetic.

"You got it, Stallion," I said. "Go do your stuff. I'll hang back in the shadows."

So I leaned back against the low wall with the skyline behind me and lit a cigarette and drank ginger ale. I caught Al Diskin's eye and he came over and I brought him up to date on recent developments.

Diskin loved the story of the poor bastard who had his tongue cut out that morning. He seemed entertained by it, as if he couldn't tell the difference between reality and a movie. And he refused my request for additional money to assemble a full executive protection team.

"The way I see it"—Diskin smiled—"is why would they bother coming out here to kill Bob when he's going back to Chicago in a couple days? No, they'll just wait until he's back on their turf."

"Everywhere is their turf, Al. Organized crime in California operates with a great deal of autonomy but it still falls under the authority of the Chicago Outfit. They don't have to come out here, all they have to do is pick up the phone."

"I'm still gonna have to say no," Diskin said, and signaled a passing waitress for another round. "See, it just plays better this way. Two guys going up against an all-powerful foe. I see you and Bob like Butch and Sundance."

"Butch and Sundance die at the end."

"Right, well you got me there," Diskin laughed. "Good one. Bad example. But you know what I mean."

"I don't give a shit how this *plays*, Al."

"Oh but you must. All the world's a stage, my friend."

He was the wrong guy to be quoting Shakespeare and I wasn't his friend. But saying so wouldn't get me anywhere. "I think Bob's life is in imminent danger and I think you're making a big mistake," I said.

"You don't like it, you can always quit," Diskin said, and his smile disappeared. "Let's see now . . . 'Small-time Private Eye Takes Big Case, Then Gets Scared and Runs Away.' How's that for a headline? I think you'll give a shit how that plays, and you know I can make it play exactly that way."

I stared at him. "You really don't care if Bob dies, do you?"

"Hey! Bob's my friend. Of course I care." And then the smile again. "I care about Bob and I care about Bob's career, which you may have noticed is getting a big boost from all this."

"Right. How's the *Final Revenge* bidding war going?"

Diskin spread his hands and shrugged. "Sure, I care about that too. Why shouldn't I?" He took a fresh drink from the passing waitress. "Ray, I know what I'm doing. Everything's gonna be fine. There'll be a piece in the papers tomorrow about this party and about Bob and you and me and *Final Revenge*. And I should have the distribution deal wrapped up in a few days. When we get back to Chicago, we'll beef up security. Between now and then, just do your job."

From a discreet distance, I watched Bob get drunk and make sloppy and unsuccessful advances toward various women at the party. After a few hours he lowered his standards to include the waitresses who, despite their beauty, had limited value because of their social status. The waitresses turned him down as well.

It was getting late. On one of the poolside beds, a popular television actress was making out with a well-known director. Another actress sat with them and traded kisses with both. Pretty soon they were really going at it, a threesome of kissing and heavy petting. There was no passion in it, or even rebellion—just performance. Instead of sexy, it looked boring.

"Got a light?"

I dug the Zippo from my pocket, flicked the lid open and spun the wheel. Virginia Lane put her hand on mine as she drew fire into the end of her cigarette. I lit one for myself and put the Zippo away.

"Are you stalking me, Red?" I asked.

"Maybe."

"Why?"

"Oh, I don't know. Maybe I'm a little homesick. How is Chi-town these days?"

"Cold and windy."

"Now I remember why I left," she said. "How do you like La-La Land so far?"

"I hate everything about this place."

"Except me."

"Except you."

"Thought so."

"Are you trying to hypnotize me," I said, "or do you always look at people that way?"

Her eyes opened wide, then she smiled with them, unafraid of the crow's-feet that showed when she did so. "I'm trying to hypnotize you. Is it working?"

"It's working."

"Good," she said, and giggled. "Would you like to take me—"

"Yes."

"—out for a drink, after this shindig breaks up?"

"Oh. Sure I would but I'm working."

"No time off?"

"Sadly, no."

"Too bad." We looked at each other some more. She broke eye contact and reached into her purse and handed me a card. Printed on the card was her name and phone number. "If you ever find yourself back in L.A.," she said, "I think I'd like to know you better."

Bob was upstairs in bed, sleeping it off. Having had nothing to sleep off, I was awake and clearheaded. In the kitchen, I loaded the coffeemaker and fired it up. Then I slipped outside and down the flagstone steps to fetch the *L.A. Times*. Next to the paper sat a small box. My name was printed in block letters on the label. Beside the address was *Delivered by hand*. The return address was Terry Green at the *Chicago Chronicle*. Under the circumstances, I doubted that Terry would send a package without telling me first but then I considered the possibility that I was being paranoid. The box wasn't addressed to Bob and didn't weigh enough to be a bomb.

I took the box and the newspaper inside and poured a cup of coffee. Using a steak knife, I cut the tape on the box and folded back the flaps. It was packed with wads of bunched-up newspaper. I removed the top layer of paper and swallowed hard. I was looking at a human tongue. The tongue was a pale pink gray and the surrounding paper was dark where it had soaked up the blood, which had dried to the color of rust.

Okay. Message received. *Fuck.*

I got the notebook and compass from my jacket, grabbed the telescope and ran upstairs. Set up in a window, I quickly calculated reverse compass directions and, with some effort, found the yellow plastic strips that marked likely sniper posts. Nothing. I trained the scope on the balconies of houses higher up the hill. Nothing.

"Bob!" No response. I ran down the hallway and into Bob's bedroom. The bed was empty but I could hear the shower running. At the bathroom door I called to Bob and told him to get out and get dressed, fast. Then I closed the blinds on all the north-facing windows and retrieved my spare magazines from the guest bedroom, fed bullets into them and put on a blazer and shoved the loaded mags into the pockets.

Within three minutes, Bob was dressed and standing before me with a questioning look.

"We're leaving now, Bob."

"What's up?"

"Do as I say, Bob. No questions. Get your wallet and whatever cash you have on hand. We have to leave, right now."

"But I don't get it. Why—"

"NOW!"

I didn't wait for more questions. Through a side window, I looked up and down the empty street. I turned off the coffeemaker and grabbed the box and closed it so Bob wouldn't see the tongue. I didn't need him going into a full-scale freakout. With gun in hand, I led Bob outside, down the flagstone steps, through the iron door and into the garage.

We got into the car and I tossed the box into the backseat and holstered the gun. I put the key in the ignition and cranked it and heard nothing but a dead metallic click.

I froze, holding the key in place.

"Get out! Run!"

Bob didn't ask questions this time. He scrambled out and sprinted across the street.

Fighting against survival instincts, I waited for him to reach the other side, my heart pounding in my chest. Thinking, *There's a bomb in this car . . . if it's a straight-contact switch, it would've blown by now or it's defective . . . if it's a contact-release switch, it'll blow as soon as I release the key and I'm dead . . . if it's a timer, it'll be set between five and twenty seconds and I've already used ten . . . okay . . . time to find out.*

I opened the door, released the key and ran like hell. When I reached the other side of the street I flung out my right arm and hauled Bob down into the ditch with me and lay on top of him.

After holding that position for a while, I began to feel vaguely foolish. Beneath me, Bob's breathing slowed to just slightly faster than normal.

"Jesus Christ, Ray. You scared the shit outta me."

"Sorry about that," I said. "I thought there was a bomb."

Just as I began to lift myself off of Bob, his car exploded. An orange ball of fire filled the garage and I ducked my head. A wave of heat rolled over us. When I looked up, the car was engulfed in flames and black smoke poured from the garage. I leaped to my feet and dragged Bob down the hill and out of range. The bomb had been under the hood but the fire would soon reach the gas tank and I have a healthy aversion to shrapnel.

"You seem pretty proud of yourself," said Deputy Mullins.

"Reasonably."

"Shouldn't be. The tongue was an obvious attempt to flush you out and get you into that car. And it worked."

We were sitting in a room at the Beverly Hills Hotel. Bob was in another room, with other cops. They'd arrived within minutes of the explosion, along with three fire engines and an ambulance. The firemen went to work immediately. A minute later two television news vans arrived. The cops whisked us out of there, first to the West Hollywood Sheriff's Station and then to the hotel, where Al Diskin checked us in.

"Bob's still alive," I said, "so I guess it didn't quite work as planned."

"Fair enough," he said, and almost smiled. "I'll give you that. But you're off this case, as of now. Bob Loniski is under police protection and you are not to interfere."

I lit a cigarette and offered one to Mullins. He shook his head. "I won't get in the way, Deputy Mullins. I'll just hang around the perimeter and be an extra set of eyes."

"That's a negative, Dudgeon. You are to stay out of it. If Diskin wants you back on in Chicago, that's up to him, but until then you are to keep your distance. Understand?"

I took a deep drag on the cigarette and nodded. "How's Bob doing?" When the police arrived on the scene, Bob had started to tremble and he was still shaking when we got to the hotel.

"He's sedated right now."

"Probably for the best. I'll drop by his room after dinner and try to cheer him up."

"Obviously I haven't made my position clear," said Mullins.

"I'm talking about having a drink with the guy, Deputy. I promise I won't try to protect him from anything."

"If you get within one hundred yards of Bob Loniski, I'll have you arrested." He stood up. "Nothing personal." This time he did let out a smile but it wasn't a friendly one.

Mullins left and I called room service and ordered a fresh pack of smokes and a bottle of Mount Gay Extra Old and some ice. The adrenaline high was gone and I had that postadrenaline hangover, which brings shakes and a feeling of nausea. A couple of drinks eased the symptoms.

My clothes smelled like Bob's burning car. I stripped and took a hot shower, using the fancy soaps and shampoos so generously provided to anyone willing to spend $450 a night for a hotel room. The towels were thick and soft to the point of decadence. I wrapped myself in a plush robe and settled onto the bed with a fresh drink. I made a mental note to steal the robe, along with a set of towels. The hotel would send Diskin a bill and he'd have no choice but to pay it and I'd have the best robe and towels in the world.

The noon news was just beginning. We were the top story. *Chicago Gangland Violence Invades Beverly Hills,* declared the plastic pretty anchorwoman, without losing her toothy smile. A slick video package followed, complete with dramatic footage of firemen dousing the burning car, police talking to neighbors and file footage of the Continental Pictures head office. A still photo of Bob that looked like a publicity head shot came up on the screen, and then one of me taken at the airport the previous day. Deputy Mullins may not have been impressed by my performance, but the male model pretending to be a reporter gave me full credit for saving Bob's life.

Of course, you can't always believe what you see on television.

Al Diskin stopped by my room and helped himself to some rum. He was thrilled by the morning's events. Insurance would take care of the fire damage and he couldn't have bought this much publicity for any amount of money. He assured me that I would be paid for the next two days even though I was not working, and that I would be back on the job in Chicago with funds available for additional security. He told me to buy whatever clothes I needed at the men's shop in the hotel, where he'd arranged a credit in my name. I didn't argue. He told me to eat and drink freely and sign everything to my room. He pumped my hand and thanked me and left and I felt like washing my hand.

I called Mike Angelo and told his voice mail about what had happened and where he could reach me. Then I called Terry Green, who had already learned of the car bomb from the news feeds at the *Chronicle*. I told him about the delivery of the tongue and about the return address on the box.

"I'm not surprised," said Terry. "I've been asking a lot of people a lot of questions. I'd actually be surprised if Tortelli hadn't heard about it yet."

"What have you learned?"

"Not much. Rumor is, Tortelli has something going that he's keeping from Biagio Amodeo. And whatever this something is, it might have to do with Johnny Greico but nobody knows what."

"Jesus. Makes no sense, Terry. Maybe if Tortelli's nuts, he goes after Greico's turf. We're agreed on that."

"Right."

"But to work behind the Don's back? Amodeo would crush Tortelli."

"Yup. But what can I tell you? That's all I've heard. So either Tortelli has a huge ace in the hole, or he's a dead man."

"Let's hope for the latter. How about Frank DiMarco?"

"Nothing yet," said Terry. "But if all these rumors add up to something, then it's a fair hypothesis that DiMarco was spying for Tortelli the whole time he was working for Greico."

"But that doesn't get us very far."

"Nope. You know they're going to come after you again, Woodward."

"They're going to come after Bob again. I've been kicked off the case. The cops are looking after him."

"Well I'm sorry for your ego but I can't say I'm sad to hear it," said Terry.

We wished each other a Merry Christmas and hung up.

There was no use thinking about it. I didn't have enough information and I wouldn't get more until I was back in Chicago and could work my own angles on the case. If I still had a case. Sure, Diskin said I'd be back on it but if Al Diskin told me the time, I'd have to check my watch. If it *played* better another way for Diskin, then I'd be out of it. Anyway, the CPD would take over Bob's protection once we got back, so I figured I really was out of a job.

I sat on the bed and drank rum. Thinking, *Who cares? Why do you even want this case? It's a no-win and you're better out of it. The Outfit is going to kill Bob. Now that they've made an attempt, they aren't going to stop until he's dead. Even if Bob were willing to develop amnesia, they now have a point to make. Hell, Al Diskin doesn't care and he's paying the bills. Mullins doesn't care. And Jill doesn't care. Doesn't care about Bob and doesn't care about you either.*

I told myself to cut it out. I was a little drunk and I was about to fall headfirst into a vat of self-pity. And that shit doesn't wash off easily. The best thing was to get some sleep. Which I did.

An hour later, I woke up, put my holstered gun in the right pocket of my robe, slipped into my shoes and left the room.

At the hotel's men's shop, a distinguished English gentleman waited on me. He acted as if it was not uncommon for a slightly drunk customer to come into the shop wearing nothing but a robe and a gun. He got me into a whole new wardrobe—jeans, chinos, some shirts, a windbreaker, a couple of ties, socks and boxers. And a very nice suit.

He assured me that the suit would be specially tailored to conceal my firearm and would be ready in twenty-four hours. I spent a little over five grand. *Thanks, Al.*

Looking dapper in my new clothes, I stopped at the hotel gift shop and picked up the day's trade papers. The clerk seemed eager to sell me cigars, so I let him. I selected a couple of Padron Anniversary Series, which I'd tried before and liked a lot.

Then up to the Polo Lounge for lunch. The People's Republik of Kalifornia doesn't allow smoking in indoor restaurants and bars, so I sat on the patio, which was nicer anyway. The patio was all shades of rose and pink—azaleas, camellias, bougainvillea, star jasmine and impatiens, the waiter told me. He added that the tree covering the patio like a giant umbrella was a ninety-year-old Brazilian pepper tree. I made appropriate noises in response and he seemed pleased that I was impressed.

I ate the most expensive burger I'd ever had. It was perhaps marginally better than a Blackie's burger at three times the price. I washed it down with fancy beer and signed everything to my room. And I read the trades. The Continental Pictures Christmas party wasn't really newsworthy but the trades gave it a lot of ink, just as Al Diskin said they would.

A tourist couple stared at me for a while and whispered to each other. I wondered if they recognized me from the noon news or if they were trying to decide if I was a movie star. There were plenty of genuine celebrities in attendance so their attention was soon drawn elsewhere and I never found out.

Back in my room, I lit one of the cigars and fixed a drink. The afternoon nap had taken the edge off my buzz but I'd enjoyed a couple of pints with my lunch and figured rum on ice would get me back into shape.

I sat on the bed and smoked my cigar. It complemented the dark rum. I reached into my wallet and pulled out a card and read Virginia Lane's name and telephone number. I had time off now, so what the hell? It wasn't like I had a job to do.

I called home and checked my machine instead, still hoping for a message from Jill. No messages. I hung up the phone. Thinking, *You're an idiot, Dudgeon. She made it clear that she doesn't want you in her life. You think she's suddenly gonna change her mind? Give it up. It's over, damnit.*

A couple of drinks later, I called Virginia Lane. A Mexican woman answered and I gave her my name and she told me to hold on and I did.

"Well hello, Chicago."

"Hello Red."

"Haven't we been busy today, playing superhero?"

"We have. But now we've got some time off."

"Then why don't we come visit us for dinner?"

"We'd love to."

Virginia Lane lived only a few blocks from the Beverly Hills Hotel, so I walked. It was a beautiful night for a walk but nobody walks in Beverly Hills and I was the only pedestrian on the street. I wondered why they bothered making sidewalks. I'd ordered a bottle of Bollinger champagne from room service and picked up some flowers from the hotel florist and I looked like a young man on his way to a first date. Except that I wasn't so young. I wondered if I had gone a little heavy with the cologne but decided that it was fine.

The house was a sprawling Spanish style mansion with an impeccably manicured garden and a black Mercedes 500SL parked in the circular drive. Every house in the neighborhood was sprawling. Every property had an impeccably manicured garden. Every circular drive had a Mercedes.

I rang the bell and Virginia Lane answered it herself.

"On the phone you sounded Mexican," I said.

"I gave Maria the night off. It's Christmas Eve, you know."

"I heard rumors to that effect." I handed her the flowers.

"Oh, how sweet!"

I followed Virginia into a kitchen that may have been a little smaller than my entire apartment. She put the flowers in water and I opened the bottle. I found a couple of crystal flutes in a cupboard and poured the champagne.

"What shall we drink to?" said Virginia.

"Long timers."

"Long timers?"

"The car bomb this morning had a long timer."

She let out a throaty laugh. "Definitely to long timers, then."

So we drank to long timers. And after that we just drank. Virginia disappeared into the wine cellar and returned with a few more bottles of champagne and put them in the fridge.

"It feels like a champagne evening," she said.

"Never mix, never worry."

In the living room, she put on a nice quiet Pat Metheny album. *Watercolors*, I think. She gave me a tour of the place and it was stunning. The photos, however, were a little unnerving. In every room there were pictures of Virginia Lane. Some were publicity stills, others were movie posters, and everywhere you looked, Virginia Lane looked back at you.

It occurred to me that it might be difficult for a woman who'd made millions on her beauty to face images of her younger self at every turn. There she was, frozen in time, ten years younger, fifteen years younger, twenty years younger. There was no escaping it. Virginia was an incredibly talented actress but she had to know that at least some of her success had come not because of her talent, but because millions of men wanted to have sex with her. That hadn't changed yet, but it was only a matter of time and the photos seemed an unnecessary reminder of what was past, and what was to come. Or maybe Virginia Lane was the most secure actress in town. Maybe.

It was an uncharacteristically warm winter evening, even for Southern California, so we sat out on the pool deck, where the music played through outdoor speakers. We flirted through the first bottle of champagne and I answered the obligatory "what's it like to be a private eye?" questions as briefly as I could.

I got a fresh bottle from the kitchen and refilled our glasses. "So what's it like to be a movie star?" I said.

Virginia let out a long breath. "Is that what I am?"

"Why not?"

"Oh I guess I am, or used to be, anyway. These days I get the *Mom* roles. Last time, I played a wife whose successful husband dumps her for a younger woman." She drank some more wine. "Not much of a stretch there, I'm afraid."

"I'm sorry."

"It's okay. He's a total creep and I don't want him back. Hollywood has been very good to me, so I can't complain."

"Do you still do theatre?"

"Oh God! I haven't been on the boards in years. How did you know?"

"I saw you play Honey in *Who's Afraid of Virginia Woolf?* at the Goodman."

She smiled and said, " 'Never mix, never worry.' "

"Exactly."

"That must be twenty years ago."

"Almost."

"That was just before I moved out here."

"You were excellent in it."

She stood and crossed to me and kissed me on the mouth. It was a good kiss and she left me sitting on the pool deck to contemplate it.

Virginia ordered a Chicago-style deep-dish pizza for dinner. "To make you feel at home," she said. I didn't have the heart to tell her that I prefer thin-crust. So we drank champagne and ate deep-dish pizza and flirted and talked about our lives. After dinner she kicked off her shoes and we curled up together in front of a gas fireplace in the living room. And necked like teenagers.

We shared an easy intimacy born of the mutually understood but unspoken fact that this night was all there would be. She was a rich actress in Hollywood and I was . . . well, I was whatever the hell I was, in

Chicago. But we were two lonely people who enjoyed each other and that would be enough to get us through the night.

By midnight we'd finished the third bottle of champagne and were well into the fourth. We were quite drunk but we both carried it well. Or so I thought.

The grandfather clock in the hall chimed twelve times and Virginia said, "Merry Christmas, Chicago."

"Merry Christmas, Red." We clinked our glasses together and drank to Christmas and kissed.

"Come here, I wanna show you something." She took my hand and led me across the pool deck and into what looked like a large guest-house but was really a six-car garage. She flicked a switch next to the door and the garage was flooded with fluorescent light.

It was a beautiful collection. A red Ferrari Testarossa, a black Bentley Continental, a white Porsche Boxter, a red 1969 Pontiac GTO and a white 1968 Shelby GT350. I guessed that the empty space was for the black Mercedes parked in front.

"You've got a definite color scheme," I said.

"My soon-to-be-ex husband says that red, black and white are the only colors for a car."

"Or for six."

"I used to call them his mistresses, until I learned that he really had a mistress."

"They're in perfect condition."

"So is she. The old ones he barely drives." She led me to the Shelby and we sat in it and I turned on the dome light. It had a black leather interior and a wood-grain dash.

"Got a cigarette?" I lit two and handed one to Virginia and she giggled.

"Albert doesn't allow smoking in his cars." We kissed a smoky kiss and I realized that we were drunker than we pretended to be. I was, anyway. Virginia looked into me with those mesmerizing brown eyes. "Do me a favor?"

"Name it."

"Drive this car into the swimming pool."

"What?"

"You heard me. The cars are all in my name. Everything is in my name, actually, so I can sink one in the pool if I like. Albert's coming over tomorrow with the divorce papers, sort of a Christmas present to both of us, and I just want to see his face." She laughed that throaty laugh again.

"I can't."

"Why not?"

"Not this car. It's a classic, and I couldn't live with myself." This time we both laughed.

"How about the Bentley?" she asked.

I thought about it for a minute. Worst thing that could happen is I'd drown.

"What the hell. It's your car."

Virginia squealed and clapped her hands together and kissed me. She showed me the way to go and I wheeled the Bentley out and slowly around the garage and she opened some gates that led to the pool deck, at the deep end of the pool. I was in no condition to drive. I buckled my seat belt in preparation for impact.

She stood beside the pool, looking radiant. I put the car in neutral and gunned the engine a few times for effect and we both laughed like hell. I stubbed my cigarette out in the never-used ashtray, reached down, and slid the stick into drive.

"Wait, WAIT!" Virginia yelled. She ran over to the car and yanked open the passenger door and I put the car back in neutral.

"Change your mind?"

"Hell no," she said, and climbed in beside me and buckled her seat belt. "I'm coming with you."

I started to protest but she silenced me with a wet kiss. "Drive me into forever, Chicago." She turned her head and looked straight at the surface of the water with a maniacal grin spread across her beautiful face. "Do it," she said. I gunned the engine a few times and jammed it into drive without letting up on the accelerator.

The rear wheels screamed against the pavement, then grabbed hold and we were thrust forward and over the water. We hit the surface with a tremendous splash and Virginia shrieked. The Bentley sank quickly for the first few feet, then stopped.

Virginia looked at me with alarm. "What do we do?"

"We wait." The car started sinking again, slowly. When the water reached halfway up the windows, we sank faster. Water leaked in through the side windows and splashed against our thighs.

"Holy shit," she said.

"Yeah."

Then it occurred to me. The Bentley had electric windows. My plan had been to wait until we settled to the bottom of the pool and then slowly crank the window down, take a deep breath and swim to the surface. I'd seen it in a movie once. But the electric windows wouldn't work and I didn't have a spike hammer handy.

"Hey, Red. What's in the glove box?" I said it calmly; there was no use worrying the poor girl.

"Um . . . owner's manual. And a tire pressure thingy." She handed me the pressure gauge. It was metal and might do the trick. We hit bottom.

"Okay, now I'm gonna break the window," I said. "Undo your seat belt. Water's gonna rush in but don't worry. Just take a deep breath and we'll swim outta here."

"God this is exciting," said Virginia. "I can hardly breathe."

We undid our seat belts and I smashed the pointy end of the pressure gauge against the side window. The window didn't seem to mind, but the pressure gauge snapped in two.

"Uh-oh," said Virginia. "Suddenly I feel pretty sober."

"Not to worry," I said, as if there was no reason to worry. I turned sideways, lying back across her lap, and kicked at the window with my heels. On the third kick, the window went away and water rushed in with more force than I would have liked.

"Deep breath!" I yelled. I took a deep one myself and braced against the turbulent rush of water as the car filled. When the water passed our heads I went through the window. It would have been ungentle-manly to shoot to the surface so I hung on to the door frame, floating in space, and reached my hand into the car. Her hand squeezed mine and I pulled her out and we both swam to the surface and gulped air. Our sodden clothes were heavy and we didn't waste time getting out of the pool. We lay on the pool deck and shivered and laughed like lunatics, looked down at the car and laughed some more.

"You sure know how to show a girl a good time, Chicago."

Inside, we stripped off our wet clothes and took the remaining champagne to the bedroom.

We were like a couple of wild animals with nothing to lose. The champagne had made us drunk and the adventure with the Bentley had given us a shot of adrenaline and it added up to a furious orgy of thrusting and biting and scratching and licking and sucking. I hadn't had sex like that since I was a much younger man. It felt dangerous and electric.

Afterward, I got up and went to the kitchen for some water while Virginia slept. Thinking, *Now that was a woman. What do I care if some timid little nurse who's afraid of her own shadow doesn't want me? There's no way she'd be as much fun as that.*

As soon as I thought it, I felt a knot in my gut that said I had be-trayed something within myself by thinking about Jill that way. Vir-ginia was a lovely woman and the sex had been terrific, but I was in love with Jill. Whatever sex with her would be like, it would be bet-ter. And as good as it had been with Virginia, it was in essence just a drunken screw between two lonely people. With Jill it would have meant something.

The morning came easy. For a while I drifted in that middle world be-tween sleep and wakefulness, enjoying the sensation. When I opened my eyes, there was no pain. The bedroom was full of morning sun and

I was glad we had been drinking champagne the night before. Good champagne never gives me much of a hangover and I'd drink it all the time if I could afford it.

I could hear the shower running, then stop. I got into my clothes and Virginia came out of the bathroom wearing a blue silk robe and a smile. I smiled back at her and knew everything was just fine. I went to the bathroom and brushed my teeth. The bruise around my eye was almost gone. A little yellow and some muted purple remained but the garish blues, browns and greens were just a memory.

I returned to the bedroom and Virginia said, "Shall we inspect the damage?" with an impish grin.

Then I remembered the Bentley. We walked, hand in hand, out to the pool deck. It hadn't been a dream. The car was sitting at the bottom of the pool, all right.

"Regrets?" I asked.

She kissed me hard on the mouth. "Thank you," she said. We stood and looked at the pool for a minute in happy silence.

In the kitchen, Virginia made huevos rancheros while I made coffee and toast and everything was delicious.

After breakfast she stood and said, "Give me a dollar." I did. "Oh, and your driver's license." I had no idea what she was up to but I couldn't resist those eyes, that smile.

Virginia left the room for a few minutes and I washed the dishes. She came up behind me and slipped her arms around my waist. The gun didn't bother her a bit. I turned to face her and she kissed me and stuck a folded piece of paper into my hand.

"You just bought yourself a classic Shelby GT350," she said. "Merry Christmas." I looked into my hand. I was holding the ownership papers for the Shelby, with all the blanks filled-in transferring ownership from Virginia Lane to Ray Dudgeon.

"No, Virginia. I can't."

"Don't spoil my fun now," she said with a playful pout. "I've been thinking about it all morning."

"The car's probably worth close to a hundred thousand."

"So? The Bentley's worth over two hundred and you see what became of it." She closed my hand around the ownership papers. "You
saved the Shelby's life last night and I want you to have it. Something
to remember me by."

"Like there's any chance I could forget."

Leaving was easier than it should have been. There was no false
talk of looking me up if she ever finds herself in Chicago or my giving her a call next time I'm in Los Angeles. No exchange of cards that
would be filed away and ignored. Virginia walked me across the pool
deck and into the fancy garage. This time we didn't stop to admire the
Bentley. I got into the Shelby and turned the key and the engine let out
a guttural roar. Virginia pressed a button somewhere and the garage
doors opened and I pulled slowly out into the sunshine. She walked to
the driver's side and leaned in and we shared one last, lingering kiss. I
looked into those brown endless eyes for the last time.

"Good-bye, Red."

"Good-bye, Chicago." She walked back into the garage, without
looking back. And the door closed.

I put on my sunglasses and hit the gas.

It was Christmas morning so I had the roads mostly to myself. Having
nowhere to be, I headed for the Pacific Coast Highway and pointed
the beast north. I put the accelerator to the floor and the Paxton su-
percharger kicked in and I was pushed back into the seat. The car was
fast. Scary-fast. In no time at all I was doing 120. The road got curvy
and I slowed to 80, getting the feel for how she handled, then edging
the speedometer up again. After playing awhile, I settled into a nice
cruising speed and took in the scenery. To my left, the highway fell off
a sheer cliff into the Pacific Ocean. To my right were steep brown hills.
The sun was bright, the car was fast and the only thing that would ruin
the moment was to *think about things,* so I decided not to. I found the
other cigar in the breast pocket of my windbreaker and lit it, listening
to the music of eight finely tuned cylinders.

Albert doesn't allow smoking in his cars . . . her cars . . . *my* car.

"Merry Christmas, Albert," I said, and pressed the pedal down farther.

On the way back to Los Angeles I stopped to top up the gas tank.

"Sweet ride, dude," said the kid at the gas station.

"Thanks, dude," I said to the kid.

Bob and I left Los Angeles on December 26, in the darkness before dawn. Al Diskin was staying in L.A. for a couple more days to close the distribution deal he'd been working on. I told him that Bob and I would also stay and fly back with him. So we were booked on an afternoon flight on the twenty-eighth. And we were still checked in at the hotel with "Do Not Disturb" signs hung on our doorknobs and orders at the desk not to let calls through. Diskin wouldn't know that we were gone until we didn't show up at the airport. Deputy Mullins was the only person who knew about it. Mullins didn't like me much but after the car bomb I sensed a slight grudging respect, and besides, he was too good a cop to blow it, regardless of his personal feelings.

Mullins didn't want me taking charge of Bob in his jurisdiction, so we met at a truck stop in Ontario, just outside the limits of Los Angeles County and into San Bernardino. Bob looked listless as he got out of the unmarked police cruiser. Mullins brought Bob's bags around and squeezed them into the Shelby's little backseat.

"I've faxed all the relevant documentation to Lieutenant Angelo at the CPD," he said.

"Thanks."

"You know, from here to Illinois you are not licensed to carry a firearm."

"I'd rather be judged by twelve than carried by six," I said. A macho cliché, but in this case it was true enough.

Mullins looked to the east, where the sky was turning pink, then back at me. "Good luck," he said. "You are definitely going to need it." He left without shaking my hand.

Bob slept for the first few hours. It was almost nine when he finally woke up and looked around.

"Isn't this Albert Westley's car?"

"Used to be," I said. Bob shifted in his seat and fell back asleep.

We stopped for lunch in Parowan, Utah. Bob apologized for all the sleeping and explained that the doctor had him on Valium for stress. I was glad for the quiet ride, so I told him that it was important to take the Valium and not get stressed.

So Bob slept a lot and I slept very little, and by the evening of the twenty-seventh, we could see the skyline of Chicago growing larger in the distance. I felt the tension leave my body. Chicago was my kind of town and I was glad to be home.

More than that, I was glad to be acting instead of just reacting. Investigative work gives you a lot to do and you feel a sense of control. It is proactive. Bodyguard work is mostly passive. You do all the things you can to head off trouble and then you wait and watch and, if necessary, react. And no matter how diligent you are in your preventive measures, you always feel like a sitting duck. I don't care for it much.

But the Chicago Police Department would be assuming Bob's protection detail and I'd be free to investigate Paul Tortelli and Frank DiMarco. And maybe I could dig up something that would put a stop to all this nonsense. If Diskin was willing to pay for it. With the CPD involved, Diskin wouldn't have to spend money on a protection team, so I figured I could convince him to keep me on in this capacity.

That's what I'd been thinking on the long drive to Chicago and it made me feel better, so I just kept on thinking about it.

I checked us into a room at the Travelodge on the corner of Harrison and Wabash. I paid cash in advance and used the name Louis Sullivan. The desk clerk didn't see anything wrong with that.

Just after noon the following day, I met Mike Angelo at the Step-Hi lounge. It was the sort of place that catered to hard-core drunks and it smelled vaguely of stale beer, vomit and ammonia bleach. It was the sort of place you go to when you don't want to be recognized.

Mike sat in a red vinyl booth at the back of the narrow room. He looked just like what he was—a cop in a room full of old drunks. The drunks in this sort of place were too beaten down by life to stop conversation just because a cop walks into the room. Booze-soaked eyes rolled in my general direction, not actually making contact with my own, then back to the square foot of bar top that was familiar territory.

I made my way to the booth and sat across from Mike and he signaled the bartender and the bartender came to the table with two bottles of Old Style. One look at Mike's eyes told me that this was not his first pop of the day.

"Drinking on duty, Mike?"

"Wow. You must be a detective."

"Something wrong?" I said.

"Only everything."

"Okay."

"Everything's wrong and nothing's right and the world is made of shit." Mike took a pull on his beer and lit a cigarette. "I think that about covers it."

I lit a cigarette of my own and waited him out.

"I've put in almost thirty years," he said. "Could've retired on full pension after twenty." It was a familiar tune, and Mike sang it often enough. But this time was different. "And I keep doing the job anyway."

"It's a good job."

"It's a shitty job. Every year since I made my twenty, Susan threatens to leave me if I don't get off the force. And every year I tell her I just gotta clear my open case files and then I'll hang it up."

"There's always gonna be open cases, Mike."

"Hell, I know that. Susan knows it too." Mike dragged on his cigarette. "In twenty-nine years I've never been shot and I've never had to shoot anyone. And I've put a lot of bad guys away." A shrug. "When is it enough?"

I didn't have an answer for that one. "I guess it's never enough. But time comes when it's enough for *you*—when it's time to hand the job off to the next guy and enjoy a well-earned retirement."

"And do what? Buy a Winnebago and see the country? Wander around museums with Susan all day?"

"Shit, Mike. Do whatever makes you happy."

"Yeah, well. Putting bad guys in prison makes me pretty happy."

We drank in silence for a minute.

"But the world is made of shit," I said, "so something else is bugging you."

"Get us a couple more barley pops."

The bartender was facing the other way, so I walked over and got a couple bottles and brought them back to the booth.

"First of all," Mike said, "we never had this conversation."

"Understood."

"I'm serious."

"I know."

"Okay. My request for a protection detail on Bob Loniski has been denied for now."

"Jesus Christ."

"They said a week or two. But right now manpower is stretched and they want to review the case file from the LASD before sending the request up the line. Meantime I'll make sure a prowl car passes his apartment building every hour or so. Best I can do."

"Someone in the CPD is setting him up."

"Watch it! I didn't say that. I didn't even imply that. And you don't know that. It's a bureaucracy and there's not enough manpower and things take time."

"Bullshit."

"You can think whatever you want. I'm gonna get him his protection detail but I'm just warning you it's gonna take a week, at least."

The world was made of shit. Which means that Mike thought it was a setup too. Bureaucracy is one thing, but only corruption makes Mike think the world is made of shit.

And maybe he was right.

CHAPTER SEVEN

I saw him, Ray! I saw the guy."

"What guy?"

"On TV, on the news . . . at a ribbon-cutting ceremony or something. He was standing right next to the mayor!"

"Okay Bob. Slow down. What guy?"

Bob picked up a notepad from the bedside table. "I wrote it down. Alderman Herman Heath."

"You saw Alderman Heath on television."

"He was the guy waiting in the car. When Frank DiMarco and I signed the contract at the warehouse. He was the guy waiting in DiMarco's car."

"Are you sure it was him?"

"Yes I'm sure! With those glasses and that orange wig, of course I'm sure." He had a point. Herman Heath was a distinctive-looking man. He always wore huge, gold-rimmed Cartier glasses and an orange toupee. It would be hard to mistake him for someone else.

Heath was a wealthy corporate lawyer with a solid reputation who represented an affluent ward on City Council. As far as I knew, he was not mobbed-up. But if he was in the car with DiMarco, he sure as hell wasn't clean.

After my meeting with Mike Angelo I'd purchased a prepaid cell phone at a shop on Dearborn. I used it now and dialed a number from memory.

"*Buenos días.*" The background noise told me that Ramon Gonzalez was in his taxi.

"Gonzo. Dudgeon. I need you."

"Kinda busy today, amigo. Where are you?"

"South Loop. I only need about an hour and my friend Ulysses Grant wants to say hello."

"Wish I could help but I'm on my way to pick up a fare on the North Side. Now, if your friend Ben Franklin wants to see me, I could turn this motherfucker right around and be there in twenty."

"Fine. South Loop Club, twenty minutes."

I didn't mind Gonzo squeezing me for the extra fifty. He was always too busy right at the moment and always said no to my first offer, so I always offered low and came up, which always made him rearrange his busy schedule to accommodate me. The dance was a little dated after all these years but we both knew the routine cold and never missed a step. Fred and Ginger would have understood.

I left Bob in the hotel room and walked over to the South Loop Club and ordered a burger, rare. The restaurant was on a corner and had large windows, so I could see Ramon as he pulled up and parked his cab with two wheels on the sidewalk. He sauntered in, sat across from me and began devouring my curly fries. I slid five twenties across the table and into his hand. He frowned at the money.

"This ain't Ben Franklin."

"One Franklin, five Jacksons, what's the difference?"

"The difference, *mi amigo*, is *style*," Ramon grinned. "Something you gringos will never appreciate." He folded the bills and slipped them into the breast pocket of his silk shirt. The silk shirt was yellow today. I had never seen him wear anything but silk.

"You own any cotton shirts, Gonzo?" I said.

"Naw, man." He rubbed the shirt against his chest. "Silk feels good against my skin, so why settle for less? All my boxers are silk too. Just like Al Capone."

"Now there's a role model."

"You got me for an hour," he said. "It goes longer, it costs more. You wanna spend it talkin' about my wardrobe, that's okay by me. You do look like you could use some assistance in that area."

"I need you to go to my office and get my laptop computer and bring it here."

"That's it?"

"That's it. And don't be followed. If you grow a tail, don't lead them here. Just cruise and pick up fares and go about your business. If you're not back in an hour, I'll call your cell and we'll make other arrangements. Got it?"

"Yeah man, no problem." Ramon finished my last french fry and wiped his hands on a paper napkin. "Greasy," he said with a frown. He picked up a small bottle of white vinegar from the table and shook a generous amount onto a new napkin, wiped his hands thoroughly and smiled. "You still protecting that movie guy?" he asked.

"I took him to Florida. He'll be safe there for a while, I've got someone looking after him." It was a spontaneous lie but it sounded good to me.

"Shit, man. Nowhere is safe," said Ramon. "This guy got some cojones, goin' up against the Outfit. You too."

There was no use explaining, so I just handed Ramon the key to my office. I reminded him to lock up when he was done and he rolled his eyes and reminded me that he wasn't an idiot.

After he was gone I ordered a beer and made a couple of phone calls.

I told Al Diskin that Bob was hiding out in Florida and I would have him back in a week or so. Diskin didn't like it. I told him that hiring a temporary replacement locations manager was a hell of a lot cheaper than hiring a five-man protection team. And I assured him that Bob would return as soon as the Chicago Police Department was able to pick up his protection detail.

Then I called Terry.

"The L.A. papers said you and Loniski had gone missing," said Terry. I thought I could hear some relief in his voice.

"We are missing," I said. "I'll tell you all about it at dinner. I'm buying."

Actually, Johnny Greico would be picking up the tab. I used the phone again to make a reservation for two at Villa d'Este. My name must have been on a list because after a short pause the woman on the phone said that Mr. Greico would be happy to have me as his guest.

Ramon Gonzales was back in thirty-five minutes. I got into his cab and had him drop me at the Hampton Inn on Illinois Avenue. It wasn't that I distrusted Gonzo, but if someone held a gun to his head, I'd just as soon have him think that I was staying there. That way he could tell the truth and keep his head and still not give me away. We weren't being tailed, but ever since my meeting with Mike Angelo, the paranoia had been growing inside me.

I checked into the hotel using a credit card in my own name. Up in the room I plugged in the computer and logged onto the Internet. At the Chicago City Council Web site I found the bio page for Alderman Herman Heath. I jotted down some details, took that information to ProInfoTrace.com and typed it in. I selected the two-hour rush service and entered my Illinois private detective's license number, credit card information and e-mail address.

ProInfoTrace combines Internet meta-searches with searches of over a thousand databases, both public and private. It isn't cheap but they could charge double and I'd still use the service. It saves days of legwork and mines databases that are usually restricted to certain levels of government. I don't know how they get such access but I suspect they have some talented computer hackers on their payroll. Anyway, two hours later an e-mail with a large attachment arrived.

I opened the attached file and read about Alderman Herman Heath. All the expected information was there—home address, unlisted telephone number, cell-phone records, driver's license and Social Security numbers. More interesting was his history. It supported his squeaky-clean image. He had never been charged with a crime, had never been sued, had been married to the same woman for twenty-two years. His children, both in their late teens, had never been in trouble with the law. His credit rating was solid and his bank balance was neither too fat nor too thin. No large money transfers either in or out of any of his accounts. No bankruptcies, no hidden assets or offshore bank accounts. His tax returns claimed no unusual or excessive deductions. He gave about 15 percent of his gross income to various mainstream charities, which is more generous than most folks but not outrageous. His favorite charitable causes were abused children, adult literacy and the environment. His insurance records indicated that he was on blood pressure medication, but he had never been treated for a serious illness. He had personally bankrolled his political campaigns and his voting record on the City Council suggested that he was beholden to no special interests. Before running for City Council, he had been elected Cook County treasurer and had served two terms without any hint of a scandal. His constituents loved him and he had won reelection to the City Council with over 70 percent of the vote.

There was nothing wrong with Alderman Herman Heath. Except that he'd been riding around in Frank DiMarco's car.

Heath was a straight guy living a straight life. He had worked hard to build a solid reputation. A guy like that doesn't suddenly decide to do business with the Outfit. So I figured it had to be blackmail. And it had to be sex. Tortelli ran the sex trade, and at fifty-three, Heath was the right age.

Most of the public officials who get involved with the Outfit are, themselves, corrupt to begin with. They're simply crooks who conned their way into public service, which is itself just another racket. Or they're latent crooks whose greed makes them natural partners for organized crime. Sometimes, however, a straight public official exposes himself to influence because of some personal weakness. He runs up gambling debts that he can't cover or he has a secret drug habit to feed or he gives his business to the wrong hooker. This, I suspected, was what had happened to Alderman Heath. And if I was right, I might be able to flip him.

I packed up my computer and left the hotel without checking out, walked to the El station and rode the train to Harrison. Bob was in the room, sitting on his bed watching television. I poured some bourbon into a couple of plastic glasses and added some water from the bathroom sink. I gave one of the drinks to Bob and turned off the television.

"How are you feeling?" I asked.

"Whenever I start getting anxious, I take another Valium," he said. "I'm okay. And I've been doing a lot of thinking."

"Me too. I may have found a way in on this thing."

"The alderman?"

"Yeah. But I need to be able to move freely and I can't stay here babysitting you." I sipped my drink. "So I'm going to take you back to Los Angeles, where Deputy Mullins can look after you."

"What about the Chicago cops?"

"It takes time to get these things approved. In a week or so I'll come get you and bring you back."

Bob thought about it. "No," he said, "I have to stay here." I looked at him and said nothing. He swallowed some of his drink. "I don't know how to explain . . . On Christmas, I wasn't able to visit Josh but the police brought him to see me at the hotel. We spent a couple of hours in my suite, just talking. And you know what he said? He said I was a hero. Can you believe that? A hero."

"He's thirteen, Bob."

"That's not the point. I've never been a hero to Josh. When I was a kid, my dad was my hero. He was strong and athletic and successful and he was my hero. I could never live up to it, you know? Our den was full of trophies he won in high school and college. Football, swim team, wrestling—he did it all. But me, I never won a trophy in my life. Look at me . . . I'm fat and clumsy and almost bald. Josh goes to school with the sons of famous actors and directors. I'm a fucking locations manager."

"This is sounding suspiciously like self-pity," I said.

"It's just the way it is," said Bob. "Now hear me out. With this Di-

Marco thing, I finally have a chance to be a hero to my own kid. I can't be a famous actor but I can be the guy who stood up to the Mob, and you can't get much cooler than that."

Or much deader. I topped up Bob's drink. "I think the Valium is affecting your judgment."

"Maybe it's allowing me to see clearly for the first time," he said. "I'm not a good father. I know that. I see my kid every second weekend and we keep in contact by e-mail, but what has he got to look up to?"

"I can't solve your family problems, Bob. I'm just trying to keep you alive."

"I've been thinking about that too," he said, "and I'm not sure how much it matters. I mean, yeah, I want to stay alive, but for what? I haven't made the kind of life for myself that I set out to make. I'm not happy. And I'm not the kind of man I wanted to be. If I stay here, I will be a hero to my son. That matters. If you keep me alive, great. If not, at least my son will be proud of me."

"And before, you were willing to risk your life for the chance to be on the permanent guest list at the Starlight Bar."

"That was before they blew up my car, it wasn't real to me then. Now I understand. And I don't give a shit if I never see the Starlight Bar again."

"Or if you never see Josh again."

"Not if I can't hold my head high and be a role model."

Bob was not responding to reason. I didn't know what approach to take next, so we sat for a while in silence.

"I don't expect you to get it," said Bob. "I bet you don't live in your dad's shadow."

Great. Now we were going to talk about *my* dad. I lit a cigarette. "My father died before I was born," I said.

"Oh. Sorry."

"Don't be, you didn't kill him."

"How did it happen?"

"He was a reporter—a stringer for AP, working out of Philadelphia. He and my mother were engaged and he was planning to move to Chicago. She didn't even know she was pregnant when he died. He was driving down to Alabama to cover the civil rights demonstrations in 1964. He stopped on the way for dinner in a roadhouse bar. Some rednecks spotted him and figured him for a civil rights worker. Another sanctimonious Yankee, come down to stir up more trouble. So they followed him when he left and ran his car off the road. He wasn't wearing a seat belt and he went through the windshield."

"So your dad was a hero," said Bob.

My dad was not a hero, and the story I told Bob was a lie. But I'd grown up believing it, so it was easy enough to tell. Bob Loniski didn't need to know the truth and I'd automatically spouted the lie I was raised on.

"Bob," I said, "I would rather have had a live father than a dead hero. And so would Josh. I want you to lay off the Valium and smarten up. We'll talk again when I get back."

I scooped the little bottle of Valium off the bedside table and dropped it into my pocket and left Bob alone with his fear.

Terry and I sat in a private booth at Villa d'Este. He had chicken Vesuvio. I had veal marsala. The waiter treated us like Roman emperors and the wine steward brought us a bottle of Gaja Barbaresco which he said was, "a complex wine of great perfume and well-integrated tannins, with a nose of tar and roses and a long finish." He added that Mr. Greico had personally selected this wine for our enjoyment.

It was very good wine.

As far as Terry was concerned, Alderman Heath fit perfectly into DiMarco's landlord scam. Before running for alderman, Heath had been Cook County treasurer, so he could easily use his contacts to compile a list of vacant commercial properties with absentee owners. But Terry added that Heath was square and he agreed that it must be blackmail. Terry shut up as Sal Greico passed the table. Sal didn't stop to say hello.

"Based on hypotheticals," said Terry, "the word is that Biagio

Amodeo would snuff Tortelli with all speed if he knew of a coup attempt against Greico. He doesn't know yet."

"But if you know . . ."

"Then he'll know soon. So for Tortelli, time is of the essence," said Terry, "and cleaning up this thing with you and Loniski is the first order of business. He won't want that distraction while warring with Greico."

I drank some wine and ate some milk-fed veal. The image of a cute little baby cow flashed in my mind. *Moo*. I told myself to have the chicken next time. "I've got Loniski hidden away in Florida," I said. "On the record."

Terry put his fork down. "On the record?"

"What?"

Terry snorted. "You want to make a fool of me? You want me to print that bullshit in the *Chronicle*?" He didn't look happy and I suddenly felt like a jerk.

"Okay Terry, don't print it. But if anyone asks, I said that Loniski is in Florida. And that's the truth. I did say he was in Florida."

Terry took the last bite of his chicken and finished his wine in a gulp.

"Thanks for dinner but I'm gonna pass on coffee."

"Terry . . ."

"And don't ever try to play me again, Woodward. You're pissing me off."

"Look, I'm sorry. But this is important. If anyone asks—"

"Yeah, yeah." Terry smiled despite himself. "If anyone asks, you said Loniski's in Florida . . . and I thought you were lying through your teeth." He stood up. "I'll see what else I can dig up on the Heath connection. Call me tomorrow."

Terry left and the waiter cleared the dishes and poured the last of the wine into my glass. A minute later Johnny Greico sat down across from me.

"Your date sure left in a hurry," he said.

"Must've been something I said."

The old man chuckled. "He don't look your type anyway." He put a cigar between his teeth and lit it using the candle on the table. He blew a stream of smoke about a foot over my head and made a hand gesture to the waiter. "Dinner okay?"

"Dinner was great."

"You like the wine?"

"The wine was fantastic. Thank you."

"Good."

The waiter arrived and put a couple of espressos on the table in front of us. Greico put one spoon of sugar in his and stirred it, then shot it down all at once. Vinnie Cosimo appeared at my side and discreetly ran the handheld bug detector over my torso, nodded once to Greico and left without a word. I took no offense.

"Mr. Greico, I want to ask you something and I also want to tell you something."

"Tell me something first and then we'll see about the asking."

"Paul Tortelli is about to go to war with you."

Whether this came as news to Greico or not, I knew he wouldn't tip his hand. His expression remained dispassionate. "That's what you want to tell me?" he said.

"I thought you'd want to know."

"And you got this information from that spade reporter?" I must have winced. Greico said, "I'm too old to give a shit, Dudgeon." I stirred a spoon of sugar into my espresso and said nothing. "Okay, doesn't matter where you got it," he said. "Do you think that it's true?"

"Yes."

Greico puffed on his cigar and gestured toward my coffee. "You oughta drink that before it gets cold." I drank the coffee. "What's the question?" he said.

"Does the Outfit own Herman Heath?"

"You mean that alderman with the orange thing on his head?"

"That's him."

"You gonna share this information?"

"This is just for me," I said. "Whatever I learn from other sources I may share. But what you say at this table is just between us."

Greico thought for a moment. "Okay kid. No, we don't own him. He's a Boy Scout."

As I slipped into my overcoat I could sense Vinnie's bulk close behind me. His mitt clasped my shoulder and he whispered into my left ear.

"Be very careful," he said. I turned to face him but he was already a few yards away, taking long, quick strides. Clearly, he was not in the mood to explain.

It was just before 11:30 when I pulled out of the Villa d'Este parking lot and onto Milwaukee Avenue. Then down Milwaukee all the way to Lake Street and east, back into the Loop. I drove slowly but my mind was racing. Thinking, *Greico doesn't know that Heath is Tortelli's boy. With the gambling and loan-sharking rackets under his control, Greico is the Outfit's big moneyman. In the chain of command, he's probably fourth, below the boss himself, underboss Chris Amodeo (the boss's son and heir to the throne) and consigliere Joe Maritote. Greico would know about every politician they owned. Which means Biagio Amodeo also doesn't know. Let's assume that Heath isn't the only one. Now it makes sense. Tortelli runs the sex trade . . . through which he often snares public officials for the Outfit. He's supposed to turn them over to the boss but let's assume he's been amassing his own personal collection. Hell, he could have cops, politicians, who knows what? That's his ace in the hole. So he snuffs Greico. Then he asks for a sit-down with Amodeo and lays it all out. Shows a list of high-ranking public officials that are under his personal control. Maybe a few names on the list to whet the boss's appetite, but mostly just office titles: three aldermen, two police captains, three statehouse representatives, one state senator . . . something like that. Offers them to the Outfit in exchange for Greico's operation. And probably offers the sex trade to Sal Greico as a concession to peace.*

Would it work? Biagio Amodeo couldn't easily overlook the fact that Tortelli had killed a made guy, broken the chain of command, held out on the Outfit and built a personal sphere of influence. On the other hand, this sort of thing had been done before, if rarely.

Whether it's called the Outfit, the Mob, the Mafia or La Cosa Nostra, people think of organized crime as a bunch of murderous thugs killing without reason. Hollywood has helped sell this image, but the truth is very different. The essential difference between the Outfit and General Electric is not violence. It is the simple fact that the Outfit does not have recourse to the courts. If a company infringes on a GE patent, that company can be sued. If an employee steals from GE, that employee can be arrested and charged with a crime. But the entire business of the Outfit is crime. If someone rips off the Outfit, nobody's going to file a lawsuit or call the cops. Violence is the only way to deal with it and the only way to make others think twice about doing the same.

The Outfit is a business and Biagio Amodeo is a successful businessman. People like Amodeo never kill without reason, or they wouldn't be in business for long. And they never fail to kill, when it is necessary to protect their position. Would it be necessary to kill Tortelli? Would it even be good business?

Good business. When a small company gains market share, sometimes it makes sense for the market leader to go to war. But if the small company has valuable proprietary assets, then it usually makes more sense to buy the small company and fold it into the larger operation.

If Tortelli's personal sphere of influence was large enough, he might just pull off this coup. I knew he had Alderman Heath as a "proprietary asset" but I didn't have any way of knowing how many others, or how significant they were. Since the CPD had rejected Mike's request for a protection detail, I could reasonably conclude that Tortelli owned at least one high-ranking police official.

My rear windshield exploded and I was jolted back to reality. *Fuck.* A black SUV was close behind, muzzle flashes coming from its rear passenger window. The two bruisers who had first rousted me were in the front seat. The little guy was driving and the big guy was in the passenger seat holding what looked like a sawed-off shotgun. I jammed down the accelerator and sped forward. From the left lane I fishtailed a hard right turn onto Wells, tires screaming, and the big guy unloaded with the shotgun, taking out the passenger-side window. But the SUV couldn't make the corner and disappeared from my rearview. I weaved through traffic, leaving a chorus of angry blaring horns in my wake. Two blocks later, the SUV swerved back into traffic three cars behind me, coming in off Randolph. I made a left on Monroe, then a quick right on Clark, narrowly missing a police cruiser that was idling at the curb. The siren howled and the roof lights came alive and the cops pulled away from the curb. From behind, I heard the squealing of rubber and then the glorious crash of metal against metal, which told me I would live through the night. The cops had pulled away from the curb just in time to be T-boned by the SUV as it came skidding around the corner. I braked and turned left onto Jackson, easing into the flow of traffic. Cold sweat trickled down my back and my hands shook as I lit a cigarette.

There was no way that the cops could've gotten a make on my car at that speed, in the dark. But DiMarco's thugs knew what I was driving and if I gave them another chance they wouldn't miss, so I drove around aimlessly for a while to be sure I hadn't grown another tail. With two windows missing, it was a wintry ride and the sweat threatened to freeze against my back but I didn't care. My legs felt like rubber bands and if I got out of the car now and tried to walk, I'd probably fall flat on my face.

I took Lake Shore Drive south to Hyde Park and stopped at an all-night coffeehouse near the University of Chicago campus. The place was full of college kids who sat huddled around tables, smoking cigarettes and solving the problems of the world and trying to grow facial hair.

It didn't seem so long since I'd been a college student myself and I envied the kids their youth and confidence. They were still at a time in life when knowledge was certain. Later they would graduate and head out into the real world and life would teach them harder lessons. I had a momentary urge to tell the students to stay in school forever but I drank some coffee and the urge went wherever urges go when they evaporate.

They'd been waiting for me outside Villa d'Este. Someone on the inside had dropped a dime on me. The image of Sal passing the table flickered in my mind. I wondered why. Was it possible that Sal would join forces with Tortelli and set up his own uncle? Sal wasn't half the man that Johnny was; maybe he knew that he couldn't handle the position for which he was being groomed. Maybe Tortelli had already promised him the sex trade in exchange for a Judas act. By comparison to the money business, the sex trade was easy and Sal wouldn't be in over his head there.

No, that didn't make sense. Vinnie didn't think Sal was such a bad guy and my judgment was clouded by my dislike for Sal. On the other hand, Vinnie had tried to warn me—maybe he had overheard Sal making the call. Hell, he could've overheard anybody. A waiter or a busboy or a dishwasher . . . Frank DiMarco had worked for Greico long enough to recruit more than one Judas.

Bottom line—I had pitifully few hard facts with which to work. What I did have were rumors and supposition. But I was out of time and I had no choice. I'd been dealt a lousy hand and I would simply have to bluff it through.

I looked up from my coffee and caught my reflection in the glass wall. The face looking back surprised me. It looked tired. It looked sad. It looked older than me.

I cracked the cap on the half-pint bottle and took a healthy swig of bourbon. *Don't do this, Dudgeon. Just go back to the hotel and get some sleep, you've got a big day tomorrow.* I took another swig and looked at the apartment building across the street.

The windows were dark. *Of course they're dark, you idiot, it's one in the morning. Everyone's in bed, like you should be.* I took another swig and felt the bourbon warm my insides. I'd taped garbage bags over the two missing windows but the car was still cold.

I sat like that and drank and smoked and waited for the bourbon to give me some courage. I drank some more and thought about what I knew of courage, and how I learned it . . .

When I was eighteen, I worked the summer on a scuba boat with my buddy Randall. Randall's dad lost an arm in a fishing mishap. Some moron laid a gaff into it by accident and infection set in and it had to be amputated just below the elbow. Randall's older brother, Clyde, took over the business but had no love for fishing, so he retrofitted the boat as a scuba charter. Randall and I both got our divemaster certifications and helped Clyde with the tourists.

We were out on the water and a storm was coming in later that afternoon. There was a surface current of four knots with three-foot seas, so we decided to go ahead with the dive. But at forty feet we were suddenly faced with about twelve knots, pulling us away from the boat. Time to abort. We rounded up our tourists, but for one. There's always one. This guy was already about thirty feet south of the group and ten feet deeper. Visibility was rapidly diminishing as the current tossed silt around—pretty soon the guy would be out of sight. He was riding the current and hadn't once looked back. I signaled to Randall and he surfaced with the group and I went after the stray. I caught up with him at about eighty feet and grabbed his tank and stopped him and we drifted together. I signaled that we had to surface but he shook his head and pulled free of me. I caught him again and he struggled against me but this time I had a good hold on him. He fumbled in the nylon mesh pocket of his BC, pulled out a white plastic diving slate and wrote on it with a grease pencil and held it for me to read. Then he snatched the regulator out of my mouth. I didn't panic. I got the regulator back in my mouth and cleared it and sucked air, but the guy was gone. I kicked my fins and went deeper but never caught another glimpse of him.

I ascended, slowly and alone, with the words he'd written on the slate echoing in my head. *I have cancer. Want to die. Let me be.*

That night after dinner, Grandpa and I sat out on the screened porch and smoked Edgeworth tobacco in corncob pipes and listened to the cricket and tree-frog music all around us.

"Took courage, what you did today," he said. "Goin' after that man."

"No, sir," I said. "Wish I had courage, but I was scared as hell."

My grandfather fixed me with his *I'm about to tell you something important* look and blew out a stream of fragrant smoke. "Listen, son," he said. "Without fear, there is no courage. Remember that."

As I knocked on Jill's apartment door, it occurred to me that I should've stopped before the bottle was empty. Still, it was only a little bottle. I tossed a piece of gum into my mouth and chewed. And knocked again, a little harder. I heard the shuffle of slippered feet behind the door.

"Go away. I'm calling the police."

"It's Ray. Please Jill, open up. Just two minutes." The door opened and I went inside and sat on the couch. Jill sat in a chair on the other side of the coffee table. She was wearing her pink robe and her hair was a mess and she had no makeup on and she was beautiful.

"Do you have any idea what time it is?"

"Late."

"Very late."

"Yeah, but . . ."

Jill lit a cigarette. "Two minutes, and then you're leaving."

It was hot inside the apartment and I felt a little nauseated. I tried to speak but nothing came out. I opened my mouth, closed it again. *You fucking idiot, just talk. This is why you're here. Let the girl in. Say something. Now. Say anything.*

"Walter Cronkite used to be my father."

"What are you talking about?"

"No, wait, that's not it," I said. "Let me start over. The day after my mother died, I found her diary. And learned the truth about my father. He didn't die before I was born. The guy my mother told me about wasn't really my father and she wasn't pregnant when he died. The guy was a reporter, traveled a lot. He was her fiancé and he lived in Philadelphia. Then he got drunk and drove himself into a ditch and went through the windshield. And died.

"My mother called his folks to find out, you know, to go to the funeral. But his dad came to Chicago instead. Sat her down and told her the truth—her dead boyfriend was already married. Wife and kids. In Philadelphia. Girlfriends scattered across the country, each believing he was gonna move to her city and marry her."

"Wow."

"Yeah, and then came the Dells. You know, Wisconsin? See, my mom, she was only nineteen. And she took it hard. She drove up to the Wisconsin Dells and checked into a cheesy resort and went to bed with the first man who bought her a drink in the bar. Didn't even know his name. And that's how I came to be. See, I'm a bastard and my father was just some nameless guy getting laid in a cheesy resort. He wasn't a hero."

"Hero?"

"Oh . . . yeah, sorry," I mumbled. "That was another conversation."

"Ray," Jill said gently, "maybe you should come back and tell me this when you're sober."

"I'm not drunk."

"I can smell it from here."

"I've been drinking, doesn't mean I'm drunk. That's not the point. I'm trying to tell you something. See, I thought my dad was this dead journalist who spent his life righting the wrongs of the world. Truth, Justice and the American Way. Rah-rah-rah, sis-boom-bah, and all that jazz. I didn't have a father, so I latched onto that, you know? That's what *I'd* be someday. My mom was out a lot and I used to eat Beefaroni out of the can and watch Walter Cronkite on television and pretend that he was my real father. Had whole conversations with him in my head. Stupid, I know. But it was a fantasy and it helped me."

"But you were still a kid when you learned the truth."

"Sure it seems weird now. But when I learned the truth, I latched onto the fantasy even harder . . . too much invested in it to let it go. My road map to becoming a man, you know? It was all I knew. So I kept at it. I wasn't blind to reality—I knew that journalism is just another business but I just didn't know what else . . . I mean, I just, I . . ." The words ran out. I waited but nothing else came. *Damn.* "Jill, I'm trying. You said to let you in, and I'm trying." I lit a cigarette.

"Ray . . . I'm sorry but I don't know what to say. I'm looking for someone to spend my life with."

"So?"

"So I read about the car bomb in L.A. How do you expect me to react to that? And I understand you're trying, but you have to get plastered in order to talk to me about your life? That's not healthy."

"I'm not plastered."

"You're smoking your filter."

"What?"

Jill pointed at my cigarette. "You're smoking your filter," she repeated. Shit. I *was* a bit drunk. Maybe even close to plastered. I stubbed out the cigarette and the ashtray slid off the table and hit the floor and broke in half. Jill stared at the broken ashtray and said nothing.

"Sorry." I leaned down and picked up the two pieces of broken ashtray and put them on the table, then scooped some ashes and cigarette butts into my palm. Jill continued to stare at the mess I'd made. Her bottom lip trembled but she didn't cry. She took a deep breath, stood and opened the door. "Go home, Ray. This can't work . . . it's over."

I stood up. "And that's the way it is," I said, just like Walter Cronkite. The door closed behind me, but I didn't hear Jill's slippered feet walk away. I leaned against the door and tried to think of something to say. "I'm sorry," was all that came out.

"Terry," I said into a pay phone outside the Walgreen's at Belmont and Broadway. "It's Ray. I just fucked up my life."

"Jesus, Ray. Go home and sober up," said Terry, understanding as always.

"No, man. I mean it. I fucked everything up with Jill. She was the only good thing in my life."

"Okay, hold on, I gotta get outta the bedroom." I held on until Terry came back on the line. "What the fuck, Ray," he said.

"They tried to kill me tonight," I said. "Almost did. Shot the hell outta my car."

"Tortelli?"

"His guys."

"And you thought the best response was to get shit-faced and visit the girl?"

"Her name is Jill."

"I know."

"I tried to explain things to her," I said, "but I got it all wrong. I drank too much and smoked my filter and broke an ashtray."

"Wait, back up a second. Are they still after you?"

"Who?"

"Tortelli's guys," said Terry. "Who the hell you think I mean?"

"Oh yeah. No, I got away. They don't know where I am."

"Okay. Now listen up, Ray. You can't worry about Jill right now. What's done is done. You gotta focus, man. Get somewhere safe. Drink some coffee. Sober up. And watch your back. We'll talk about Jill another time."

"No, we won't," I said, and hung up the phone.

CHAPTER EIGHT

Bob still refused to go back to California. When I got to the hotel room at 4 A.M., stinking of fear and failure, I thought he would change his mind. But the attempt on my life actually strengthened his resolve. I was risking my life to protect him, he said, and he was determined to "become a new kind of man." I wasn't prepared to have that argument, at that hour. I gave him a couple of Valium to help him sleep and got a couple hours' sleep for myself.

Two hundred dollars motivated Sasha Klukoff to come into work early, take my car and set me up with a loaner. So my car was at Franz Motorwerks for repairs and Bob Loniski was still hiding out in the hotel room and I was sitting in a borrowed Volkswagen Jetta, parked down the street from Alderman Herman Heath's house.

It was 9:37 on a clear Monday morning. I'd been sitting there since 7:00, drinking black coffee from a thermos and swallowing aspirin and trying to ignore my hangover. The City Council was on Christmas recess and Alderman Heath's Audi was in the two-car garage. I'd spotted it at 9:22, when Mrs. Heath opened the electric door and loaded two teenagers into her Land Rover and drove away. As far as I could tell, Alderman Heath was alone in the house. It was time to play poker.

I rang the doorbell, and through a little speaker next to the button, a man's voice asked who was there.

"DiMarco," I said, having no idea what Frank DiMarco's voice sounded like, "we gotta talk." I turned my back to the door and waited. From his arrest records I'd learned that Frank DiMarco was seven months younger and three inches taller than I, so I tried to look young and tall. The door opened behind me.

Alderman Heath said, "I told you never to come here—" and stopped short as I turned around. "What the hell is this?"

I put my hand on my gun and said, "Please step inside, Alderman. I need a word with you."

In the study, Alderman Heath started toward his desk. I clamped my left hand on his shoulder and his whole body stiffened.

"Not there," I said. "Sit on the couch." I didn't think it likely that Alderman Heath had a gun in his desk and even if he did, I seriously doubted that he would go for it. He could have a panic button, which would bring armed security. Again, not likely but I was taking no chances.

Regardless, I needed to strip away his sense of authority. We were on his turf but taking away his ability to make choices would remind him that he was not in charge of the situation. Humiliation would help reinforce the point, so I snatched the orange toupee off his head, dropped it on the floor and pointed at the couch.

"Sit," I said. He did. I took the desk chair for myself.

Alderman Heath sat wringing his hands. I tried to see him as a sexual deviant and a crooked politician but all I could see was an insecure and frightened man. I had prepared a speech but now it didn't seem appropriate. So I just stared at him.

"What can I do for you, Mr. Dudgeon?" he said.

"That's good, you know me," I said, feeling ridiculous. "So you know that Paul Tortelli and Frank DiMarco have been trying to kill me." I lit a cigarette. "And you know they've failed."

Alderman Heath looked at his hands. "I saw your picture in the newspaper. And I'm not familiar with those names," he said weakly.

"Of course not. But you told DiMarco never to come here," I smiled.

"You don't know anything," said Heath, but his voice quavered and it sounded like wishful thinking.

I smoked and looked around the desk for an ashtray and didn't find one. I knocked the ash off my cigarette onto the mahogany desktop and locked eyes with Heath. "You like them young, don't you Alderman?" I said, as if I had any idea what I was talking about. Sure, it was a guess but a pretty safe guess; it was unlikely that he had requested old whores and I hadn't specified male or female.

Heath blinked rapidly and his eyes ran away from mine and his face flushed bright red. "I don't know what you're talking about," he said with a complete lack of conviction.

I searched for another guess that would clinch it. Might as well bluff it through. I looked at Heath. Something about him said *adolescent girls.*

"She was a *child,*" I said, "younger than your own daughter."

I'd guessed right. Alderman Heath slumped into the couch and covered his face with his hands and sobbed. I waited.

"I insisted that the girls be at least eighteen," he said. "I swear I did." He removed his glasses and put them on the coffee table and wiped his eyes with his sleeve. "I insisted upon it. I just wanted them to look young. That's what I told her."

I stubbed my cigarette out on his leather desktop blotter. "She wasn't even close to eighteen, you fucking pervert," I said.

Heath's bare pate turned red to match his face. "No," he said, still looking at his hands. "She wasn't. But I was drunk and . . . Jesus, I didn't know . . ." He choked it off with another sob.

He didn't know. Sure he didn't. Maybe he didn't want to know, but he knew. Deep down, they always know.

I let him cry for a while. Without a partner, I was running a multiple-personality-disorder version of the "good cop/bad cop" routine—and it was time to bring in the "good cop." From a bar in the corner of the study I poured three fingers of Oban into a heavy crystal rocks glass. I handed it to him, along with a box of Kleenex. He wiped his eyes and blew his nose and drank some Scotch and pretty soon had himself under control.

"I can help you, Alderman," I said.

"No one can help me," he muttered to himself, eyes fixed on the floor.

"Herman," I said, "look at me." He turned his wet eyes toward mine. "I can help you," I repeated. "Tortelli and DiMarco have tried for me and failed—"

"They'll get you eventually," he said.

"Maybe. Or maybe I'll get them."

"You can't be serious."

"Serious as a heart attack," I said. "If Tortelli wins, then I'm dead and they still own you . . . but if I win, I may be able to give you your life back. Either way, they'll never know you put in with me."

Heath finished his drink. "You can't beat them," he said. "It's not just Tortelli—you're taking on the whole Outfit."

"Don't be so sure."

"What are you saying?"

"There's a lot I can't tell you," I said, lighting a new cigarette, "but let's just say that Tortelli is pissing off the powers that be and will likely be cut adrift in the coming days. To survive, he'll use everything he's got on you and a dozen other public officials."

"Oh my God." Heath sat staring at nothing. I refreshed his drink and returned to the desk.

"You may not like my chances," I said, "but I'm the only chance you've got. I'm going to save myself. If you don't side with me, that's fine, I'll just move on to the next name on the list. But there's only room on the ark for one of your sorry asses. The rest I hand over to the FBI, along with Tortelli and his cousin. You seemed like the least degenerate of the lot, so I'm giving you the first shot at it. But this is a limited-time offer."

Heath said, "Who else is on the list?"

I smiled at him. "Not a chance," I said, and glanced at my watch without actually registering the time. "I need an answer. Now."

"What is it you plan to do?" he asked.

It was time to bring in the "bad cop" again. I ground the new cigarette into his desk blotter and sent him an unpleasant look.

"You don't get to know what I plan to do, asshole. And you don't get to know who else is on the list. I ask questions and you answer them. You do as I say and you don't ask why. Those are the rules. You work with me, maybe you get your life back. You don't, you drown. I've been very patient with you but time's up." I stood and glared down at him. "One word—yes or no."

Heath sat with his mouth hanging open. His entire head was covered in a sheen of perspiration. I knew I couldn't stand there very long or he might suspect the truth—that I didn't really have a list. Just as I started for the door, he spoke up.

"Okay," he said. "I mean, yes."

For the next hour I took notes as Heath told me the story of how he got involved with the Outfit. A friend in the State's Attorney's Office had recommended Premiere Escorts, a high-priced call-girl service. He had assured Heath that Premiere was very discreet and paid off the police department. He'd been using them for years, he said as he pressed a referral card into Heath's hand. He said that Premiere was not listed in the phone book and they would accept as new clients only those who arrived with such a card. Heath feigned disinterest, saying that he was happy in his marriage. But he kept the card and two months later he called for an appointment.

Heath became vague at this point. He didn't want to talk about what came next. I told him that some minor detail might be the very thing that enables me to save him from this situation. I reminded him that I already thought he was a lowlife, so he didn't need to worry about losing my respect. And finally, after another drink, he told me the rest of the story.

At a luxury high-rise condo on Lake Shore Drive, Heath met with Gloria Simpson, the madam of Premiere Escorts. As they chatted over coffee, Heath found it hard to believe that this woman was a madam, or had ever been a prostitute. She seemed to him like a financial planner or the chief executive of a designer clothing firm. She seemed both educated and incredibly self-assured, not characteristics he associated with prostitution.

She was a smooth operator and she convinced Heath that there was no risk in becoming a client. She told him that Premiere's files were indexed by number only; his name would not appear on any piece of paper in their records. The charges on his credit-card statement would appear as "Renfrew & Sons Rare Books," "AC Communications Consultants," or "Cambridge Men's Clothing." He could choose one, or change each time from one to another. He chose to rotate among the three. To further avoid suspicion, the fee would vary. A random number between 700 and 850 would be generated each time, and that would be the amount charged to his credit card.

Premiere was an expensive agency, Gloria Simpson reminded him, so he might as well get exactly what he wanted. Heath was reluctant but she cajoled him into revealing his sexual desires.

He admitted that he wanted a girl who looked young, because he had never been able to get a girl in high school and it remained an unfulfilled fantasy. He insisted that the girl be over eighteen but he wanted one who could pass for a high school cheerleader. She asked him what name he would like for his cheerleader. He chose "Kimberly." Hair color? Blond. Dominant, submissive, playful? Playful. Vaginal, oral, anal? Vaginal and oral. And so on.

After Heath revealed his fantasy, the madam told him to give her a week to find just the right girl. She gave him a card with a phone number and a five-digit membership number. Nothing else was printed on the card. He was to call and give the operator his membership number and a location and his girl would arrive within two hours. He could call any-time, day or night. If he had a good time, he was expected to tip the girl at least $200. If he was unhappy, he could simply call the office number and Simpson would make arrangements for a different girl the next time.

Heath was very happy with the first Kimberly and he saw her every three weeks or so, for a few months. But on their fifth "date" a differ-ent Kimberly arrived at his hotel room. She said that the first girl was on vacation visiting her folks for a week. But she told him that she was a very good Kimberly and would make him happy. She even brought along a cheerleader's uniform. The girl was very small and seemed impossibly young but Heath was drunk and horny and convinced him-self that she was over the age of consent.

A few weeks later he called again and expected the original Kim-berly to arrive at his hotel room. Instead, a couple of tough guys showed up. The larger one never spoke. The other introduced himself as Frank DiMarco. DiMarco said that he represented Paul Tortelli. He didn't have to tell Heath who Tortelli was; Heath had seen the name connected to the Outfit while reviewing research material for a new antiprostitution bylaw. DiMarco spread some color photographs on the bed. The photos showed Alderman Heath in all his glory, violat-ing a schoolgirl. DiMarco showed Heath photocopied enlargements of the girl's birth certificate and student identification card. The girl was thirteen years old.

DiMarco laughed as Heath broke down. He said that the photos were just a taste of what was on the videotape. Then DiMarco and his henchman picked up the photos and departed without another word.

"After they left," Heath said, "I just lay on the bed and stared at the ceiling until morning. Then I went home. A month passed by. I could barely eat and I didn't sleep more than a few hours a night. I waited for them to call with their demands. I sold a few paintings and some jewelry and put fifty thousand dollars cash in my safe, to pay them off. Finally DiMarco called but he didn't want money. He instructed me to vote in support of a rezoning ordinance that would ease the way for commercial developers. What could I do? I voted for it."

Then came the landlord scam. On DiMarco's orders, Heath compiled a list of vacant commercial properties with out-of-state absentee owners. He initiated a few informal discussions with fellow aldermen about changing the property tax structure for real estate speculators, which he hoped would provide cover in case anyone looked into his information request from the county treasurer. And he turned the list over to DiMarco.

They had thirty-two tenants in nine buildings, generating $29,000 a month in rental income. The operation had been going for almost a year. DiMarco planned to expand the scam to sixty tenants, generating just over $650,000 a year, gross. After expenses and payoffs, DiMarco and Tortelli would clear about half a million dollars a year.

DiMarco only rented ground-floor units, leaving the buildings mostly vacant to minimize electricity consumption. In order to reduce the paper trail, the tenants were all renting without leases. They were small business owners who were willing to rent month to month and pay cash in exchange for a discount.

Each month, DiMarco gave $3,000 cash to Heath. Heath tried to refuse the money but DiMarco explained that it was not an option; the money served to solidify their relationship. So Heath took the money and added it to the fifty grand he had stashed in his safe, which had now grown to over $80,000.

"They don't need me anymore," Heath concluded, "since they already have the list. So I was hoping that maybe I could buy my way out when I get to a hundred thousand." He went to the bar and refreshed his own drink. "But they aren't ever going to let me out, are they?"

"No, they aren't," I said.

"Okay," said Heath. "Now you know everything. What do you want me to do?"

"Buenos días."

"Gonzo. Dudgeon. I need your hack."

"No can do, amigo," said Ramon Gonzales. "Just finished my icebreaker and it was a big fare. Know what that means?" Gonzo continued without waiting for me to guess. "It's an omen. It means that I'm gonna have a very big day. I can feel it in my bones."

Occasionally Gonzo rented me his taxi. Unlike most cabdrivers, he owned his car, so he could just take the day off and pocket the cash. He didn't have to worry about odometer readings and he didn't have to explain anything to anyone. As long as the meter stayed off and I didn't pick up fares, there was nothing illegal about borrowing a friend's cab. And there was no better vehicle for tailing someone in downtown Chicago than a taxi. Like vagrants, billboards and litter, taxis just blend into the scenery and become part of the visual background noise of the city.

"Listen Gonzo. I don't give a shit about your bones. I need the cab and I don't have time to dance around. I'll give you two large for twenty-four hours."

"Two grand? You gotta be in some heavy shit," said Gonzo. For a twenty-four-hour rental, I normally offered four hundred and came up to eight. "I like the money, but I gotta visit my sister in La Grange tonight. You gotta rent me a car too, 'cause my plastic is maxed out."

"I've got a car you can borrow," I said.

"All right," Gonzo said, "but I still don't like the sound of your voice. I want the cash in advance and I don't want to be seen with you."

"Fine. We'll do it cloak-and-dagger. Meet me at the dog pound in one hour," I said.

"You're makin' the wrong kind of enemies these days, amigo."

"One hour," I said. "If I'm not there, wait for me." I broke the connection.

Back in the study, Heath sat at his desk, memorizing the index cards I'd prepared for him. There were ten cards in all, lined up in two rows of five. On each index card in the top row, I'd written one main point that I wanted him to convey to Frank DiMarco. On each card in the lower row was a response to whatever DiMarco might say when he heard each of the main points. Since I couldn't really know what DiMarco would say, the responses might not match his objections but it didn't really matter as long as Heath stuck to the cards and didn't start improvising.

We ran through it a few times with me playing the part of Frank DiMarco and Heath's performance got a little better each time. But he was nervous and his hands and voice both trembled.

"I don't think I can pull it off," he said, dropping his glasses on the desk.

"You're doing fine. You're just anxious. So acknowledge that right off the top. Start the conversation by telling him you're scared as hell. It fits into our story, and then you don't have to worry about it. You can sound as nervous as you like and it won't matter."

I poured Heath another drink. This was his fourth and I didn't want him getting too loose, but in the tug-of-war between adrenaline and alcohol, adrenaline was clearly winning. Another drink might even things out.

I brought the cordless phone from the kitchen into the study. I stood next to Heath with the cordless phone to my ear and my thumb over the mouthpiece. Heath used his desk phone and dialed Frank DiMarco's number.

There was no answer. Heath told DiMarco's machine to call him back at home; it was an emergency. Then we waited.

Sixteen minutes later, the phone rang and the call display panel showed that it was coming from DiMarco's apartment. Heath took a deep breath and looked at me. I nodded at the phone. He picked it up and I engaged the cordless at the same time.

"Heath, here."

"Yeah, it's Frank. What's the big emergency?"

Heath glanced at the first index card. "That detective . . . Dudgeon. He was just here."

"Jesus. How long ago?"

"He left about a half hour ago. Frank, I'm scared shitless, he knows everything."

"You asshole," said DiMarco. "What did you tell him?"

"Nothing . . . I swear, not a thing. But it didn't matter, he already knows. He even knew the addresses of all the buildings. I—I acted like I didn't know what he was talking about but he didn't believe me."

"Christ. Why didn't you keep him there and call me?"

"I couldn't. Look, I can't take this anymore. I have to get out."

DiMarco snorted. "Don't be such a pussy. We'll take care of Dudgeon." I pointed at one of the index cards and Heath's gaze followed my finger.

"It's too late, Frank. He said he's going underground and giving everything to the feds."

"Shit."

"Look, I want out. I can give you a hundred thousand dollars, cash."

"We don't want your money," replied DiMarco.

I pointed at another card. Heath said, "I can give you Dudgeon. The cash is just extra. I'm supposed to meet him at midnight."

"Where?"

"No. I'll meet you first, give you the money, and you give me the photos . . . and videotape . . . everything," said Heath. "Then I'll tell you where Dudgeon is."

There was a silence on the line. I pointed at a card that read, *Now or never—Dudgeon going to FBI*. Heath said, "If you don't get him tonight, he's gone. He's going to the FBI. You've got plenty of other politicians. All I want is my freedom. I'll never say a word to anyone, and I'm getting out of politics."

"Shut up, I'm thinking," DiMarco barked. Heath shut up and we waited. "How do you know he'll show up at this meeting?"

Heath's eyes darted down to an index card. "Because I'm supposed to pay him off. That's what he wants. I agreed to give him thirty thousand to keep my name out of it."

Another long silence. I jabbed my finger at another card.

"If you're thinking of coming over here, forget it," Heath said, with more strength than I thought possible. "I'm leaving right after this call and you won't find me." I pointed at another card. Heath read it. "You need to resolve this thing with Dudgeon and Loniski more than you need me, Frank."

"I'll have to call you back."

"No!" shouted Heath. "Right now. I'm leaving after this call."

More silence. "Okay," said DiMarco, "how do I know this ain't all bullshit? I show up, give you your home movies, and you send me to a meeting spot and Dudgeon don't show up because there never was any meeting. Huh?" I was relieved that he asked because I needed Heath to give him the information I'd written on the appropriate response card.

Heath glanced down at the card that was titled, *Lying?* and said, "Dudgeon gave me his cell number, in case I need to change the meeting. You can call it if you want. If he answers, you'll know I'm telling the truth." He read the number into the phone.

"Hold on, I gotta get a fuckin' pen." Heath waited and then read the number again.

DiMarco said, "Okay Alderman, you got a deal."

Heath let out a long breath. "Okay," he said, looking at a card, "there's an underground garage on the corner of Polk and Spaulding. I'll be parked on level two at 11:00. I'll leave my lights on so you can find me. If you're not there by 11:30, I'm leaving and I'll pay off Dudgeon."

"I'll be there," said DiMarco.

Heath started to hang up and I stabbed frantically at another card. "Wait," he said, "one more thing. I'll have a lookout waiting outside. Park your car on the street and walk down. If you're not alone, I'm calling 911."

DiMarco laughed into the phone. "Where'd you get the brass balls all of a sudden, Alderman?" I didn't have an index card for that one.

"I just want out," said Heath wearily.

"I'll come alone," said Frank DiMarco with a chuckle. "You don't scare me that much."

The phone clicked over to a dial tone. Heath broke down in tears but it was just a release of tension and didn't last long. I poured some more Scotch into his glass and he drank it.

"You did very well," I said. "Now about that thirty thousand dollars . . ."

Heath's eyes grew wide and he gestured to the index cards on his desk. "But—but . . . that was just for DiMarco."

"Operating expenses," I said. "Look at it this way, you were willing to pay them a hundred to get free so, at thirty, I'm a relative bargain. Besides, it's dirty money. You don't want to hang on to it, it'll only rot your soul." *Ray Dudgeon—The Soul-Saving Detective.*

Heath crossed to an oil painting of an equestrian scene and pressed on the frame and the painting hinged away from the wall. He punched some numbers into a keypad on the safe door and it opened. He removed three stacks of bills and handed them to me, then closed the safe and pushed the painting back into place. They were hundred-dollar bills, held together by rubber bands.

"You can count them," said Heath.

"That's okay," I said. "I don't doubt your ability to count to a hundred." I shoved the bundles into the patch pockets of my blazer.

Heath looked at me for a long moment and said, "You're going to kill him, aren't you?"

"You watch too much television, Alderman," I said. "I'm going to make an arrangement with him."

Heath looked shocked. "You're going to sell out your client?"

I'm no Mona Lisa, but I think I managed an enigmatic smile. "Don't worry about what I'm going to do. Frank DiMarco may very well come over here to see if you were bluffing and if you're here, your afternoon will be infinitely worse than your morning. I suggest you go for a very long drive and don't return for a day or two."

I stood at a counter in the Greyhound bus terminal, looking up at the arrivals-and-departures board. A man walked up beside me, dropped a newspaper on the counter and also examined the board.

"Schaumburg, Schaumburg, Schaumburg . . ." I said.

"Hey buddy, you got a schedule I can look at?" asked Ramon Gonzales.

"I've got an extra, you can have it." I handed Gonzo a bus schedule that was wrapped around $2,000 cash and the keys to the loaner car. "Silver VW Jetta, parked around the corner on Wells," I added quietly.

"Thanks," said Gonzo, and tapped on the sports section of the *Chicago Tribune* that lay on the counter. "Damn Blackhawks just keep on losing," he said, and walked away.

I picked up the newspaper and walked in the opposite direction. Opening the paper to the hockey scores, I found the key for Gonzo's cab taped to the page. Above it was written, "Franklin Avenue, back of the taxi stand."

Cloak, I'd like you to meet Dagger.

Parked on Damen, a half block from Frank DiMarco's apartment building, I had that nagging feeling of having forgotten something. It was the same feeling I got on the way to the airport, whenever I went on a trip. The feeling was usually right and I'd forgotten a belt or a toothbrush or some item that could easily be replaced at my destination. Sometimes the feeling was wrong and I'd packed everything. I hoped that this was the case now because there would be no returning home before my meeting with DiMarco.

From the Greyhound depot, I'd gone to my apartment for supplies, which was risky but unavoidable. There were no thugs waiting to greet me but it was probable that they just hadn't yet arrived. Heath had told DiMarco that I was about to disappear . . . it was a reasonable assumption that I might need to stop at home before heading underground. If DiMarco could find me before his meeting with Heath, he could keep Heath under Tortelli's thumb, so it would make sense for DiMarco to station a couple of guys at my place, just in case. I'd gotten in and out as quickly as I was able and I sure as hell wouldn't risk it a second time.

Why hadn't DiMarco called? I had bet that he would, not because he didn't believe Heath's story but because he was, as Johnny Greico had said, braggadocio. I didn't think he could resist the temptation to act like a big shot; to let me know that he had the upper hand and to hear the dread in my voice. Calling would also boost my motivation to get the payoff from Heath and get out of town quickly, increasing the odds that I'd show up at the midnight meeting. So Frank had plenty of reasons to call. It was important that he call.

Another hour passed. The phone remained silent and DiMarco didn't emerge from his apartment. My watch said 4:52. The lights were on in his window, so he was probably home. Or maybe he just wasn't energy-conscious. *Name: Ray Dudgeon. Sign: Capricorn. Turn-ons: Moonlit Walks on the Beach, Driving Cars into Swimming Pools, and Women Who Aren't Afraid. Turnoffs: Pimping, Blackmail, and People Who Waste Electricity by Leaving the Lights on When They Go Out.*

Maybe DiMarco kept the videotape and photos at home, but I doubted it. He was smart enough not to have anything incriminating in his apartment when the cops had searched the place and I doubted he had grown seriously stupid since then. Or maybe he had gone out immediately after speaking with Heath, collected the evidence and returned home before I arrived. I was hoping that I could tail him to his blackmail stash, but if not, the evening would still proceed as planned. *If only he would call.*

I adjusted the rearview mirror and checked to see that everything was in place. I wore black-rimmed glasses with lenses made of plain glass, and an old Chicago Cubs baseball cap. Gray hair protruded from under the cap and hung down to just above my shoulders. A bushy gray mustache adorned my face. I'd gotten the disguise from a friend who worked as a makeup artist at the Victory Gardens Theatre. She showed me how to put the facial hair on with spirit gum and she showed me how to remove it with cold cream. It looked real, even from a few feet away.

The cell phone rang as I put the mirror back in place. I pressed the answer button.

"Ray Dudgeon," I said. Silence. "Hello?"

"I just wanted to hear the voice of a dead man," said Frank Di-Marco, always handy with a cliché.

"Who is this?"

"Can't you guess?"

"Ooh, I love guessing-games," I said. "Let's see now . . . it's either Paul Tortelli or Frank DiMarco, and since Frankie is the bigger knucklehead, I'll guess DiMarco. Am I close? Do I win a prize?"

"When the time comes," said DiMarco, "remember this: it can be very long and very painful, or you can choose quick and painless, just by telling us where he is."

The line went dead before I had a chance to advise DiMarco about his tendency to talk like he's in a 1940s gangster movie. I made a mental note of the time: 5:04.

Frank DiMarco emerged from the building seven minutes later. He was a handsome man with a thick mane of black hair that flowed straight back from his tanned face. He must've spent fifteen minutes working with a hair dryer each morning and an hour a week stretched out in a tanning bed. He wore a black cashmere overcoat, which he left unbuttoned. Under the coat he wore black chinos and a green Tommy Bahama Hawaiian shirt with tan palm trees printed all over it. I recognized the shirt because I'd admired the same one in Marshall Field's, but I'd demurred at the $110 price tag. So Frank DiMarco and I both liked the same shirt. It didn't mean anything.

DiMarco got into a black Nissan Maxima and pulled away from the curb, heading north. I followed at a prudent distance. He stayed on the main roads, making it easy for me to follow without being made. I changed lanes frequently and stayed three cars back. One time he blew through a yellow light and the red caught me but it only took a few blocks to close the distance and I settled into place again. He turned west on Fullerton and stayed on it past the Kennedy, then turned north onto Rockwell. I pulled to a stop on Fullerton and idled at the curb for a full minute before making the turn. Rockwell was not a busy street and I now had a pretty good idea of his destination.

Between Fullerton and Belmont, there were six self-storage facilities on Rockwell. I cruised slowly up the street and spotted the Nissan parked in front of Rockwell U-Store-It. I parked in an alley across the street, from where I could keep an eye on the entrance, and turned on the radio.

The radio told me that Chicago would be hit with the first major snow of the season later that evening. Then the radio said a new scandal was brewing in City Hall's Hired Trucks Program. Chicago politics: another day, another scandal. I suppose that shows some progress. They've always pulled the same crap, but in the good old days, they never got caught. Now at least some people were trying to keep things on the level. Noble, if naive.

The next story was one of my favorites. The Gold-Coin Santa had struck again. Every year for the last dozen years or so, someone dropped solid gold coins in various Salvation Army red kettles around the Loop. South African Kruggerands and Canadian Gold Maple Leafs. This year's total was seventeen one-ounce coins. Despite the best efforts of the local press, the Gold-Coin Santa had maintained his anonymity. Or hers.

Frank DiMarco appeared carrying a large manila envelope, got into his car and drove away without looking in my direction. I took off my cap-wig and snatched the fake mustache from my face. From a kit bag on the passenger seat I grabbed a small tub of cold cream and a handkerchief and removed the remnants of spirit gum. Then I crossed the street to Rockwell U-Store-It.

In the grimy vestibule, I smiled through a two-way mirror and gestured toward the inner door. After a moment, the door buzzed open and I was allowed into an equally grimy office where a Latino girl in her twenties sat chewing gum. Her dyed-blond hair, showing about two inches of brunette at the roots, was pulled back into a ponytail. She wore a red, low-cut V-neck sweater that couldn't quite contain her ample breasts. Not that I noticed. She wore too much makeup and her eyebrows had been plucked almost into nonexistence. She didn't seem able to keep her mouth closed while chewing the gum and it made a *smacking* sound with each bite.

"We're 'bout to close for the day," she said. *Smack, smack, smack.*

"That's all right, darlin'," I said, adopting a Southern accent that passes for authentic anywhere north of the Mason-Dixon. "I'm just checkin' the place out . . . my belongings haven't arrived yet from Georgia."

She pointed at a stack of brochures. "Everything's 'splained in there," she said with total indifference. *Smack, smack, smack.* I plucked a brochure off the pile and looked at it. A five-foot-by-ten-foot locker rented for sixty-five dollars, due on the first of each month. Customers supplied their own padlocks and the facility did not keep a key. Management was not responsible for loss or damage but insurance was available for an additional fee. Storage of firearms, explosives or "illegal items" was forbidden. If rent fell two months past due, management would cut the lock and sell the contents at auction.

"That all looks fine," I said. "But how 'bout security? Is a guard on duty at all times?"

The girl lit a cigarette without getting rid of her chewing gum. "No," she said, as if my question had been completely unreasonable. "You can't get in unless we buzz you in. *Smack, smack.* During business hours there's always a couple of guys in the loading bay. *Smack.* You have to sign in and out. *Smack, smack.* When we close up for the night, there's a burglar alarm. And we got video cameras, *smack, smack, smack,*" she concluded, waving her cigarette at a video monitor on the desk.

The monitor displayed four camera views, and each segment of the multiplexed screen changed from one camera to another every thirty seconds or so. The girl hadn't glanced at the monitor once since I arrived. There was no way to know if the video signal was being recorded on tape, so I would just have to assume that it was. I nodded in mock satisfaction and gestured to a clipboard hanging on a nail by the door.

"And this is the sign-in sheet?" I asked.

"Uh, yeah," said the girl. She made sure to put emphasis on it so I'd know what a stupid question I'd asked.

" 'Course it is," I said, and picked up the clipboard. Frank DiMarco had signed in at 5:43 and back out at 5:50. His locker number was K-25. "Well this all looks fine," I said. "I know you're about to close for the evenin', so I won't take up any more of your time, but can I just take a quick boo at the locker areas?"

"What's a boo?" she said. *Smack, smack.*

"A boo," I said. "A gander, a look-see."

"Oh," she said. "Hold on." She picked up a walkie-talkie and pressed the button. "Martinez to the office," she said.

Martinez arrived in less than a minute. He was a small man, with deep craggy lines in his face and laborer's hands. He wore an old and oil-stained windbreaker with a Chicago Bears logo over the left breast. His hair looked like a badger shaving brush and he had a mustache to match.

The girl said, "Show this guy a locker."

Martinez nodded. To me he said, "You wanna see the loading bay first? We can take the freight elevator up."

"No," the girl said harshly. "He doesn't care about that. Just show him a locker like I told you."

Martinez bowed his head like a schoolboy reprimanded by the teacher. "Sorry," he said.

"And hurry up, we close in four minutes," said the girl.

"Yes . . . sorry," said Martinez.

The girl's disdain was obvious. Their exchange told me that Martinez commonly suffered such emasculation and countless other indignities, because he was living in the country illegally and couldn't afford to make trouble. Bubblegum Girl knew it, and to her he was a man without pride, deserving of contempt. I wanted to smack the gum right out of her painted face.

Martinez led me up a staircase and through a doorway. He pointed at the metal door. "Each night, this is locked."

The entire second floor was dark. Martinez turned a dial on a timer set into the wall and the ceiling flickered to life with fluorescent light and the timer started ticking. Martinez said, "You gotta come back and turn it each time it's thirty minutes."

There was no climate control in the storage area and I could see my breath.

"This would be a good place to store a side of beef," I said. Martinez started to tell me that perishables were not allowed but he stopped halfway into the sentence and a wide smile broke out on his face.

"Ah, cold like a meat locker," he said. He thought about it for a few seconds and giggled, but in a masculine way. "Good." I smiled back at him and made a mental note to cultivate a manly giggle. My giggle sounded like a little boy, so I hadn't used it in years.

Before us stood row upon row of storage lockers, their doors and walls made of quarter-inch plywood. The lockers were ten feet in height and another ten feet of empty space stretched above them to the old warehouse's twenty-foot ceilings.

The doors were flimsy enough; exterior hinges could easily be removed with a screwdriver, or a crowbar would pop the hasp without difficulty if you weren't concerned about your invasion being detected later. But to get in that way, you'd have to stand in view of the video cameras. There was a camera at the end of each row, mounted about eight feet from the floor and angled slightly downward to cover the entire hallway. The lockers were five feet wide and the hallway was six feet across.

Martinez stopped at a vacant locker in the B-section. He opened the door and I looked inside. Chicken wire served as a crude ceiling for the locker. The walkie-talkie hanging on Martinez's belt crackled to life. "Tour's over, Martinez. Start your rounds, I wanna get outta here," said Bubblegum Girl.

That was fine with me. I'd seen all I needed to. I fished a ten-spot out of my pocket and stuck it into Martinez's hand.

"Thanks for your help," I said.

I cruised level 2 of the underground garage at Polk and Spaulding, looking for a suitable car. Near the southwest corner, I found it. A blue Chrysler LeBaron that was about a decade old. I donned a pair of Isotoner gloves, pulled my kit bag from the passenger seat and approached the car. It had at least a few days' worth of dust on it. There was no flashing light on the dash or any window decals to suggest that the car had an alarm. There was a steering-wheel lock in place, but I wasn't taking the car for a joyride. A quick *push-hook-pull* with a Slim-Jim unlocked the door. Once inside, I jammed a flathead screwdriver into the ignition and turned it just enough to engage the electrical system. Chryslers from the early 1990s were notorious for their friendliness in this regard and I didn't want to disassemble the ignition switch, leaving obvious evidence of my visit.

I'd chosen this garage partly because it had no video cameras or security guard. And it wasn't close to anything except the CPD Area 4 Headquarters, which had plenty of its own parking. So the garage was only half occupied and most of the cars parked there were not leaving until morning. Still, I worked quickly and kept an ear open for approaching cars or footsteps.

I put the kit bag back into Gonzo's taxi and lifted Bubba from the trunk. Bubba was a legless mannequin I sometimes employed when on an extended tail job. I would periodically reposition him on either side of the backseat or the front passenger seat. I'd also lay him down out of sight for a while. There were other things I would do to give the surveillance subject different "looks" over the course of a long solo tail job. Simple clothing changes, both for me and for Bubba, were essential. Baseball cap, no cap; light shirt, dark windbreaker; sunglasses, no sunglasses . . . that sort of thing. At night, I would routinely change the car's appearance simply by running the headlights only, or headlights and fog lights together. Easy changes that would not register consciously in the mind of the subject but worked together to ward off the thought *Hey, there's that car again.*

Anyway, I placed Bubba behind the wheel of the Chrysler and put a thick sweater and a windbreaker on him to approximate Alderman Heath's shape. Then I put Heath's orange toupee on Bubba's head and the outsize Cartier glasses on his face. Heath hadn't been happy about lending them to me but I hadn't offered him the option of refusal.

Standing on the hood of the taxi, I used a crowbar to break the fluorescent tubes nearest to the Chrysler. I put the crowbar back in the kit bag and grabbed a roll of duct tape. I switched on the Chrysler's headlights and stepped back about thirty feet up the ramp to see how it would look to Frank DiMarco as he entered the garage.

It looked pretty good. With the nearest overhead lights out and the car's headlights on, I could just make out Bubba sitting behind the wheel. If I didn't know better, I'd have thought Alderman Heath was sitting in the car. I walked closer, squinting against the head-lights, and stopped walking as soon as I could discern that it was just Bubba in disguise. About twenty feet from the Chrysler. I tore a piece of duct tape from the roll and stuck it to the garage floor, marking the spot.

I extinguished the Chrysler's headlights and drove the taxi down to level 3 and parked it near the staircase, then took the stairs back up to level 2. It was 10:15.

I waited. I hated the stillness of the garage, and I hated waiting. But Frank DiMarco might arrive early and I could take no chances. I thought about Bob Loniski, waiting in the hotel room, stoned on Va-lium and staring at the television and trying to become a better man. Staying in Chicago wasn't really going to make Bob a better man, or a better father, but in a strange way I liked him for the attempt. The real work would come when he got back to Los Angeles and tried to build a genuine relationship with his son. If he lived that long. I'd left him with plenty of canned food and snacks and soda pop. I told him he'd have to sit tight on his own for a few days and I just hoped he didn't get cabin fever and go for a walk.

Control the things you can, and don't be distracted by the things that you cannot. So I pushed Bob Loniski from my mind and focused on the immediate situation. I remembered the cell phone in my pocket and turned it off. And waited.

I decided to see if I could sing all the words to Peter Tosh's "Step-ping Razor" in my head, without missing any. I found that I could. Round Two . . . Dylan, "Tangled Up in Blue." No sweat. Time for a challenge . . . something I hadn't listened to recently. Lou Reed. For no good reason, he had fallen out of my regular rotation. That's the downside of having a large music collection—sometimes even the best get neglected for a while. I sent a silent apology to Lou and took a shot at "Home of the Brave." Tough one. I think I scored about 75 percent. Or maybe a little lower.

At 10:40 I turned the Chrysler's headlights on and retreated into the darkness behind the car. And waited some more.

At 10:54 I heard the footsteps. I held my gun in my right hand and crouched by the Chrysler's rear fender. My heart beat against my ribs and I could feel the blood pulsing in my temples. I forced myself to breathe, deep and slow. Frank DiMarco appeared at the top of level 2, walking confidently and with purpose. He held the manila envelope in his left hand. His right hand was empty. He strode toward the Chrysler and entered the bright beam cast by the headlights. He was slightly less than forty feet away.

"Jesus Christ, Alderman," DiMarco called. "You wanna shut those off? You're blinding me over here." He kept walking . . . thirty-five feet away . . . thirty . . . twenty-five . . . DiMarco stopped and I stepped out in front of the car. I held my gun in a modified Weaver stance, aimed square at his chest.

"Not a muscle, DiMarco," I said. "You move, you die." I continued walking forward and stopped about fifteen feet in front of him.

"Holy shit," said DiMarco, and shook his head. "I shoulda known." He held his arms out away from his sides in an exaggerated shrug. "What the fuck is your problem, buddy? What's Loniski to you? He's nobody. I got no beef with you, why don't you just walk away from this thing?"

I shot him twice in the chest. He looked surprised. He took one and a half steps toward me, dropped the envelope and fell forward. I was standing over him by the time he hit the concrete. I holstered my gun and rolled him on his back and searched under his shirt and found a revolver stuck in the waistband of his pants.

DiMarco regained consciousness and writhed under me as I

took his revolver. His hand reached for mine and I slapped it away. I stuck his revolver in my own waistband. His shirtfront was already soaked bright red and a horrible gurgling sound came from his throat. I hadn't hit him in the heart but I had obviously hit a large artery, and a lung.

I pulled the cell phone from my pocket and held it in front of his face. His hands grappled at the air but he'd already lost a lot of blood and most of his strength and he couldn't reach the phone. His hands dropped down to his sides. "Frank," I said. "You want an ambulance? Just tell me when the hit on Greico is going down."

DiMarco's eyes moved to the cell phone, then back to mine, comprehending. His lips curled back and his teeth were swimming in blood. "Fuck you," he gurgled, his gaze growing more distant by the second. A cupful of blood erupted from his mouth and flowed over his cheeks, staining them crimson.

I stepped back and watched Frank DiMarco die. It took about six and a half minutes but felt like twenty. Probably felt even longer than that to Frank DiMarco. After his chest stopped heaving and his bladder emptied and the twitching finally ceased, I checked his pulse to be sure.

I put the revolver in his right hand. I forced his finger to squeeze off a shot in the general direction of where I'd been standing. Then I shook the revolver from his hand and let it clatter to the floor a few feet away. I ripped the duct tape off the floor, picked up the envelope, turned off the Chrysler's headlights and ran down the stairs. I drove Gonzo's taxi back up to the Chrysler and put Bubba back in Gonzo's trunk. I removed the screwdriver from the Chrysler's ignition switch, locked the door and closed it. I returned the screwdriver to the kit bag and drove the taxi down to level 4 and parked it.

I had brought along a little *drop piece*—an unregistered gun that I'd taken off of a street punk years earlier—just in case DiMarco was unarmed. I hadn't needed it, and now I took it from my back pocket and dropped it in the kit bag with everything else. I put the bag in the trunk, beside Bubba. I closed the trunk. I put the key to Gonzo's taxi in a little magnetic box and stuck the box up inside the rear passenger-side wheel well.

Back on level 2, I placed my gun on the floor and, beside it, my badge and identification. Then I stepped back and called 911.

CHAPTER NINE

Detective Lance Santos was playing it "bad cop" all the way. After two hours in an interrogation room at Area 4 Headquarters, I was still wearing handcuffs. Santos hadn't offered me a cup of coffee or a cigarette or a lawyer. And I hadn't asked. I had requested that he remove the bracelets but he only sneered and told me that they were for his protection. I wouldn't have minded so much, but my arms were cuffed behind the back of the chair and my shoulders were beginning to ache.

"Your PI ticket doesn't get you special treatment around here, fuck-head," said Santos. He put his face about an inch from mine. "And your story reeks of bullshit." Santos slammed his palm on the table.

My ears were still ringing from the gunshots in the garage and it sounded far away. I looked at his hand. "That must have hurt," I said.

Santos moved behind me, slapped the back of my head, and tilted my chair onto its hind legs. He said, "Okay, tough-guy, how about I just drop you and we'll see how much a couple of broken arms hurt?"

"I wouldn't love that a lot," I said.

The door opened and Mike Angelo walked into the room and Santos shoved my chair back into place. I'd told the 911 operator that Lieutenant Angelo should be called at home because he was familiar with the situation. I hadn't mentioned that to Detective Santos.

"He's extremely uncooperative Lieutenant," said Santos.

"I'm sure he is," said Angelo, "but lose the bracelets." Santos removed the handcuffs. "There's been a development, I need you for a minute." They left the room and I rubbed my numb wrists, trying to bring the blood back to them.

On television, the interrogation room (or, as cops prefer, "interview" room) is always clean, with freshly polished stainless steel furniture, and there's a big two-way mirror that connects to the hallway. Nice dramatic lighting too. In Chicago's Area 4 Headquarters, the "interview" rooms are brightly lit, cramped and dirty, with old metal benches bolted to the wall, accented by iron bars similarly bolted and handy for handcuffing the "interviewees." If you're lucky, you get a room with a beat-up table and a couple of wobbly chairs. If you're *really* lucky, you get the room with the two-way mirror, which in real life is only about a foot square and connects to another "interview" room—not to the hallway, where passersby could see how you're getting along with your "interviewers." I was really lucky, so I got the room with the table and chairs and the two-way mirror.

With nothing but time to kill, I read the walls. The graffiti consisted mostly of street-gang symbols. The Outfit was the only Mob in America that held true to the "no narcotics" rule, so the drug trade was left to the black and Latino street gangs, which had grown into a major force over the years. The street gangs called themselves "sets" and collectively made up two alliances—the People Nation and the Folk Nation. Tagging was a way to mark turf, to share news, or simply to say hello. Reading the tags was like reading a community bulletin board in a foreign country. I wasn't versed in much of the code so most of it went over my head, but I could read a bit.

On one wall was a large bunny head with a small five-pointed star in his left ear and wearing a bow tie, and a top hat and cane to one side. A symbol of the Vicelords set, part of the People Nation. Beside it was a pyramid with an eye in it and BPS underneath—a complimentary greeting from a member of the Black P-Stones, one of the most feared and respected Chicago gangs—one of the originals. Beside the pyramid was a lion wearing a five-pointed crown with the number five in it, and LK on either side: Hello from the Latin Kings. Beneath these symbols was written ALL IS ALL, a motto of the People Nation. Someone else had added the People's other motto: ALL IS WELL.

On the opposite wall was a six-pointed star with two raised pitchforks and BGD. This was a calling card of the Black Gangster Disciples—a leading member of the rival Folk Nation alliance. Nothing wrong with that tag—it was on the opposite wall and showed no disrespect, while proudly announcing itself. Near it was written ALL IS ONE, the Folk Nation motto. Next was a heart with horns and a devil's tail, and a raised pitchfork on each side. This was a complimentary greeting from the Latin Disciples. There was also a cobra with pitchforks and the number six: Greetings from the Spanish Cobras.

But the symbol next to the cobra was a problem. An upside-down dead bunny head with little crosses for eyes and his tongue hanging out, suspended over a trash can. Yikes. Someone from a Folk Nation set was showing serious disrespect to the People, and blood would flow in the streets as a result. You could count on that.

There were also some RIPs for various gang members, but I didn't know enough to decipher the rest of the coded messages.

There were a few protestations of innocence and some admonitions to follow Jesus, but they did nothing for me. Luckily, the cops had detained two poets, and each left a piece of verse for my edification and entertainment. The first read:

> *Big Cheese*
> *Suck Ass,*
> *Dick, Cow,*
> *Cat, Horse Balls,*
> *And that's not all.*

Maybe not Carl Sandburg, but it showed promise. The second read:

I like my mother to suck
My big white dick
As she give birth
To my baby

Gross. I didn't want that image in my head any longer than necessary, so I looked for something else to read. Someone had written "I love you" just below the two-way mirror. Much better.

Mike Angelo returned and sat across the table from me.

"I was starting to think you'd never come," I said.

Mike smiled. "Your PI ticket doesn't get you special treatment around here, fuckhead," he said.

I glanced at the little two-way mirror set into the wall. "How long were you watching?"

"Awhile. I wanted to know how you'd tell it to a stranger," he said. "And Detective Santos is right—your story does reek of bullshit. They're typing it up now but I can tell you that your statement, as it stands, raises more questions than it answers." Mike leaned across the table and his voice was just above a whisper. "Ray," he said, "as far as I'm concerned, you did the world a favor by icing Frank DiMarco. He was a first-class asshole and deserved far worse than the quick death you gave him. But there's a state's attorney involved—Sam Kingman— and he's calling for your head."

"Jesus," I said, "I'm glad he doesn't hold a grudge." A few years earlier I'd been hired by a defense attorney whose client was being prosecuted for a double murder on the South Side. The prosecutor was Sam Kingman. I was able to dig up some solid sober citizens—one of them a judge—who testified that the defendant was at an AA meeting in Elmhurst at the time of the murders. The fact that the defendant was innocent was of little concern to Kingman. He just didn't like losing and I was the guy who lowered his batting average.

Mike said, "He wants charges pressed on this thing and he wants your ticket revoked. Says you're a public nuisance." I started to protest but Mike cut me off. "Yeah, I know, Kingman's a prick," he said, "and I'd love to tell him that this is pure self-defense but you're not giving me a lot of help, here."

The circulation had returned to my hands and brought with it a rush of pins and needles. I opened and closed my fists a few times to hurry the process along. "That's the problem with telling the truth," I said testily. "Anybody can make up some shit that plays better. If I had planned to kill DiMarco, you can bet that I'd have prepared a better story."

Mike looked unimpressed. "Don't get too clever with this," he said. "You'll only end up hanging yourself."

A uniformed cop entered and put two cups of coffee and a tin ashtray in front of Mike and said, "Statement's almost ready, sir." He left without glancing at me.

"Ashtray?" I said.

"We relax the rules when interviewing suspects. Offering them a smoke makes them feel indebted to us and helps build a bond. We can't let the puritans compromise our interviewing techniques, now can we?"

Mike plucked a pack of Marlboro Lights from his shirt pocket, lit a cigarette and held it out to me. I took it and he lit another for himself and dropped the pack on the table.

"Well thanks for the smoke," I said, "I'm indebted to you."

"Don't go away," he said, and got up and left the room.

I ran over the story again in my head. For the cops to rule that the killing was justified, a number of conditions had to be present. Frank DiMarco had to have the *motive*, *means* and *opportunity* to kill me. His motive was well established since I was the bodyguard of a witness against him in an impending trial. He had a gun, which gave him the means, and a paraffin test would verify that he had fired it. I wasn't claiming that he fired first, just that he drew first. Since he had fired it after taking two hollow-point .45s to the chest, it would be reasonable to suspect that he had already drawn the gun before I shot him. And we were face-to-face in a deserted underground garage, so he certainly had the opportunity. With the holy trinity of motive, means and opportunity all present, the police then had to answer just one question: *Would a reasonable person in my situation reasonably believe that his life was in imminent danger and that shooting was the only way to survive?* I didn't see how they could come to any conclusion other than self-defense.

Then I thought about what had really happened. From a legal perspective, I'd committed murder. Premeditated murder. But from a moral perspective, had I not acted in self-defense? DiMarco's thugs had twice tried to kill me, first with a bomb and then with guns. And when a guy like Frank DiMarco tells you that you're a dead man, you can take it to the bank. What he'd said in the garage about not having a beef with me was garbage. He knew that Loniski had seen Heath at the warehouse and it would be logical for him to assume that Loniski had told me about it, as indeed he had. Frank DiMarco would not have let me live. No, he wasn't trying to kill me at the instant I shot him. His hand was nowhere near his gun when I dropped the hammer. But he would have killed me eventually.

In military jargon it was called *first-strike self-defense*. But I wasn't in the military. In the eyes of the law, I'd committed murder.

And I felt okay about it. In fact, I felt fine about it. I felt neither guilt nor regret. And I knew that I had to maintain a sense of indignation for my story to ring true. I was the victim here. I had been forced to kill Frank DiMarco in self-defense and now the cops were treating me like a criminal.

Mike Angelo returned. In his hand was my statement, typed on yellow paper. He flipped through the pages while making incredulous sounds.

"Okay. Let's start with last night," he said. "You say that DiMarco's men chased your car, took shots at you and then smashed into a police cruiser on Clark Street. You didn't bother to file a complaint or even report the incident, but a cruiser was hit at that location and three knuckleheads were arrested. Then you say Frank DiMarco called you this afternoon and told you to meet him at the garage tonight. If they were gunning for you, why would you go?"

"To set him up," I said, and gestured at the pages in his hand. "Look, DiMarco called and said I was a dead man. I told him that I would trade Loniski for my life. And he told me to meet him at the garage. I planned to meet him and set a time and place tomorrow where he could take out Loniski. Then I was gonna call you and set up a sting."

"Reeks of bullshit," said Mike.

"I'm not saying it was a good plan," I said. "But it was the best I could think of at the time." Mike winced. I added, "I didn't know DiMarco was gonna call, did I? I had to think quickly."

"Which leads me to the next point," said Mike. "You said it was a prepaid cell phone that you've only had a couple of days. How did DiMarco know the number?"

"I have no idea." I said, "Maybe he's got a friend at the phone company. But it doesn't matter, you have my phone and you can verify his call easily enough. Look at my phone records. He called sometime around five o'clock. Maybe he called from his apartment, or his cell phone, or Tortelli's office."

"Or maybe he called from a pay phone."

"And maybe someone in the vicinity of the pay phone will recognize his picture, if you take the trouble to check it out."

"Thanks for the tip," Mike sneered. He drank some coffee. "Okay . . . where were we? Yeah, DiMarco somehow learns the number of a prepaid cell that you just got . . . he calls sometime around five o'clock . . . he tells you that you're a dead man . . . instead of calling the cops, you decide to run a Hardy Boys sting operation on him. And despite the fact that his guys tried to clip you the night before, you agree to meet him at an underground garage at eleven. How am I doing so far?"

"Except for the insinuation, fine," I said, and drank a little brown water that called itself coffee.

"Fine. Then you say you took a taxi to the garage. Why?"

"Because my car was in for repairs, they shot a couple of windows out."

"Get a receipt from the cabdriver?"

"I didn't think of it."

"Legitimate business expense," said Mike.

"Yeah, my accountant will be pissed," I said.

Mike sent me a deadeye cop-stare, then shrugged. "Don't matter," he said. "Which taxi service did you use? We'll just call the company and check it out."

"I flagged it. It was a gypsy cab," I said. "No company."

"How convenient."

"No, Mike. It would be convenient if it had been a company taxi." I said it with a good deal of anger. "Then you could check it out and stop acting like I've done something wrong." Mike dragged on his cigarette. I couldn't tell how much he believed.

"Okay," he said, "so you flag a mystery cab and go to the garage . . . how you plan to get home is another mystery but we'll leave that one for now . . . once at the garage, you wait for DiMarco to arrive, which he does within a few minutes. But DiMarco parks on the street and walks down the ramp to meet you. Why'd he do that? Why not just drive down?"

"You'd have to ask DiMarco," I said.

"Very funny."

"What can I tell you?" I said, my voice rising. "I don't know why the fuck he walked down, now do I?"

"Don't you?" asked Mike.

"No, I don't. Shit. I already told you." I ground my cigarette out in the ashtray. "You know, if the CPD had acted on the report from the Los Angeles Sheriff's Department, Loniski would've gotten a protection detail and none of this would have happened."

Mike Angelo's eyes flashed fire. "Not one more word about that," he spat. "I'm serious, Ray. Not a fuckin' word." He got up and stormed out of the room.

He left his cigarettes on the table, so I lit another smoke and waited.

By mentioning the police protection issue I'd reminded Mike that the CPD also had something to lose in all this mess. I knew he wouldn't like it, and he didn't. But I'd put the request in through proper channels, and if this thing ever came to a trial, I'd lean on that, heavily. Hell, I'd have my lawyer subpoena Deputy Mullins if necessary. Mullins would testify that Angelo had told him the threat against Loniski was real and about the car bomb too. He'd testify that the LASD had assigned a protection detail to Loniski after the bomb and that they'd recommended the same to the CPD. The idea didn't make me happy but I wanted Mike to know that I was willing to go there, if necessary.

Mike Angelo returned and said, "You caught a break. We checked your cell-phone records and DiMarco called your cell from his apartment at five-oh-three."

"Lucky me," I said.

"Okay. Why do you think DiMarco would tell you to meet him at a garage only four blocks from here?"

"I have no idea. Maybe he felt safer meeting near a cop shop."

"Or maybe it was you who set up the meeting," he said. "You set it up and you chose the location so that this case would fall to me. You put it right on my fucking doorstep."

"It was DiMarco's meeting," I insisted. "I don't know why he chose that garage."

"Like I said, too clever. Too cute." Mike stubbed out his cigarette. "Okay, take me back to the garage. DiMarco walks down, we don't know why, and meets you. Then what?"

"It's like I told Santos," I said. "I tried to convince DiMarco that I would deliver Loniski to him. He laughed at me and said, 'That's okay, we'll find him without your help. But thanks for delivering yourself,' and then he reached under his shirt and I saw a gun coming up. I drew mine and shot him, twice. He fell forward, rolled over and squeezed off a shot at me and then he dropped his gun and lay back. He was trying to speak, so I went to him. He said that Tortelli would take care of me after he was done with Greico."

"Really," said Mike.

"Really," I said.

"He didn't happen to say when and where Tortelli was planning to hit Greico, did he?"

"He just said, 'Paul's gonna take care of you, you fuck, soon as he's done with Greico.' That's all. Then he lost consciousness and I called 911."

"That's a nice story," said Mike. "DiMarco was good enough to confirm your suspicions about Tortelli, and good enough to die so I gotta take your word for it."

"What can I tell you, Mike? That's what the man said."

Mike Angelo let out a long sigh, then locked his eyes onto mine. "Here's what I think," he said. "I think you lured DiMarco into that garage and killed him in cold blood. Don't know how you got him to call, don't know what you said to make him go alone to that garage and leave his car on the street. But that's what you did. Maybe you and DiMarco rode there together, parked the car and walked down together . . . maybe you told him Loniski was in the garage . . . or maybe you had an accomplice drive you there and hang around long enough to make sure DiMarco was alone, then split. You knew you wouldn't need a ride home, because you knew you were gonna ice the bastard and then call 911 and claim self-defense. How am I doing so far?"

"Lousy," I said. "Look at it from Paul Tortelli's perspective. I kill DiMarco. Is that gonna make Tortelli less motivated to clip me? I just killed his cousin. Now he's gonna want my blood more than ever. And Tortelli's got the kind of professional killers that Frankie only dreamed about. So what good could it possibly do for me to kill DiMarco?"

Mike turned it over in his mind for a moment. "Granted. This doesn't improve your chances with Tortelli . . . and maybe that's why you're trying to make me believe that he's going after Greico, which is more bullshit. On the other hand, killing DiMarco does help your client's chances, doesn't it? DiMarco's dead, so there'll be no fraud trial and now your client doesn't have to testify."

I couldn't offer a rebuttal without bringing Heath into it. I'd made a square deal with Heath and I intended to stick by my word.

"Okay, it helps my client," I said, "but you don't think I'd intentionally draw a death sentence for myself just to help a client. I'm the asshole who asked Greico for permission to protect the guy, remember?"

Mike chuckled without any humor. "You are some piece of work, Dudgeon. I can't figure you out."

"So why not take me at my word?" I drank some more brown water, which was now cold. "I was hired to protect a witness against DiMarco. You've got the deaths of the other witnesses against him. You've got the car bomb. You've got the report from Mullins at the LASD. You've got his guys making a play for me the night before. You've got DiMarco's phone call to me. You've got his gun. And you've got my statement, which fits with the physical evidence. It's a clear case of self-defense."

Mike leaned back and cracked his knuckles one at a time. He stood up and so did I. "I'm gonna retype your statement to emphasize things in your favor," he said, "and expunge the fairy-tale bullshit about Tortelli going after Greico. Then you'll sign it. I can sell it to Kingman but it's not gonna be an easy sell. And you're gonna owe me, big-time."

Mike turned to go. I should have said *thank you very much, sir,* and then shut my yap. But I didn't.

I said, "I don't owe you a damn thing," which spun him around. "I came to you from the beginning. And I killed DiMarco to save my own life, because I had to. Now I'm giving you information about an Outfit war that's getting ready to explode, and you don't want to know about it? What the fuck is—"

Mike was fast for a fat man. He crossed the room in a blur and clasped his right hand over my mouth and shoved me hard against the wall, his left forearm against my throat.

"Ooomph," I said.

"I warned you to shut the fuck up," Mike said in my ear. He dropped his forearm, but kept his cold hand over my mouth until he was sure I wasn't going to reply. Then he let go completely and shook the tension out of his arms and let out a long breath. "I'm trying to help you, Ray"—his voice had lost its rabid intensity and now sounded almost caring—"but you won't listen." He reached over to the table and lit another cigarette. "Has it ever occurred to you that there might be more to this than you can personally observe, you arrogant motherfucker?" he asked.

"Why don't you tell me about it?" I said.

"Why don't you grow up?" he countered.

It was a good question, and I didn't have a good answer.

Just after 3 A.M., Mike Angelo left me alone in the interrogation room. He took his cigarettes with him, but he left his pen. I took the pen to the wall and beneath "I love you" wrote "I love you too." No disrespect. Just love.

It occurred to me that, as little as I knew about street gangs, I didn't know a hell of a lot more about the Outfit. More than the average civilian, but not nearly enough. Not if I was going to stay in this business for the long haul. So far I'd done a pretty good job steering clear of cases that could bring me into contact with organized crime. But sooner or later, everyone does business with the Outfit.

Pornography, prostitution, strip clubs . . . all obvious Outfit industries. But the Outfit has its fingers in a lot of pies, some less obvious than others. Restaurants, hotels and hospitals all need linen service, glassware and cooperation from the unions. Property developers need on-time delivery of construction materials, need to minimize shrinkage of materials on the job site, need construction workers to keep working on schedule. Trucking, dry cleaning, professional sports and gaming—you name it. Even the music industry is rife with Outfit influence. From liquor to law firms, mortgage companies to movies, everyone does business with the Outfit eventually. They invest in so many legitimate businesses, control so many unions and own so many politicians that doing business with the Outfit is an unavoidable fact of life.

But I could've avoided this mess. I told Loniski that I'd protect him and there was no way I'd cut and run. My mistake wasn't seeing it through—no, my mistake was taking the job in the first place. Next time I'd know better. Next time, at the first hint of connection to the Outfit, I'd do better due diligence.

Next time.

At 4:00 I stretched out on the floor for a while but sleep wouldn't come. I was grateful that they hadn't put me in the holding pen. All it would take is one bent cop to tell one scumbag in the cage that I'd capped DiMarco. The news would travel from scumbag to scumbag, like an electrical current running around the room. A couple of the scumbags would see an opportunity to make their bones with the Outfit and I'd never see morning. By comparison, the interrogation room was downright homey. I considered moving in permanently.

At 5:30 I gave up on the idea of sleep and went back to the chair. The uniformed cop delivered more bad coffee. I drank it anyway. I felt numb, inside and out. I felt disconnected from my body. It seemed like years had passed since I shot Frank DiMarco in the underground garage. Lies and truth mingled freely in my mind, dancing around each other, coming together, moving apart. I couldn't remember exactly what had happened. It was like a movie that was still being rewritten as it played. It started, stopped, rewound and played again, slightly different each time. The projectionist was nearsighted and the images out of focus.

God I was tired. I told myself that things would make sense again after I got some sleep. Whenever that would be.

The medical examiner would conduct a paraffin test on DiMarco's hand, confirming that DiMarco had been holding his gun when it was fired. Then he'd open up DiMarco's chest cavity and dig out the slugs that I'd put there. He'd send the slugs to ballistics, where they'd be compared with a slug test-fired from my gun into a tank of water. After dusting DiMarco's gun for prints, ballistics would then test-fire it. They would compare that slug to whatever was left of the one I'd forced DiMarco's dead hand to fire into the wall of the garage. Mike would wait for the results of all these tests and more. He'd make sure that all the *t*'s were crossed and the *i*'s dotted and then he'd write it all up and present it to Sam Kingman. And he'd make sure that Kingman was convinced.

All I could do is wait. So that's all I did.

At 7:15 Mike Angelo returned and placed my revised statement on the table in front of me. "Read it and sign it," he said.

I read it. It contained no mention of Paul Tortelli or Johnny Greico. I signed it. Mike picked it up, took the pen and left.

At 8:40 the door opened again and Mike Angelo entered, looking as tired as I felt. Assistant State's Attorney Sam Kingman was with him. Kingman didn't look tired at all. He wore a crisp light blue double-breasted suit with dark pinstripes, shiny black loafers with tassels, a gleaming white shirt and a tie of alternating stripes, burgundy and navy blue, to match the pinstripes. He held a legal form in his hand. His fingernails looked like they'd just come from the manicurist.

Kingman placed the document on the table and stared down at me for a while. The stare was supposed to be intimidating. Or maybe Kingman had indigestion. I couldn't be sure. Anyway he just stood there squinting at me and not saying anything for a while.

"You're going to have to speak louder," I said. "My ears are still ringing from the gunshots." Back near the door, Mike let out a tiny smile.

"I'll make this brief," Kingman said. "The police have determined that this was a justifiable homicide."

"I prefer the term *self-defense*," I said.

"I'm sure you do," said Kingman, "given the frequency with which the term appears on your record."

"I believe this is the third," I said.

"That we know about," said Kingman. He was right, there. "Anyway, that's more than most cops have in a career."

"Bad guys are more hesitant to shoot at cops," I said.

"And let's not forget the retarded kid you crippled," said Kingman with a sick smile. The kid's name was Glen Warren and I'd been avoiding thinking about him all night. I sent Kingman a stare that was supposed to be more intimidating than his. His eyes left mine and darted down to the paper on the table. He said, "Well congratulations, you've gotten away with another one."

I kept my eyes on his until he looked back at me. "Are you suggesting that the CPD investigation was in some way faulty?"

Kingman bristled. "Nothing of the sort. But you should be aware that I'll be keeping a very close eye on your actions, in future."

"It's a comforting thought," I said.

Kingman turned the paper around and told me to read it. In short, it said that I understood that, based on available evidence, the state's attorney had decided not to press charges at this time. I would make myself available for further questioning in this matter, should the police deem it necessary. Furthermore, I understood that this was not a ruling from the bench and did not preclude the state's attorney from filing charges at a later date, should new evidence arise in this matter.

"You want me to sign it in blood," I said, "or do I get a pen?" Kingman reached into his breast pocket and withdrew a silver Waterman, reconsidered, and returned the pen to safety. To Angelo he said, "Lieutenant?"

Mike came forward and dropped his disposable Bic on the table. I signed the form and Kingman snatched it up and left without telling me to have a nice day.

The uniformed cop entered and handed a bulging manila envelope to Mike. My heart leaped into my throat until I noticed that the envelope was clean; DiMarco's had been splattered with blood. This envelope contained my holster, badge and wallet, cell phone, keys and money.

"What about my gun?"

"I'll see what I can do," Mike said. "Call me in a couple of days."

I signed for everything and Mike led me out of the room, at last. We crossed the floor, past the detectives on the morning shift. A small poster, taped to one of the cubicle dividers, caught my eye. It was a Rockwell-style drawing of a smiling police officer holding a coffee cup. Above Officer Friendly was HOW ABOUT A NICE BIG CUP OF SHUT THE FUCK UP. At the bottom was THINK BEFORE SAYING SOMETHING STUPID. Good advice for someone giving a witness statement or signing out a complaint. Or for anyone.

At the end of the hallway stood a tall, athletic man wearing wingtip shoes and a dark blue no-nonsense suit with a lapel pin. He wore it like a uniform. I turned to Mike. "Feds?" I said.

"I tried to warn you," Mike said, "but you're gonna have to stop breathing before you realize you're in over your head."

The fed stepped forward to meet us. "Special Agent Holborn, FBI," he said, without offering his hand. "I'll be taking you home."

Home. Sleep. Good.

CHAPTER TEN

I stood outside an upscale coffeehouse on Dearborn Avenue and studied my reflection in the window. Greasy hair hung down past my shoulders and a long matted beard covered my face. My clothes were soiled and ragged, my fingernails impacted with black dirt. It occurred to me that I was homeless. The people inside the coffeehouse looked warm and happy. I shivered and my stomach ached from hunger. A bitter wind howled down Dearborn and rushed into my lungs, taking my breath away.

I shuffled inside and approached the counter. A beautiful woman with sympathetic eyes stood behind the cash register. Jill.

I felt ashamed. I dug into my pocket and pulled out a single dollar bill and held it between my hands. It was all the money I had in the world. Someone had left the cappuccino machine's milk frother on and it gave off a piercing and unrelenting squeal.

Jill said, "Can I help you?"

I tried to speak but nothing came out. Vinnie Cosimo walked past and whispered in my ear, "Frank DiMarco is off the leash," and then disappeared.

I held out the dollar bill and said to Jill, "I'm sorry."

She understood, looked over her shoulder and called through a doorway, "Honey, do we have any day-old for this guy?"

Embarrassed, I looked away from her face. A few of the patrons were staring right at me, while most tried to steal a quick glance without being obvious. Their discomfort was a living entity that filled the room and increased my shame. A few customers seemed oblivious to my presence. Terry Green and his wife, Angela, sat holding hands and staring into each other's eyes, a couple in love. Glen Warren was in a wheelchair in the corner, breathing with the aid of a respirator. Alderman Heath sat, bald-headed and weeping, at a table near the window.

A bright light shone through the doorway to the kitchen. Frank Di-Marco came through the doorway with a manila envelope in his hand. He kissed Jill lightly on the mouth and handed her the envelope, then turned to me and said, "I'm sorry for your troubles buddy, but this is the last time. You can't come back here again."

Jill gave me the envelope and an apologetic smile. The envelope was full of bacon. I held out the dollar bill but Frank said, "We don't want your money."

I looked at Jill. "I'm sorry," I said. "I'm sorry."

"Go take a shower, you smell awful," said Jill. "You can use my robe, it's hanging on the back of the door."

Frank DiMarco opened his mouth and blood flowed down his shirtfront and splashed onto the countertop.

A bear claw clamped down on my shoulder and rocked me back and forth.

"Nice dream you were having."

I was in my bedroom, sprawled across the futon. My skin was clammy and my ears were still ringing from the gunshots.

"You want this, or what? I'm not going to stand here all day." I lifted my head and raised a hand to take the coffee mug from Special Agent Holborn.

"What time is it?" I said.

"Just after seven."

"Morning?"

"Night. You've been sleeping a little over nine hours. I was going to let you go twelve but when the nightmares got really bad, I figured you'd had enough."

"Thanks." I sipped some coffee. It was strong and black and there was no sugar in it. "How'd you know?" I asked.

"No milk in the fridge, no sugar bowl on the counter," said Holborn. "Hey, I am with the FBI."

"And a damn fine detective," I said.

"Did Frankie Fingers accept your apology?"

"What? Frankie Fingers?" I sat up.

"Frank DiMarco," said Holborn. "You kept saying, 'I'm sorry.' "

"Naw, man," I said. "I was talking to my ex-girlfriend."

Holborn rolled his eyes. "Figures." He turned toward the living room. "I've made bacon and eggs, hope you like them scrambled."

I sat at the dining table and ate. Holborn had cooked the bacon crisp, the way I like it. And the eggs were done up just right, with some chopped green onion and sharp Cheddar cheese and a good measure of Tabasco. White buttered toast on the side. I made quick work of it all while downing a second mug of good coffee. Holborn sat across from me and watched the gluttony. It seemed to amuse him. I finished the last piece of toast and wiped my mouth with a paper towel.

"You'll make someone a fine wife someday, Special Agent Holborn," I said. Holborn went to the kitchen and brought back the coffeepot and refilled our mugs.

"Your refrigerator is a disaster," he said. "I had to send out for groceries."

"I haven't been here for a while."

Holborn nodded and sipped his coffee. He put the mug down and picked up a newspaper from the table, tossed it over to me. "Read this, then we'll talk," he said.

The killing of Frank DiMarco made the front page of the *Chicago Chronicle*. It was a big story. So big that they'd printed a special afternoon edition. The bold headline shouted, LOCAL PI IN DEADLY GUNFIGHT.

The photograph below the headline showed Holborn and Mike Angelo leaving the police station. Between them was a man who looked a lot like me. Holborn and Angelo were both looking toward the street but the guy who resembled me was looking right into the camera lens. His face wore an empty expression. I looked at him as if he could tell me something about the mess I'd gotten myself into. He just stared back at me, frozen in time with nothing to say. All around him, large snowflakes hung motionless in midair.

I tried to remember leaving the Area 4 Headquarters, flanked by Angelo and Holborn. I remembered the snow-blanketed street, how new and pure and quiet it seemed. And I remembered some flashes from photographers' strobes. And then voices. Reporters barking questions.

As if reading my mind, Holborn said, "You didn't say anything to the press. You were practically walking in your sleep."

The story, which ran under Terry Green's byline, said exactly what you'd expect. The gist of it was that Frank DiMarco, cousin of reputed Outfit capo Paul Tortelli, was shot dead in an underground garage on West Polk around 11:30 last night. The shooter was a Chicago private detective named Ray Dudgeon, who was working as a bodyguard for Bob Loniski. Loniski was a witness in an upcoming fraud trial, in which Frank DiMarco was the defendant. Four days ago, while parked in the garage of his Hollywood Hills home, Loniski's BMW had been destroyed by a car bomb. Dudgeon had gotten Loniski away from the car before the bomb exploded and no one had been injured. Three other witnesses against DiMarco had all died within the last month. One was killed in an apparent mugging, the second an apparent suicide and the third gunned down on the front steps of his West Side town house. Police were investigating all three deaths but had no tangible leads, according to unnamed sources within the department.

There were no witnesses to last night's shooting, which police believe was a gunfight instigated by DiMarco. The police held Dudgeon overnight for questioning. After reviewing the results of ballistics testing and forensic examination, they determined that Ray Dudgeon had acted in self-defense. Upon leaving the police station this morning, Dudgeon had been unresponsive to reporters' questions.

Both Lieutenant Mike Angelo and Assistant State's Attorney Sam Kingman were quoted in the article but both had obviously tried to be as uninteresting as possible, so their quotes were brief and didn't say a hell of a lot.

Then the article went further. According to unnamed sources, Frank DiMarco had, until recently, been working for Johnny Greico, another reputed Outfit skipper. DiMarco had reportedly quit and gone back to Tortelli. There was talk on the street of a power struggle brewing within the Outfit.

It was bold. I wondered why Terry's editor had allowed the piece to go to press with so much speculation and I guessed that they'd gotten some confirmation from a high-placed source. I needed to talk with Terry. And I needed to get my hands on DiMarco's blackmail stash. Getting that evidence was my only chance of survival. But I had to get rid of Special Agent Holborn before I could make a move for the storage locker.

Holborn poured the last of the coffee into my mug. "Okay," he said, "let's start with the article . . . the part about an Outfit war . . . you were Terry Green's source for that?"

"Nope. I may have hypothesized but I couldn't have been his source because I didn't have any knowledge until DiMarco told me. And obviously I haven't had a chance to talk with Terry since last night."

"Do you know who the source was?"

"Nope." I drank some coffee.

"Do you have a guess?"

"Why don't you ask Terry Green?"

"I did," said Holborn. "He went into that song-and-dance number about freedom of the press and anonymous sources."

"Is that the FBI's official position on the First Amendment?"

"Whatever. Green's not going to tell us. Now, do you have a guess?"

"Nope."

Holborn sighed dramatically and sipped his coffee. "Ray," he said, "I read the early version of your statement to the CPD. In fact I'm the one who told Angelo to edit it."

"I didn't know the CPD took orders from the FBI," I said.

"All right. I asked Angelo politely and he agreed. Better?"

"Why'd you want it changed?" I said.

"Because it would get leaked to the Outfit in about five seconds and that would jeopardize an ongoing federal investigation. Now, I've been tasked with keeping you alive until I learn what you know. Which means you don't leave my sight until I'm satisfied. So the sooner you drop the tough-guy act, the better for both of us."

"I don't see how that's better for me," I said. "As long as you're here, I'm relatively safe. As soon as you go, Tortelli's gonna kill me."

"You should have considered that before you murdered his cousin." I started to respond but Holborn cut me off with a wave of his hand. "Oh, don't bother," he said. "Nobody believes your story. Anyway the point is, the moment you dropped the hammer on Frankie, you ceased to be a citizen. See, I'm not a citizen but I've got an army behind me called the Federal Bureau of Investigation. Angelo's not a citizen but the CPD is his army. Tortelli's not a citizen, but the Outfit is his. And you . . . you're no longer a citizen either. But you've got no army." He looked at me with what seemed like genuine sympathy. "Sorry, but that's the way it is. Soldiers without armies don't live long." Sure, he was trying to scare me but I didn't need his help.

"Yeah," I said.

"Look, just tell me everything you know. If it helps us, it might help you." Holborn rose and went into the kitchen. He put another pot of coffee on and returned to the table with an ashtray and a pack of cigarettes. I lit one.

Then I told him all about the Loniski case, including the trip to California. It took a while. I stuck with my official version of the previous day, leaving Alderman Heath out of it and maintaining my self-defense position. And when he asked, I assured him that Frank DiMarco had really said that thing about Tortelli going after Greico. Holborn took notes as I talked.

"I believe you," he said when I finished. "I don't mean I believe you about yesterday. You set Frankie up and killed him. I don't care, but I just want you to know I'm not a dupe. Anyway, I do believe the rest."

"You should, sweetheart," I said, doing my best Bogart, which wasn't very good.

Holborn didn't look amused. "You really don't have any idea when Tortelli's planning to dance with Greico?"

"Wish I did, but I haven't got a clue," I said.

"Where's Loniski now?"

Someone dragged an ice cube down my spine. "In a safe place," I said.

"Well you might want to let him out now that Frankie Fingers is deceased," said Holborn. The tingling in my spine settled down, just a bit. Loniski had seen Heath with DiMarco, so he could still unravel Tortelli's operation, but Holborn had no way of knowing that.

"Why'd they call him Frankie Fingers?" I asked.

"Oh, that. Before my time, but the story is Frankie's father, Stefano, was consigliere when Frankie was a kid. And Stefano promised his wife that Frankie would not grow up to be an Outfit guy. They wanted better for their children. But the kid became enamored of all the flashy thugs hanging around the house, you know? He found it glamorous. So around the age of thirteen he started stealing shit and showing up at Tortelli's place to offer it as a gift to the Outfit, hoping they'd let him in. He'd show up with watches, jewelry, wallets, cases of liquor, whatever. Sometimes he'd show up with cash. And the wiseguys thought this was hilarious and they started calling him Frankie Fingers. Then when Stefano died, they let Frankie in. And the name stuck."

"You said Stefano wanted better for his children. What happened to Frankie's brothers?"

"No brothers. He had a sister, a few years older. She went off to some Ivy League college and married a big-shot New York Mob lawyer. About five years ago I heard they divorced but nothing since." Holborn got up and refilled our coffee mugs. He sat back down and blew on his to cool it. "What I would do, if I were you," he said, "is move to another state, change my name and learn a new trade." He looked at me like he was trying to decide something, then nodded. "But you're not going to do that, are you?"

"No."

"Why not?"

"I really don't know," I said. I thought of Jill, but I knew that my decision would be the same whether she was in my life or not. "I can't spend the rest of my life looking over my shoulder."

"So what are you going to do?"

"Take sides," I said. "Put in with Greico and hope he wins."

"And if Greico doesn't want your help?"

"Then I'll have to think of something else."

Of course I wasn't just relying on Greico. Getting my mitts on Tortelli's blackmail files would give me some leverage. I hoped it would be enough.

It was just before midnight when Holborn left. I called Terry and told his voicemail to meet me in his office at 8 A.M. I looked up Yoshi Inoue in my address book and dialed the number. Yoshi Inoue was the owner of Doctor Ink, a fountain-pen repair shop located a few floors below my office in the Richmond building. He was also the most talented forger in the Midwest.

My call woke Yoshi, but nothing in his voice suggested irritation. We talked as if I were looking for a set of rare collectible pens. I told him that I needed a standard set for tomorrow and a full set the following day. I understood that it was an unreasonable time frame but I was happy to pay extra for rush service. He said that he'd seen the news and he understood my urgency.

"You know what I look like, right?" I said, asking if he still had my photo on file.

"Oh sure, I remember your face," he said, confirming it. "Which commemorative sets are you looking for?"

"I'm looking for the Peter Dunbar set and the Austin Clarke set." These were the names I wanted for the identification. In a week, Yoshi would call and leave a message on my machine, saying that I must be misinformed because he can't locate any such pens. Just to make things tidy.

He asked if I knew the issue dates, meaning dates of birth, and I told him. He said he'd get right on it and I should stop by the shop around 4:30 tomorrow afternoon, meaning 2:00, and we hung up.

Before Holborn left, he'd speculated that Tortelli wouldn't make a play for me until after Frank DiMarco's funeral. So that gave me a couple of days to make my move. Maybe. Or maybe not. Maybe I was screwed. Maybe I should have left this whole goddamn mess alone. Maybe I should have told Bob Loniski and Alan Diskin to get stuffed. Maybe I wasn't too bright.

There was no percentage in thinking that way. I cracked open a new bottle of El Dorado and poured some into a glass and threw a few ice cubes into the glass, just to be fancy. It helped. Then I opened a can of Beefaroni and ate it cold, right out of the can.

When I was a kid, my mother used to make a big fuss out of letting me "eat like a cowboy," right out of the can. Saved her a lot of dishwashing. And later, when she wasn't home much, I knew how to open my own can. I also knew how to use a bowl, but for some reason I preferred to eat like a cowboy. Still do.

I refreshed my drink and added more ice. I noticed that there was a message waiting for me on the answering machine. How long had it been there? Since yesterday. I hadn't checked my machine when Holborn and I arrived in the morning. *Jill.*

"It won't be her," I said aloud to no one. I drank down the rum and pressed "play."

"Hello, son," said my grandfather's voice. "It's the old man calling. I'm sure you're out celebrating, but I just wanted to say happy birthday . . ."

I hit "stop" and looked at the magnified date window on the face of my diving watch. Shit. Yesterday had been my birthday. I guess it was understandable, with everything that was going on . . . but still, I forgot my own birthday. What was that? Thirty-eight. Shit. Celebrating. Whoop-dee-fucking-doo. What was there to celebrate? And with whom?

In the kitchen, I refilled my glass and brought the bottle with me back into the living room. I didn't bother with the ice this time.

I searched through my CD collection for the right mood. My mood was self-pity, and I was looking for something to lift me out of it. Call it counterprogramming. I chose Lee Morgan's funky album *The Rumproller*. It was a good choice but my mood was stubborn.

Sitting on the couch, I toasted the four dead guys hanging on my living-room walls. Dexter Gordon and Thelonious Monk and Dizzy Gillespie and Hal Russell. I drank the rum and poured another and my eyes were drawn to the photo of Hal Russell.

Hal was a local jazz legend and had been one of my more patient music teachers. I used to go to his gigs at Club Lower Links, and after closing time we'd sit in the empty bar and get drunk on Pernod, which causes an evil hangover. But Hal was a musical genius and I was young and impressionable, so I never questioned his choice of poison. Hal died about a dozen years ago. Now he seemed to be staring at me.

"What the hell do you want, Hal?" I said.

Hal didn't answer me. But he didn't look away either.

When the music ended I put on Keith Jarrett's *Staircase* and turned the volume up. I took my drink into the bedroom. Maybe Keith Jarrett's piano would keep the ghosts away.

As I drifted off, my mind again showed me the killing of Frank DiMarco, this time playing it without lies or rationalizations. Maybe it was self-defense, but the truth was, I was not dispassionate about it. The truth was, I wasn't detached at all.

Truth was, I liked it.

CHAPTER ELEVEN

Ramon Gonzales met me on the corner of Michigan and Twentieth at 6:15 A.M. I walked there from my apartment building. No one had been waiting outside for me. No one followed me.

Gonzo slid over to the VW Jetta's passenger seat and I got in behind the wheel. I drove us to the parking garage on Polk. Gonzo cursed at me the whole way there. He'd read the newspaper and seen the reports on television, and he was not pleased that I'd gotten him involved. I did my best to assure him that as long as he didn't say anything to anyone, he was not involved. I wasn't completely successful. He even cursed my mother. On the brighter side, the same no one was still following us.

We pulled to a stop a few blocks from the garage. I told Ramon where to find his cab and where to find his key. I gave him money for the parking and he cursed me again, and then disappeared around the corner. I drove north to Harrison, then east to Wells and south past River City to the end of the road. From the end of Wells Street to the Roosevelt Road Bridge stood an empty lot about the size of two football fields.

The unpaved lot was surrounded by concrete highway barriers that were once painted yellow but had since developed a skin condition. I found a gap in the barriers and pulled into the lot, avoiding the large slushy puddles which masked depressions large enough to swallow half a car.

At the south end of the lot stood six derelict cranes that someone in city government had forgotten about. Piles of rubbish were scattered around. About fifty yards in front of me was a miniature mountain of junk, about the size of a one-car garage. Beside it, smoke rose from a small mound of burning debris. A black man warmed himself by the fire. Closer inspection through field glasses confirmed that the man was exactly what he appeared to be, although perhaps younger than he looked. If you cleaned him up and put him in a suit, I'd have guessed him at about sixty-eight. But he could've been forty, or anywhere in between. Living on the street ages a man fast. He sat on a tattered blanket, its corners anchored to the ground with a large rock, a table leg, a cracked toilet bowl and a shopping cart filled with his worldly possessions. The mountain provided some protection from the wind but little eddies of snow swirled around the lot and the man's old army coat fluttered in the breeze. Every so often, he would stand and flap his arms over the fire and yell at the invisible people around him. Then he'd move to the mountain and carefully select a new piece of junk and add it to the fire and sit back down on the blanket to continue his argument with the invisibles. Although warm by late-December Chicago standards, January was approaching fast and there was a threatening sky above and I didn't like the man's chances.

Ramon arrived and parked beside me, as instructed. We stood together between the cars. Ramon's anger had given way to fear, and he was done cursing. He said that he didn't want any part of this. His eyes darted around the lot, never settling on any one spot. I told him to walk straight forward and not to look back until I called his name.

Ramon walked straight forward. I opened the trunks of both cars and transferred Bubba from the taxi to the Jetta. Then my kit bag. I slammed the trunks and called to Gonzo. He came back and got into his cab and peeled away without a word. Grumpy.

I found a pay phone and dug a calling card out of my wallet and placed a call to my grandfather's home in St. Simons Island, Georgia. As the phone rang, I found myself hoping for the machine. But he answered on the third ring.

"Hi Pop," I said.

"Ray, it's good to hear your voice," said my grandfather, with an accent like a coastal Southern breeze. "How you doin'?"

"Fine," I said. "Good. Just wanted to thank you for the birthday wishes."

"Don't bullshit me, son," he said. "You know I subscribe to the *Tribune*." Which was true. As far back as I could remember, he had taken the Sunday *Trib* so he could keep track of current events in the city where his daughter lived, and later, his grandson.

"I don't want you to worry," I said.

"Bullshittin' only serves to make it worse," he said. "You're a grown man and I know you've got a good head on your shoulders, but do you really want to square off against the mafiosi of Chicago?"

"Wasn't my intention," I said. "It'll be over soon."

"Well when it's over, you wanna come down for a spell and visit with your old grandpa?"

"I'd love that. What's biting?"

"Hell, son, everything. Tarpon longer than your leg, jacks, forty-pound red bulls practically leaping into the boat and beggin' to be invited home for dinner."

I swallowed hard to get rid of the lump in my throat. "Save some for me. I'll be down as soon as I wrap up this case."

"From what I read in the paper, it sounds less like a case and more like a war."

"You know how it is Pop, they're just trying to sell papers."

"Ray . . ."

"It's okay, really," I said.

"I already had to bury my daughter," said my grandfather. "Don't you make me bury my grandson."

"No, sir," I said. "I won't."

An hour later, Terry Green and I sat drinking coffee in the editorial boardroom at the *Chicago Chronicle*. On the table before Terry sat a stack of file folders and a notepad. Before me was just my notebook. Terry asked how I was feeling. I was feeling fine. He asked if I wanted more coffee. Maybe later. He knew better than to ask if I'd told the truth to the police and he seemed to be searching for a line of questioning that would satisfy both his professional responsibilities and those of a friend.

The room was long and narrow and white, with a stretched-oval table that could seat all the section editors and their boss. A glass wall divided this room from the city room. You could have a private conversation, as long as you kept the volume reasonable and turned your head away from the lip-readers on the other side of the glass. Large windows on the north wall looked out over the Chicago River. Across the river stood the Tribune Building and the Sun-Times Building. The view was a nice visual reminder to the *Chronicle* workforce. A reminder of who the big boys are. Nobody slacks off at the *Chronicle*.

I hadn't been to a meeting in this room for eight years . . . almost nine. The last time was the day that I quit my job and told journalism to go to hell. Colm Stanwell, our editor, had called Terry and me in to hear the bad news. We were being pulled off the *union pension scam* story. I think Stanwell held the meeting in this room, rather than his private office, to keep my temper at bay. In addition to being a great newspaperman, Stanwell was an adroit manager of egos and insecurities.

He knew that I would not take it well and I didn't. I kept my voice down all right, but my words were choice. And I walked out of there an ex-reporter.

A lot of blood under the bridge, since then.

"How about I go first?" I told Terry. "I need to know the name of your anonymous source from yesterday's piece."

"Jesus, Ray. You're kind of missing the point of an *anonymous* source."

"Yeah, but I need to know. To the rest of the world, he can be anonymous."

Terry glanced at the file folders on the table. "You know I can't help you with this, right?" I returned his look and said nothing. He continued, "I'm going to get us some coffee, which will take ten minutes. While I'm gone, you had better not look at my interview notes."

"Cross my heart," I said.

Terry grinned. "You had especially better not look in the green folder," he said and left the room.

I looked in the green folder. The first two pages were telephone logs that told me nothing. At the top of the third page was written *Incoming Call, Re: DiMarco, From:* followed by a name, which had been scratched out. Next to the scratched-out name was written, *Insists Anonymous.*

I removed the page from the file folder and held it up to the light but I couldn't make anything out. Terry was a good scribbler. I used the high-powered miniflashlight on my key chain, holding it against the paper from behind.

And there it was. *Holborn—FBI.* Well, well, well. Holborn had pressed me for the source, when in fact he was the source. *Why? First . . . if I offered a name, even as a guess, that name might give him a new direction to investigate, or a weak link to try to turn informant. Not unreasonable. Second . . . asking me could help to establish that he didn't know, which might give him some deniability if he were ever accused of being the source. But why would he call Terry with this information in the first place? Maybe he wanted to send a heads-up to Greico. Couldn't do that, officially. But Greico would certainly be on guard after reading the article in the* Chronicle. *Makes sense. Maybe. It wouldn't be the first time that a G-man broke the rules for a good cause . . . if you can call Greico a good cause.*

I returned the page to the folder and the folder to the stack. Terry came back and we drank coffee.

"Anything surprising crop up while I was gone?" Terry asked.

"Shocking," I said.

"We never know what we know until we know it," said Terry.

"And even then we are confused," I said.

"A lot of that going around, these days." Terry opened a yellow file folder and reviewed his notes. "First, Alderman Heath . . . I think I've found—"

"Forget Heath."

"No, I think you were right about him," he said. "I've been looking at his voting record, and—"

"Forget Heath," I repeated, with a little more emphasis this time. Terry's eyebrows danced and he looked up from his notes.

"Okay, let's look at this carefully," he said carefully. "I'm a reporter, following a story about Frank DiMarco's real estate scam and the dead witnesses and Bob Loniski, who saw Heath in DiMarco's car. Heath is the connection to the larger scam. Heath is the reason Loniski's life is in danger. And you want me to forget Heath? DiMarco's dead. There is no story without Heath."

"Heath's story died with DiMarco," I said. "Don't chase it."

"Bu—"

"Terry, you won't get there without me and I won't take you there." He looked dismayed. "Not to worry," I assured him. "There's a bigger story that I will take you to. Much bigger."

Terry took notes while I told him my theory about Tortelli collecting public officials under his own personal control, to leverage his way out of trouble and into Greico's office.

"That would take a lot of leverage," he said. "What makes you think he's got them?"

"First, it's the only way he could go after Greico. Second, and I can't tell you why, but I have strong reason to believe he's got at least one very high-placed cop."

"But you can't tell me why."

"Nope."

"Look, man, this story is wide open," Terry said. "My editor wants new developments every day. I can't sit on Heath just because you tell me to."

"Let's go off the record," I said.

Terry put his pen down. "We're off."

"I mean completely. This is just us talking."

"Hey, we're always off the record unless you see me taking notes, partner," said Terry, with a little hurt in his voice. "You ought to know that by now."

"Okay. We're off. I wouldn't have gotten to DiMarco without Heath. Heath stays out of it."

"Shit. I knew it," said Terry. "Fuck, Ray . . ."

"I know. It's bad."

"What are you gonna do?"

"I'm going after DiMarco's blackmail stash tonight. I can bring you the bigger story tomorrow. And it'll be huge, Bernstein."

Terry sighed, "Here we go again, just like before."

"Don't do that to me, Terry. Now is not the time . . ." I drank some coffee while forcing my preferred response back into the dark cave from which it was trying to crawl. "I only need one day and I guarantee you won't get the story without my help."

"Oh? We're playing hardball?" Terry asked.

"Just trying to stay alive, partner," I said.

Terry thought about that. "I still need something new for tomorrow's paper," he said.

"Okay. I'll give you an interview about California and the car bomb and defending myself against DiMarco. Tomorrow you can run a big color piece, bringing readers up to date with the *human interest* side of the story. Your editor should love that and it'll buy us the time we need."

Terry made a face. "Sounds a little lame," he said.

"You can visit with Bob," I said, "and really flesh it out."

Terry beamed. I thought he might kiss me. "Well why didn't you say so, Woodward?"

As we drove to the hotel where Bob Loniski was hiding, I gave Terry his interview. And he took notes. It was what reporters call a *puff piece*—long on colorful descriptions and short on news. But readers love stories with *fleshed-out* characters and Terry would score points by bagging an interview with a man in hiding from the Outfit.

I didn't mind Terry coming to the hotel. I needed to check on Loniski and I'd decided to move him, anyway. Keeping him in one place too long wasn't the smart play. Staying in that room day after day, never leaving, never accepting maid service, never using the phone. It wouldn't be long before hotel staff got curious or Bob went stir-crazy. Time for a change.

I didn't want to give Bob a heart attack by flinging the door open, so I knocked our prearranged pattern on the door and then used my key and entered, with Terry right behind me.

"Oops," said Terry. There was no one in the room but us.

On the desk lay a note, written on hotel stationary. It read:

> Dear Ray,
> I can never repay what you've done for me. You saved my life, and you showed me what is important in life. I don't have the words to thank you and I'll always be in your debt.
>
> > Your friend,
> > Bob

Goddamn.

Terry went back to the *Chronicle* to write up our interview and I promised to call him as soon as I learned anything. I used the hotel phone to call Bob's apartment but there was no answer. Then I called the *Final Revenge* production office and asked for Bob. Bob couldn't come to the phone right now, and would I like to leave a message? Hell yes, I'd like to leave a message.

"It's Ray Dudgeon calling—"

The receptionist squealed in my ear. "Oh my God! The Gunslinger! I mean, that's what they're all calling you here. You're, like, a hero or something."

"Something," I said. "I need to speak with Bob."

"Oh and I know he wants to see you! He's been talking about you nonstop. But he can't come to the phone. You have to come down to the studio. He'll be thrilled! Everyone will. I'm about to go back down myself . . . I just popped up to check messages."

"Then let me talk to Al Diskin."

"He's down there too. Everybody is. I mean, it's out of control! You just *have* to come down! Studio B, look for the nightclub set. See ya!" And she hung up.

The nightclub set in Studio B was in full bloom. Movie people drank at the bar and laughed and shouted their conversations over the pop music that blared through a powerful sound system. Some of the cast and crew gyrated spastically on the dance floor, where overhead lights spun, flashed and changed color. The art department had covered the wall behind the bar with a hand-painted sign that said WELCOME HOME BOB! YOU BEAT THE MOB! NOW DO YOUR JOB! Poets. They'd also made life-size stand-up photos of Al Capone, Vito Corleone and John Gotti. Gotti was a New Yorker and Corleone was both a New Yorker and fictional, but maybe that was nitpicking. I wasn't in a party mood.

I spotted the receptionist laughing with some women at the bar and made my way through the crowd. She saw me and waved and heads turned in my direction.

"Hey! It's the Gunslinger!" a man's voice hollered behind me.

"Gunslinger!" shouted various movie people, raising their glasses in a drunken toast.

When I reached the receptionist, she shot me with her finger and said, "Nice shootin', Tex." Her eyes were cocaine-bright.

"Christ," I said. "Where's Bob?"

"Somewhere 'round here," she said. "Have a drink, they're free! Al is such a great boss, he gave the whole crew a day off so we could have a party for Bob. You want to get high, just go to the bedroom set and they've got everything and everything's free. How great is that?"

A man's voice behind me said, "Want to ride me, cowboy?" I turned to face the voice. A young man with a golden tan and Venice Beach muscles and unnaturally blond hair smiled at me.

"Flattered, but no thanks," I said.

"Don't know what you're missing," he teased.

As I made my way through the crowd, strangers shook my hand and patted my shoulder and called me Gunslinger, which made me want to shoot them. The fourth to approach was Al Diskin. He grinned at me with his fake teeth and pumped my hand like he was trying to draw water.

"Ray, great of you to come! We tried to reach you but your cell is off. I'll take you to Bob. We're on the lounge set, it's a little quieter there." His eyes were as bright as the receptionist's.

We walked away from the nightclub set and down a wide hallway toward a pool of light in the opposite corner of the soundstage. Our footsteps echoed along behind us.

"That's a hell of a party for ten-thirty in the morning," I said.

"Well, they're good kids and they deserve it," said Diskin. "We've all been under a lot of stress with Bob's situation. A good producer recognizes when his crew needs to let off some steam and if I'm not a good producer then I'm nothing. And with distribution sealed, we can afford a day." There was a speed and intensity in his speech that confirmed my suspicion. Diskin was coked, all right. His hand patted my shoulder. "And it's all thanks to you, Ray. I want you to know that. And there'll be a substantial bonus added to your check. We're all very grateful and—"

I stopped walking and Diskin stopped talking. I said, "Bob isn't out of danger yet. This is premature."

Diskin stared at me and then let out a laugh. "Good one, Ray. You had me going there."

"I'm not kidding, Al." I held his gaze. After a few seconds, his mouth turned down at the corners.

"Oh come *on,*" he said. "You're being very well paid and I've just included a bonus. Let's not have it end badly. I know it's a lucrative gig but, *really.* Don't pad your part."

"Al, I'm not trying to stretch the gig."

"Sure you're not," said Diskin.

"I'm not. Bob saw something that goes higher than Frank DiMarco. He's still in danger."

"And I say, Bob saw nothing," Diskin spat. Then his anger suddenly vanished and he put his arm around my shoulders. "Let me tell you a little something, my friend. I guess you didn't hear me the first time. We create our reality. The truth is a lie, agreed upon. If I say Bob saw nothing and Bob says he saw nothing, then he saw nothing. And if I tell everyone that you're Superman, then you are. On the other hand, if I say you're a two-bit chiseler who tried to squeeze us for more money when the job was finished, then *that's* what you are." His eyes blazed. "Got me?"

"I can't talk to you while you're juiced, Al." I turned away from him. He didn't follow and I found the lounge set by myself.

The lounge set smelled of fresh paint. Other than the missing ceiling and the massive lighting grid suspended above, it looked just like a piano lounge you'd find in any elegant hotel. There was even a piano. A man with wild hair and a scruffy beard sat at it, noodling around with some Nat King Cole tunes. He wasn't a professional but he was pretty good. Movie people were scattered around the lounge in little groups of four or five. One of the groups passed a joint around. Bob sat in a leather wingback chair in the corner. Alone. He held a bottle of Pol Roger in one hand and drank straight from the bottle. As I approached, he stood and raised the bottle in my direction and spoke to the room.

"Attenshun, good people!" Bob was hammered and his eyelids were riding low. "Can I have your attenshun for a moment?" Conversations stopped and heads turned to look. "Thank you. I just want everyone here to know that *this* is the man"—he thrust an arm out toward me—"who saved my life. Let's all raise our glasses, to my good friend Ray Dudgeon." People raised their glasses and made pleasant noises and the guy at the piano bashed out the riff from "For He's a Jolly Good Fellow" before returning to "Portrait of Jennie."

But Bob wasn't done. "I just want everyone to know that I love this man!" He tried to give me a hug and almost fell into me. "I love you, man!"

I took hold of his shoulders and eased him back into his chair. "Okay Bob, okay."

"Great party," he said.

"Swell. We have to get you back under wraps. You're not in the clear yet."

"Aw, now Al said you'd say that."

"I'm not looking for more money. I'm in this too, so from now on we're off the clock. But you've got to listen to me."

"Naw, see, I talked with Al and everything's fine. I didn't see anything and he'll swear I told him so. I just saw DiMarco, there was nobody in his car."

"You're whistling past the graveyard," I said. "It won't work."

"You can stop worrying, Ray." Bob took another swig of champagne and dribbled some onto his knee. "I know you mean well but Al's taken care of it. He knows this lawyer in New York, see, who is someone connected to the Mob. And he's gonna spread the word to the right people in Chicago, that I saw nothing but DiMarco and I'll swear on it on a stack of Bibles. Then there's no reason to kill me, right? It's even better for them if I'm alive."

"And this was all Al's idea," I said.

"No, now . . . no, we both thought of it together." Bob's eyelids slid passed half-mast. Further discussion was pointless.

If Diskin really did ask a New York Mob mouthpiece to pass the message along to the Chicago Outfit, he needn't have bothered. Quicker just to send a telegram straight to Paul Tortelli, informing him that Bob was now available for slaughter at his convenience.

I didn't have time to wait for Bob to drink himself unconscious, sleep it off, wake up, and recover from the hangover. I'd try him again tomorrow. I found a pay phone and called John Stone at Stone Security and told him that, in my opinion, Bob Loniski was still a target and Stone's men should be extra careful. He said "ten-four."

Then I called Terry and told him about Bob. To his credit, Terry didn't gripe about not getting the interview. He said that my interview would suffice for now, and he had a source on the other line. I said I'd call back later.

I stopped at a hardware store for supplies. A stepladder, sleeping bag, padlock, heavy wire cutters, small pry bar, two knapsacks, a roll of twenty-gauge wire, a new flashlight and a battery-powered lantern. At a shipping store, I bought a dozen medium boxes, a roll of packing tape and a Sharpie. I was the model of efficiency and I arrived at Doctor Ink just before 2:00.

Behind the counter, Yoshi Inoue stood at his workbench, adjusting the gold nib of an old orange Parker Duofold. A true classic. He didn't seem to hear me enter and I knew better than to interrupt, so I waited and watched the master at work. Yoshi gazed through the lighted magnifier and his rock-steady hands tweaked the nib with two pairs of miniature needle-nose pliers.

"We are concerning ourselves with three-tenths of a millimeter," Yoshi said without looking up, "and that makes all the difference. I beg your indulgence and I assure you that your pen will receive the same care and attention."

"Take your time, Yoshi," I said.

Yoshi grinned but his head didn't move and he continued his work. "Ray," he said, "come through. I have some new first-flush gyokuro that you'll want to try."

I lifted the hinged section of countertop and went to the kitchenette in back. I poured water from the filter pitcher into an electric kettle and measured two teaspoons of the expensive green tea into a little cast-iron teapot. Watching the surface of the water, I waited for the "shrimp eyes."

Yoshi had taught me all about the shrimp eyes. When making green tea, you don't use boiling water. For a delicate grade like gyokuro, you want the water at 160 degrees. Some people use a thermometer but Yoshi had a better way. He had categorized the different sizes of bubbles that rise to the surface as the water temperature nears boiling. At 160 degrees, you see hundreds of tiny bubbles forming on the bottom of the kettle and breaking free. These are shrimp eyes. At 180 degrees, the bubbles are larger and more distinct when they break on the surface. These are crab eyes and are suited to medium-grade teas such as sencha. A few degrees below boiling, crab eyes grow to become fish eyes, perfect for oolong. And so on.

The shrimp eyes came quickly and I poured the water into the little pot and noted the position of the sweep second hand on my watch. For gyokuro, I waited 110 seconds and then poured the tea into two cups. I placed one of the cups on the workbench beside Yoshi and warmed my hands on the other.

Yoshi finished tweaking the Duofold's nib, put the pliers down and tested the pen, laying a smooth blue squiggle onto a thick sheet of white paper.

"Medium-broad, no rough spots, nice angle . . . perfect," he said with a nod. He laid the pen on a little velvet pillow and clicked off the magnifier lamp and picked up his tea and sipped. "Very nice," he said with a nod in my direction. "I'll make a Buddhist out of you, yet."

"That'll take a lot of work," I said.

"Lot of work, little work . . . no difference," said Yoshi, with a serene Buddha smile. He rose and hung a "Back in 5 Minutes" sign on the door and locked the door and led me into a small office just off the kitchenette. I tasted the tea. It was very nice.

"Peter Dunbar," said Yoshi. From a drawer he produced some identification cards and spread them on the desktop. "Illinois driver's license. You'll want to memorize all the information on it. The signature is easy but you'll want to practice it, of course. Visa card, valid for the next thirty days, same signature, credit limit of one thousand dollars and I'll need cash to cover it. Spend it all because there are no refunds. Chicago Public Library card, valid forever. AmEx, Diners, Exxon, MasterCard . . . all dummies. Don't even try to use these, they just fill out your wallet. I left these unsigned. Once you've got the signature, sign them. It is good to have slight variations."

I gave him $4,000 cash for his work and another thousand to cover the Visa card. I put the cards in my pocket. Yoshi looked disappointed.

"I know how good you are," I said.

"Please. It gives me pleasure." So I compared the Peter Dunbar driver's license to my own. Yoshi's work was flawless, of course.

"You are a true artist," I said.

"Yes." He sipped his tea. "Thank you."

After practicing my new signature and signing the dummy cards, I dropped my prepaid cell phone in a Dumpster. The cops had been in possession of it and I wouldn't be surprised if they decided to listen in on my calls for a few days. Or maybe my new friends at the FBI. Anyway, I was taking no chances and I hadn't used it since I got it back from the police. Using Peter Dunbar's driver's license and Visa card, I bought a new phone with a new number. I kept the charged battery from the discarded phone and also bought a couple of disposable "emergency power" batteries, just to be safe.

Then Peter Dunbar rented a cube van, transferred everything from the car to the van, and parked the car in a garage around the corner from the U-Haul outlet. In the back of the van, I assembled the boxes and filled them with bunched-up paper. I put my kit bag in one box and the hardware supplies in others and taped them shut. On each box I wrote *Peter Dunbar / 23 Main Street / Wrens, Georgia.*

At a medical supply shop, I picked up two stiff EMS spineboards and added them to the payload. At Central Camera, I bought some colored lighting gels. My checklist was complete. I parked in the loading bay behind Rockwell U-Store-It and went through my checklist a second time. I had everything. It was 4:56.

I called Terry and left my new cell-phone number on his voice mail. I checked messages at home and at the office. I didn't know there were that many reporters in Chicago. Everyone wanted to talk to me. Everyone was my buddy. Since killing DiMarco, I'd become a very popular guy. Maybe I should shoot people more often. I erased all the messages, put on my Southern accent and went inside to rent a locker.

Bubblegum Girl sat in the grimy office as before, smacking her gum and smoking. Her dye job still needed a touch-up and I still didn't notice her ample breasts. She didn't seem to remember me from my previous visit. Nor did she seem to recognize my face from the newspapers. If she did recognize me, then she was a hell of an actress and was wasting her talents in the self-storage business.

Bubblegum Girl acted terribly inconvenienced by having to rent me a locker only one hour before closing time. She told me that six o'clock was six o'clock and that's when they close, and if I wasn't finished unloading, I'd have to come back tomorrow. I promised that it wasn't a problem. And she rented a locker to Peter Dunbar, of Wrens, Georgia. Wrens ain't a whole lot to look at, but it's the pecan capital of the South. There are worse places to pretend to be from.

I told Bubblegum Girl to charge my credit card for the first four months in advance and she did. The first locker she offered was too close to the freight elevator and susceptible to theft. The second was too close to the windows and susceptible to water damage. I examined the floor plan on the wall and innocently suggested that K-section looked good. She produced a melodramatic sigh to let me know how difficult I was being, but she rented me locker K-32, which was almost directly across the hall from Frank DiMarco's. Sometimes you just get lucky.

I wrote the appropriate things on the sign-in sheet hanging by the door and thanked Bubblegum Girl for being so helpful. She didn't tell me that I was welcome.

Martinez stood in the loading bay, smoking a cheap cigar by an open door. He smiled and said that it was nice to see me again. If he recognized me from the papers, he didn't show it. Martinez was accustomed to keeping things inside, but I didn't figure him for a bigmouth anyway, so I didn't let it worry me. Much. I declined his offer of help and told him to enjoy his cigar.

I loaded half the boxes and the spineboards onto a rusty flatbed dolly and dragged the dolly on its uncooperative wheels to the battered freight elevator, which was large enough for a midsize car. With a pull on the strap, the elevator's outer doors closed from the floor and ceiling, crashing together at waist height like the jaws of a large animal. Then I pulled the inner cage shut in the same manner, and the animal was a shark with two rows of teeth. I held down the appropriate button and the shark began to rise. It was sluggish and noisy and lurched a couple of times along the way, but it lifted me to the second floor without snapping its cables.

I got lost only twice while looking for my locker. I made sure to memorize the route for next time. K-32 was in the sixth row of K-section. The place was even colder than I'd remembered.

Inside K-32, I opened the boxes and placed my supplies to one side. The open door blocked the video camera's view as I loosened the hinges.

Back at the loading dock, I stacked the remaining boxes and the stepladder onto the dolly and repeated the trip to my locker, getting lost only once this time. The lights were still on in K-section but the timer was running down. I did not turn the knob to refresh it. I loaded everything into the locker and closed myself in, unpacked the boxes and broke them down flat and stacked them out of the way. I put the padlock in my pocket and returned the dolly to the loading bay. Then

I left by the front door, signing out on the way, and walked around outside the building for the cube van in the loading bay.

I parked the van a block away and walked back to Rockwell-U-Store-It and entered through the back door, where Martinez had been smoking. It was 5:54.

The plan was to hold up the padlock and look sheepish and tell Martinez that I forgot to lock up and I'd be in and out in a jiffy. Martinez would assume I'd left again via the front door. But Martinez was not in the loading bay. I guessed that he'd probably started his closing rounds, since the freight elevator was not on the ground level. I took the stairs.

The timer had expired and the lights had gone out and K-section was darker than a politician's heart. I felt my way along, counting the rows until I reached mine. I stepped inside the locker and closed the door behind me. In the distance, I could hear Martinez's footsteps and the keys jingling on his belt. The lights were still off, so he hadn't reached K-section, but the sound was getting louder. With the hinges loosened, I could push the door out just enough to slip my hand through and secure the padlock. I got my hand back inside as the fluorescent lights flickered to life.

Martinez jingled up and down the hallways, occasionally stopping to rattle a padlock. I held my breath as he passed my door but he didn't stop and I resumed breathing and avoided passing out.

A few minutes later, I heard the freight elevator clanking and groaning. And then there was only silence and darkness.

After Martinez was gone, I turned my new cell phone on but I was in a dead zone and couldn't pick up a signal. Although there was no chance of sleep, the sleeping bag at least kept me from freezing to death as I lay on the floor of my locker. Waiting.

Several eons passed until the luminescent hands of my Rolex lined up at midnight. A Rolex is a pretty expensive watch for a guy like me, but I had a good reason for buying one. While serving in Korea, my grandfather had bought the original Submariner model at the PX, and he wore it for thirty years. Then he passed it to me on my eighteenth birthday and it was my proudest possession. But a year ago, a nervous junkie pointed a gun at me and demanded the watch. On television, the PI would deliver a swift roundhouse kick to the wrist and knock the gun flying and then say something witty. In real life, when someone points a gun at you and demands your watch, you just give him the damn watch. Still, it broke my heart to give it up and there was never any question of what I would buy to take its place. So I'd put off the new car purchase a little longer and bought a new Rolex Submariner.

Now that watch told me it was midnight. The numbers in the date window changed from 31 to 1. *Happy New Year.*

The battery-powered lantern provided plenty of light for inside my cave but too much for the hallway. With rubber bands, I secured a red lighting gel over the lens of my flashlight. It was still a little too bright, so I added another. Too dark. I removed one of the red gels and added a yellow. Perfect. I stood on the stepladder and used the wire cutters to make a large flap in the chicken-wire ceiling, cutting right at the edge of the walls. I bent the flap back and secured it open with duct tape. Then I switched off the lantern and lifted the spineboards and laid them across the top of the adjacent locker. I didn't think that the chicken wire would hold my weight, but the spineboards were long enough to cover the five feet between plywood walls. I loaded my supplies on one board and slid it ahead and then hoisted myself up onto the other board, on my hands and knees, with the flashlight clamped in an armpit. I crawled along to the end, moving slowly to keep my balance. Then I carefully moved from one board to the other, pulled the trailing board forward and transferred my supplies to it, then pushed it ahead and shimmied forward again. And then repeated the whole procedure.

It was slow and strenuous work, and despite the cold, I worked up a pretty good sweat. I was now directly across from K-25. But I couldn't be positive that the wide-angle lens of the video camera wouldn't reach the top of the lockers at this point, since I was still four lockers, or twenty feet, from the wall where the camera was mounted. So I resisted the urge to traverse right there and instead continued my slow crawl toward the end of the hallway, where the camera was mounted. Somewhere along the way, it occurred to me that I should have considered kneepads.

Twice I thought I heard something and held my position each time, my heart pounding, until I was sure I was mistaken. Finally I reached the end of the hallway. The luminescent hands of my watch said 12:32. I placed one board spanning the hallway, directly above the video camera, and tossed the knapsacks across to the chicken wire on the other side. I slid the other board ahead of me and inched across. It was only a ten-foot drop to the floor but I couldn't have been more careful if I'd been negotiating an icy gorge in Nepal. Maybe if I'd had a Sherpa leading me I'd be able to relax, but there's never a Sherpa around when you need one. At least not in Chicago. Anyway, I made it across without scaring myself to death.

Then another long slow crawl. And I was above Frank DiMarco's locker. Shining the flashlight down through the chicken wire revealed a black metal two-drawer filing cabinet and a chair of the sort you'd find at the kitchen table of any modest home. That was all. But that was enough for me. I cut a flap in the wire and secured it open as I had with my locker. I dropped the two knapsacks down into DiMarco's locker and lowered myself in after them. I removed my gloves, wiped my sweaty hands on my jeans and put the gloves back on. I opened my jacket and wiped my face on the inside of my sweatshirt and took a few deep breaths. I removed the lantern from one knapsack, turned it on and placed it on top of the filing cabinet.

The cabinet's drawers were locked. I got the pry bar from the other knapsack, jammed the bar in beside the lock and pushed to the right. The metal cabinet groaned and warped. I forced the bar farther. Thinking, *Screw you, Tortelli. You bastards may run this town but you don't run me, and I'll be damned if I let you kill me. I won't run from you.*

Another shove and the lock popped. I put the bar down and pulled the drawer open.

The filing cabinet was empty. Empty as a gangster's conscience. Empty as a cheerleader's head. Empty as . . . shit. It was empty. Completely empty. Nothing in the world could ever be emptier than that filing cabinet. I sat on the little chair for a while and pondered complete emptiness. If I weren't such a tough-guy, I would've even shed a few tears.

By 2:30 I was back in my locker. I'd used the twenty-gauge wire to secure the chicken-wire ceiling back in place over both lockers, and it would take very close inspection to notice anything had been altered. More likely it would be assumed that his padlock had been picked. How the intruder got past the video camera would be a mystery. Anyway it was doubtful that anyone would investigate. Paul Tortelli would probably get a kick out of the fact that I'd tried and he'd been a step ahead.

I had almost seven hours to kill until I could get out of there. I took the padlock off the door. In the morning, I'd simply walk out with my supplies in the knapsacks and my kit bag. If asked, I'd say that I'd just popped in through the loading bay and forgot to sign in. Maybe Martinez would get in trouble for that. Maybe not. And in six months, my rent would be sixty days past due and they'd cut the padlock and find a stepladder, two spineboards and a dozen flattened boxes. They could have them.

With my exit strategy planned, I wrote some ideas in my notebook and then I ran out of ideas and I still had almost seven hours to kill. I tried to sleep. I was plenty tired but sometimes tired isn't enough. I looked at my watch. I tried again to sleep.

The hours crawled by like a procession of wounded turtles. I thought sleep would never come. I was wrong.

It was a dream I was having, about the first time I killed someone. *This hot summer day, sunny and blue-skied. The man works under a rusty Trans Am. You've been served, sir, have a nice day . . . and walk away.*

Blinding flash. Sharp pain. Hit pavement. Roll over. Draw pistol. Front sight. Squeeze trigger.

Bright red blood against a sapphire sky. Ruby rain on a cloudless day. Blood shower shimmers in the sunlight. Sun so bright. Sky so blue.

Blood so red.

I awoke with a single word on my lips . . .

Beautiful.

CHAPTER TWELVE

How's it going, killer?" said Lieutenant Mike Angelo as I entered his office.

"Don't start, Mike," I said, and dropped into a chair.

"What? You're making Chicago a better place to live," Mike said with a shrug. "Hey, I got a whole stack of files you can clear for us . . . pimps, drug dealers, gangbangers, rapists, wiseguys . . . take your pick. Maybe you can kill 'em all and save the justice system some trouble . . ."

"Only if they're trying to kill me."

Mike snorted, "Yeah, right."

"Shit, can we just drop it please?" I said.

"Three, 'that we know about,' " he added, mimicking Assistant State's Attorney Kingman.

"Really, Mike. Don't."

"Know what you are, Ray? You're an addict." Mike twisted the knife a little deeper, grinning. "What's that old saying? Oh yeah: 'One's too many and a hundred's not enough.' That's you, my man. That's you all over."

"Fuck! Drop it, Mike." I'd never spoken to him in that tone and the room was suddenly airless. There was a half-empty coffee cup on the desk, so I lit a cigarette. Thinking, *He helped you get away with murder, Dudgeon. He knows what really happened in that garage—he made that very clear. But he sold your story to Kingman anyway. Remember that.*

There was no way to know what would have happened without Mike's help. I might've gotten away with it—or not. So he'd earned the right to needle me. "Sorry," I said. Mike stood and cracked open a window and sat back at his desk. The chair squeaked.

"Someone woke up on the wrong side of the bed this morning."

"No bed."

"Not unreasonable," said Mike. "A hunted man gathers no moss."

"Holborn doesn't think they'll make a play for me until after the funeral."

"That's the general etiquette but I wouldn't bet my life on it if I were you." Mike lit a cigarette and crumpled the empty pack and tossed it in a wastepaper basket behind his desk. "I pulled some strings and we delayed the release of DiMarco's body as long as we could. But he ships out this afternoon, so I'd expect a funeral tomorrow or the next day."

"Thanks, Mike," I said.

"Now about your gun. It'll be a few days. I assume you have others."

"I'm sentimental about that one."

"By the book, it would take six to eight weeks, minimum."

"Well I do appreciate your help."

Mike held my gaze. "Of course you do. And you're about to ask for more?"

I was, and I did. Mike called down to evidence and found out that, yes, Frank DiMarco did have keys on his person when he was killed, and that DiMarco's personal effects were collected by next of kin yesterday, just before noon.

Mike cupped the phone as I asked, "Next of kin?" and then repeated the question into the receiver, waited for an answer and chuckled.

He said to me, "Sister. Apparently a knockout." His attention was drawn back to the phone. "A what? Oh, okay," then back to me, "I'm sorry, not a knockout, a hot piece of classy ass."

"More?"

"Keep going," Mike said into the phone and then listened. "Uh-huh." Back to me, "Late thirties or early forties . . . says she looked like a sexy LaSalle Street executive."

And the pieces started falling into place. "Gloria Simpson?" I guessed.

"Can I get a name on that ass?" Mike said into the phone. After a moment, he nodded across his desk at me.

As I left Area 4 Headquarters, I had that feeling. I was being watched. It was a relief to see Special Agent Holborn idling at the curb across Harrison in a black Mercury Grand Marquis. I crossed the street and Holborn told me to get in and I did.

"Any news?" Holborn asked. He handed me a paper cup of coffee. He'd remembered—black, no sugar.

"No news," I said. "You?"

"It's a two-way street, Ray."

"Sure, fine, but I just don't have any news. If I get some, you'll be the first to know."

"After Angelo."

"Okay," I said, "you'll be the second to know."

"All right, let's play it this way," said Holborn. "You think that Loniski is still a target. Why?"

"John Stone?" I asked.

"Or someone who works for him. The question stands."

"Yeah, okay. Let's say Paul Tortelli is after Greico's turf. He wants out of the sex trade and he wants to be the moneyman. But that's a no-go with the Outfit, because Greico's grooming Salvatore to take over."

"Heir apparent."

"Right. So Tortelli puts cousin DiMarco in Greico's crew, as a mole. In the meantime, Tortelli and DiMarco use the sex trade to build Tortelli's sphere of influence, bagging public officials without passing them on to Amodeo."

"Suicide," said Holborn.

"Unless they get away with it long enough, and their sphere of influence grows large enough."

"That's a lot to assume."

"But let's. And DiMarco getting busted for the landlord scam is the trigger. DiMarco knows too much and he's already proved that he's a blabbermouth inside the joint. So Tortelli pulls him out of Greico's crew, lends him some muscle and orders him to get rid of the witnesses, while Tortelli plans his offensive strike against Greico."

"But then you kill DiMarco," said Holborn, "so there's no chance for him to blab in the joint and Tortelli can forget about Loniski. Which leads us back to my original question, which you're not-so-skillfully avoiding."

It was a tough one. Holborn was playing from a position of strength. He could have me thrown in jail whenever he wanted, which wouldn't increase my chances of survival any. Or he could order an FBI surveillance team to shadow me around the clock. Then I wouldn't be able to get to Gloria Simpson and the blackmail stash, and I'd be dead as soon as he got bored and pulled the surveillance team off me. But I couldn't give him Heath. I knew that Holborn had been Terry's source, so I figured that he had a rooting interest with Greico. And I knew he was willing to bend the rules for the greater good. But could I trust him?

"You want my help, Agent Holborn, and I want to help. But I have to draw the line at why Bob Loniski is still a target. It isn't important. You want the sharks and you're focusing on the minnows."

"Convince me," said Holborn. I lit a cigarette to give me time to think. "Roll down the window if you're gonna smoke that," he said. So I rolled down the window and he cranked the heat to maximum, which wasn't enough.

"Okay, let's say Tortelli is a smart guy," I said. "He nabs public officials through the sex trade but then goes one step further. He involves his suckers in some illegal activity, to solidify the relationship. And let's say that DiMarco's landlord scam was one of those activities, and Bob Loniski saw the public official involved."

"Now we're getting somewhere," said Holborn.

"But in Loniski's case, let's say that the public official was just a minnow. A meter maid."

"Meter maid?"

"Whatever . . . too low on the totem pole for you to care about. Let's keep focus on the big picture."

"Because you don't want to give up the meter maid."

"I can't."

"So what are you offering?" said Holborn.

I let him wait for it, then said, "Let's say I can give you the whole shebang."

"Can you?"

"Not yet. But I will very soon, if you leave me free to move."

Holborn was silent for too long. I sat and smoked and realized, once again, that I'd stopped enjoying cigarettes a long time ago. I tossed it out the window. Holborn still didn't say anything, so I decided to assume the sale.

"And you, Agent Holborn?" I said. "Any news on your end?"

Holborn laughed. "You know, Ray, you're a bit of a prick, but you're hard not to like."

I blew him a kiss. "That doesn't mean we're going steady," I said.

Holborn stiffened. "What the fuck was that?"

"What?"

"That. Fucking homophobe."

I tried to stop it. I swear I did. But I couldn't help it. I burst out laughing. "Oh my God," I said. "Agent Holborn. I had no idea."

"Yeah," he said. " 'You'll make someone a fine wife, someday.' 'Sweetheart.' 'Going steady.' Asshole."

"No really," I said, "I swear. I didn't know. And I don't care."

"I don't care if you care," said Holborn.

Now it was my turn. "Yeah, right," I said. We looked at each other for a while.

"Okay," said Holborn, "you didn't know."

"So are you in or out?" I asked.

"What difference does it make?"

"If you're out, I'll know that I can use my fag jokes in front of the other kids," I said. That did it. Now he knew I really didn't care.

Holborn smirked. "I'm out in my personal life, but my professional life is a little more complicated."

"I bet it is," I said, "especially with J. Edgar as a role model."

"You can't begin to imagine," said Special Agent Holborn.

I felt a little better after my meeting with Holborn. Six hours earlier, I had nothing. Now I had a pretty good idea of where the blackmail stash was, or at least a line on someone who could lead me to it. Holborn had become at least a marginal ally and I'd stood my ground where it counted.

Before we parted ways, Holborn had given me his news. Four respected guns had arrived in Chicago in the last two days. One from Los Angeles, two from Miami and one from Kansas City. Could be that Greico was calling in chits to bolster his defense. Or Tortelli was hiring guns for the attack. Holborn offered a third scenario—Tortelli could be bringing guns to deal with Bob Loniski and Ray Dudgeon. But that seemed far-fetched to both of us. There were plenty of local guns who could make quick work of Bob and me. This was bigger than that.

I called the *Final Revenge* production office but there was no answer. Probably all nursing hangovers. No answer at Bob's apartment either.

Then I got Terry on the phone and told him that I needed to meet with Delwood Crawley, right away. Terry told me that Crawley was a lowlife and any help he could give me wouldn't be worth what he'd ask in return. But he agreed to set it up.

Since 1958, the Old Town Ale House has been the favorite watering hole of Chicago's well-watered news scribblers. Reporters tend to prefer dives, and this was one of the best dives in America. And one of my favorite bars in Chicago.

I passed through the battle-scarred front door and into the darkness. Nothing ever changes in the place and I could probably find my way around blindfolded, but I stood and waited for my eyes to adjust. No use taking unnecessary risks.

The front windows wore a thick coat of nicotine residue that effectively filtered the daylight. Dim globe lights hung on chains from the brown pressed-tin ceiling. Everything was dark wood and decrepit.

Along the east wall was a mural, painted thirty-odd years ago, depicting the bar's regulars of the time, including many of Chicago's most famous scribes. Like the windows, the mural had yellowed over time. Framed portraits of bar staff and more recent regulars covered the back wall. Beneath the portraits, scores of books crowded built-in shelves.

Behind the bar, a hundred bottles of liquid relief shared space with peculiar artifacts. Among them, a Kabuki mask, some Mardi Gras beads, a human skull, about a dozen doll heads, a Swiss cuckoo clock, a pink feather boa and the Maltese Falcon. Bogie should have stopped chasing that fake and come to Chicago instead.

Perhaps the best thing about the place was its jukebox. Browsing through pages of CD covers was an invitation to terminal indecision . . . Billie Holiday, Carmen McRae, Mel Tormé, Sinatra, Ella, Satchmo, Duke, Miles, Bird, Jimmy Smith, Stan Getz, Dr. John, Lurrie Bell, Buddy Guy, Junior Wells, Otis Rush, Muddy Waters, Hound Dog Taylor, Bob Dylan, Tom Waits, John Prine, Fats Domino . . . and so on. An embarrassment of riches. If you don't find some of your favorites here, you just don't like music.

I fed quarters into the beast and flipped the last coin to decide between Marcus Roberts and Art Tatum. Tatum won. I exchanged greetings with a couple of reporters I knew and took my place at the front end of the bar and Davey set me up with a pint. But he cut short his hello when a young woman passed on the other side of the dirty windows.

"Oh come in, come in, come in . . . *please* come in," he whispered. She passed on by the door. "Damn."

"Hard up?" I said, just to be saying something.

"It's been brutal. We've had a total of one woman in here all day. I mean, nothing against you guys. I love you all, but I need to see some tits before I go crazy."

"Scenery could stand improvement," said Sun-Times Phil from halfway down the bar. "Maybe we can talk Tribune John into getting a sex change."

Without pausing his conversation at the other end of the bar, Tribune John raised his middle finger at Sun-Times Phil.

Davey made pleading eyes in my direction. "Ray, why don't you bring a date here sometime, give me something to look at?"

"First he's got to get a date," called Tribune Larry from the other end.

"More truth than poetry in that," I said, and lifted my glass.

"Hey, Ray, where's Chronicle Terry?" asked Tribune John.

"Working, like you should be," I said.

The guy-banter went on like that for a couple of pints. During a lull, I stepped outside to the paperbox and picked up that morning's *Chronicle* and brought it back.

Terry's coverage had slipped to page five, bumped by yet another contracting scandal at City Hall. Beside my interview, Terry had a small piece quoting unnamed law enforcement sources. Several suspected Mob hit men from other cities had arrived in Chicago in recent days. The CPD had no official comment about ongoing investigations.

Davey put an unasked-for third pint on the bar top in front of me. "This one's on me," he said. Maybe he'd read the paper.

Delwood Crawley arrived late and without apology. Trim and gray-skinned, he looked about seventy but, making allowances for drinking, was about sixty. He wore a blue pin-striped three-piece suit, a light blue shirt with white collar and cuffs, and gold cuff links that bore some kind of club crest. He was taking no chances, and completed the look with a paisley bow tie. It seemed his worst fear was that somebody might mistake him for an American. His well-cultivated accent said *Dry martinis at Ascot,* but something in the background said *Newcastle Brown Ale at the dog track.*

A veteran of the London tabloids, Delwood Crawley had been part of the Chicago scene since the early 1980s. He wrote a gossip column called "Chicago After Dark," which had no real news value but was very popular with *Chronicle* readers. From power brokers and society dames to students and secretaries, everybody read "Chicago After Dark" for a glimpse at the dirty laundry of the rich and famous. No one would ever replace Irv Kupcinet in this town, and if Crawley didn't have the style or decency of Kup, he certainly had as extensive a network of sources.

Crawley ordered a double Johnny Black with exactly two ice cubes. I told Davey that Crawley was on my tab and Davey looked at me with, perhaps, a slight loss of respect.

Crawley suggested that we repair to a table for privacy and we did. He produced a cigarette from a monogrammed silver case and lit it with a matching Dunhill lighter.

"Mr. Green conveyed your request for this meeting," he said. "I assume you wish to insert something into my column?"

"I have a news tip for you," I said.

"That is amusing," Crawley said, and sipped his drink. "But let's not pretend that I am in the news business, shall we?"

"Okay."

"Very well. Now, how much space do you require?"

"One 'graph," I said, "maybe two."

Crawley slid a small notepad across the table to me. "Just the points to be covered. I'll put it into my own inimitable prose and you'll read it in tomorrow morning's *Chronicle.*" I wrote on the pad and slid it back to him and he read it. "Very good," he said. "Of course, I am not a charity."

"Of course. How much do you want?"

"No, no," Crawley chortled, "nothing like that." He drank off most of his Scotch and signaled Davey for another. "There are a couple of story leads I've been following, but to go further may require someone of your particular skills. I've researchers working for me, naturally, but they're not comfortable moving in certain circles, you understand."

"You want to barter for some investigative work."

"Exactly."

"I'm not available right at the moment."

"That's fine," he said with a soothing smile. "There's no hurry. These stories aren't going anywhere, as long as you can get to it by summertime."

I felt like Eve, negotiating with the Serpent of Eden. But what the hell. I didn't care for Diskin's implied threats and I'd seen how he could manipulate the press. This way, Diskin would be reading my spin, instead of the other way around. Would it motivate him to put me back on the job? Probably not. But it might motivate Bob to go back underground, where he'd be safe.

"All right," I said. "How about forty hours of my time, in exchange for two paragraphs in your column?"

Crawley stubbed out his half-smoked cigarette and lit a new one. "The poisons become more concentrated as you smoke them down," he explained. "I may smoke three packs a day but I only smoke the first half of each cigarette, so it is the equivalent of less than one pack."

"If you say so."

"I do say so. I've researched it," he said. "As for your proposal, I cannot agree. You may sit in your car for forty hours and turn up nothing. But I'm giving you definite value, so I wish to receive definite value in return. Why don't we say, once your investigative work produces two publishable items, your debt will be absolved?"

"What if we disagree about what constitutes a publishable item?"

"My dear boy, we are reasonable men. We shall be reasonable, when the time comes. Or should I say, *if* the time comes. After all, the odds are not good that you'll even live to repay this favor."

"How do you figure those odds?"

"Well I hate to be the bearer of bad news but in the office pool your life can be measured in days. Mr. Green is the only one who's put money on the proposition that you'll live through this trouble."

"Where'd you put your money?" I asked.

Crawley sniffed. "I'd rather not say."

If Terry had arrived thirty seconds sooner, Crawley could have held the chair for him. As it was, the chair was still warm.

"I hate that," said Terry, squirming in his seat. "Makes me feel like I'm touching asses with somebody." He drew the day's *Chronicle* from his satchel and dropped it on the table in front of me.

"I saw it," I said.

"Page *five*," said Terry. "My editor thinks the story has crested, but I told him you're bringing me something today that's gonna blow the doors off. Tell me I didn't lie to him."

"Terry—"

"Don't 'Terry' me," he cut in. "Yes or no."

"Not yet," I said. "The files had been moved but I've got a new lead on the location and I'll have them tomorrow."

"Yesterday you said tomorrow. And I sat on the Heath story for you yesterday, which would've kept me on page one."

"Trust me on this. Another day and you'll be back on page one, big time."

Terry poked the newspaper with his finger. "See, there you go again, Woodward. Same bullshit as when we were working together. We had a perfectly good story that would've bagged a bent union treasurer—"

"A *local* treasurer," I interrupted. "There was a national story there."

"But we didn't have the national story, did we? And as soon as we got close, the motherfuckers shut us down. We could've done a little bit of good and taken a pat on the back for a job well done and moved on to the next one. But not you. No, you gotta save the whole fucking world. So in the end, we did no good and got shit."

"Ancient history, Terry."

"No man, you're wrong. You act like you've changed but you're still doing the same old thing, just in a different job. You should've dumped this case a long time ago. What are you gonna do, put the Outfit out of business? In the real world, Goliath always wins. You oughta know that by now."

"I took the case. I'll see it through. That's it. I'm not trying to do anything more than that."

"This quixotic bullshit is gonna kill you, Ray."

"I'll see you tomorrow," I said. I stood and left the bar without finishing my beer.

Today is the tomorrow you worried about yesterday, and all is very far from well.

Quixotic bullshit.

I drove across North Avenue, trying to shake Terry's accusations. A voice kept telling me that Terry was right, and the harder I tried to ignore it, the louder it got. Maybe that's all it was in the end—quixotic bullshit. The sum of my life's choices. But I didn't know any other way to live. Even if I could, I didn't know if I'd want to. Maybe I just wasn't built to fit in with practical society.

Or maybe I should just quit navel-gazing. I called the *Final Revenge* production office again and this time they answered but Bob had not come to work today.

"Did he call in sick?"

"No, he just hasn't shown up," said the receptionist. "Neither has Kathie, and there's no answer—"

But I'd already dropped the phone and screeched a U-turn across traffic. With a sour taste rising into my mouth, I burned rubber to the Balderstone Apartments. All the way there I told myself that it didn't mean anything and I was overreacting. But I didn't believe myself.

I pulled up to the building and left my car on the sidewalk. Let them tow it. Inside, the lobby was quiet and the security desk was vacant and I knew that everything was wrong. I drew my gun and peeked over the desk. Nothing but an empty chair. A sheet of paper on the desk said *Back in 10 minutes*. I walked around the desk and looked under it. On the floor, nestled deep under the desk, Major Sylvester lay curled with a confused look on his face and a bullet hole in his forehead.

Shit. The answer was obvious but I went up anyway. I let myself into Bob's apartment with Major Sylvester's passkey.

Bob Loniski lay naked in the bathtub and he couldn't have been more dead. There was a lot of blood. His face was frozen terror and his body was not something you could look at for long. It had been done with a knife and they'd taken their time with him. They'd even cut off his dick. Was it a message, or did they just send a sadist? No way to know. *Shit*.

Kathie was in the living room, slumped facedown on a heap of location scouting reports spread across the coffee table. She still half sat on the couch where I'd watched television with Bob a hundred years ago. I lifted her by the shoulders. She'd been shot twice—once directly through the heart and once in the forehead. Her body was somewhat stiff and her skin was cold. Blood pooling was also evident, but not complete. I'm not a forensics expert, but judging by the degree of rigor mortis and livor mortis, I guessed that she had been dead between five and eight hours.

I called Mike Angelo. "It's Dudgeon," I said. "I'm at the Balderstone Apartments." I gave him the address and apartment number.

"Good for you," he said.

"Mike, I'm up to my ass in dead people."

Mike sighed hard into the phone. "Wonderful."

"Security guard under the desk in the lobby, Bob Loniski and his assistant up here in the apartment."

"Hang tight and don't touch anything."

"Sorry Mike," I said, "no time for that. I never called you—this was an anonymous phone tip." I hung up on him and got the hell out of there.

———

I called Terry from the car and got his voice mail. "This is an anonymous tip and you don't recognize my voice," I said. "Bob's dead. His assistant's dead. Security guard's dead. Balderstone Apartments. That should get you back on page one, asshole."

I hit Lake Shore Drive and headed north. But I wasn't seeing the road. I was seeing Bob, in his final indignity. His final horror. And I was seeing myself in the Old Town Ale House, drinking with Delwood Crawley.

There was no way around it. I'd been playing media-spin poker against Al Diskin while someone was cutting Bob to ribbons. I'd taken my eye off the ball and Bob had paid for my pride with his life.

Goddamnit, Dudgeon, don't be an idiot. The job was over. Diskin ended it and Bob agreed with him. Not your fault, you can't be responsible for the decisions of other adults . . . No, you're rationalizing, I should've been there. Bob was weak and I shouldn't have given him the option . . . What were you gonna do, kidnap him for his own safety? . . . Maybe, if that's what was required . . . Come on, be reasonable . . . No, you be reasonable. I should've known when there was no answer at the production office this morning but I was more interested in showing Diskin up . . . That's not fair, you didn't know anything this morning . . . Bullshit. I had a feeling and I should've paid attention to it . . .

Speeding up Lake Shore Drive and arguing with the voices in my head, I felt unlike myself. I felt disconnected. I felt cruel. I wanted to kill something. Something inside was about to snap.

The gun was in my hand, and my hand pointed it at the security guard.

My voice said, "We're going up to see Gloria Simpson. If you do anything I don't like, I'm going to shoot you in the face."

"Yes, sir," said the security guard.

As we rode up in the elevator, the guard made noises about being from Greece, supporting his family in America, a daughter in high school and not wanting to die.

I told him to shut up. I took the handcuffs off his belt and cuffed his hands behind his back.

Then we stood at the door of Gloria Simpson's condo. The guard asked me what I wanted him to do. My head hurt and my ears rang and I swallowed hard. For a moment, he almost became human to me. But the moment passed.

"Tell her there's a gas leak and you need to check the apartment," I said.

I knocked and stood to the side and the guard did as instructed and the door opened. I sent him tumbling through the doorway and went in after him and swung the door shut behind us. Gloria Simpson stood with a drink in one hand and her mouth open.

I pointed the gun at her. She didn't faint.

"Why don't you put that away and join me in a drink," she said. "I make a terrific Brandy Alexander."

"Shut up," I said.

The guard was still lying facedown on the deep pile carpet. I told him to stay where he was, and he did. I told Gloria Simpson to sit on the couch, and she did. So far, so good. I stood where I could keep an eye on both of them and I kept the gun on her.

"I'm going to ask you a few questions," I said, "and your life depends on giving me honest answers."

Gloria Simpson sipped her drink. "I'm sure it does," she said.

"Is there anyone else in the apartment?"

"No. Just you, me and Captain America down there," she said, nodding toward the guard lying on the carpet.

"You're positive," I said. "Because if someone enters the room, the first thing I'm gonna do is shoot you."

"I understood you perfectly well the first time."

"I want the files," I said.

"You killed my brother," said Gloria Simpson.

"Self-defense."

"I have no doubt." She sipped her Brandy Alexander again, then licked the creamy drink from her upper lip. The cop on the phone was right—she was a knockout. "I don't blame you, really," she continued. "I blame Paul. He never should've put Frankie in over his head."

"We're agreed on that," I said. But I didn't believe her. She was playing me as best she could under adverse circumstances.

"I'd love to see Paul get what he deserves," said Gloria Simpson. "Now, I can get you a sit-down with Don Amodeo, and you can make a deal. The boss will take care of Paul. You see, the files won't help you. But I can."

The throbbing in my head was getting worse, and I was becoming disconnected again. "Just give me the files," I said.

"The files won't save you," she said.

My head pounded and I was dizzy and felt like I was watching myself from above. I heard myself say, "Just get the files."

"Mr. Dudgeon, you must listen to reason—"

My right arm flew in an arc and the barrel of my gun caught Gloria Simpson on the cheekbone. She swayed sideways on the couch and dropped her drink. The security guard on the carpet started whimpering.

I'd never hit a woman, and I didn't like it. I didn't like myself. I didn't want to be there. I didn't want to be anywhere. I wanted to disappear.

Gloria Simpson sat up and wiped the blood from her cheek. She looked at me and her face had changed. In her eyes I saw the realization that her life could end right now. She looked down at the blood on her hand and back to me, and her face changed again. The fear had become hatred. "I bet you enjoyed that," she said.

"No more talk," I said. "The files. Now."

CHAPTER THIRTEEN

There were forty-one files in all, stuffed into a leather duffel bag that I'd taken from Gloria Simpson. The bag sat beside me on the passenger seat. I didn't glance at it more than two or three times a minute as I headed south on Columbus Drive.

I needed some time. But time was not on my side. I called Special Agent Holborn's cell phone.

"Ray Dudgeon," I said.

"Jesus, Dudgeon. You are in a world of shit," said Holborn. "Your buddy Angelo put an APB out on you. You better turn yourself in."

"I've got Tortelli's files," I said. "How soon can you be next to a fax machine?"

"I'm five minutes from my office. I've got a fax on my desk."

"Call me when you're standing next to it," I said, and gave him my cell number. I broke the connection and found a small copy shop and parked outside.

Flipping through the first few files, I stopped at the name of a high-ranking state legislator. Inside the folder was a detailed report covering the history of his association with Tortelli and company.

Dates and times of meetings, votes influenced, and some photographs of a young, leather-clad woman flogging the naked lawmaker. That should get everyone's attention. There was also a small digital videotape and an audiocassette but I couldn't fax those, so I left them in the car.

The Korean woman running the copy shop explained that customers were not allowed to operate the fax machine, but that she'd be happy to send anything I needed. I opened my jacket enough to accidentally expose the gun on my hip, palmed my wallet and flashed my badge at her for a nanosecond. The badge could have said *Dog Catcher* and it wouldn't have made a difference. She stepped aside and I went behind the counter. We stood for a long minute, smiling awkwardly at each other until my phone rang.

"Dudgeon."

"I'm in my office," said Holborn, and gave me the fax number. I punched it into the machine and put the pages into the sheet feeder and hit "send." I collected the pages as the machine spat them out, dropped a ten-spot on the counter and headed back to the car. As I turned the ignition over, I heard Holborn say, "Holy crap," on the other end of the phone.

"That's just a taste," I said as I pulled away from the curb. "I've got lots of 'em."

"You'd better come in, Ray," said Holborn.

"Not bloody likely," I said. "Not until I can look through the files and figure out what's what." I turned onto Jackson and headed deeper into the Loop, where I could get lost in the crowds.

"We can look through them together," said Holborn.

"Nothing personal," I said, "but I can't trust anybody right now. Hell, there could be a file on you, for all I know."

"Don't be a dickhead, Ray."

"Can't help it," I said, "it just comes naturally."

Holborn didn't laugh. "So how do you want to play this?" he said.

"Call Angelo and get that APB lifted," I said, "then we'll talk."

I hung up and then called the *Chicago Chronicle* and asked for Sid

Schwartzman on the fourth floor, hoping he hadn't retired since I last saw him.

Sid's job at the *Chronicle* was to listen to the scanners. He monitored the police, fire and aircraft frequencies and directed reporters to hotspots of breaking news around the city. Most of the younger *Chronicle* staffers were nervous around Sid—he was the longest-serving *Chronicle* employee and he was very old, which gave him license to be permanently cranky. But there was no bite behind his bark and we'd gotten along fine when I worked there.

After listening to a Muzak version of "The Night They Drove Old Dixie Down," I heard Sid cough three times into the receiver. Just the coughs—he didn't say hello.

"Ears," I said, "it's Ray Dudgeon."

"Hey, kid." Another cough. "You locked up yet?"

"Not yet. That's why I'm calling. I'm expecting the APB to be lifted anytime—"

"Yeah, that'll happen when the pope converts to Judaism," barked Sid.

"Wanna bet?"

"Betting is for suckers."

"I need to know when it's clear," I said.

"Gimme your number. I'll call you when I hear the good news." He still didn't believe me, but that didn't matter. I gave him my cell number.

"Thanks, Ears."

"Yeah, okay." Sid coughed twice and hung up.

I considered my options. There would be cops stationed at my apartment and my office. Cops, or worse. What I needed was a safe place to go through the files. A quiet place to get my head together and figure my next move.

And then I thought of Gravedigger.

Gravedigger and I were born in the same year and grew up on the same street and had been friends since we'd lived in diapers. As a child,

Gravedigger had a normal name—Mark Tindall. When we were four years old, Mark hit me over the head with a hammer. A few years later, he taught me how to climb up on the school roof. He also taught me how to throw a baseball, how to pick a lock and how to stand up to authority. In many ways, Mark was my older brother.

Mark looked like a little blond monkey and he was a lot smaller than the rest of the kids our age. But he was the toughest sonofabitch in the schoolyard. He fought often and always won. He even fought kids a year ahead of us and he beat them too.

In the sixth grade, there was a new kid in school who decided that he had to fight his way to respect. He started midway up the totem pole and fought his way higher. Since I was not near the top, my turn came after only a few kids. I was afraid, but chickening out would be worse than taking a beating. So I accepted the challenge at recess and we duked it out behind the school portable at the end of the day, with spectators cheering all around us.

The fight commenced, and in no time, blood was dripping from my nose and my lip was bloody and swollen. But I pressed on. And it turned out that, against an opponent who fought back hard, the new kid wasn't as tough as he seemed.

The kid went down on his back and I straddled his stomach and pummeled his face. I hated it. I yelled at him to call *Uncle* and I kept on hitting him, wondering why it was taking so long. Finally, the new kid called *Uncle* and cried. I got off of him and the other kids crowded around me, cheering and laughing and backslapping. I'd maintained my position in the schoolyard hierarchy. That stuff matters to a kid.

A teacher arrived on the scene and hauled us both down to the principal's office. In those days, *he started it* was a perfectly valid defense and the principal was not oblivious to what the new kid had been up to. So I was warned to stay out of trouble but I was not disciplined. The new kid was suspended for three days.

When the new kid returned from his suspension, Mark Tindall was waiting in the schoolyard. Mark walked straight up to the kid and told him to *put 'em up*. They fought. Mark beat the hell out of the new kid, and when the kid fell to the asphalt, Mark stomped repeatedly on his head. As the kid lay unconscious, Mark shouted a warning never to mess with his best friend. Everyone in the schoolyard heard it. The new kid was sent to the hospital in an ambulance and Mark was suspended for a month.

And that's the way it was with Mark. For the rest of us at that age, fighting meant bloody noses and black eyes and calling *Uncle*. For Mark, it meant breaking bones.

Mark had never lost a schoolyard fight and after that incident nobody would fight him. But he showed up occasionally with a black eye or a split lip, and a variety of bruises. He told exciting stories about fighting tough kids from the housing projects and we believed him. We later learned that it was his father who caused the injuries. When he was twelve, he showed up with a broken arm. That was finally enough for Mark's mother, and his father moved out of the house for good.

Mark and I got into a lot of trouble together, but more times than not, he could talk us out of it. Adults did not intimidate him and he could talk his way out of almost anything. He was smarter than me. He was, in fact, the smartest kid I ever met.

When I was thirteen, my mother died and I moved to Georgia to live with my grandparents. At nineteen, I came back to Chicago to attend college.

While I'd been living in Georgia, Mark had dropped out of high school and worked at a series of dead-end jobs while staying drunk much of the time. Whenever a boss reprimanded him for calling in sick or showing up late, Mark would tell the boss to fuck off and go looking for another job. We had little in common, beyond the shared adventures of childhood. We got together occasionally, but after we exhausted the *remember when* stories, our relationship became awkward and we saw each other less often.

Six years later, I heard that Mark had finally given in to his anger and was working as a mercenary in Africa. He was gone a couple of years, ended up spending six months in a Kenyan prison and finally returned to Chicago, in very bad shape. And for some reason, he called my number.

I let Mark live with me while he recovered, to the extent that recovery was possible. In the ensuing months, his body healed but his mind was still a mess. We had a lot of all-night amateur psychoanalysis sessions, fueled by bourbon and friendship. It was a rough time and I fully expected to come home from the *Chronicle* one day and find him dead by his own hand. Instead, I came home one day and found a polite note thanking me for my generosity and wishing me well.

Mark got a job at Mount Pleasant Cemetery and the job somehow helped him make sense of his life. He rose to the rank of head groundskeeper and, in a bizarre move, legally changed his name to Gravedigger Peace. He would never again answer to the name Mark Tindall.

I pushed these memories from my mind as I drove through the main gates of Mount Pleasant Cemetery and past silent fields of snowcapped tombstones, to the old stone building that served as the groundskeeper's residence.

Gravedigger opened the door and grinned out of one side of his mouth—a familiar expression that made him look every bit like the kid in the schoolyard so many years ago. He shook my hand. His hair was still blond, still cut short and still curly. And despite his thick Aran sweater, I could see that he was still compact and muscular. No middle-aged spread on Gravedigger Peace.

The residence was simply furnished, warm and comfortable. Gravedigger made instant coffee and we sat in the living room. It had been a few years, but the awkwardness of earlier times was absent and it didn't take long to catch up.

After the preliminaries were over, I cut to the chase. "I need a place to stay, Gravedigger," I said.

"I've read the papers," he said. "You can stay here as long as you want. The couch is a pullout." He stood and got a twelve-gauge pump action Mossberg 500 from the coat closet. "Anybody wants to fuck with you, they'll have to get through me first."

"I don't think anyone will find me here," I said.

"If they do, they better bring friends," said Gravedigger Peace. It wasn't boasting; it was a statement of fact. Gravedigger only stood five foot six but he was a battle-hardened soldier. And if he found peace living in the cemetery, he could still tap into the deep reservoir of rage that lives beneath the surface calm.

His reaction hadn't surprised me. In fact I'd expected it. We had a strange friendship and years would pass without contact between us but if I ever needed someone to break me out of a Mexican jail, Gravedigger Peace was the only person I'd call. Terry was my closest friend, and he'd work diplomatic and legal channels to try to secure my release, but I knew the limits of what he would do and what he was capable of doing. Some friends would have good intentions and offer little more than sympathetic noises. While they were busy wringing their hands and fretting, Gravedigger would load up and come break my ass out, pure and simple. And I would do the same for him. It was that kind of friendship. I didn't understand it, but I knew it was there.

Gravedigger left to take care of his groundskeeping duties and I made another mug of instant coffee and got to work. I opened Gloria Simpson's leather duffel bag and stacked the files on the kitchen table.

Each file folder had a name written on the index tab. Some I didn't recognize, but many I did. Too many. It read like a Who's Who of Illinois politics. As I moved the files from one side of the table to the other, I transcribed the names and job titles into my notebook.

Three Chicago aldermen, four Cook County Circuit Court judges, two federal judges, two assistant state's attorneys, one Illinois state senator, two Illinois state representatives, a high-ranking aide in the governor's office, a mayoral aide, a senior customs inspector, three Catholic priests, a handful of Illinois state troopers and Cook County sheriff's deputies and a few government administrators. There was a lot of clout in those files.

And then there were the Chicago cops. Only a half dozen. Not too bad, considering that there are almost fourteen thousand cops in the CPD. Of course there was no file on Mike Angelo, but two of the six were captains. The first deputy would decide Mike's request for a protection detail for Bob Loniski, if it got that far. But either of the two captains could have derailed his request along the way.

I found myself wanting to know which one had done it, but even if I knew, what the hell would I do about it? *Just give them over to the feds and wash your hands of it, Dudgeon. It won't bring Bob back.*

I sipped my now-cold coffee and moved on. The next file was a whopper—a real, live member of the U.S. Senate. Yikes.

But it was the last file that felt like a kick in the gut. Written indelibly in block letters was the name Vinnie Cosimo. Damn. Vinnie. I don't know why it hit me so hard. Twice I looked away and back again, perhaps hoping the name on the index tab would change. It didn't.

I opened the file. Like the others, this one contained a mini-DV videocassette and a dozen eight-by-ten color stills that looked like frame-grabs from the video. In the photos, a woman was giving Vinnie a blow job. I'd seen Vinnie's wife, Mary, in a picture that he kept in his wallet. The woman in these photos was not Mary.

I turned the photos facedown and read the accompanying report. Three meeting dates were detailed and each had a noted conclusion. The first said *won't play*. The second said *loyal to G—be careful*. The third said *some help on outsiders*.

Some help on outsiders. So it was Vinnie who had dropped a dime on me while I was having dinner with Terry at Ville d'Este. He'd tried to warn me but, still, it was Vinnie who set me up. Damn.

I put Vinnie's file aside and went through the others in detail. I didn't have a DV deck handy, so I couldn't screen the videos, which was probably for the best. The frame-grab photo enlargements were more than I wanted to see anyway.

Vinnie had broken his marriage vows but at least he was into normal sex. The others were something else, altogether. Pedophiles, piss-drinkers, shit-eaters, infantilists, sadists, self-mutilators and a surprising number of masochistic discipline freaks . . . the photos made for a catalog of neurotic sexual fetishes. I'm no Sigmund Freud and I didn't bother to try to make sense of it.

With the exception of the pedophiles, I'm really not concerned with what turns other people's cranks. None of my business. But the reports made clear the pernicious nature of their sexual peccadilloes. By exposing themselves to blackmail, these civil servants had breached the public trust and their subsequent actions represented all manner of public corruption.

Cops had sabotaged investigations and tipped off Tortelli about impending vice raids, judges had made egregious rulings, state's attorneys had tanked airtight prosecutions, legislators had held up pending bills in committee and voted as their Outfit masters dictated, and various government officials had taken part in money laundering, fraud and other criminal activities. The list of their sins was long and the evidence was all right there in the files.

In addition to the videos, most of the files contained audiocassettes. I listened to portions of each on Gravedigger's little stereo. Tortelli had recorded conversations between Frank DiMarco and his victims, detailing much of the corruption ahead of time and the payoffs later.

Tortelli was a smart bastard. The audiotapes firmly established that the public officials were taking orders from the underworld and that they'd accepted money for services, leaving no wiggle-room whatsoever. And it was always DiMarco's voice on the tapes, never Tortelli's.

My cell phone rang and I answered it.

"Like I said, betting is for suckers," said Sid Schwartzman.

"They lifted the APB?"

"Wouldn't have believed it, if I hadn't heard it myself. I guess you're in the clear."

"Thanks Ears."

"Yeah, okay." He hung up.

I turned my attention back to the files. Seven of the blackmail targets had not engaged in any form of public corruption. Not yet, anyway. One was a pedophile. I put his file on the large stack. But what to do with the other six? Their screwed-up sex lives were none of my business and I wasn't about to bring them to ruin on the basis of what they *might have done* if I hadn't got their files. I did have their files and they were now free of Tortelli's blackmail scam. That was what mattered.

I phoned them and offered them a choice. I could pass their files on to the FBI, who would prosecute Tortelli for extortion, or I could simply destroy the files and they could get on with their lives. All six wanted me to destroy the files, which was no surprise. A few of them had a difficult time accepting the fact that they were now free of Tortelli, but they got it eventually. Two of them actually broke down in tears and one offered me money, which I declined.

Sifting through the large stack, I selected two files that suited my purposes. One was the U.S. senator, Stanley Roach. The other was a federal appellate-court judge named David Miller. These two files were the key to my survival and I hoped that I'd chosen wisely.

I checked my phone messages. Reporters were still calling and there was a message from Sasha Klukoff saying that my car was ready. The fact that there was no message from Jill still bugged me and the fact that it still bugged me, bugged me even more.

Gravedigger returned, shook new snow from his pea coat and removed his watch cap.

"I need to burn these," I said, holding up the six files of the blackmail victims I'd called earlier. "And I need to hide the rest."

Gravedigger didn't ask why. "Get your coat," he said.

The sun was down and snowflakes danced in the beam of the flashlight as Gravedigger and I crunched through the snow to the cemetery's incinerator. Gravedigger brought the thing to life and when the fire was raging, I tossed the six files into the flames. We watched the fire consume the files and Gravedigger pushed the iron door shut with the butt end of his shotgun and we trudged across the lawn to a small family mausoleum that stood about twenty yards from Gravedigger's residence. Engraved in granite above the mausoleum's door was the name Andersen.

I aimed the flashlight for Gravedigger as he selected the appropriate key and removed the lock from the heavy wrought-iron gate. He pulled the gate open and its old hinges creaked like in a horror movie. A lesser detective might have found it creepy, but I don't believe in ghosts.

Inside, there were two granite crypts. A four-foot crucifix hung on the wall facing the door. Under the crucifix was a brass plaque that identified one of the occupants as Mr. Alfred Andersen—born in 1878 and died in 1921 and now dwelling in the loving embrace of Jesus Christ, Our Lord. Below Alfred's message, there was an empty space on the plaque.

"Poor old Alfred died of TB," said Gravedigger. "His wife was sick with it too, and he had this place built so they could spend eternity together. But instead of following him to the grave like a dutiful wife should, she had the nerve to recover. Then, add insult to injury, she marries some rich guy from Cleveland. I suppose she's buried with Husband Number Two." He pointed at the crypt to my left. "Anyway she never came back, so that one's empty. No kids, no visitors. Poor old lonely Alfred."

I wondered how many people would visit Bob Loniski's grave, and for how many years.

Gravedigger used a crowbar to shift the lid of the empty crypt. I dropped the duffel bag inside and we closed it up again.

Gravedigger made Kraft Dinner with sliced wieners stirred in, and we sat at the kitchen table and drank a bottle of cheap red wine with our meal. He told me about some of the prominent Chicagoans he'd recently buried and I told him about my trip to California, and about my failed relationship with Jill.

After dinner, Gravedigger put a Bob Marley cassette into the stereo and we sat in the living room and smoked cigarettes and drank instant coffee with bourbon in it. The music was good and the bourbon was warm and the conversation flowed freely.

"I don't drink like I used to," said Gravedigger, after refilling our mugs, "but after work is done for the day . . . I like a few before bed."

"Me too," I said. We looked at each other for a moment and Gravedigger shrugged.

"It's weird, Ray," he said. "I never figured you'd get yourself into this kind of jam, people gunning for you. I don't get it."

"I didn't plan it that way," I said.

"Well, I gotta call Bullshit on that." He smiled out of one side of his mouth. "You can stop me if you don't want to talk about it."

"It's okay. Say what's on your mind."

"You just always seemed so . . . I don't know . . . together. And no, you didn't plan it this way but you didn't have to do this for a living, as far as that goes. I mean, what are you trying to prove with all this private-eye shit?"

"I'm not trying to prove anything," I said.

"The hell you're not."

"The job isn't like this, most of the time."

"No, but it's bad enough that you can't keep a romance going with a normal woman," he said.

I stubbed my cigarette out in an ashtray. "What about you? Living in a graveyard must be a real draw for the ladies."

"I'm not very good at relationships," said Gravedigger. "Whenever I get desperate I can always go out and pick up a Goth chick—they get off on this place. But it doesn't last. Anyway I'm better off alone. I read a lot, tend to the grounds. I'd make a lousy father and I'm honest enough to realize that I'm fucked up about women. I'm attracted, you know, sexually . . . but I don't really like them, to spend time with."

"You want to do something about that?"

"Hard enough just to stay sane. I've found my place in the world. I'm okay this way."

"Okay."

"But I believe we were talking about you," Gravedigger said.

"Yeah, why is that?" I said. I could feel the alcohol in my system, smoothing out the rough edges. I was a little bit drunk but I wanted more. I reached for the bottle and topped up our drinks. At this point, adding coffee would be mere pretense. From the stereo, Bob Marley was warning me about running away. He said I couldn't run away from myself. Bob Marley was a wise man.

"You could've gone somewhere else," said Gravedigger. "You could've taken a hotel room. But you came here. You knew what you'd get, just like I knew when I came to live with you after Africa."

"I guess."

"So, what is it with you? Why not just live a normal life, like normal people?"

"I don't know," I said.

"Anger," said Gravedigger.

"Not really," I said. "Yeah, maybe . . . some."

"More than some," he said. "You found the body, right?"

I didn't have to ask which body he was talking about. "Yeah, I found it."

"You were just a kid."

"Yeah."

"That would make you angry."

"Sure."

"You know why she did it?"

"Why does anyone?" I said. "I guess she was unhappy."

"She had a thirteen-year-old son to look after."

"I guess that wasn't enough," I said.

CHAPTER FOURTEEN

I awoke feeling foolish and guilty but I couldn't remember the dream that made me feel that way. It skipped around the edges of my consciousness, taunting me. Hard as I tried, I couldn't bring it into focus. The feeling finally receded as I drove to Franz Motorwerks and gave $5,500 to Sasha Klukoff, in exchange for my repaired Shelby.

In addition to the repair work, Sasha had installed a good stereo system, without my having asked. We'd had long discussions and debates about our favorite jazzmen in the past, and the stereo was a thoughtful touch. Sasha charged me for the labor, naturally, but sold me the stereo at cost.

I parked the Shelby on Indiana Avenue and walked around the corner to the entrance of Pearl's Place, on Thirty-ninth Street. Gravedigger was somewhere nearby. He'd insisted on shadowing me and I didn't put up a fight. Tortelli's thugs could be anywhere and it did make me feel better to know that Gravedigger was watching, even though I couldn't see him.

Inside Pearl's Place, I made straight for the buffet and loaded up a plate with some of Chicago's best soul food. Mustard-fried catfish, collards, fried chicken, black-eyed peas and cornbread. Breakfast of Champions.

"If Tortelli doesn't move fast, the cholesterol will get you first." Special Agent Holborn gave my plate a disapproving look as I slid into the booth next to him, across from Mike Angelo and a beautiful black woman I'd never met before.

"Ray Dudgeon, Sergeant Vicki Pickett," said Mike Angelo. I had no idea why Mike had brought her along, but it wasn't my place to ask.

I shook hands with Vicki Pickett and felt the tingle that men sometimes feel when they shake hands with certain women. Her smile said that she was accustomed to having that effect on men, and she liked it.

"Put your tongue back in your mouth," said Mike.

I ignored him and reached into my bag and dropped seven file folders on the table and said, "Show of good faith. Thanks for lifting the pickup order." Mike examined the names on the index tabs and he didn't look happy. "There's a lot more," I said, "but that's all of the CPD, and the State Rep that I faxed you yesterday." I ate while they each looked at the files, then pushed my plate aside. "You'll get the rest soon. In the meantime, if I get arrested, or get dead, they disappear."

"Christ-In-Heaven," said Mike. "Don't fucking *hotdog* us, Ray, I'm not your biggest fan right now." His eyes were blood red but he seemed completely sober and I supposed he'd been up all night with the fallout from the Balderstone Apartments massacre. The image of Bob's mutilated body returned and I pushed it away, with some effort. Major Sylvester and Kathie each made a brief appearance and I shooed them away too.

"We're not interested in prosecuting people for visiting prostitutes," said Holborn. "Unless there's serious public corruption involved, we view these people as victims, period."

"Listen to the tapes," I said, "and read through the files. You've got a boatload of public corruption."

"What about the other files?" said Holborn.

"All of them. Nobody's a victim here." I didn't see any reason to mention the files I'd burned.

"And these are all the Chicago cops?" asked Mike.

"Yeah."

"Okay, then," Holborn said to Mike. "We'll work with your IA guys on these, the others we'll take care of ourselves."

"That's more than okay with me," said Mike. "I've got enough shit to deal with. Just keep me in the loop, so I'm not in for any unpleasant surprises."

"Of course," said Holborn.

Mike picked up the CPD files and looked at them again, skipping the photos this time and reading the reports in detail. "Fuckin' assholes," he said.

"Mike, listen," I said, "about yesterday . . ." Mike held up a hand and turned to Vicki Pickett.

"Don't look at me," she said with a twinkle in her eye. "I'm not even here."

Mike held Holborn's eyes for a few seconds, then turned his glare on me. "I got an anonymous phone tip yesterday," he said. "But since you weren't there, you wouldn't know anything about that, would you?"

"No."

"Besides," he continued, "I read the *Chronicle* this morning. You were busy playing footsie with that faggot from England. Nice priorities you got, Ray."

I didn't look at Holborn but I doubt I'd have seen any reaction.

Mike leaned forward and planted his hands on the Formica tabletop. His voice was quiet. "The feds seem to have some use for you, so I'm playing nice. But you've exhausted my goodwill and if you fuck around with me in future, I will be displeased." He stood and left the restaurant and Sergeant Pickett followed after him.

I moved to the other side of the table as a waitress cleared the plates and refilled our glasses with iced tea. Holborn put a paper bag on the table and slid it across to me. Inside was my .45.

"You might want this," he said.

"Thanks."

"Thank Angelo," he said. "He's a good cop, you know."

"I know."

"And he's right to be pissed at you."

"I know."

Holborn sighed and stuffed the files into his briefcase. "It's gonna be a real shitstorm," he said. "When do I get the rest of them?"

"The feds have a use for me?"

He shrugged. "We managed to establish electronic surveillance on one of the hired guns I told you about. For a while, anyway. He melted this morning. But while we had him, he called home, said he's going dancing tonight, and he'll be back in K.C. in the morning."

"So the hit on Greico is tonight," I said.

"That's what we think."

"What do you expect me to do about that?"

"Well I don't expect you to pull a John Wayne," said Holborn. "But maybe there's an IBM you'd like to notify." "IBM" was a slang cop term for any member of organized crime. It stood for Italian Business Man.

"Why are you taking such an interest in his well-being?"

Holborn thought for a minute. "It's like this," he said. "There's bad guys and then there's Bad Guys. I'd like to put them all away but I know that's not going to happen. So we focus on the psychopaths and the amateurs. Nobody gets a free pass, but those who run a professional shop and keep the violence mostly in-house . . . you get rid of them and sometimes you end up with something much worse."

"And Tortelli's worse than Greico," I said.

"Like night and day," said Holborn. "But it goes beyond that. If Tortelli gets away with this, who knows where it ends. Right now we've got stable leadership in the Outfit, and we didn't have that for years. Biagio Amodeo is a blessing compared to the gang of morons and nut-jobs who came before him.

"The last real pro we had before Amodeo was the Big Tuna . . . Tony Accardo. He was the real deal. After the Big Tuna it was a nightmare for a while. But Amodeo's been a solid boss. He's not as bright as Accardo was, but he's predictable, he has a code of conduct and he keeps his Capos in line. And his son is even better."

"Chris."

"Yeah. Twenty years ago, Biagio sent Chris to Northwestern and the kid got an MBA, for Christ's sake. He's smarter than your average bear. And he'll be taking over soon, if Tortelli doesn't fuck things up. Actually Chris is pretty much running the show now, and he's been making a lot of upperworld investments."

"Don't tell me you think they're going legit," I said.

"Never." Holborn drank down his iced tea and signaled the waitress for the check. "But the more upperworld interests they have, the more important it is to keep the underworld controlled and professional. And then the citizens don't complain, and we all go home happy.

"Like I said, nobody gets a free pass but you pick your battles. That's why your buddy Angelo wouldn't be any good in the OCD—he's a good cop but he doesn't pick his battles, he just wants to go after everybody."

"Maybe that's a virtue," I said.

"Yeah, very nice, but we're not in the Virtue business," said Holborn. "We're in the putting-bad-guys-away business. We make practical choices and we win more than we lose. We chase Virtue, and we end up with our dicks in our hands."

I considered sharing Benvenuto Cellini's thoughts on Virtue with Holborn, then decided against it. But I think Mike would've understood. Mike *was* in the Virtue business, which is probably why I liked him better than I liked Holborn. I used to be in the Virtue business too. Holborn wasn't a bad guy, but he was a little too mature for my liking, if you define maturity as the willingness to compromise. Anyway, his practical reasons for warning Greico were solid enough and it was a nice bonus that he could offer moral justification. But for me, it was about survival. If Tortelli ascended to the throne, I was as dead as Duluth on a Sunday night.

"I'll warn Greico," I said. "Anything else you need?"

"Just the files," said Holborn.

"Give me a day or two," I said. "You'll get them."

———

I pulled the Shelby into a gas station and popped the hood and checked the oil—a signal for Gravedigger to surface. Within a minute, a brown pickup truck pulled up to the pump behind me and Gravedigger hopped out, wearing a long Australian oilskin overcoat.

"Nice wheels," he said.

"Thanks."

"That a '68?"

"Uh-huh."

"Supercharged?"

"Sure is," I said.

During this exchange of banality, we scanned over each other's shoulders. We had no company, and we nodded that fact to each other.

"I need to get into my office," I said, and told him the address. "You go ahead and open my window if it's clear."

"No problem," said Gravedigger as I handed him the office key. "If it isn't clear, you want me to clear it?"

"Negative," I said. "Just get out. If the window's closed, I won't come near."

The window was open. I headed up to the thirteenth floor where Gravedigger was waiting in my office.

"Nice digs," he said.

"Everybody seems to think so."

Gravedigger reached under his coat, behind his back, and withdrew the shotgun and then stretched his back. "I'll wait in the hallway."

"Keep it out of sight," I said. The shotgun disappeared under the coat and Gravedigger stepped out into the hallway.

I always kept a suit in my office, just in case I was expecting fancy visitors, and now I changed into it and shoved the tie into a pocket. It was no match for the new suit I'd bought at the Beverly Hills Hotel, but I couldn't risk another visit to my apartment. Fashion be damned.

I took my pistol from the paper bag, threaded the horsehide holster onto my belt and slid the .45 into its familiar position. It made me feel only slightly better.

I pulled back the rug and opened the floor safe under my desk and pulled out $17,000 in cash. It was my life's savings, which probably said something significant about my life. But I had neither the time nor the inclination to ponder the significance. I closed the safe and took a good look around the office. The oak desk . . . the Declaration of Independence . . . the old map of Chicago before the Great Fire . . . the current map of my city. If Tortelli came out on top tonight, I'd never see this office again. I'd never see Chicago again. I was fond of the place, but I had to balance that against my fondness for breathing.

I picked up *The Autobiography of Benvenuto Cellini* and a framed five-by-seven photograph of my grandfather and put them in my bag. Ernie Banks smiled at me from the desktop.

"Tell me, Ernie," I said, "and be honest. Am I ever gonna see you again?" I flicked the bill of Ernie's bobblehead baseball cap. His head bobbled, but not straight up and down. Nor did it go side to side. Instead, it bobbled around in a circle. Ernie Banks was undecided.

"Can't blame you," I said. "I don't know either."

Vinnie Cosimo lived in a third-floor walk-up in Wrigleyville. It was the wrong neighborhood for a Wiseguy but Vinnie Cosimo was a reluctant Wiseguy, at best.

In the alley behind the building, I picked the lock on the gate and climbed the wooden staircase, which led to a porch outside Vinnie's kitchen. I knocked on the kitchen door and called his name.

Vinnie appeared in the doorway, wearing navy-blue sweatpants and a white undershirt. A layer of perspiration covered his skin and engorged veins showed on his muscular arms.

"Hey Ray. Nice to see ya," he said. "I was just working out, I didn't hear the doorbell."

"Why aren't you at work?" I said.

"Day off." He stepped back from the door. "Come on in."

"Sick day?"

"No man, it's my day off. What's wrong?"

I passed Vinnie and sat down at the kitchen table. "Where's Mary?" I said.

"Visiting her mom," said Vinnie. "What's wrong with you, Ray? You're makin' me nervous." He wasn't lying.

I put his file folder on the kitchen table. He sat across from me and I opened his file and spun it around to face him. I lit a cigarette and waited.

Vinnie stared down at the file for a long time. He didn't flip through the photos. He didn't read the report. He just sat and stared at the top photo. His neck and cheeks turned red and he cleared his throat.

"Sorry Ray," he said.

"But why, Vince? Mary's a beautiful woman," I said.

"You've never been married," said Vinnie.

"No."

"You think it's gonna be something, and it's something else," he said. He stood and got a couple of beers from the fridge, handed me one and sat back down. He took a long pull from the bottle. "When Mary and I were dating, she was saving herself, she said. Okay with me, I said. I was a football star and there was plenty of girls at the college to show me a good time. I could wait.

"Then, right after we get married, her father dies. She just wasn't feeling sexy right then, she says. Okay with me. I wait. Then her mother gets a heart condition and needs a lot of looking after and it's a stressful time for Mary. Okay with me," he said bitterly.

He cleared his throat again. "I love her, you know. And it's not like we don't ever have sex. We do. But not as much as I need. And it's me on top or her on top, and that's it. At first she says, 'Be patient, I'm new at this, I just have to get used to the idea of oral sex.' Okay, I'm patient. I'm the most patient fucking guy you ever met. Then one day I realize, it ain't never gonna be like it was with all those other girls. She'll do it, sort of, but she ain't never gonna like it. And that makes it no fun. It just ain't never gonna be like it was."

Vinnie drained the bottle. "And then there's Frankie. Sometimes we go out drinking after work and all the time Frankie's offering me a freebie with his girls and I'm always saying no. And finally one night, I think, 'Shit, I've been patient long enough. I just want a fucking blow job.' What the hell is so wrong with that?" He tossed the empty bottle across the room, into a garbage can. It didn't break. "Why can't Mary just like it, the way most girls do, you know? It's supposed to be fun."

"Okay, Vince," I said. I excused myself to the back porch and smoked my cigarette and drank my beer. Vinnie came out on the porch and leaned his massive forearms on the railing beside me and we watched the sky turn red, blood clouds silhouetting the church steeples and low-rise apartment buildings west of Wrigleyville.

"Now what do we do?" he asked.

There was a question. I couldn't see any point in turning Vinnie's file over to the feds. Yes, he dropped a dime on me to DiMarco, but he didn't owe me loyalty. He owed loyalty to Greico and as far as I knew, he stayed loyal even under pressure. He was trying to save his marriage and so he tossed DiMarco a fish. An outsider. Me. And then he took the risk of warning me—a risk he was not obligated to take. He was, I thought, a good guy in a bad jam. And he wanted out of the Outfit. He wanted to live on the level. Maybe if I could help him get out, then he'd owe me some loyalty. Or maybe I was giving him too much credit, but sometimes you have to trust your instincts. Sometimes you have to take a leap of faith.

"It's up to you, Vince," I said. "The file's yours. I'm going to warn Greico. You can come, or not."

"Warn him what?"

He really didn't know. *Sometimes a leap of faith is all it takes.* "Tortelli's been assembling a squad," I said. "There's a hit going down on Greico tonight."

"What the fuck?! Why didn't you say so?" Vinnie dashed into the apartment and returned a minute later wearing jeans and a sweater. He held the file folder in one hand and a stainless Colt .357 in the other. "Let's get going," he said.

In the parking lot of Villa d'Este, Vinnie used my Zippo to burn the photos and the report. He pulled the videotape from its casing and burned the tape. Then he burned the file folder and stood staring at the smoldering ashes on the pavement.

"Goddamn," said Vinnie.

"Give it time, Vince."

The sentry stood in his usual position at Johnny Greico's office door. "Whatcha doin' here, Vinnie?" he said.

"We gotta see Mr. Greico," said Vinnie. "It's important."

The sentry turned his hooded eyes on me. "You're Dudgeon, right?" The edges of his mouth turned up slightly, hinting at his opinion of the recently departed Frank DiMarco.

"Right," I said, "I'm Dudgeon."

Vinnie and I waited in the fragrant hallway and I inhaled the kitchen smells. I could never work here and maintain my girlish figure. That sentry must have had an iron will.

Johnny Greico sat at his desk. "You shouldn't a brought him here Vinnie," Greico said.

"Yes, sir. Sorry. But Ray, here, brought me some information," said Vinnie.

"Make it quick."

"Mr. Greico," I said, "Paul Tortelli's been importing some hired guns—"

"I can read," said Greico. "You got something more?"

"Yeah. They're coming for you tonight."

"Says who?"

"Holborn."

"Ah," said Greico. "Special Agent Holborn, of the Famous But Incompetent."

"They intercepted a phone call," I said. "It's tonight."

Greico picked up the telephone receiver and punched a button. "Sal, get in here," he said, and replaced the receiver in its cradle. Then to me, "You think Holborn's jerkin' you around?"

"No."

"He order you to tell me about this?"

"Not exactly, but he knew that I would and he wanted me to."

Johnny Greico nodded but said nothing. Sal entered and closed the door.

"Salvatore," said Greico. "Call in Tommy Two Guns and Sam and Freddie. Take Dom off the floor and put him on the door and put Pietro on the floor. Get Joey, Anthony and Little John back from the yards. Vests for everybody. And get the guns ready."

"Yes sir," said Sal. He glanced in my direction.

"Sometime today would be nice," barked Greico, and Sal left in a hurry.

Greico pushed his chair back from the desk, stood and removed his shirt, and draped it over the back of the chair. From a closet he retrieved a bulletproof vest and slid it on over his undershirt. It didn't quite cover his girth. He reached in vain for the Velcro straps and grunted, "Vinnie, help me with this." Vinnie rushed to Greico's side and got the vest fastened properly. Greico slipped his shirt over the vest and started working on the buttons and gave a small nod in my direction.

"Thanks for the information, kid," he said. "Now get outta here."

Yoshi Inoue lived in a white, ranch-style house in Evanston, just north of Chicago. I rang the sonorous bell and Yoshi's wife, Charmaine, opened the door and welcomed me inside. She had about three inches and thirty-five pounds on Yoshi but she was comfortable with her body and she radiated loveliness.

"Hey, darlin'," Charmaine said, her voice like a New Orleans evening stroll. "Ain't you a sight for sore eyes? Yoshi's in the workshop. Sit yourself down and I'll tell him you're here." And she hip-swished out of the room.

I sat on the tan leather sectional and took in the living room. A mix of Far East and Modern America, it didn't try too hard to be anything in particular but somehow managed to look *inevitable*. I never could figure how some people achieved such perfect harmony in their personal spaces.

Charmaine poked her head into the room. "Coffee?" she said.

"Thank you." She disappeared into the kitchen and I found a copy of that morning's *Chronicle* in a magazine rack and read Terry's page-one story.

It was accurate and it was ugly. I didn't need to read the gory details but I read them anyway. Terry had handled it as well as could be expected. A Continental Pictures spokesman expressed "deep sadness" about the death of Bob Loniski; his assistant Kathie Craig; and the unfortunate doorman at the Balderstone Apartments. Apparently mired in his deep sadness, the spokesman hadn't bothered to learn the doorman's name. Alan Diskin was suffering from emotional shock and could not be reached for comment. Production of *Final Revenge* had been put on hiatus until after Bob's funeral, "so cast and crew could have time to properly grieve the loss of such a valued member of the Continental Pictures family." Where the hell do they get these spokesmen?

I flipped to Delwood Crawley's "Chicago After Dark" column. Crawley gave my piece twice as much ink as I'd asked for, which wasn't surprising given recent events. He hit all the points that I'd given him. Against the strong advice of local PI Ray Dudgeon, film producer Alan Diskin had terminated Bob Loniski's bodyguard detail. Continental Pictures no longer felt that Loniski was in danger. Crawley said that "multiple sources" backed up Dudgeon's dire assessment of the situation. That part was probably a fabrication but I wasn't about to call the *Chronicle* and lodge a complaint. Then Crawley finished with his own personal anguish about "an entirely avoidable tragedy" and he placed the blame squarely on the doorstep of Hollywood. According to Crawley, Loniski's death "put a spotlight upon Hollywood's disconnect from the reality of contemporary American life." Ugh.

Great going, Dudgeon. You covered your ass. You must be very proud.

I looked up from the newspaper and Yoshi smiled at me. "It's just a newspaper," he said, "and tomorrow there will be another one. And another the day after that."

I put the paper away. Yoshi sat next to me and displayed his latest work of art.

"Your passport," he said. It looked exactly like the one issued by Uncle Sam. "You are Austin Clarke. Just like Ray Dudgeon, you were born December twenty-ninth, but two years earlier . . . so you have neatly escaped the trauma of anticipating your fortieth birthday." Yoshi smiled at his little Buddhist joke. "You are now from Savannah, Georgia, instead of Chicago. I chose it because you had only said Georgia and I know that you are familiar with Savannah."

Yoshi flipped to the pages designated for immigration stamps. "Now this is some of my best work. These stamps will pass any inspection but you must memorize the dates and places you've traveled. For those places with which you are unfamiliar, you must study a tourist guidebook. I know that you're a scuba diver, so I've given you trips to Barbados, the Caymans, Bonaire, Trinidad and the Bahamas."

"I must be wealthy."

"Perhaps you simply prioritize travel over other things," said Yoshi. "Passports with too few stamps are suspicious, just as those with too many or those with the wrong countries." He flipped a few pages. "I've also put you in Britain four times in the last six years. You entered through Glasgow. Perhaps you have family there."

"It's perfect," I said.

"Naturally," said Charmaine as she carried a tray into the room and poured coffee into fine Wedgwood cups. "Yoshi's the best, aren't you, baby?" Yoshi smiled back at his wife, and something beautiful passed silently between them. I wondered what it would be like to have that kind of connection to another human being. That kind of union. I'd never felt it, myself, but it looked like something that I could feel. Maybe I'd come close with Jill. Or maybe I was kidding myself.

Charmaine put two sugar cubes and a lot of cream in Yoshi's coffee and I held up my hand to stop her from doing similar violence to mine. She put just a splash of cream into her own and settled on a nearby hassock.

The coffee was strong and had chicory in it and I liked it.

Yoshi went through the routine with my new birth certificate, Social Security card, Georgia driver's license, credit cards and so on. "Only the driver's license is signed," he said. He put a blank piece of paper in front of me and handed me a blue Parker Duofold ballpoint. "Practice."

The signature was easy to master and I repeated it until the sheet was full and the signature consistent. Then I signed all pieces in the appropriate places, using a different pen for each.

"Very good," said Yoshi. "Is this a temporary change of identity, or permanent?"

It was a good question, and the answer was almost certainly tied to Johnny Greico's fate. "I don't know yet," I said.

Yoshi nodded. "If it is permanent, then once you arrive at your destination, you must first open a bank account and rent an apartment. Then you use the birth certificate, Social Security card and an electric bill to apply for a new driver's license. Then use the new driver's license and apply for new credit cards."

"Got it," I said. I handed Yoshi $8,000 cash and stood to go. We shook hands and he wished me well and Charmaine showed me to the door.

"Good luck, honey," she said. "Take care of yourself."

The overnight drive to Washington, D.C., was made easier by music and caffeine pills, both of which I picked up at a truck stop along the highway.

The music selection at most truck stops is limited but I got lucky and found enough CDs to fit a variety of moods. Little Richard, Jimmy Buffett, Al Green and Van Morrison. I was all set.

It was a marvelous night for a moondance, and the Van Morrison album brought back a college romance. Linda Quijada was a dancer. No, not a peeler—a real dancer. She was working on a master's degree in the Columbia College theatre department. Being a journalism major, I was somewhat skeptical about the idea of a master's degree in *dance,* and our relationship started as verbal sparring in the college bookstore, where she worked part-time. The sparring led to friendship and we spent a lot of time together.

I saw her perform with a number of artsy modern dance companies and she was very good, even if I didn't catch some of the deep symbolism involved. Maybe I'd need a master's degree in pretentiousness to get it all.

Still, I had to admit that I was becoming smitten, and friendship quickly led to romance. Van Morrison provided the sound track, but even with Van's help, our romance was not without its challenges.

Linda's upbringing had been decidedly average but for some reason she was in therapy and she found it *liberating.* She thought everyone on earth should be in therapy. That included me. She insisted that I'd never become *fully self-actualized* until I'd been through therapy. She thought that I was in *denial,* which was one of her favorite words. And I thought that she should lighten the hell up and try to enjoy life without analyzing everything to death. Call it a stalemate.

So it ended and we didn't see each other anymore. A few months later, we ran into each other on the sidewalk outside the Fine Arts Building and I suggested lunch, hoping that we might rekindle things. We ate spanikopita at the Artist's Café and Linda told me all about her new boyfriend. He was an English professor and writer of deep poetry.

"He's very sensitive, very open," Linda said. "He's sexually non-functional but he's willing to weep openly about it and we're working on it together, in therapy." She seemed thrilled about that.

It would be easy to conclude that we just weren't right for each other. But I also remembered the exquisite silences. The times together, lying in bed with Van Morrison on the stereo. The feeling, on the edge of sleep, when I couldn't quite make out the end of my body and the beginning of hers. Somewhere in those silences, I'd felt the potential for the kind of union that I saw in Yoshi and Charmaine.

Mawkish doesn't look good on you, Dudgeon.

I ejected the *Moondance* CD and put Little Richard on. And sang "Keep A-Knockin' " at the top of my lungs.

Just before noon, I hit Washington, D.C. Most of the city wore a thin blanket of snow but it was warmer than Chicago and there was a bright sun in the cloudless sky above, so the streets were wet and clear. I parked in an expensive garage on G Street and locked my gun in the glove box.

I walked a block to Union Station and ducked into a men's room, where I dug the tie out of my pocket and put it on. I was calling on a real, live U.S. senator, so I'd better look respectable. Having spent a day in my pocket, the tie was hopelessly wrinkled but the senator was hopelessly corrupt, so I figured we were even.

Near the men's room was a newsstand that carried the *Chicago Tribune*. I bought a paper and, looking for a place to sit, was struck by the magnificence of my surroundings.

Washington's Union Station was a striking example of Beaux Arts architecture at its finest. Daniel Burnham, Chicago's celebrated architect and city planner, had designed it. Burnham was also famous for saying, "Make no little plans, they have no magic to stir men's blood." Probably good advice.

On a bench in the train station's Great Hall, I scanned the *Trib* for any mention of an Outfit battle the night before. There was none. There was mention of a memorial service for Bob Loniski, to be held the following day in Beverly Hills. I'd have to miss it.

I left my paper on the bench and took my little plans to D Street, where I stopped at the Monocle for lunch. I sat at the bar and drank coffee and ate an ambrosial crabcake sandwich. That sandwich alone would have justified the trip to D.C., even if I'd had no other reason for being there.

But I did have another reason. I used the phone behind the bar to call Senator Stanley Roach's office and learned that the senator was expected back from lunch in about forty-five minutes.

The Monocle was a favorite of Washington's top politicos, so I passed the time playing Name That Legislator. I was pretty good by Chicago standards but a Washington schoolboy could've beaten me without breaking a sweat.

I quickly grew tired of the game, settled my bill and went to see The Man.

U.S. senator Stanley Roach couldn't meet with me today. He was always happy to meet with his constituents but he was a very busy man and I'd have to call ahead for an appointment.

So said Alice, the senator's pretty and able receptionist. I dug a business card out of my wallet and on the back I wrote, *I have Tortelli's file. Meet with me now.* Alice took the card in to the senator and two minutes later I was sitting on a six-foot sofa in his expansive office. The sofa had green patterned upholstery and a dark wood frame and Senator Roach sat on a matching sofa across a black marble coffee table.

The office had hunter-green walls and dark wood trim and light green carpeting. One wall sported built-in bookshelves filled with important leather-bound volumes, and the other walls were decorated with diplomas and citations and photographs of the senator with presidents and prominent Illinoisans and fellow Washington lawmakers. Although Stanley Roach was a Republican, the photos were almost evenly split between members of each party, reflecting his reputation as a moderate. Two oil paintings hung on the wall behind the senator's substantial desk. They weren't to my taste, but they looked like big money.

I reached into my breast pocket and pulled out a photo I'd lifted from Roach's file. I handed it across to him and he unfolded it and there was something like pain in his eyes. But he didn't flinch.

"I do not have to apologize to you for my private behavior," he said.

"I'm not looking for an apology, Senator."

"What, exactly, are you looking for?"

"A way to survive," I said.

"I see."

"You read the Chicago papers?"

"Sure."

"So you know what I'm up against."

"But I really don't know how I can help you," he said.

"It's simple," I said. "I have Paul Tortelli's blackmail files, and Tortelli's going down. I'm turning the files over to the FBI."

"But not mine."

"Right."

"If I do what?"

"Call Biagio Amodeo on my behalf."

"I've never even met Amodeo."

"Doesn't matter," I said. "You call Amodeo and tell him who you are. You tell him that you are taking a personal interest in my well-being. You tell him that if anything happens to me, you will make it your mission in life to fuck with his interests. He's a businessman. He'll get the message."

Roach stood and walked to the window. The window looked out over a park. Beyond the park, Daniel Burnham's Union Station shimmered in the sunlight. Maybe Roach was considering the merits of

Beaux Arts architecture. Maybe he was considering the folly of making little plans that have no magic to stir men's blood. Or maybe he was just stalling.

"Senator Roach," I said, "your file is safe. But if anything does happen to me, it'll be released to the CPD and the FBI, and to the press. You really don't have a decision to make."

Roach returned to his place on the sofa. "And if I do this, what then? When do I get the file?"

"Never."

"That's insane," he said. "I'll have only traded masters. Instead of Tortelli, you'll have control of me."

"Yes, but I'm one of the Good Guys," I said with a virtuous smile. "Your file will never see the light of day, so long as I'm alive."

"But anything could happen. You could get hit by a bus."

"I'll look both ways before crossing."

"No. That's not acceptable. I can't live like that."

"Oh come off it, Senator," I said. "Compared to the way you *have* been living? Give me a fucking tax break."

He thought about it. "I don't know," he said. "There's got to be a better way." But his tone told me that he was resigned to it.

I said, "I know that all telephone activity from this office is logged, so I'll give you until midnight tonight to make the call. End of story."

Roach checked his watch. "That's just not possible," he said. "I mean . . . I will make the call, but I need until tomorrow evening. I have the Turkish ambassador in twenty minutes and then I'm on a flight to Cairo with Senators Snyder and Burke for the Foreign Relations Committee. We'll have journalists with us and I don't know when I'll be able to slip away."

It wasn't completely implausible. I told Roach to use his intercom and ask Alice to bring his schedule in. She appeared promptly and read from an agenda. He thanked her and she left the room.

He'd been telling the truth.

"I promise you," Roach said, "I'll make the call by midnight tomorrow . . . midnight at the latest. I just can't say exactly when."

"Okay. Midnight tomorrow. If the call hasn't been made, your file goes to the feds and to the press and you burn with Tortelli. If the call has been made, I'll keep your file under wraps. And in a few years, when the dust has settled, I'll destroy it."

"How will I know when it has been destroyed?"

"You won't."

Getting in to see Judge David Miller was not as easy. Unlike members of Congress, judges of the federal appellate court are under no obligation to make nice with the public, and Miller's secretary seemed to know that. So I was not going to get an appointment without being screened. Not even a telephone appointment.

I drove to the edge of town and checked into a motel. I needed to keep the Austin Clarke name pure, to preserve the option of a permanent change of identity in case things went wrong. So I checked in as Peter Dunbar. I'd brought my laptop with me, and I logged onto the ProInfoTrace Web site and ordered a report on Judge Miller. I called the front desk and asked for a wake-up call four hours later. I hadn't slept in thirty-three hours and I knew that I'd crash soon if I didn't get some shut-eye. Eight hours would be ideal, but four would have to do.

There was a little coffeemaker in the bathroom and the coffee helped clear the cobwebs. I checked my e-mail and read the report on Miller. I called his unlisted number at home and got one of his teenage boys, who volunteered that Miller and his wife were dining at 1789 this evening and would not be back until late.

I surfed the Web and found that 1789 was considered one of the finest restaurants in town. Located in a nineteenth-century Georgetown Federal house, 1789 catered to the well-heeled of Washington and men were required to wear a jacket. The Web site didn't say anything about a tie but I pressed my tie with the motel's complimentary in-room iron, just to be safe.

I spotted Judge Miller and his wife at a table near the fireplace in the John Carroll Room. Miller wasn't dining naked but I had no trouble recognizing him from his sex photos. Like most of us, he looked better in clothes, although perhaps a little less happy.

I made a pretense of scanning the room for someone and, not seeing my imaginary party, retreated back into the foyer. To the right of the entrance was the restaurant's cozy Pub Room. At the back of the pub was a little bar with four bar stools. Sitting on the stool closest to the wall, I could see through a stained-glass window and into the John Carroll Room. Behind me, a picture window looked onto the foyer. Restrooms were upstairs. So if either the judge or his wife paid a visit upstairs, I'd know it.

I ordered a glass of Australian Shiraz and the soft-shell crab tempura appetizer. The bartender was friendly and professional and didn't chastise me for having red wine with seafood. The soft-shell crab was served with wild mushrooms and seaweed salad, and it was perfect. I considered going on an all-crab diet.

After I'd cleaned my plate and emptied my wineglass, I ordered coffee and waited. Frédéric Chopin kept me company.

Finally, Miller's wife went upstairs. I dropped enough money on the bar and slipped into my overcoat and joined Judge Miller at his table.

He looked mildly surprised when I sat next to him. I offered him a quick glance at the photo from his file and said, "Come walk with me." He did.

We stepped outside and strolled to the end of the block and back. Judge Miller seemed cold without his overcoat.

Miller had read the papers and understood my situation. But, in sharp contrast to Senator Roach, Miller seemed relieved that I had his file and he agreed to call Amodeo the following day. No hesitation. I told him that I would protect his file and destroy it when I decided that I was safe. He didn't question it.

"Thank God you got it," he said. "Paul Tortelli is a monster. My life has been hell since this all began." He held out his hand and I took it in mine. "And thank you for coming," he said.

Judge Miller stepped back inside the restaurant and I gave the valet my ticket and he fetched the Shelby and I headed for the highway. My work in D.C. was done and I still had a half bottle of caffeine pills, and Jimmy Buffett to sing me back to Chicago.

CHAPTER FIFTEEN

Greico won," said Special Agent Holborn. "No contest, it was a slaughter. Not one of Tortelli's guns lived. Not one." With a mortician's smile, he added, "Somebody must have tipped the old man about the timing of the ambush."

"Somebody must have," I said.

We were standing on the curb of Lower Wacker Drive, which runs alongside the Chicago River. Not surprisingly, Lower Wacker Drive runs directly underneath Wacker Drive. Like so much of downtown Chicago, the tunnel system was designed by Daniel Burnham—the man with the very big plans that had magic to stir men's blood.

Locals called the tunnel *Emerald City*, because the lighting cast a greenish glow over everything. Emerald City is populated mostly by deliverymen and homeless people. And maybe the occasional FBI agent or private detective. I'm not sure about the Wizard. I've never seen him down there. I considered asking Holborn if he'd ever seen the Wizard in Emerald City but I thought he might take it as a gay joke, so I kept it to myself.

Instead I said, "What about Tortelli?"

"Gone underground with some of his crew. He's now officially a *problem* for the Outfit. But don't start getting comfortable, we don't think they'll skip town. Tortelli will stick and fight." Holborn pulled his overcoat collar up around his neck. It was too damn cold. "And he's gonna want his files back, so you'll want to get them to me sooner rather than later."

I nodded and shivered. *Damn, it's cold.* "And Greico?"

"He's at home," said Holborn. "His three bodyguards are licensed. More than three guns were fired from Greico's side but all the guns were registered to the bodyguards and there's no law against picking up someone else's gun and defending yourself. It was clearly self-defense, so Greico's not in any legal trouble. But Sal got hit."

"Dead?"

"Not yet. He's at Rush. Circling the drain. Doc says it'll be a miracle if he makes it."

I wondered if Jill had been on duty when they brought Sal Greico into the hospital. Would she have made the connection? Did she think of me? *Oh Dudgeon, that is pathetic . . . Who the hell asked you? . . . Well, somebody's gotta snap you out of it . . . Why don't you fuck off? . . .*

"Hello? Earth to Ray, come in Ray," said Holborn.

"Sorry. Too much stress and not enough sleep."

"Yeah, well, don't crack up on me until you hand over those files."

"Tonight," I said. "Midnight." *Ray Dudgeon—the Midnight Detective.*

"Fine," said Holborn. "Where?"

"Don't know yet. I'll call your cell."

"And you'll bring the files?"

"Yep."

"All of them?"

"Yep."

"Except those on your buddies in Washington," said Holborn.

Damn. "I must have lost a step, I never spotted the tail."

"There wasn't one." Holborn stepped to the front of my car, reached behind the chrome front bumper and removed a tracking device. "I had one of my associates place it while we were jawing at Pearl's Place. Pretty cool, huh?"

"Cool," I said.

"Yeah, I thought so." Holborn put the rectangular black metal box in my hand, magnet side up. It felt like a block of ice. "You can keep it as a souvenir. And whenever you look at it, I want you to remember. I'm smarter than you, Ray. Maybe you're better than most private dicks, which I don't suppose is saying very much. Anyway I can work with you. But you play too loose with the system and I don't really care for that. As soon as you got to D.C., I knew you'd kept a few files for yourself."

"Not a few," I said. "Two."

"You parked next to Capitol Hill," Holborn said. "I can canvas area restaurants and check the sign-in sheets at government buildings and pretty soon I'll know where you went and who you saw. Later you were in Georgetown, at 1789. I can get their reservation list and inter-view the waitstaff."

I lit a cigarette. "I'll save you some trouble. I was in the Dirksen Senate Building visiting Stanley Roach. But I think you'll find the sena-tor less than obliging when you come with your questions, and last time I checked, high-ranking senators swing a little more clout than FBI agents . . . or maybe I'm mistaken. Later I made small talk with probably a dozen important people at 1789," I lied. "Judges, U.S. at-torneys, congressmen. So you'll have to harass a whole lot of clout. Which might prove to be an interesting career move." I handed the tracking device back to Holborn. "You may or may not be smarter than me, but I'm nowhere near as dumb as you think I am." I smoked and tried to look smart and waited for Holborn's answer.

He stuffed the tracking device into his coat pocket. "I guess we'll call this one a draw," he said.

I headed back to my car. "You'll hear from me before eleven."

Why had Holborn removed the tracking device from my car? Why not leave it there and let me lead him to the files? Maybe he wanted to make a point and establish his authority over me, but that wasn't enough. There had to be another reason. He wanted me to see him remove the tracker. Why?

There's no better way to convince you that you don't have a tracking device on your car.

Damn. I drove south to the Hilton & Towers and parked on Balbo. And sure enough, there was a second tracker under the front bumper, next to where the first had been.

I walked around the corner to the taxi stand outside the hotel's main entrance and hopped into the backseat of the first taxi in line.

"Hi," I said, using my Poindexter voice. "Take me to Milwaukee?"

"I'll take you to Alaska if you got the bread."

"I only need to go to Milwaukee," I said. "How's fifty dollars?"

"Are you on drugs?"

"Okay, seventy-five," I said, "but not a penny more. And you pay for the gas."

"Get the fuck outta my cab."

"You don't have to be grouchy," I said, and got out of the taxi, leaving the tracking device under the front passenger seat.

Terry Green sounded happy to hear from me and downright joyful to be getting Tortelli's blackmail files. He even apologized for his churlish behavior at the Old Town Ale House. I told him to forget it.

I told him to get his hands on twenty-six mini-DV dubbing decks and set them up in the editorial boardroom for ten o'clock. Also twenty-six audiocassette dubbing decks. And I told him to make sure his editor stayed late, because there would be cops who might take exception to the *Chronicle* keeping copies of everything.

"If you're inviting cops to the party," said Terry, "I'm sure we'll also invite one of our lawyers to sit in."

That was fine by me.

The meeting with Mike Angelo went reasonably well. He was still angry with me but he didn't mention it and neither did I. It would pass, in time. And inviting him to the midnight meeting was a good first step. It was Holborn's case now but I wasn't sure he'd invite Mike, so I took it upon myself. Mike accepted the invitation. I said I'd call him around eleven with the location. He said that he'd still be in his office at eleven.

I left the Area 4 Police Headquarters and walked east, feeling pretty good about things. I decided to pick up a late lunch at Pearl's Place on the way back to Gravedigger's. I walked around the corner and continued south on Albany to the spot where I'd parked my car.

An unmarked police cruiser pulled up to the curb beside me and two plainclothes cops stepped out. I didn't know them but I'd seen the older one in the lobby of the station house. He was in his late forties, mostly bald, about my height, with at least twenty-five pounds on me. The junior partner was about six-one and he looked like a bodybuilder.

The older one said, "Ray Dudgeon. I'm Detective Layton and this is Detective Dunn."

"What's up, guys?"

"You know a Booker T. Washington?"

"I know of him."

"He turned up dead about an hour ago."

"I don't know anything about it," I said.

"Yeah, well Lieutenant Angelo asked us to bring you back for some questions." He got close and took hold of my right wrist. "We're gonna have to take your firearm." Detective Dunn moved behind me and was probably pointing his gun at my spine. I lifted my arms and let Layton take the pistol off my belt. He dropped it into his blazer pocket and then produced a pair of handcuffs from behind his back.

"Now wait a second," I said. "You don't—"

Fireworks exploded behind my eyes and there was a deep *whoosh* in my ears and then I wasn't there.

I was scuba diving. Exploring a coral reef. I loved diving. I felt more at home underwater than on dry land. I could always find peace underwater. Underwater, the critics in my head were silent. Underwater, I liked myself.

Underwater, I lost the distinction between what was *me* and what was *not me*. There were brown-spotted grouper and silver barracuda and multicolored parrotfish—and they were all part of me. Orange tube sponges swayed gently and fan coral waved in the current and I became orange tube sponges and fan coral waving in the current. For some reason, the air in my tank tasted like chocolate as it passed through the regulator and over my tongue.

And I became the taste of chocolate.

I was in the backseat of a car. Bound and blindfolded. My head throbbed. I could smell chocolate, so I knew we were near the Blommer factory on West Kinzie. It was late afternoon. I tried to determine the direction of the sun's heat and I figured we were driving west.

And then I wasn't there again.

I was strapped to a chair. My ankles were tied to its front legs, my wrists to its arms. I wasn't going anywhere.

I didn't want to go anywhere. My head hurt like hell and it was hard to stay conscious. I was still blindfolded but my ears told me that I was in a large room with a high ceiling and hard surfaces. Probably a concrete floor. I could smell gasoline. No, not gasoline—diesel.

"I think Jerry sapped the fucker too hard." It was Detective Layton's voice.

"I told you, I need him to talk," said a voice I didn't recognize. Then I was gone again.

Someone had removed the blindfold. I was in a nondescript warehouse. There was an overhead rolling service door on one wall, so I was in the loading bay. Another wall was lined with metal shelves. Wooden crates sat on the shelves and a small forklift was parked next to a stack of skids.

Past about twenty feet, my vision was blurred. There may have been printed signs on the wall or stencils on the crates that would've identified the place, but I couldn't bring them into sharp focus.

To my right, a metal door opened and two men entered and came closer and one of them was Detective Layton. The other was about forty years old, five-foot-seven, with a rugged, handsome face, short salt-and-pepper hair and a cigarette in his mouth.

"You know me?" he said.

I tried to speak but my throat was dry. "Water," I whispered. He nodded at Layton, who went away and returned with a paper cup. Layton held the cup to my lips and I drank. "I don't know you," I said.

"Chris Amodeo," he said. "You took some files from an associate of ours and we want them back. Where are they?"

"Paul Tortelli's disloyal," I said. "He's been working off the record and he hired the hit on Greico."

Amodeo held up a hand. "I thank you for your concern," he said. "If we gotta break an egg, we'll break an egg. But Paulie is our problem, not yours. And his sins, whatever they may be, don't give you a pass."

I couldn't think of an answer for that. I said, " 'Whithersoever the wheel of Fortune turns, Virtue stands firm upon her feet.' Do you agree with that?"

"What the hell is that?"

"Something I read."

"You're trying to lecture me about virtue?" said Amodeo.

"I'm asking if you agree."

Amodeo said to Layton, "Take a walk for a minute."

Layton stopped at the door. "I'll be just outside," he said. "Knock when you need me."

Amodeo turned his attention back to me. "I went to school too, smart guy. So let me educate you about virtue. Yeah, Virtue stands firm upon her feet. But not in the house of hypocrisy. Virtue does not live in the house of hypocrisy.

"See, we came to this country with nothing, because this was the Land of Opportunity. Come make your fortune in America. Bullshit. Come make your fortune in America if you're a white Anglo-Saxon Protestant, is more like it. Us greasy dagos never got any opportunity. We were blocked. So we made our own opportunity where we could. And we made our fortune. The upperworld was off-limits, so we thrived in the underworld. You wanna judge me for that?" He tossed his cigarette down and stepped on it. "And don't fool yourself that there's a dime's bit of difference between us and the country-club billionaires. How about the robber barons? The strikebreakers? The stock manipulators? The J. P. Morgans, the Du Ponts, the Fords. Where do you think the Kennedys got their money? You oughta learn a little history before you sit in judgment."

I'd hit a nerve and the longer I could keep him talking, the better. "All that stuff was a long time ago," I said.

"Bullshit. That's right now. It never ended. They just got better PR firms. You got the big banks, Fortune 500s laundering drug money, the S&L scumbags, BCCI, junk bonds, the pharmaceutical companies, the oil giants, chemical companies, defense contractors—"

"Maybe so, but they don't have me tied to a chair right now," I said.

"See, there's where you're wrong. Those motherfuckers have the whole goddamn world tied to a fucking chair. And you think they haven't killed millions for their fortune?" Amodeo worked himself into a fury as he counted off the upperworld's sins on his fingers. "Oil spills, unsafe products, crap pharmaceuticals, secretly dumping nuclear waste and toxic chemicals. Love Canal, Bhopal, and a hundred others you never heard of. You should do some research, find out what went down in Midland, Michigan, or Rocky Flats, Colorado, it'll blow your mind. And the cover-up? Yo. The cover-up is massive, engineered by our own government."

Here's an idea for a bumper sticker: I'D RATHER BE RESEARCHING MIDLAND, MICHIGAN, OR ROCKY FLATS, COLORADO. *No, it would never outsell* I'D RATHER BE FISHING. *How about* THE COVER-UP IS MASSIVE? *Bumper stickers—are you completely cracked? . . . Pay attention to the little man, he might be saying something you can use . . . Use for what? He's gonna kill me . . . Shut up. Pay attention, don't drift.*

". . . and don't even get me started on the government," Amodeo continued, his face flushed by fervor. "Our entire economy is fueled by graft and corruption and large-scale murder by big business and the G." He lit a new cigarette and said, "I can't believe you're really this naive."

I wasn't really this naive, but if I agreed with him, we'd have nothing left to discuss and my date with Layton would resume. I tried to think of something to keep him going without sending him over the edge. "So, 'we kill a lot of people but they kill even more people' is your argument?" I said.

"We don't kill that many," said Amodeo, "and those we kill got it coming to them. You don't think we use restraint? Let me tell you something about the Outfit. Unlike those uncivilized East Coast bastards, and unlike our own government, the Outfit has never dealt drugs. Never. We could've made billions in narcotics, but we never got involved. We don't kill children. They do."

"Okay, you're the good guys," I said. "Let me go and I'll nominate you for a Nobel Prize."

"Don't you get sarcastic on me," said Amodeo. His tone had changed and I knew I'd pushed it too far. He stepped forward and knocked the ash off his cigarette. "This conversation is over." He ground the cigarette out in the back of my left hand. He did it slowly so the ember would stay alive for a while and it hurt. He walked to the door and opened it and Layton stepped in.

"Keep him awake," said Amodeo, and left the room.

Layton used an electrical cord. He flogged my calves and thighs until they went into spasm and wouldn't let go. The shins were a special treat. Then he whipped my chest for a while, and went back to the legs. It continued for a long time. I wasn't a tough guy and I hollered from the pain. But I didn't beg him to stop. He applied himself with great enthusiasm. He spent some time working on my gut and I retched and vomited but I hadn't eaten in a while and it was mostly water. He hit me across the face and I pretended to pass out and he stopped. My mouth was full of blood and my bottom lip had split wide open.

I heard him breathing heavily from the workout. Then I heard him light a cigarette. I opened my eyes.

"Having a good time?" I mumbled.

"Sure. You?"

"Not so much." Blood ran down my chin and dribbled onto my shirt. I spit out a tooth.

Layton dragged on his cigarette. "You'll break," he said. "Everyone breaks."

"I know."

"So why put yourself though the aggravation? Just tell Amodeo what he wants to know and we'll whack you nice and painless."

"Mike Angelo will be displeased," I mumbled. "He'll get you."

"Angelo's an idiot." Layton dropped the cigarette and ground it under his heel and picked up the electrical cord. "So you wanna spill, or are you gonna make me work up a real sweat?"

He came closer and I couldn't take my eyes off the electrical cord. That cord in his hand was the most terrible thing I'd ever seen and I was consumed by dread. I wanted to beg for my life. I wanted to tell him where the damn files were. I wanted him to shoot me in the head. I wanted anything but another flogging.

"The cord's not working," I said. "Maybe you should try something else."

"Ooh, you are such a tough guy," said Layton. He whipped the cord across my chest and I thought my heart would explode but I held it in, didn't scream.

"Be right back," he said, and left the room.

I focused on my breathing. I wondered what time it was. I looked at my watch. It was covered with blood and I couldn't read it. I wondered when Holborn and Angelo would start looking for me, and if they'd know where to look. Gravedigger was expecting me back hours ago and he'd be searching by now. Maybe he looked at the files for clues. But they wouldn't lead him here. I wondered how long I could hold on before breaking. *Cut it out, Dudgeon. Just pick a point of focus and hold it. No thinking allowed.*

Layton came back and his partner was with him. Dunn stood in front of me. Layton untied my right wrist and pulled my arm behind my back as far as it would go. He shifted his position, leaned into the arm and pushed it farther, and I realized that the chair was bolted to the floor. As he pushed, pain shot into my chest and up my neck and into my head. I focused on my breathing.

"Ready?" said Layton.

"Go," said Dunn.

Layton rammed his chest against my arm, forcing the shoulder joint open, and the arm dislocated, jumping out of its socket with a loud *pop*. I screamed.

"Now," said Layton. Dunn stepped forward and kicked my shoulder joint. A strange sound erupted from me. The atavistic howl of a seriously wounded animal.

"Again." Dunn kicked me in the same spot and I slipped off the face of the earth.

I was scuba diving, deeper than before. I swam beside a vertical wall of coral. About 40 feet below me was a shipwreck. I kicked my fins and headed for the wreck. Deeper, until all color was absorbed by the sea and everything was blue. I checked my depth gauge . . . 170 feet. Euphoria embraced me, signaling the onset of nitrogen narcosis.

I knew what I had to do. I'd always wanted to do it, but I'd never been able to follow through. This would be the time. I passed the wreck and continued, deeper still. My depth gauge said 200 feet and the pressure gauge read 900psi. But I didn't stop. I let go of the gauges. I wouldn't be checking again. Soon I'd run out of air. That didn't matter.

I was happy underwater and I wasn't coming back.

My shoulder had been popped back into joint and my wrist tied to the arm of the chair again. The pain in the shoulder was bad, but by now everything hurt and I couldn't play favorites.

I wasn't *in* pain—I *was* pain.

Dunn was gone and Layton stood before me with a butterfly knife in his hand. Chris Amodeo stood beside him with a disgusted look on his face.

"Dudgeon, let me look at you," said Amodeo. "You're a mess. Now me, I don't like this shit. Can't even watch it." He jerked his thumb at Layton. "He likes it." Layton grinned as if he'd just received a compliment. Amodeo continued, "He'd be happy if you held out awhile longer. Me, I'd just like to spare you any further discomfort. So whaddaya say, hey? Where are the files?"

I couldn't think of anything clever to say, so I just sat there and drooled some more blood on myself.

"Okay, have it your way." Amodeo stepped to one side and Layton approached with the knife. He grabbed the index finger of my right hand and stuck the tip of the blade under the nail and pushed the blade forward. Then he pried the nail off. I tried to scream but all that came out was a low growl.

I looked down at my trembling hand. Blood oozed from the end of my index finger and the nail stood up vertically from the quick. And then it hit me. I'd seen that before. I'd seen it on Bob Loniski's mutilated body.

I looked up at Layton and said, "I'll kill you," but it didn't sound like me.

"Oh-ho," Layton laughed. "You hear that? This guy's got some balls, man." He put his face close to mine. "Tell you what I'm gonna do next, tough-guy. I'm gonna cut those balls off and feed 'em to you."

The metal door opened and Biagio Amodeo shuffled into the room. He was old and obese and he walked with a cane in each hand.

"Stop this," he croaked. He pointed a cane at Layton. "You, take a break. Chris, come with me, we gotta talk."

Chris Amodeo looked at his father.

"Got a call from Washington," the old man said.

It could've been hours, or just minutes. I'd lost all sense of time. I may have passed out once or twice but I couldn't be sure. I was alone in the room and that was fine with me. That was enough for now.

But they'll come back. If the door opens and it is Biagio Amodeo, then you get to live. If it is anyone else, game over. Was it Roach or Miller who called? Or both. What did it matter? Would it be enough? Now, there's a question.

The door opened. It wasn't Biagio Amodeo. The blurry figure walked closer. It had a knife in its right hand. It was Vinnie.

"Aw, shit," I said. "Vinnie. Don't."

"Shut up," said Vinnie. "I'm here to spring you." He bent over me and cut the ropes. "And don't call me Vinnie." He put the knife in his pocket, wrapped his left arm around my back and hauled me to my feet. I coughed up some blood and struggled to get my legs working.

Vinnie dragged me around the room until I found my footing. My legs were not much use but I could stagger, and with Vinnie's support, I didn't fall down.

"Ready?"

"As I'll ever be," I mumbled.

We got to the door and stopped. Vinnie's left arm was around my rib cage and his right hand was now filled with a gun.

"Hold this," he said, and stuck the gun into my hand so he could turn the doorknob.

"I can't see past ten feet," I said.

"Just hold it, I'll take it back if we need it."

Vinnie opened the door and we stepped into a dim hallway and something strange happened. A rush of adrenaline. I was surprised that I had any left. The adrenaline blocked the pain and I felt numb and my legs worked a little better. We turned left and headed toward a fire door at the end of the hall. About seven feet from freedom, we came to an abrupt stop as the fire door opened and Layton stepped inside.

"What the fuck is this, Vinnie?" Layton reached for his belt and the gun in my hand barked twice. Layton crumpled to the floor in the fetal position, moaning and holding his gut.

"Shit," said Vinnie. He snatched the gun from my hand.

I must have lost my mind for a second because I stopped and dug my Para-Ordnance from Layton's blazer pocket. Vinnie heaved me off my feet and dragged me out the door and down some iron stairs. I don't think my feet touched the ground as he hauled me across the darkened parking lot.

Bright lights swept across us and Gravedigger's pickup truck tore into the lot and skidded to a stop beside us. The tailgate was down and Vinnie tossed me, like a bag of cement, into the payload and jumped in after me.

Gravedigger hit the gas. The fire door opened and Vinnie unloaded at the door as we flew off into the night.

"You stopped for your gun?" yelled Vinnie.

"I'm sentimental about that gun," I said. Then I passed out.

CHAPTER SIXTEEN

I came around in Gravedigger's living room. I was on the pullout bed. Gravedigger sat on a chair beside the bed. Vinnie paced the room. A gray-haired man with bushy eyebrows and a French accent cut the clothing off me. The fabric stuck to my wounds and I made an inelegant sound. He stopped pulling on the fabric and jabbed a needle into my arm and I went away again.

Then it was morning. There was an IV drip connected to my arm. I lay on my back and Gravedigger sat in the same chair as before. Vinnie was not around. The man with the eyebrows checked my pulse. I blinked at him and he put my wrist down.

"Welcome back," he said. He held a glass to my mouth and said, "Only a sip." I drank a little water. My bottom lip was large but it had been stitched shut and it didn't hurt. In fact, I couldn't feel much.

"What's the good news, Doc?" I said.

"Good news is, you'll live." Thick eyebrows came together and then moved apart. "When the medication wears off, you'll have pain. But you will live. I suspect that the shoulder will require surgery. Perhaps not. Let it heal for a month and then see a doctor."

I tried to sit up but my limbs were disobedient.

"Lie still," said the doctor. He prepared another syringe and stuck me again.

I wanted to explain that I didn't have time to lie around, that I had *very important* things to do. Instead I said something like "Mumu-mumph," and fell asleep.

Another day passed without any help from me. When I awoke, the IV was gone. So was the doctor. Vinnie stood in the kitchen, stirring sugar into two mugs. Gravedigger sat in the chair beside the bed. My right arm was in a sling.

"He's awake," said Gravedigger.

"Don't you ever move from that spot?" I said. Gravedigger gave me his crooked smile. He stacked some pillows and helped me sit up. I could now feel the pain that the doctor had talked about.

Gravedigger handed me a couple of pills. "Percocet," he said. I tossed them into my mouth and he handed me a glass of water.

I waited for the Percocet to take the edge off while Vinnie and Gravedigger recalled the details of their daring rescue.

Gravedigger had gone looking for me, as I thought he would. Not knowing where to look, he considered the places I'd gone while he was shadowing me a few days earlier and decided that Vinnie was his best bet.

"I go to take the garbage out," said Vinnie, "and the midget, here, puts a fucking twelve-gauge to my head." He chuckled. "Shit, for a second I thought Tortelli sent him. Almost messed my pants."

Gravedigger shrugged. "I didn't realize Glandular Case was gonna help willingly."

"Anyway, I had some ideas of where we could find you," Vinnie said, "and we did."

"Yeah, only the sixth place we checked," said Gravedigger, and shot Vinnie with his finger.

"Yeah, like you'd a found him without me," said Vinnie. It was nice to see them bonding.

"Is the doctor coming back, or am I good to go?" I said.

"Uh, no, you're good," said Gravedigger. "He said to take it easy for a while, but you'll be fine."

"Tell him the best part," said Vinnie, and Gravedigger gave him a look.

"What's the best part, Gravedigger?" I said.

"Well, to tell the truth, he's not really a doctor," said Gravedigger. "I mean, he used to be a doctor but his patients kept dying, so they took his license away. He's sort of a mortician now."

"You got me a mortician?"

"Limited options," said Gravedigger.

Vinnie laughed out loud. "A doctor and a mortician. Can you believe that? The best part is, if you died, we had our bases covered."

Vinnie and I sat at a table near the back of Manny's on South Jefferson. A local institution since 1942, Manny's is the best deli in Chicago. The corned-beef sandwich is their signature dish but everything on the menu is great. Since my mouth was tender, I skipped the sandwich and ordered liver and onions with matzo ball soup on the side. Vinnie had the Salisbury steak. Good food for a cold January day.

I'd chosen Manny's not for the food, but because there were at least a half-dozen cops eating there at any one time. It was also a favorite spot for local politicos. Even "Hizzoner" the mayor was a regular and there was always some clout in the room. So it would not be a place where I'd expect to run into Paul Tortelli's crew, and it would be unwise for Chris Amodeo to start shooting the place up.

Gravedigger came along, just in case. He sat a few tables behind us, his shotgun hidden in a soft guitar bag slung over the back of his chair.

While I'd been sleeping, Vinnie had gone out and bought me some clothes—blue jeans, a Chicago Cubs sweatshirt and a matching ball cap. Manny's is south of the Loop and caters mostly to White Sox fans, so I couldn't be sure if the looks I attracted had to do with my clothing, or my battered face and the sling on my right arm. I suspected the latter.

With only my left hand working, I had to sit like a child while Vinnie cut my liver into bite-size pieces. Eating was slow and a little messy. I got through the liver and was just about to splash soup near my mouth when Chris Amodeo arrived. Amodeo didn't stop at the counter for food. He walked straight to the table and sat across from me. He didn't even glance at Vinnie.

"You're looking well," Amodeo sneered at me.

"Better than Layton, I imagine."

"Yeah, that guy's no longer with us." He sat and didn't say anything else. I wondered how long he was going to make me wait.

I gave it a while and then said, "It's your meeting, Chris."

"All right. It seems you have a couple of friends in high places. And Big John told us what you did for him. So we're gonna give you a pass on this one. Now what do you plan to do with the files?"

"Turn them over to the feds."

"That's not smart."

"It's not negotiable," I said. It occurred to me that the Percocet was giving me an unnaturally cool demeanor. Under the circumstances, it was a blessing. "The files don't implicate anyone but Tortelli and Di-Marco. The feds can't hurt your operation much."

"Unless they get hold of Paulie."

"Like you told me, Tortelli is your problem, not mine."

We sat for a minute and then Amodeo said, "Okay, you gotta forget all about the other night. Somebody asks what happened to you, you say you fell down the stairs."

"I've got a good memory for forgetting," I said.

"Fine."

"But not about Detective Dunn. Anybody asks, I don't remember where I was and I don't remember you or your dad, but I do remember Dunn. He has to pay." I hadn't planned on saying that. *Ray Dudgeon— Nerves of Steel. With a little pharmaceutical help.*

"It wasn't personal, he was doing his job."

"Oh? I thought he was a cop."

"God, you really are naive," said Amodeo. I didn't answer him. "Say nothing to anyone about Dunn, then check the obits tomorrow." He shrugged. "It's on your head."

"I'm sure I won't lose any sleep over it," I said.

"Fine. Then we're square. But know this—you just got a onetime pass, not a lifetime pass. If you ever become a problem for us again, I promise we'll take care of you, and then worry about your boyfriends in Washington after."

"Understood."

For the first time since he arrived, Amodeo looked at Vinnie. "As for you, you got a lot to answer for."

"Wait a second," I said. "This includes—"

"Shut up, Dudgeon," said Amodeo. "Count yourself lucky and keep out of what's got nothing to do with you. Vinnie, you—"

"This has everything to do with me," I said. "It's a package deal."

"What the fuck are you talking about?"

"The deal includes Vinnie. He's making a career change."

Amodeo looked at me as if I'd just spoken Urdu. I don't suppose anyone had ever suggested something so ridiculous to him and he seemed at a loss for words. Vinnie looked at the table, beads of perspiration visible on his forehead. Finally he made eye contact with Amodeo and nodded.

"Listen, Chris," I said, "Vinnie's not a rat. You have nothing to worry about. He gets a pass, along with me. That's the deal."

"Or what?"

"Or my boyfriends in Washington start turning up the heat. And their boyfriends too."

Amodeo pulled a cell phone from his pocket and left the table. Vinnie blew out a long breath. After a minute, Amodeo returned.

"Here's the way it is," he said, and pointed his finger at Vinnie. "You are officially chased. You will have no contact, ever again, not even with Big John. Don't ever call us for help, for a job, for anything. You are dead to us. You do not exist. Your wife will have to get a new set of friends. She is dead to our wives. She does not exist. Got it?"

"Yeah," said Vinnie, "I got it."

Chris Amodeo nodded at me and said, "Then we're done." He stood and left the restaurant. Vinnie looked stunned.

"You okay?" I said.

"Yeah, I'm okay," said Vinnie. "I just don't know what I'm gonna do with my life."

"Welcome to the club," I said.

Vinnie went home to explain things to Mary and figure out what to do with his life. Gravedigger drove me back to Mount Pleasant Cemetery, where we paid another visit to the final resting place of the lonely Mr. Alfred Andersen. I retrieved the files, except for those on Senator Stanley Roach and Judge David Miller. Those would stay in the mausoleum. In the event of my death, Gravedigger knew what to do with them.

Then Gravedigger drove me to the Chicago Chronicle Building. He offered to wait and drive me home but I told him I'd be okay. He hopped out of the truck, came around and opened the passenger door and helped me down.

I held out my left hand. "Thanks, Gravedigger. For everything."

Gravedigger smiled out of one side of his mouth. "Don't go soft on me, Ray," he said. "I had a blast." He shook my hand. "You're welcome," he said.

As Gravedigger's old pickup truck sped away, I looked north across the Michigan Avenue Bridge. On the other side of the Chicago River, the Tribune Tower reflected white in the cold winter sunlight. Across Michigan stood the Sun-Times Building, soon to be replaced by Donald Trump's newest monument, the appropriately named Trump International Hotel & Tower.

So Chicago would finally be part of Trumpworld. And why not? Since the late eighties, corporate America had been buying up Chicago's soul and sterilizing it, one piece at a time. Now there were corporate monsters everywhere you turned, and the old independent downtown joints were becoming an endangered species. ESPN Zone and Hooters and Planet Hollywood and there was even talk that Marshall Field's might become Macy's. Now people went to places like the House of Blues, Inc., because they were too scared to venture out into Real Chicago and experience the living, dirty, red-blooded thing. And then they headed back to the suburbs, where they talked about how Chicago is such a great blues town.

Chicago was becoming a movie set for a Disney film about a fake Chicago that's good clean fun for the whole lily-white, Jesus-fearing, Old Navy–wearing, McDonald's-eating, SUV-driving mutant inbred family.

And soon the *Sun-Times* would be a tenant of Trumpworld. If they even survived. The newspaper had been raped and bled almost dry by "Lord" Black and his corporate cronies—and was looking for a buyer.

But that's okay, because Mayor Daley promised that Trump's new tower would stand even taller than the Sears Tower. Tears of joy, Chicago. Trump wasn't yet sold on the extra expense of building that high, but I was sure they'd work out the details in a back room somewhere. Not to worry.

Maybe Chris Amodeo was right—maybe the corporate giants and the government really did have the whole goddamned world tied to a fucking chair.

Christ, Dudgeon. Get over it. All you can do is put one foot in front of the other and do the right thing . . .

So I put one foot in front of the other and took the files into the Chronicle Building.

Terry got busy dubbing the audiocassettes and videotapes and photocopying the pictures and reports. I sat drinking coffee in Jim Barker's office.

Barker was Terry's editor and he was definitely *old school*. He re-minded me of Colm Stanwell, our old editor when I worked at the paper. Barker was only in his late forties, but he had the quality of that dying breed of newsmen who ran things before the bean counters and ad salesmen took over the industry.

"It looks like you paid a heavy price for this one, Ray," said Barker. "Could be that maybe you're ready to hang up the badge and gun? We could use a man like you at the *Chronicle*."

"Thanks." I'd been thinking about a change, even more seriously since my tryst with Detective Layton. I didn't know if I could go on being a private detective anymore, and I didn't know if I could give it up. In the fashionable vernacular of pop psychology, I was *conflicted*. "I don't really know what I'm going to do next," I said.

Barker smiled like an indulgent uncle. "Take some time to think about it. I'll leave the offer open"—he nodded at my Cubs sweatshirt—"say, until the start of spring training."

Everybody's a smart-ass.

Special Agent Holborn, his partner Special Agent Jordan, Lieutenant Mike Angelo, *Chronicle* lawyer Fran Read, Jim Barker, Terry Green and I sat around the table in the editorial boardroom.

"This entire situation is counterproductive to the service of jus-tice," said Holborn through clenched teeth.

"We disagree," said Jim Barker. "Publication in the *Chronicle* doesn't destroy the evidence and doesn't stop you from investigating or prosecuting those responsible."

"And you say that from all your years of experience in law enforce-ment?" Holborn was not happy. "Of course we'll investigate, but with the information public, we'll have lost leverage. As a result, the strength of any subsequent prosecutions will suffer. Is that in the pub-lic interest?"

Now Barker wasn't happy either. "The only thing you lose is the ability to cut a deal that hides evidence of public corruption in order to get one to roll over on another," he said. "So I would say that publication is totally productive to the service of *equal* justice. And yes, that is in the public interest."

"You haven't got a clue," said Holborn.

"Agent Holborn," Fran Read cut in. "You gentlemen can debate this all day, but the *Chronicle* has made an editorial decision to run the story and we're within our rights to do so. We've turned all original materials over to you and we'll cooperate in every way possible, short of compromising our journalistic ethics or our responsibility to the public interest."

The conversation bored me. I looked out the windows and across the river, at the big boys who were missing this scoop. Thinking, *Yeah, maybe Chris Amodeo is right but there's still a Real Chicago out there and you can still live in it, for as long as it lasts.*

Holborn's voice brought me back. "I'm disappointed in you, Ray," he said.

"I'm on Percocet," I said with a silly grin. "So your disappointment probably hurts me less than it would otherwise. But think of it this way—there are twenty-six files here. Let's say, for every file Tortelli kept for himself, Biagio Amodeo has three. That's a very conservative guess, so let's say Amodeo's got at least a hundred files. Maybe just one of them could be someone at the Bureau who lives higher on the totem pole than you? It's not impossible. And maybe just one of them lives higher on the CPD totem pole than Mike."

"And maybe," said Holborn, "just one of them is the publisher of the *Chronicle*. It's not impossible. Ever think of that?"

"Sure," I said. "So I'm hedging my bets. Between everyone at this table, the chances are pretty good that at least some justice gets served."

Mike Angelo hadn't said a word since he sat down. Now he chortled. "Ray, you're an idiot, but your heart's in the right place."

"Thanks Mike."

"What happened to your face?" Mike Angelo said.

"I fell down the stairs."

"And you liked it so much, you climbed back to the top and fell down three or four more times," said Holborn.

"And now he wants to see justice served," said Mike.

"Doesn't everybody?" I said.

Terry Green gave me a lift home. He spent the ride pressing me to take the *Chronicle* job that Barker had offered, and I spent the ride being evasive. But none of the glib answers I offered would satisfy Terry and I didn't really want to get into it. The truth was, I once made an enormous emotional investment in what journalism is *supposed* to be, and reality never stood a chance. And I couldn't get over it, or maybe I just couldn't grow up. Either way, I'd learned that lesson once. *Fool me twice, shame on me.*

We pulled to a stop in front of my apartment building and Terry put the car in park. "You know, Ray. You've got no reason not to take the job. Think of Jill. Maybe—"

"Jill's gone," I said.

"Then think of the next girl who comes along," said Terry, "and plan for the future. You're almost forty, man. You don't want to grow old alone."

"I'll make you a deal," I said. "I gave you twenty-six files today. If I see all twenty-six names in the *Chronicle* tomorrow, I'll take the job."

Terry beamed. "That's a no-brainer."

"We'll see. My bet is, someone higher on the *Chronicle* totem pole than Jim Barker pulls at least one name out of the story."

"Cool," said Terry. "You're on. It's gonna be fun working together again, Woodward."

CHAPTER SEVENTEEN

Four names were missing from the story in the next morning's *Chronicle*. So I wouldn't be a reporter. I was okay with that.

Anyway, twenty-two corrupt public servants made for a huge story and Chicago was buzzing. My phone rang every few minutes, with intrepid reporters looking for quotes, benign well-wishers wishing me well and angry lunatics calling to threaten my nonexistent children. Halfway through the first day, I unplugged the phone and I left it unplugged.

In other news, the body of CPD detective Jerry Dunn was found in the trunk of his car, parked at O'Hare. I was okay with that too.

A big snow came and covered the city and I spent the next ten days at home, healing and following the story in the newspapers and on television, like everyone else. On the third day, I made it all the way down to the mailbox in the lobby of my apartment building. A check had arrived from Continental Pictures and it was twice what I'd been expecting, but somehow it still didn't feel like enough.

Meanwhile, the FBI made a lot of arrests. One of the people they arrested was Gloria Simpson. Terry told me that she rolled over on everyone and entered the Federal Witness Protection Program. Gloria Simpson was a survivor.

When news of Simpson's arrest got out, the feeding frenzy began in earnest. It was a race to sell out the other guy before the other guy shops you first, and public officials were tripping all over themselves to cut deals with the feds. Others called press conferences to declare their innocence, even though nobody had accused them of anything.

Then Paul Tortelli's body washed up on the shore of Lake Michigan and three of his top soldiers turned up dead in an abandoned van parked across the street from the Cicero Town Hall. The message had been sent, and nobody came forward to cause Biagio Amodeo any trouble.

My shoulder improved and I got limited use of my right hand, which expanded the choices of food available to me. After a week of soup and apples, it was nice to cut into a steak. By day seven, I was even able to lose the sling and shave the hair off my face.

On day nine, I managed a walk to the newsstand around the corner, where I picked up a copy of *The Hollywood Reporter*. It caught my eye because there was a small picture of Alan Diskin on the front page. Unnamed sources said that he suffered some sort of a breakdown after Bob was murdered but Continental Pictures would only say that he was on indefinite sabbatical for health reasons. Production on *Final Revenge* had resumed without him and the movie was on schedule for a summer release. Near the bottom of the article, there was a generic quote from the CEO of the New York distribution company that had won the bidding war on *Final Revenge*. The CEO's name was George Simpson. The article didn't say if he was a lawyer.

Simpson is a common name, so it could've been a coincidence. Or perhaps George Simpson was Gloria's ex-husband. Perhaps he outbid the competition and made my dismissal a condition of the deal. And Simpson assured Diskin that he could send the message that Bob Loniski was no danger to the Chicago Outfit. Then Diskin had fired me. After I'd spoiled Tortelli's elaborate plans with the tongue and the car bomb, getting me fired would've been a top priority. Tortelli and

Gloria were cousins. Tortelli could've picked up the phone and called New York, collecting on a favor owed or offering an IOU for a future favor. It made sense.

Or not. Layton had killed Bob and Layton was dead and I'd managed to survive a showdown with the Outfit. That was enough. I had no desire to take on the New York Mob as an encore.

By the eleventh day, Chicago's attention had shifted to the next big story and I was able to plug my phone back in. But nobody called. My right arm was now fairly serviceable and I was walking like an injured thirty-eight-year-old, instead of a half-crippled eighty-year-old. So I selected a bunch of CDs, loaded my car and headed south to visit my grandfather. At a Cracker Barrel in Kentucky, I used a pay phone to check my messages.

And there was a message. It was Jill. She'd read about me in the papers and she just wanted me to know that she was glad I was okay. She didn't say to call her back. Then again, she didn't say not to call. It was a strange message and I didn't know quite what to make of it.

I hit the road again and put on a Bob Marley CD—*Uprising*. It was too damn cold in Chicago and I was looking forward to finishing my convalescence on the south Georgia coast.

Maybe I'd settle down there and take tourists fishing on Grandpa's boat. Help them pretend to be Great White Hunters of the sea. Or maybe I'd sign on with my buddy Randall and babysit the scuba tourists as they pretended to be Jacques Cousteau.

Or maybe, after licking my wounds for a month or two, I'd go back to Chicago and try to pick up where I left off.

There was no rush. I could decide later.

I spent the night in a highway motel and, just before noon the following day, crossed the bridge from Brunswick to St. Simons Island. I rolled the window down and the salty sea air was like the warm embrace of an old friend. I parked in the Pier Village, locked my gun in the glove box and removed my jacket. It was sixty-eight degrees and sunny. Not bad for January.

I stopped at Brogen's and ate on the porch. I had a rare cheeseburger and onion rings on the side. Maybe not quite as terrific as the Blackie's burger back in Chicago, but not far off. And there was the balmy winter to consider. The old oaks draped in Spanish moss and the palm trees on the beach. The view of the pier, the blue water beyond and Jekyll Island in the distance. Maybe I could settle here.

There was no rush. I could decide later.

I finished my burger and left the restaurant. I stopped at a pay phone by the front door and called Grandpa and told him I'd be there in a few minutes. I hung up the phone and stood there, staring at it. I picked up the receiver and began dialing Jill's number but stopped before the final digit, and hung up. I watched my hand pick up the receiver . . . put it down . . . pick it up again. I tried to hang up the phone, but my hand wouldn't cooperate.

What would I say to her? More to the point, what did I have to offer? Nothing. Not yet. I needed time to recover. I needed to get my head together.

I left the receiver dangling by its cord and headed for the car.